THE LOST
STEERSMAN

BY ROSEMARY KIRSTEIN

The Steerswoman's Road

THE LOST STEERSMAN

ROSEMARY KIRSTEIN

BALLANTINE BOOKS
NEW YORK

A Del Rey® Book
Published by The Random House Publishing Group
Copyright © 2003 by Rosemary Kirstein

www.delreydigital.com

Library of Congress Cataloging-in-Publication Data

Kirstein, Rosemary.
  The lost steersman / Rosemary Kirstein.—1st ed.
    p.   cm.
  ISBN 0-345-46229-7
    I. Title

PS3561.I78L67 2003
813'.6—dc21

2003045344

Book design by Kris Tobiassen

Map by Rosemary R. Kirstein

Manufactured in the United States of America

First Edition: September 2003

10 9 8 7 6 5 4 3 2 1

FOR LAURIE MARKS,
DELIA SHERMAN, AND DIDI STEWART

"The Fabulous Genrettes"

ACKNOWLEDGMENTS

*T*he author wishes to thank all the friends and associates who helped and supported her during the writing of this book, including Sabine Kirstein, Brian Bambrough, Shelly Shapiro, Ann Tonsor Zeddies, Geary Gravel, Laurie Marks, Deb Mensinger, Delia Sherman, Didi Stewart, and Lisa Bassi.

And special thanks to Mary Ann Eldred, for certain arcane technical assistance.

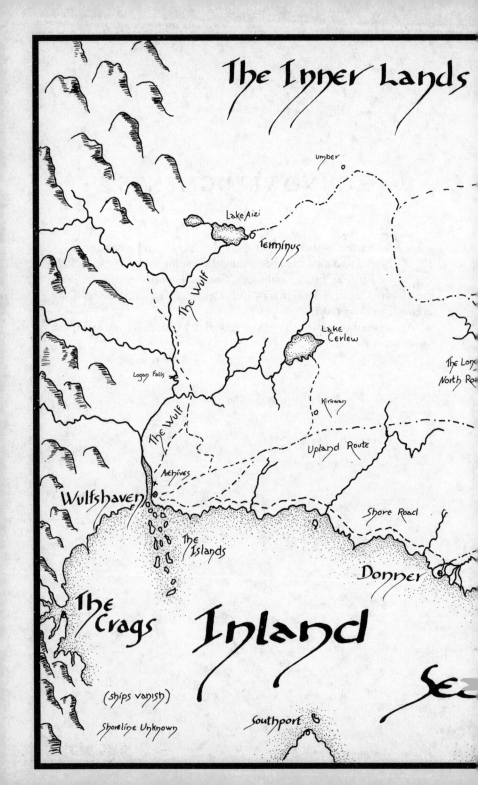

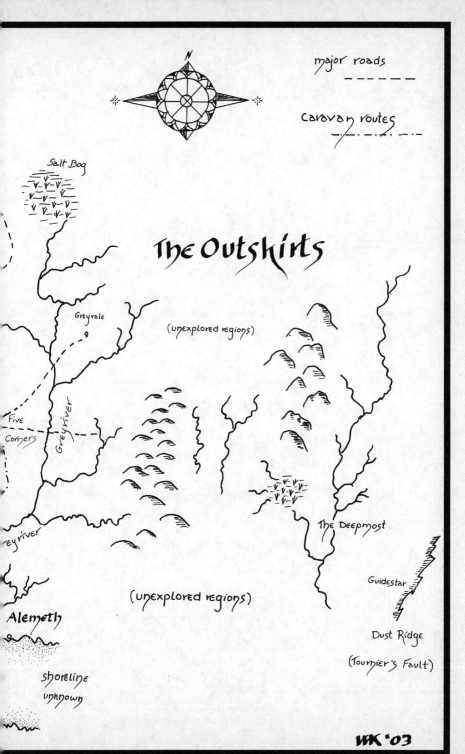

major roads

- - - - - -

caravan routes

Salt Bog

The Outskirts

Greyvale

(unexplored regions)

Five Corners

Greyriver

Greyriver

The Deepmost

Guidestar

Alemeth

(unexplored regions)

shoreline unknown

Dust Ridge

(Tournier's Fault)

WK '03

PROLOGUE

From the steerswoman Rowan
To Henra, Prime of the Steerswomen, residing at the Archives, north of Wulfshaven, I send greetings.

Henra—
I reached the fallen Guidestar.
I enclose fragments.
I enclose my logbooks, with sketches, and analysis of other findings I made in the Outskirts. I enclose maps.
It is absolutely urgent that you examine this material immediately. Matters are far worse than we suspected.
There is trouble in the Outskirts, and that trouble is going to move out of the Outskirts and enter the Inner Lands, and I cannot guess how it all will end—
But I think I know how it will begin.
There will be war.
And the wizard Slado is behind it. I'm certain.
This is what I learned:
We know that the area called the Outskirts moves, and always has been moving; we know that the Inner Lands expands in its wake. But I have discovered that this process is and *always has been* absolutely dependent upon the intervention of magic.
The country that lies beyond the Outskirts is stranger than we guessed— poisonous plants, dangerous animals, even monsters. It is hard to enter, difficult to survive in, and impossible for humans to thrive there.
Magic has always been used to destroy the native life, to clear the way for the Outskirters to enter new land (see pages 535–542 of my logbook, under the heading "Routine Bioform Clearance"). The critical spell was applied in a repeating twenty-year cycle.
But the Outskirters themselves know no magic. Someone else, some wizard or series of wizards, has been maintaining the magic.

But no more. Regular use of the spell ceased, decades ago.

Without Routine Bioform Clearance to destroy the worst of the native life, the Outskirts cannot expand and shift eastward. The land the Outskirters now hold will be required to support a population outgrowing its resources.

There is already famine among the easternmost Outskirter tribes (see pages 311–321: "The Face People"). They have begun preying on each other.

When life in the Outskirts becomes unsustainable, all the tribes will begin to move back, toward and into the Inner Lands.

The Outskirters will do what they need to survive. And they are warriors. I hate to think what will happen to our people, and to theirs . . .

Because the last proper usage of Routine Bioform Clearance took place before the previously unknown Guidestar fell to earth, and because we know how concerned Slado was at my discovering that a Guidestar had fallen, I must conclude that Slado is behind all this.

At first I assumed that the Guidestar's fall itself somehow destroyed the spell, somehow rendered its magic unusable. But I now know that is not the case.

Because Routine Bioform Clearance has been used again.

Not against the wild lands and monsters beyond the Outskirts: against the Outskirts itself. Against the land, and its people. I do not know how many died. Bel and I barely escaped with our lives.

See my maps for the location and size of the area affected, and pages 601 through 615 of my logbook for descriptions of the attendant phenomena. And, Henra, be aware as you read them that my estimates are *conservative*.

That such a power exists in the world, has always existed, and has now been used against human beings—it's almost inconceivable. I would hardly accept it as true myself had I not witnessed it.

For your part, you must trust my Steerswomen's training in observation and analysis. You taught me well. The information is correct.

Slado must be stopped. I do not know how, or by whom. But before anything can be done, he must first be *found*.

I think that the Steerswomen are uniquely suited to this task. We may be the only people who can accomplish it.

I beg you, lady, put every steerswoman residing at the Archives on the problem, immediately. Search our records and charts and, as quickly as is possible, pass word out to the traveling steerswomen. Slado must have left some trail. Once we discover his location, we can deal with the question of what to do next . . .

But as I see it, possibilities are three:

Approach him openly, on the chance that he does not understand the full effects of his actions.

Infiltrate and subvert his plans covertly.

Assassinate him.

Henra, if you had seen what I have seen, you would not be shocked by this last option. Whether it will ultimately prove wise, or necessary, or even possible, remains to be seen. But I happen to know just the woman for the job . . .

Bel has remained among the Outskirters. She will rejoin me at a future date. I cannot be certain when, and I find myself half at a loss without her. I've come to depend on her friendship, her quick mind, and her sword. But Bel thinks that it may be possible to prevent the conflict Slado is forcing upon us. To that end, she is warning and organizing the tribes . . . I hope that she is right, and that Outskirters and Inner Landers can stand together against what may come next.

But so much remains unknown. And I still cannot imagine what it is that Slado hopes to accomplish . . .

I apologize for writing so briefly, and so urgently, with such alarming news. But a ship is sailing today, and this letter and package must sail with it.

I also enclose a second letter, which I feel that you ought to forward, as discreetly as possible, to the wizard Corvus.

I realize that he is under the Steerswomen's ban for withholding information requested of him in the past, and I am thus not permitted to answer any question he asks of us—but by strict interpretation of the ban, one can volunteer information unasked. I did so for Corvus once before. I think that the Steerswomen should do so again. If Slado is still hiding his actions from Corvus and the other wizards, then those acts must be against the wizards' interests as well as ours.

We may find ourselves working on the same side as wizards, an astonishing thought in itself. But, for the hope of any possible future assistance from Corvus, we must let him know what is happening now . . .

I leave this to your judgment. Evaluate my findings, then read the letter and decide for yourself. We may be too late: it's possible that Corvus has already thrown in with Slado and Slado's plans. I can only hope he has not . . .

I am now in Alemeth, at the Annex, and intend to remain for several months, at the least. I know this was not planned, and I apologize for abandoning my assigned route.

But this matter must supersede all other concerns. At the Annex, I might be able to make progress on the question myself.

Although, unfortunately, the situation here is not the best . . .

1

The paper was wrinkled and torn down one side; the ink was smudged, and the lines weren't exactly steady. There was something that looked sort of like a street, but it looked like *this* street only if you already knew that it was. The little square blocks on both sides were buildings, but there was only one of them labeled at all . . .

Steffie watched sidelong while Gwen, her arms all full of dirty dishes, looked from the paper up to the face of the steerswoman. "It's a map," Gwen answered to the question she'd just been asked.

"I can see that," the steerswoman said. "But what I cannot see is what it is *for*."

"Mira carried it," Steffie put in. He went back to sweeping, bringing up a cloud of dust off the old rag rug. "All the time. She said it helped her find her way."

"To where?"

"To the tavern."

The steerswoman blinked at him. "The tavern," she said, "is around the corner."

"Well, yes." He grinned and kicked up the carpet's edge. "I guess she mostly used it to get back from the tavern, of an evening. When she'd had a few, see? She used to make a big show of pulling it out, and say, 'When you can't tell where you're going, get a Steerswomen's map.' And that since she was a steerswoman herself, and she made that map, she could always trust it to get her home."

That got him a blank stare. And then the steerswoman shook her head and sighed through her nose. "Well." She looked at the map again. "I suppose Mira must have been a steerswoman—" and then she looked up and around at the room "—but I can't help myself doubting it."

Too damn right, Steffie thought—except, the other way around.

Gwen traded a glance with Steffie, like she was thinking just what he was thinking, and then carried off her dishes. The steerswoman gave up on the map and went back to sifting through the piles of loose papers on the table. And Steffie kept on sweeping.

When the news had gotten around town that there was a steerswoman at the Annex again, everyone was glad enough. What with old Mira gone, it had been like there was a big hole right in the middle of Alemeth. And even though the new steerswoman said she could only stay for a little while, people pretty much expected things to go back to normal.

But the last thing Gwen and Steffie expected was to be put to *work*.

Steffie stopped at the edge of the rug, wondering if it would be enough to just sweep away the dirt that showed on top; but with a whole day of the new steerswoman's company behind him, he figured Better Not, put the broom aside, and set to rolling the thing up. Gwen clattered the last load of dishes into the tin bathtub and said, not being quiet about it, "If you find any more than these, I won't wash them!"

The steerswoman didn't even look up from the worktable. "If we find any more," she said, in exactly the same kind of voice, "throw them away!"

Gwen snatched up a bucket and went to the front door, growling to Steffie as she passed him, "If I'd wanted to wash dishes, I'd have stayed at home."

Steffie watched her go, then tried to shift the rolled rug to the back door by kicking it along the floor. No good: it was too heavy. He gave up and hefted the thing over one shoulder and carried it out, coughing from the dust in his face and trailing bits of dirt behind, some of which were big enough to rattle when they hit.

Just before he reached the door, he heard the steerswoman mutter, "It's just as well Mira and I never met. I'm sure we wouldn't approve of each other."

That was for sure, Steffie thought.

Outside, the yard was the same old tangle of weeds, cast-off furniture, and broken crockery. The only clear area was the muddy path to the outhouse. It crossed through three different permanent puddles; whenever she used the path, Mira had always put on a pair of huge, old boots that she kept on the back stairs just for that.

The boots were still there, crusted with dry mud. Steffie sat down beside them.

Crazy old woman, he thought. He missed her.

Steffie had been just a tyke when he'd first heard about how a steerswoman always has to answer whatever question you ask, no matter what. Seemed funny, so he decided to test it out, just to see. So he walked right up to old Mira, in the middle of the street, and started asking her every personal question he could think of—all the nasty and rude things that make a little boy snicker but no grown-up in her right mind would ever answer.

But Mira had just looked him straight in the eye and answered each and every one—some of them at length and with lots of details—while her friends stood by laughing and making saucy remarks, which Mira didn't mind one bit, either. Pretty soon it was little Steffie who was squirming, going red as a petunia, and finally fleeing.

Except, he came back. And he kept coming back. He followed her like a shadow.

The next thing he knew, here he was, all grown up to twenty-one years, still spending most of every day at the Annex. And what kept him coming back was Mira.

No one else was like Mira. No one was as honest or as unafraid. She did not care at all what people thought about her. She kept her house a mess; and she ate and drank what she liked, carried on, and talked about things no decent old woman would think of. She used to say that she had spent most of her life being decent and working hard, and she was tired of it. She figured she had earned the right to have some fun.

Sometimes someone would get Mira to talk of her times on the road; and Steffie had to admit that the way Mira told it, it didn't sound very nice: being cold and often hungry, usually alone, and always with work to do, never any real rest. And often in the middle of talking, her voice would trail off, and she'd look off into the distance or down at the ground, sort of sad and far away—

Then she'd suddenly jump up—they were usually in the tavern—grab someone, like old Brewer, and haul him out to the floor. Then skinny Belinda would pull out her fiddle; Brewer's fat son would start clapping a rhythm; Janus, so usually quiet and courtly, would start making up the most *scurrilous* lyrics—and the two old people would set to dancing, stamping their rickety bones around the floor, always off the beat, and everyone laughing, Mira the loudest of all . . .

For as long as Steffie had been alive, it was Mira who lived in the Annex, and it was Mira and Mira's ways that meant "steerswoman."

He couldn't figure out this Rowan person at all.

The rug was still slung on his shoulder. He heaved it off into the yard, and it thumped to the ground in a cloud of dust. Out in the light of day, he could see it was hopeless. It would be a job of a year to get it clean. He gave it up.

When he came back into the room, he felt at first that it was altogether empty, like a snail shell found on the beach, its little dweller dead and gone. It was proper for it to be empty.

But there was that Rowan, sitting at the worktable as Mira never did, poring over those books, as Mira never had done. It felt wrong; it felt like an insult.

She did have the right to be there. This was the Annex, and she was a steerswoman: so she said, and she wore the little gold chain and the twisty silver ring, like they all did. But she did not look like a steerswoman to Steffie, not at all; she looked dangerous.

She sat at the old table, where the sun slanted down, dusty, through the high front windows. There was a pile of loose papers on the table and three stacks of books, each book looking exactly like the others, all bound in red leather.

Her right hand was on top of the papers, holding them down, and that hand was splotched with ink stains, new ones and old ones together. Her left hand, the one with the silver ring, was holding the book open; that hand looked like it had been through a little war all by itself, because it had small scars crisscrossed all over it, maybe a dozen of them.

Her short hair looked like it had been trimmed with a knife; and it was a dry, harsh yellow on top, darker under. Her skin was sunburned and weather rough. And at first Steffie had thought her much older than he, from the lines about her eyes. But close up, you could see that the wrinkles weren't real—just pale lines on darker skin, as if she had spent a long time squinting into the distance against bright sunlight. She looked like a woman from a land with no shadows.

And there was something about the way she sat, too, forward from the back of her chair, both her feet on the ground. It was like she figured she might need to move somewhere else quick, and she thought she should stay ready. Except, not really thinking about it, because her mind was all on her work, you could see that from her face. So it was like her body had a mind all its own, and by itself it made her sit that way, all ready to go, just in case.

And that sword—seemed like her body really wanted to keep that sword nearby. One time Rowan was reading at the table, got up with the book still in her hand, went to the sword where it leaned against the hearth, brought it back, and laid it right down on the table in front of her—and never stopped reading once all that time. It was spooky.

It was like some kind of instinct. It was like she had taught her body to take over and protect her whenever her mind was busy someplace else.

It made Steffie queasy to watch her. It made him remember that there were places out in the world where life was not safe.

But he did watch her—he just couldn't help it, it was all so odd—so now, when the front door opened with a bang and the steerswoman looked up, Steffie saw that her hand went right to the hilt of her sword, slung on the back of her chair. He couldn't help wondering what trouble it was that her body, if not her head, expected.

But it was only Gwen, lugging the bucket she'd filled from the well out in the square and trailing a half dozen children of all different ages, each toting a jar or pot. "I found help," Gwen said gruffly, and she led her helpers in like a stream of ducklings up to the hearth, where each one added to the cauldron.

The steerswoman had a way of smiling that happened in two steps, almost too quickly to separate: first her eyes, then her mouth. It was when her mouth smiled that her hand left the sword, and Steffie was surprised to see a big grin.

She liked the children; you could tell. "Thank you so much," she said to them, like they were each special. "That's very helpful."

They shuffled their feet, made shy smiles, then lined up in front of her, waiting.

Rowan glanced at Gwen. "They're expecting a reward," Gwen told her. "I see . . ."

One girl spoke up. "Mira used to give us sweets."

Rowan winced. "Are there any on hand?"

"None," Steffie said.

"Or beer."

"Beer!" She leaned back in her chair. "Are the people of Alemeth in the habit of giving their children beer?"

"Yes," Gwen answered straight off, and Steffie nodded along. And there was plenty on hand, since Brewer had taken to sending over Mira's usual daily ration, which Rowan hardly touched.

But you have to be honest with a steerswoman. "Well," Steffie said, "I guess really, it depends on the parents . . . Some do and some don't . . ."

Rowan nodded and turned back to the children. "I'm sorry, I can't give you beer unless I know that your parents approve. But here—" She shuffled the papers before her, found one that was blank, and began to fold it. It grew smaller and smaller in her scarred and stained hands, until at last she held a little triangle.

"Like this." She moved her hand: a sharp downward flick. The thing let out a sudden loud *pop,* and everyone jumped. The children shrieked and giggled, and nothing else would do but that Rowan make one for each child. Then the whole bunch of them boiled out into the street, snapping and popping like chestnuts in the hearth.

Rowan watched them go, smiling a little, like she was thinking of something similar but from long ago, or maybe very far away. "Well." She turned back and looked down at her work, and her mouth twisted. "I'm getting nowhere with this." She pulled the pages together, stacked the books, and stood up. "I think I have time to see about organizing that second shelf. Gwen, please let me know when the water is ready. I can't have you scrubbing all those dishes by yourself; you've done far too much already. I hardly know how to thank you." She turned away and took a half dozen steps toward the aisles of dusty bookshelves that filled the rest of the room, then stopped. She looked like she thought something might be lurking back there, and frankly Steffie didn't blame her.

He took the chance to say, "I think we should give up on that rug. Just chuck it out."

"It's just as well," the steerswoman replied, sort of far-off. "Unfortunately, we can't chuck out the entire house."

Steffie jumped at a clang from the bathtub. Gwen had kicked it. "Mira liked things just the way they are!" she declared.

In the space of that clang, Rowan had come back to her chair, putting her right next to her sword again. "I'm sure she did," she said to Gwen, seeming not to notice where she was or how she got there, "but I don't, and no good steerswoman would. However much you may have liked Mira, the truth is that she simply wasn't doing her job."

She waved one hand at the shelves behind her. "Taking care of the Annex is an honor and a trust," she said. "All of these books are careful copies of books in the Steerswomen's Archives. If something should ever happen to the Archives, these books may become the only place where this information is held. The steerswomen have worked *hard* to gather all this." She was angry now. "There are facts in these books—there are *lives* in these books," she told Gwen, "years—*centuries* of individual human lives. Look—" She stormed over to one shelf in the first rank and came back with a book that she had put by earlier. She opened it toward the middle and held it up for Gwen to see. "There. That's me, at the age of twenty-two. My first year as a steerswoman; and everything I learned or discovered in that year is right here." Gwen gave the book a blank stare. She couldn't read.

"The original is in the Archives," Rowan went on. "There's a copy here and another in the Annex in the western mountains. And that is all." Then she riffled the pages at Gwen. From the middle of the book, all the way to the back, the pages were moldy and bored through with wormholes. "*That's* what Mira thought of my life."

She put the book down and rested one hand on it, the hand that had the scars. "Most of the books are in that condition, or worse," she said, still looking down, like she was talking to the book. "They're moldering in dust; they're fused shut with damp. There are entire cratefulls still in the boxes they arrived in. They're not cleaned, they're not shelved, and nothing's been catalogued for what looks like thirty years."

She looked up at Gwen. "And in return for this service, Mira received a home, a stipend—and apparently a position of some respect in this town. Had Mira not been a steerswoman, I would care not at all how she lived her life. But apparently her work, and her sisters', meant nothing to her."

But trust Gwen to give no ground. She tossed her head. "Paper and ink and books aren't lives. Mira's life was her own, and she was alive and living it, and that's more important than dusting and organizing. It's mostly dead people's lives in those books, isn't it? Dead and gone, and who cares what they did?"

The words seemed to surprise Rowan, and she stood with her brows knit, thinking hard. After a while, she said, "Mira was a steerswoman, correct? And if you ask any steerswoman a question, she must answer, isn't that true?"

Gwen crossed her arms. "She always did."

"That's the rule," Steffie put in. He couldn't see what Rowan was driving at.

The steerswoman drew in and let out a long breath. "I," she said, "have questions. I have a great many questions. And, unfortunately, the people I would most like to ask them of"—and here she threw out her arms suddenly—"happen to be *dead*!" She snatched up one of the other books on the table, held it tight in her two hands. "The steerswoman who wrote this book traveled more in one year, and saw more, than either of you will in your entire lifetimes. Somewhere in here or there"—and she turned back toward the shelves, angry—"someone might have an answer for me, or part of an answer or a clue or even a rumor . . . They'd tell me if they could."

Dead people, talking; the idea sent a chill up Steffie and down again.

"If the catalog and indexes had been kept up," Rowan went on, "I might have a chance of finding likely subjects quickly . . . proper abstracts would give me some idea of where at least to begin looking . . . even shelving the books in chronological order would help. Instead"—and she set the book down with a little slam—"I'll have to look at every book that comes to hand, one by one, and set them in order myself. A proper search would take years. I'll be doing Mira's job at the same time I'm doing my own."

Dead steerswomen, still answering questions. Like ghost sailors still sailing, ghost blacksmiths still pounding away, invisible. But think of that: imagine liking something so much that you'd keep right on doing it, even after you were dead. "Does Mira have a book in there?"

"Possibly." The steerswoman did not sound much interested. "Very likely, I suppose. Something from her early career, perhaps. I certainly haven't found her current logbook about anywhere."

"Waste of time, if you ask me. Mira had other things to do," Gwen said. "I never saw her bothering about writing in some old book!" Then she snatched up the kindling carrier from the hearth and stomped straight out the back door.

"And I am not in the least bit surprised!" Rowan snapped back; then she stormed off herself, not down the bookshelves but upstairs. Steffie heard her feet crossing Mira's room overhead and then some bangs as she shifted something or other, more footsteps, creaks, and then nothing. Leaving Steffie standing alone in the middle of the empty room.

"Right," he said to no one in particular. Two women arguing; leave it alone. He'd learned that one early on, house full of sisters and all.

That sword had gone upstairs with Rowan, somehow. He didn't see it happen, but it was gone now. Figured.

He went back to sweeping.

After a while, Gwen came back in with the carrier jammed full of kindling—which they didn't really need, because there was plenty by the hearth. And she bumped right into Steffie on the way, too, and shoved him aside with her shoulder, even though there was plenty of room to go around him.

Which naturally sent his mind off in a whole other direction, knowing her like he did. As signals go, that one usually worked pretty well, and he started laying out a few plans in his head. Gwen peaceful was nice enough, but Gwen angry could be *really* interesting, if you came at it right.

Of course, Rowan was up in the bedroom. Still, she had to leave it sometime . . .

So Steffie played innocent while Gwen clattered with the kindling, grumbling and sounding like she was making a mess of it, which she never did for real. He let it go on for a while, sort of building up to a nice boiling point, and just when she got to sounding really frustrated, he set his broom aside and made to go over and help her—

Overhead, Rowan started moving again, toward the bedroom door. Good timing, Steffie thought.

But then it came to him that while Mira never minded when he and Gwen slipped upstairs, Rowan might be a whole other matter . . .

Better Not, he decided. So he just stayed put. Which wasn't easy, now that he'd got his mind set on things, so to speak, but there you are.

Then Rowan came down the stairs, slow, carrying something, and using both hands to do it, even though it was small enough to carry in just one.

"Gwen," she said, when she got to the worktable, "I'm sorry we argued." She sounded a bit stiff, but she went on. "It was entirely my fault. Mira's choice of habit had nothing to do with you. The fact that it makes my own work difficult isn't your fault or your concern." She put the thing in her hands down on the table, but carefully, like there was a spider inside. It turned out to be a little, dusty box.

The sword was slung over her arm by its belt; she put it back on the chair. "The Annex seems to be a second home to you, to both of you, and I hope you'll continue to consider it so. I'm sorry you lost Mira; I hope she was as good a friend to you as you are to her. It was very kind of you to give so much help to an elderly woman."

It was a pretty speech, but Steffie still wished Rowan was someplace else—out of the house altogether, in fact.

Gwen straightened up from the hearth and eyed her. "Mira was a steerswoman. You're supposed to help a steerswoman." Her head tilted, one eyebrow up, and she looked Rowan up and down. "*Any* steerswoman."

Steffie could see something go *thump* inside Rowan, and right then he wondered if maybe it was him who should leave the house. Out the back. Fast.

"Yes," Rowan said, even stiffer than before. "Well." Then—moving so small and careful that Steffie just knew she really wanted to do something big and wild—she turned the box around so it faced Gwen, and lifted up the lid. "A steerswoman," she said, "cannot do *that*," and she pointed inside, "and remain a steerswoman."

Then, like something inside of her let go, she was moving quickly, snatching something up off the table—a wrapped package—and then she grabbed her sword and was gone, straight out the front door.

Leaving a lot of silence behind. Which went on for a while.

Then Gwen walked wide around him to get to the table, so wide he couldn't have touched her even if he reached out. "What's this, then?" she said.

"A box," Steffie said stupidly, feeling all off balance; but the mood was gone, now, he knew that. He looked again. "A trinket box?"

A cheap-looking one, at that, and little and dusty, though not as dusty as most things in the house. Remembering how Rowan had acted with it, he stayed far back and had to lean way over to look inside . . .

What had Rowan just said? "Does it mean that?" he asked out loud, "if you take them off? That you're not a steerswoman?"

"Make sense," Gwen told him, and picked up the box and dumped it out, exactly the way he hadn't.

There on the tabletop: puddle of gold, twist of silver. A steerswoman's chain and ring. "Mira took them off," he said.

"Never. We buried them with her, like we're supposed. I should know, I helped lay her out." Gwen picked up the ring, looked at it closer, and made a noise. "Not Mira's, any fool could tell. It's too big." And with a flick she tossed it up in the air toward Steffie.

"Whoa, hup!" He snatched at it, missed it with his right hand, caught it with his left.

But when his hand closed around the ring, it didn't feel big at all. He opened his hand and looked; and it seemed normal sized, lying on his palm.

Which was funny; so, sort of to prove it to himself, he slipped it on. And, sure enough, it looked just right on his own big hand—

Then he slipped it off again quickly, feeling spooked, like it might be haunted.

Thing was, though, it fit. "Well, that's a man's size," Steffie said. Had to be. Big for almost any woman's hand; not big for his own.

Gwen laughed out loud. "A *man* steerswoman?"

"Well. Guess not." But too big for Mira, that was sure.

Then the water was hot, and Gwen rolled up her sleeves and set to work, ignoring Steffie just like he wasn't there at all. Which put an end to those plans he'd been laying, no doubt about that.

So Steffie gave up, heaved a sigh, and went back to work himself. But first he put that ring and chain back in their box, wiped the dust off the box with his sleeve so he wouldn't be told to do it later, and put it up on the mantelpiece.

And he forgot all about it, until much later.

2

*H*ow do you find a man?

The steerswoman moved quickly down the street, long, angry strides.

How, if you have never seen him, never heard him described, did not know where he lived? How, if he *wished* not to be found?

And how, most especially, if he were the most powerful wizard in the world?

For all Rowan knew, the wizard Slado might dwell on the opposite side of the world; he might assume any number of disguises; he might render himself invisible or so cloud Rowan's mind that he could stride down the street at her side, unseen, undetectable—

This thought brought her up short, and she stopped in the middle of the street. She looked about.

On one side of Old High Street, four houses attached each to the other, with four doors in four different, faded colors; on the other, single houses, of plastered brick washed with pale colors.

The street was empty. There was no one else present.

The steerswoman took the moment to set her package on the ground, then carefully strapped on her sword, recovered the package, and resumed walking, somewhat more slowly.

No person could render himself invisible; she was certain of it.

But, magic, a far corner of her mind reminded her.

To be unseen was to be either absent, blocked from view, or somehow disguised—

But, it came again, *magic.*

For most of her life, Rowan had doubted the very existence of magic. She had been proven wrong, again and again: a tiny statue that moved without life, a room that filled with light at the turn of a wheel, gates that opened in the presence of an amulet—

The great fortress of the wizards Shammer and Dhree, shattered by the touch of a flaming arrow sent by a boy only fourteen years old—

And Slado's killing heat, pouring down from the sky.

Magic was real. And the steerswoman must believe.

But surely—and Rowan held tightly to this thought—surely even magic must have limits. If an invisible watcher were nearby, his or her presence must still leave some clue.

Rowan paused again, stood perfectly still, and closed her eyes.

The light breeze brushed her throat and forearms, bearing a hint of the coolness of water, brought up from the harbor. The air moved toward her in a smooth sweep, with no little gusts and eddies. No one was in front of her for a distance of at least twelve feet.

Behind her, heat rose from the sun-warmed cobblestones. No shadow blocked that warmth, and there were no rustlings of clothing, no hiss or motion of air from a person's breathing. No one stood behind her.

There was a still, cool area on her right, and she snapped her fingers once. The sound was sharp and immediate; no human body stood between her and the shadowed brick walls of the row houses six feet away.

To her left, a small, silken flutter, but high up: a banner, constructed—as she had seen before—of silk scraps, pole hung over the door of the fragrant bakery. Voices escaped from its open door—a small, clear discussion of weevils found in a sack of wheat—no one stood between Rowan and the conversation.

Further off: the sound of children playing, squeals and giggles thin with distance, almost ghostly; up and behind her, a door quietly thumped, slammed in some upper storey. More distantly: a jingle of harness, a clang of hammer on anvil. And at the threshold of hearing: rattles, splashes.

There was no one nearby.

The steerswoman opened her eyes to sun dazzle and went on, following Old High Street on its canted run down to the harbor.

She wished Bel were here. She very much wished that Bel were here.

She and the Outskirter had parted nearly a year before. Bel had her own work to do among the Outskirters. Bel knew her people, knew how to approach the tribes safely, knew what to say, knew how to convince them of the present and coming threat to their way of life.

But more important, Bel knew what to be. The Outskirters had no knowledge of steerswomen and cared nothing for Inner Landers. Only a warrior could unify the warriors.

Rowan found herself grateful, deeply grateful, that she was not herself, and would never be, a great leader.

Bel had her job, and Rowan had her own: Locate Slado, discover his plans, learn how to stop him. Everything depended on this.

But how do you find a man?

By logic.

For a wizard, look for magic. And for a wizard whose very existence was secret, look for any magic that could be attributed to no other source.

And no need to go hunting the wide world for some sign or rumor of magic; Rowan had, at her fingertips, the lives of the steerswomen. If one of them had seen magic, or heard of its use, there would be record of it.

But the contents of the Annex had no index.

The earliest event that Rowan could connect to Slado's plans was the fall of a Guidestar, not one of the two that stood apparently motionless in the night sky, familiar even to children, but a distant, secret Guidestar, unseen from the Inner Lands, hanging over a far and unknown part of the world.

The Guidestar had fallen some forty years ago, and magic must have been involved in that event. So, look in the logbooks dating from that time.

But the books in the Annex were not in chronological order. And there were thousands of them.

It might take months to locate even one useful logbook—and all the while, Slado's plans, whatever they might be, would continue to advance to their unknown end.

Mira had a great deal to answer for. Fortunate that the old woman had already passed away; feeling as she did right now, Rowan suspected she might slay the woman on sight, for so stupidly placing the entire human race in danger.

Old High Street stopped at the waterside, and Rowan turned left onto Harbor Road. Here, warehouses and offices and provisioners crowded shoulder to shoulder, facing a line of huge, old trees standing between the edge of the road and a narrow, rock-riddled beach.

Half the trees had lost their smaller branches. Six were splintered down their lengths. A jagged stump showed where one had been lost entirely.

Rowan considered the damage silently.

At a half-tumbled building nearby, a crew of burly men and women were hauling wreckage onto a horse-drawn wagon. Scaffolds were under construction, rising beside pale new walls. Pine resin scented the air.

A man and a woman stood by a stack of fresh lumber, the man holding forth with gusty authority, the woman listening with visibly patronizing patience. Rowan decided that one of them, at least, would not mind being interrupted.

"Excuse me." Both turned. "I was wondering, is this damage from two autumns ago?"

They stood regarding her; then the man said cautiously, "Planning to kill someone?"

"What?" She followed the direction of their gazes. "Oh." Her sword. "A habit. I've been traveling in dangerous lands." They were reassured, and she repeated her question.

"Year and a half ago, yes," the man replied. "A run of nasty weather and high seas. Smashed up the docks, waves halfway up New High Street, made a mess of everything. We lost two buildings and most of this one." Behind him, the woman had taken the opportunity to call over several workers and give out detailed instructions.

The man, tall, blocky, and oddly graceful for his size, arranged his features in an amiable expression. "Now, haven't seen you around. Off the *Beria*, then? Ho!" This as he noticed Rowan's chain and ring. "A steerswoman, is it? That's right, I heard you'd come to town. Just passing through? Old Mira will be glad to see you—no, wait, old Mira's gone now. But you knew that already, didn't you?"

Rowan put up a hand to slow him down. "I was planning to pass through, but it seems I'll be staying for a while, possibly until the Archives sends a replacement for Mira."

"Oh." Then a two-toned, "O-oh." He scanned her, the nature of his speculation noticeably altering. "Well, you're an improvement, I'll say that. Tell you now, I could take an hour or so right now, show you around town—"

"Actually, I have some business to tend to at the moment—"

He took this in stride. "Just as well, really; I'd best be keeping an eye on this lot— Here, you two! *That* over there, and *that* one goes *up*. But hang about"—this to Rowan—"let's say later, then, about sundown?" Behind his back, the forewoman, by gesture only, exactly reversed his instructions.

Rowan moved back a step. "In fact," she said, "I expect to be busy in the Annex well into the night; there's a lot that needs to be done there."

"At the Annex?" The idea surprised him. "Can't say I ever saw Mira do a thing there."

"I'm not much like Mira—"

"But you eat."

"Excuse me?"

He cocked his head. "You must have your dinner sometime. Now, there's a fine place right harborside, the Mizzen, it's called. Best food in town, and quiet tonight with the *Beria* heading out at noon."

"Another time, perhaps."

"But you'll keep it in mind?"

"Yes, I'll do that . . ." She managed another step back. "But if the *Beria* is leaving so soon, I really must get to the harbor."

"Of course—wouldn't want to hold you up. Come by the shop one day or ask for me at the Mizzen of an evening. I'm there most nights, with the other bosses . . . Dan the cooper, that's me."

"Rowan," she supplied. "I'm certain we'll run into each other again." It would surely be impossible to avoid him entirely.

When she turned away, she was facing the water—and abruptly, it caught her again. She stood, all else forgotten, her heart filled only with light, motion, and joy.

Out past the harbor, on the far horizon, the sea glittered with sunshine, like diamonds cast on liquid silver; she felt the motion of the waves and the mass of the water below like a pull on her bones. The air was thick with damp; rich with the scent of salt and wrack and sea grass; alive with the slap of water, the call of gulls, and the wind from the wide, clear skies.

After so long in lands far away from the sea, the steerswoman found that she could hardly believe its beauty.

Rowan had been raised in flat farmlands at the edge of the Red Desert, far from sight or sound of the Inland Sea. But she had met the sea in the course of her training, learned how to mark her course across its open face, learned the beat and flow of its elegant logics, struggled against the turn of its whims.

In the end, she had come to know the sea as the home of her spirit: free, open in all directions, the widest road that a steerswoman could travel . . .

She took two steps forward, half dreaming, and rested her hand on something nearby—

The oak stump. She drew back her hand.

Waves halfway up New High Street . . . even here, so far from the Outskirts, Slado's spell had had an effect . . .

On the weather. The air connects everything to everything else. Really, she ought to give more study to weather.

She turned away from the bright sea, returned to the dusty road, and made her way toward the docks.

Alemeth's harbor was modest, merely a pair of piers and five wharves. Only one cargo ship was present, large enough that its draught kept it out in the deeper water. A barge was being loaded at the second pier; Rowan hurried to catch it.

She called to the small, wiry woman who appeared to be in charge. "Is that your ship?"

The woman slapped her tally board on her leg and looked up, eyes crinkled. "Captain Carlin's. But still, mine, too. My home. For now."

Rowan placed her accent. "Are you going straight back to Southport?"

"Just come from there. Donner next, send these clothes up the caravans. After that, don't know."

"Can you take this?" Rowan passed the package down to her, quelling a brief urge to snatch it back, to clutch the paper-wrapped box protectively.

The woman pursed her lips. "Need to see the mate for the charges . . . hm . . ." She read the address. " 'Archives—' " And she looked up at Rowan again, taking in the ring and chain. "You're a steerswoman?"

"That's right."

"Good enough." No ship would charge a carrying fee to any steerswoman. "Someone at Donner'll hold these for a ship to Wulfshaven, if *Beria* doesn't head there herself." Rowan grit her teeth at the thought of fragments of the shattered, fallen Guidestar sitting untended in some harbormaster's office.

The crewmember ticked off crates on her board. "If you've got time, navigator'd be glad to see you." Ship's navigators always welcomed the opportunity to have a steerswoman update their charts.

Rowan shook her head. "I'd be no use, I'm afraid; I'll have nothing new to add. I've been away from the sea and the Inner Lands for two years."

"Away from the sea?" The woman seemed to find the idea incomprehensible. "And the Inner Lands? Where else is there?"

"Well, there's the Outskirts."

She squinted in thought. "No sea there?"

"None that I found."

While they conversed, a sailboat rounded a woody spit, moving fast and light. By the time the barge pushed off, the sailboat had neared enough that its master was visible in the distance: a dark-skinned figure in a loose white shirt, a broad straw hat keeping off the sunlight. Rowan shaded her eyes to watch his nimble movements, appreciating his skill as he rounded the harbor buoys.

The sailor paused his work, then suddenly swept one arm back and forth in a broad, exaggerated wave. Without thinking, Rowan smiled, started to lift her own hand to wave reply.

But a small commotion burst out behind her; she turned to find that two fishing children had abandoned their poles and catch, and were shrieking happy giggles, flapping their hands wildly at the returning sailor. Then they thumped away, shuddering the pier with their footsteps, laughing a breathlessly incoherent conversation.

A small arrival, Rowan thought; a large event. A single person returning. The sailor had family or a lover or friends who would be glad at the news the children would bring.

Perhaps there would be a celebration, a gathering of laughter and greetings; and all the small events of the separated and now reunited lives would be brought out and displayed, remarked upon. They would be traded, each to each other, like small pieces of gold: treasured and cherished, then stored away safe in the hoard of favored memories.

It all could come to an end in a moment.

Slado could as easily target Alemeth as the distant Outskirts.

Instead of being overrun by hungry warrior nomads, this town, these people, could be destroyed directly, immediately, by magic.

She had to find Slado.

How do you find a man?

The steerswoman turned back, turned away from the clean, wide sea that she loved, and slowly made her way toward the dark and squalid chaos of the Annex.

3

The next morning, as she was walking by the mulberry groves, a man attacked her with a hoe.

Her parry gouged the haft through half its thickness. The man pulled back immediately and gaped at the handle. "Look what you've done!"

"Yes," Rowan said, bemused. "Fortunately, my sword isn't damaged."

"Who are you?" he demanded; Rowan explained. "What are you doing here?" She explained further. He was astonished. "Walking? What for?"

"Because I thought I would enjoy it."

He shook his head. "A walking steerswoman . . ."

Rowan was affronted. "Steerswomen spend most of their lives walking. We're rarely comfortable staying still for long."

His dubiousness was extreme. "Well . . ." He winced. "Well, I'm sorry, lady, but I took you for some hireling of Karin's. That's next plantation over." He indicated direction with a jerk of his head. "She's always at me one way or another, checking my progress and all. Wouldn't put it past her to do some harm, and that's what I was thinking, then, when I saw you."

Rowan laughed a bit, sheathed her weapon. "I understand. Competition must be fierce. But I assure you, I'm utterly harmless. Good morning to you." And she stepped around him, to continue on her way.

He called after her. "Here, lady; are you going to be coming by here often?"

She turned back, one brow raised. "Every morning, I expect."

He shook his head in dissatisfaction. "Mira never did that," he said, turning away.

"I'm not Mira," she told his departing back.

It was a statement she would make often in the coming days.

* * *

When she returned to the Annex she found that Gwen and Steffie were already present, discussing in subdued voices whether it was late enough to go upstairs to wake the steerswoman.

"How long have you been up?" Gwen asked when she had mastered her surprise.

"Since dawn," Rowan replied. She unslung her sword and laid it on the table, then shifted it to hang on the back of her chair as Steffie began bringing plates of food. "I was taking a stroll by the mulberries." There were warm rolls, dried apples, bacon, and gruel. "I expect that I keep earlier hours than Mira must have. I don't often sleep past dawn."

"At least you don't need Gwen helping you dress," Steffie commented.

Breakfast proceeded, with Gwen and Steffie chatting desultorily to each other, Rowan lost in her own thoughts. Eventually, in a lull in the conversation, Steffie addressed her directly. "Well, what's on for today, then?"

Rowan had a ready list of necessary chores already in the back of her mind, and she found herself reciting it with only a fraction of her attention. She was halfway through it when she realized, in retrospect, that Steffie had jumped just a bit after speaking, apparently because Gwen had kicked him under the table. Rowan stopped in mid-sentence, recovered her balance. "Or you could do whatever you usually do—or whatever you please . . ."

"Market day," Gwen pointed out.

"Fine." She paused again. "How did Mira handle the money?"

"Generally," Steffie put in, "if we say it's for the steerswoman, people just let us have it. They know us. But if it's a lot we're getting, Mira gives us coin to pay. Sometimes people will take it."

Rowan opened her mouth to ask, but Gwen guessed the question. "Money's in the jar," and she indicated with her head a blue-and-brown pottery jar with a lid, resting on the mantel.

Mira's trust had apparently been complete; Rowan decided she would act no differently and allow Mira's permanent replacement to deal with any possible pilfering. "Very well. And since the people don't know me, why don't you take whatever you think will cover the cost of everything— if there's enough."

"They'll give it," Gwen replied, offhand, then passed her empty plate to Steffie, who seemed inclined to linger over his meal. He took the hint, stuffed a heel of bread in his mouth, and stood to clear the table.

Rowan did not watch as Gwen went to the jar, but rose to attend to the books.

She paused one step away from the center aisle, feeling like a diver about to enter a pool whose water was of dubious quality.

Such an immense job.

She found herself wishing she could go outside again and simply walk, observing. She would make notes: bits and pieces of this town, this area of the world. Perhaps she would see something missed by the other steerswomen who had passed this way, perhaps discover something new, some new object or way or idea. Adding, incrementally, to the body of all knowledge.

That was the proper work of a traveling steerswoman: to discover, to chart, to explore . . .

Time enough later, to stay in one place. Time enough, when she was elderly, or when injury ended her traveling days. And even then there would be exploration, delving by thought and reason into the deeper questions of the world. With decades of experience behind her, with knowledge she had gained for herself, and more knowledge waiting in the ordered volumes at the Steerswoman's Archives.

Instead—

Stay here. Find Slado. Look for the clues of magic in these books.

And these books were all in chaos.

The steerswoman sighed and forced herself to enter the dusty stacks.

She sorted by decade. When the piles became waist high, she shifted them to the floors of other aisles, assigning the row nearest the front window as the most recent. Lunch, announced by Gwen, came and went; Rowan ate but hardly noticed.

In the afternoon, she did come across two logbooks covering the relevant period; and unable to restrain herself, she sat down on the low stepladder to scan through them.

The first was written by Helen, whom Rowan had met briefly at the Archives, and it began with Helen's embarkation on a sailing ship bound for Southport.

Rowan had herself originally planned to go to Southport, to "lay low," as Bel had put it. But laying low could be accomplished in Alemeth as well as in Southport; and Southport had nothing like the Annex.

Helen had sighted dolphins on her journey, which intrigued Rowan. Dolphins were rare enough to be considered legendary by most common folk. But such an event was hardly magical.

Rowan passed those pages by.

Once in Southport, Helen's entries continued in the standard steerswoman's fashion: descriptions of the local plant life; Helen's surprise that the only wild animals present were feral descendants of escaped domestic animals and imported pests, especially cats and rodents . . .

Not relevant. Move on.

Rowan heard the door open. She hesitated, hearing friendly greetings and conversation.

Mira had been a popular figure. Likely the residents of Alemeth were accustomed to dropping by.

"I'm not Mira," Rowan muttered, and she read on.

Helen's notes continued with detailed observations of the clearing of some land for a new home at the southernmost edge of the town. The process included the removal of a patch of bushes that clearly, and startlingly, were a form of tanglebrush—a plant Rowan had thought existed only in the Outskirts. How odd . . .

Out in the room, the conversation abruptly moderated to whispers. The visitor had apparently been told that the steerswoman was absorbed in work, and he or she was politely attempting to be unobtrusive. Rowan felt a twinge of guilt but continued to read.

Helen's sketches showed other plants and three insects, all of which Rowan recognized as native to the Outskirts. And Southport marked the southernmost known human habitation . . .

The whispers were continuing.

Rowan suppressed a sigh. The visitor intended to stay. A guest was being inconvenienced. Rowan, as host, was behaving rudely. Carrying Helen's book in one hand, Rowan emerged from the stacks and made her way to the hearth.

"And there she is! Good afternoon to you, lady." The speaker was a woman of middle age, with the lively face and youthful eyes of an avid gossipmonger.

They had been introduced briefly the previous day. "Good afternoon"—Rowan sought and found the name—"Lorraine."

Pot and teacups were arrayed on the worktable. Steffie lifted the lid, peered inside. "Tea's up," he announced and set to pouring and passing.

The largest and most comfortable of the chairs had been left empty. Rowan took the cue; she draped her sword belt over the wing chair's back, took a cup from Steffie, and sat, book in one hand, cup in the other. The permanent depression in the seat cushion left by decades of contact with Mira's bottom in no way matched Rowan's own bottom. She shifted awkwardly from edge to edge, her teacup rattling. Eventually she brought her feet up onto the wide seat and sat cross-legged; the pose immediately reminded her of Bel, who habitually sat on chairs exactly as she sat on the ground, if the seats were large enough.

Rowan wished Bel were here.

Whatever conversation had been ensuing during Rowan's absence now ceased in her presence. She suspected that the subject had been herself.

Lorraine rearranged herself in her creaking wicker chair, adopting a waiting expression of cheerful interest. Steffie handed Gwen a cup, then hunkered down by the hearth, sitting on his heels, blowing across his teacup. All were quiet for a long moment that began to teeter on the edge of becoming an awkward silence.

The steerswoman was expected to take the lead; Rowan quickly tried to think of something to say. "And how are you today, Lorraine?"

"Oh, busy as always, and isn't that the way when you've got such a family? I've been baking to feed a year's famine, and would you believe I'll do the same tomorrow? Now, if I hadn't set this aside—" she reached to the floor for a large wooden bowl covered with a cloth and offered it to Rowan. "As I was working anyway, then, I thought to myself, wouldn't them over at the Annex like some of this for their dinner afters?"

Rowan tucked her book between one knee and the chair arm, reached down to set her cup on the floor, and accepted the bowl. It proved to contain a number of small fancy pastries. "Thank you, that's very thoughtful." Rowan smiled a bit uncomfortably. Despite her years in the order, she always felt faintly embarrassed by the largesse customarily granted to steerswomen.

"My pleasure." Lorraine subsided again, smiling and nodding. Gwen quietly sipped her tea. Steffie rocked on his heels musingly.

The subject was spent. Rowan cast about for something that might interest this woman. She looked at the bowl in her lap. "Perhaps you'd like one of these with your tea?"

"No, thank you."

"Gwen? Steffie?"

"None for me."

"Later, maybe."

A pause.

"These cups are rather nice."

"Been here forever. Don't know where they came from."

"I see."

Quiet.

"Steffie, I don't believe I've asked you—what is your real name?"

"Real name?"

"Well . . . 'Steffie' is a nickname, isn't it?"

"No . . ."

"He's always been just 'Steffie.' "

"Oh."

Silence.

Rowan's mind ranged wildly. She was required to be entertaining. Half a dozen fascinating events from her personal experience occurred to her, but she found herself unable to baldly trot them out, like boasts. She wished someone would ask a question or express an opinion. She found she was gritting her teeth. "This morning I noticed that they're stripping the leaves in one of the mulberry groves," she said at random.

Success.

Lorraine's mouth dropped to become an open O; Steffie hooted a laugh and cried, "Lasker!"; and Gwen declared with delight, "He's mad!"

"Thinks he'll get the jump on us all," Steffie said.

"The jump on Karin, more like."

"It's his pride, that's what it is," Lorraine put in, leaning forward, her bright eyes wide with scandal. "He'll make not a penny extra, cause himself grief with hard work, but he'll have sales before Karin has promises, and that's what he's thinking of."

"What a fool." Steffie grinned. "More work than people when the season comes—why hurry it up?"

Gwen turned to him. "He'll want workers quick—you should tell your cousin."

"What, him? He gets fed, try to make him lift a finger past that—"

The door opened to admit an elderly man with a little girl in tow. Before he could speak, Gwen announced, "Spring silk!"

"Lasker," he said immediately, and everyone laughed.

Lorraine relinquished her seat to him. "It's a chill spring. Now, who's got the firewood for him, after that winter we had?"

The man snorted. "Everyone. Wrap ourselves in blankets and gloat over the coins he'll give us."

"I'm not freezing for Lasker's worms," Gwen said.

Steffie nudged her. "Saw you eyeing that frock in Tarry's shop."

She tossed her head. "Figuring the making. I can do as well myself . . ."

"And you can use spring silk!"

More visitors arrived, singly and in pairs. Each was told the tale of Lasker's conceit, each expressed an opinion, and the conversation continued under its own impetus.

At the end of two hours, the little parlor area held eleven persons, standing and sitting, and had gone through three more pots of tea. Looking around, Rowan realized that this was what the room must have been like while Mira lived: an open gathering place, for news and entertainment, with Mira in her stuffed chair with the sagging seat, the source and controlling center of it all.

But in Mira's place sat Rowan, quiet, attempting to listen politely and wishing that she could return to her work.

Rowan was perfectly capable of enjoying cheerful company and idle conversation. But she had an ominous feeling that she was going to be required to enjoy it, exactly like this, every single day.

She realized that the talk had died down, and she wondered if she absolutely must get it moving again or if there were any polite way to clear so many friendly people out of the Annex.

The problem was solved by Steffie. As if on cue, he slapped his knees, rose, and said, "Well, who's for a few, then?"

Some took up the idea; others declined. But all, blessedly, dispersed to their homes or to the taverns, bidding the steerswoman a polite good-bye—after making absolutely certain that she definitely did not wish to join them at the Mizzen or at Brewer's. Their expressions of puzzlement as they left told Rowan that Mira would have behaved very differently.

"I'm not Mira," Rowan informed the empty room.

There were teacups in every corner; Rowan gathered and washed them. Six different varieties of pastry, each with one bite taken, were discovered beneath various articles of furniture; the little girl had tested each and found them wanting. Rowan cleared them away, placed the bowl with its single remaining custard tart on the worktable next to her sword, wiped her hands on a cloth, and looked around.

The room was quiet, comfortable, the light from the tall windows slightly dim from the overcast sky. There was a sense of immanence, of the anticipation of work to come, work that mattered, and would be done well. Rowan paused a moment to savor the solitude.

Then she brought the selected logbooks to the table, gathered fresh paper, trimmed two pens, and settled to a seat. She opened a book flat before her, picked up a pen with one hand, the custard tart with the other, dipped the nib, and took a bite.

Sweetness filled her mouth, so strong and pure it seemed to run down her veins to her fingers. She had a sudden vision: wide, wide blue sky, roiling red and brown covering slow, low hills, swirling down a valley to embrace with shuddering color a single quick stream that glittered with speed. She heard a sound—a rattling hiss like rain on rooftops—felt the walls of the room open to the horizon, and she almost put out her arms, merely to feel the pleasure of space, almost turned around to speak to the good comrades standing just behind her . . .

She set her pen down carefully and looked at the pastry in her hand.

Why would a custard tart make her think of the Outskirts?

Fletcher.

I can make a custard tart that you wouldn't believe, he had said once, supporting his claim to humble origin as a baker in Alemeth. Whether or not it had been true, Rowan did not know. She would never have the opportunity to ask him, never be able to give him the chance to set right the lies he had told her, to become as true in words as he had always been in act.

It came to Rowan that custard tarts would now forever remind her of Fletcher.

She had no intention of avoiding custard tarts for the rest of her life, nor would it help her to do so. Every accoutrement of her work or habitual action she undertook had the potential to remind her of him. He had been that constant a presence, from the day she first saw his gangling, unlikely form amid a crowd of barbarian warriors, to the quick, shocking instant his life ended.

But it was not that ending that held her now, alone, motionless in the wide, empty room nor was it the beginning. It was single, sharp-felt moments in between.

How he had walked among the herds with her, wading the rattling redgrass, spouting now nonsense, now wisdom, both in the same canting Alemeth accent. How they had stood back-to-back awaiting battle, unseen by each other but sensed and known, and trusted. How he sat close behind her as she wrote in her logbooks, playing at distracting her, but waiting quietly and companionably when he saw she needed silence.

How, in the darkness of the tent at night, she listened to his long, sleeping breaths among the breathing of the other warriors and how, in the light-spattered brightness of the daytime tent, and they two alone together, his long, angular body a lattice around hers, they had spoken and not spoken, touched and moved . . .

And this is how people come to believe in ghosts, Rowan told herself: when memory and imagination are this strong. Imagination, inspired by longing, gifted with all the remembered details, abruptly presenting a perfect re-creation—in sound and sight and scent, in the very pressure of the departed one's breath upon the still air.

Were she a far simpler soul, she might almost believe *This is real*, almost think *He is here*, now, almost expect, at any moment, the sound of his voice just behind her.

Almost wait, and wait, for the touch of his hand on her shoulder—

She found that she had risen; and she discovered in herself a sudden, urgent need to be surrounded by people.

Nonsense. She had practically chased her visitors out.

Rowan stubbornly seated herself again, carefully rearranged her work, picked up her pen, and began a list: names of the writers of the selected logbooks, date ranges, assigned routes.

Halfway through, she idly and unconsciously took another bite of the tart.

She stopped. She set it down again. She sat regarding it.

Then: a few coins from the jar, Mira's cloak from the hook by the door, her sword—and she was out in the gray and drizzling street, swinging the cloak about her shoulders, pulling the door closed behind her.

4

$\mathcal{B}$rewer's Tavern was one left turn and four doors down, with its entrance and windows pulled half closed against the rain. Rowan entered the sea of murmuring voices, found a seat: a high-backed carved wooden chair at the empty end of a long table. Adjusting her sword to one side, she settled herself and with relief allowed the quiet conversations around her to lap gently at the edge of her consciousness.

A sudden pocket of silence formed at the other end of the table. Rowan looked. A group of mild-seeming men were eyeing her with alarm. One glanced at her sword.

The steerswoman gave a small smile. "It's a habit," she explained simply. "I've been traveling in dangerous lands." The men muttered among themselves, then returned to their drinking.

The tavern was busy, more than half full, with most of the customers gathered together in knots, as if they expected it to get fuller yet and wished to avoid being separated from friends yet to arrive. Two servers moved among the tables, and Brewer himself was pressed into duty, bustling about the room, bent but spry.

A serving girl with a full tray passed by Rowan and paused to place a mug of beer in front of her. She was about to accept payment when Brewer signaled vigorously from the far side of the room. "That's the steerswoman," he called, and the girl politely refused Rowan's coin and went on her way.

"Thank you," Rowan called after her, then caught Brewer's eye and raised her mug to thank him as well.

She leaned back, sipping, viewing her surroundings. There was only one room to the establishment, a long, low-raftered hall, whitewashed walls and smoke-blacked wood. Battered furniture of every description crowded the floor, few pieces matching: tables of rough plank and tables of old curly maple, low benches, high stools, chairs, a few worn armchairs. A pair of ancient divans were pushed against adjacent walls in a corner, seeming settled and frowsily comfortable, like elderly uncles. Apparently Brewer's was the final repository of much of the town's cast-off furniture; but far from seeming seedy, the effect was oddly pleasant. Rowan suspected that everyone present recognized at least one object in the room, and perhaps was made more comfortable because of it.

She could not imagine surroundings more homely or people more harmless. She felt rather a fool for being armed.

Brewer had worked his way around the room, and now stood passing mugs to the customers at Rowan's table: one to each of them and one more to Rowan. "Excuse me, but I already have one—"

He paused long enough to wink. "But you'll be wanting another."

"Eventually, yes . . ."

"It's here when you want it— Hey, no, you!" Something by the entrance caught his outraged attention. He dropped his empty tray with a clatter and hurried off at his best speed. One of the men at the table nudged his neighbor; the signal was passed down, finally reaching a severely inebriated man at the end, who roused himself with a sleepy smile, saying, "Here we go, then, here we go." All rearranged their chairs to acquire the best view of the proceedings.

Brewer had reached the door. "Out, out, then!" he shouted. "Out with you!"

The cooper was standing in the entrance, ostentatiously confused. "What?"

"You!" Brewer flapped his apron at the man, as if chasing geese. "You coming by here, some gall you have—"

"What, me? Passing by, wanted a drink— Hey, ho, stop! Do you flap at all your customers? No surprise your business is so poor—"

"Poor, this? But that's no thanks to the likes of you, telling tales, coaxing folk down to your brother's place."

"Now, Brewer, the Mizzen is a fine old inn, no reason not to say so—"

"Saying so *in* my place *to* my customers, while they're already having the best time to be had in Alemeth—"

"I think it's Maysie's house for that, you know," someone called out, and the room responded with laughter.

Something nagged at Rowan's mind; she could not place it.

The cooper drew himself up to his full burly height. "Now, look at this." He held it up. "Plain copper coin, as good as anyone's here, I should think. If you want it joining its friends in your till, you'll bring me a mug of your beer, which I freely admit is the best in town. In fact, with two beers for the same coin, I won't mention to everyone here how my brother's got a good dozen ducks on the spits at the Mizzen, sizzling since morning and just about done now—"

Brewer threw up his hands. "Two beers, and you shut up entirely!"

"Not a word? Who comes to a tavern just for drink?" He pushed the coin into Brewer's hand and backed away. "Now, I have to say a good day to my friends, don't I?—like the steerswoman there. Hey-oh, Rowan, and good afternoon to you . . ."

"Dan," Rowan acknowledged. The cooper reached her table and pulled up a chair.

"I see you've come out of hiding," he said, a broad smile on his broad face. He sat. "A musty old room like that's no place for a person like yourself. You should get a little sunshine, see a little life—and what about that dinner we planned together?"

Rowan sipped her beer, its mate still untouched before her. "With more work, that musty old room won't be quite so musty. And as I recall," she added, "the dinner was not planned but only suggested."

He was not put off. "Then may I also suggest," he said, folding his hands, "duck?"

"Perhaps another time—" She broke off. Laughter, off to her right, at the far corner of the room. The steerswoman sat, listening, puzzling.

Dan watched her. "Lady? Rowan?"

His voice caught her attention, but for a moment she found no words. Then she stood, abruptly, catching at the back of her chair to prevent it falling, suddenly clumsy. "Excuse me." Pushing her second beer toward Dan, she said, "Help yourself," and left, half sidling, half scrambling through and around the chairs and tables toward the back of the room.

The laughter had died down at the corner table, and the occupants were now conversing quietly, except for one dark man, his chair tilted back against the wall. Gloved hands steadied a mug on his knee. He watched her entire approach across the room, his expression unreadable.

Arrived, Rowan discovered that she had not the slightest idea what to say.

Apparently, neither did he. As the silence lengthened, his companions at the table grew still, then puzzled. "What's this?" she heard one of them ask another; she ignored them.

At last, the dark man winced. "I've been wondering when we'd run into each other. I heard that you were in town." He looked away, uncom-

ROSEMARY KIRSTEIN
35

fortable. "I admit I've been avoiding you. I've been trying to plan out what to say when we finally did meet. I'm afraid I couldn't come up with anything." He looked back. "Rowan, please—say something."

"Janus."

He grinned weakly. "Well, you remember my name, at least."

The words spoke themselves: "Why did you resign?"

The grin vanished. "I assume Ingrud sent word back to the Archives."

"I met her on the road."

"How was she?"

The steerswoman opened her mouth to reply, and closed it just in time. She said nothing; the sensation was almost physically painful.

Her silence had a similar effect on him; he looked as if he had been struck. Then he nodded slowly. "I see. I'm sorry about Ingrud. I treated her . . . well, 'badly' hardly covers it." He became intent. "Will you give me a chance to explain?"

Again she stopped herself just before speaking; but Janus had already raised one hand. "I'm sorry—I'll phrase that differently." He took a deep breath, then released it. "Rowan, my old friend, I'm very sorry that I've acted so stupidly. I regret it deeply, and I hope you'll give me the opportunity to explain myself." He studied her, tilt headed, a glint of humor in his eyes. "Will someone please find the steerswoman a chair? I think her knees are about to give."

Rowan sensed a movement to her left, heard the scrape of a chair behind her; but at that moment, her emotions resolved themselves, and she found herself not moving back, but forward, with what was without a doubt a very large and idiotic grin on her own face. Janus rose and met her halfway, and then they were laughing, pounding each other on the back, shouting for joy.

"Janus, you incredible imbecile. Gods below, it's good to see you alive!"

"I wasn't all that certain you would be glad to see me . . ."

"Of course I am!" All of a sudden, this strange town, where she had been feeling so awkward, was transformed. She had been so long in the Outskirts that the Inner Lands itself felt foreign; and she had not been aware of this until now. But here was a friend, and somehow that gave balance to the world.

She pulled back to look at him. "How long has it been?" It felt like decades, half a lifetime. She counted. "Six years." She stopped short. "You look terrible."

"Oh, thank you so much."

"You're so thin!" And his beard, she noted, was prematurely salted with gray.

"And you look as if at some time in the past you'd been dipped in vinegar and left to dry on a rock. Tell me, did you use your knife to cut your hair, or was it actually chewed by badgers?"

She laughed out loud, discovered a wonderfully witty answer, prepared to deliver it—and only just halted its escape by sheer force of will.

They stood regarding each other across the silence. "Well. Sorry," Janus said. "And here I'd been feeling as if the years had rolled back on us . . ."

"I'm afraid not."

"Apparently."

Rowan noticed that the silence that surrounded them was somewhat larger than could be generated by two people. Looking about, she discovered herself and Janus to be the center of rapt attention. As she watched, the inebriated man at the end of her former table received another nudge from his crony, and with no attempt at dissemblance whatsoever, that entire group once again readjusted their chairs to face the action, making rather a lot of noise doing so. The act was not lost on the rest of the crowd, inspiring laughter and some wry remarks that evolved into a spate of banter, under cover of which Rowan leaned close to Janus to say, "You mentioned an explanation."

"Yes."

"A long one?"

"As long as you require."

"Here?"

"Preferably not."

"Good." At which point the crowd ran out of witticisms and returned its attention to Rowan and Janus. The steerswoman had the bizarre sensation that she was facing one single, curious, many-eyed creature.

"There's . . . no way to exit discreetly, or unobtrusively, is there?"

Janus seemed to be enjoying himself. "If those are the only options, no." She noticed that he pitched his voice to carry.

She ought to be playing along; she ought to try to fit in. These people meant her no harm and were giving her the opportunity to either perform or participate, as she chose. She found such ostentation difficult. "What other options do you suggest?" she said, managing a more normal tone.

He made a show of deep thought. "Under the circumstances . . . I believe 'with dignity' is the best we can hope for."

She sighed, winced. "I shall follow your lead."

5

*R*owan's last contact with Janus had been not sight but sound.

She had been walking in a forest, along a route more game trail than path, that slanted and wound up a woody hill. As she walked, a part of her mind was measuring her own steps, noting with pleasure their swing and pace; another part was studying the land about her in what was already a reflexive, half-conscious contemplation; and a third part, that part of herself to which she put her own name, was realizing with joy and wonder that this would be her life: forever walking across the wide face of the world.

It was the first time she was doing the things of which her life would now consist: it was the first hour of the first day that she was traveling entirely alone, as a newly qualified steerswoman.

Four of them, freshly graduated students all, had journeyed together from the Archives on the way to their separate, assigned routes. An hour ago, they had reached the point where they must split and continue each alone. Their good-byes had been strange and almost tentative; the fact of their separation had seemed not quite real. Then each turned and walked away, into the hilly woodlands: due north, northeast, due south, southwest.

Rowan worked her way uphill in close pine forest, and eventually reached a crest, where rock bared the face of the hill to the open sky. She paused and turned around to view the land, checking it against the map in her memory, noting elevations—that craggy hill to the south was perhaps a bit higher than charted—gauging distances—she might make that distant saddle by nightfall—marking how the little brook in the floor of the dell meandered down from the northeast—its source was unknown; perhaps Rowan would be the one to discover it! . . .

She was completely alone.

As her gaze swept the entire landscape, there was no sign of human presence, no sign of her former companions. Even the little path where they had parted had been swallowed by overhanging pines. There was only the cloud-crowded sky above her; the soft dark green of the piney hills all around; the glitter of water far below; and close beside her, the liquid twitter of a song sparrow.

And it seemed then to Rowan that a door had closed and that she now stood on the one side, and her Academy days; the companions of her youth; the bustling seaport of Wulfshaven; the cool stone corridors of the Archives; the wise, worn faces of the elder steerswomen, her teachers, whom she loved so well—all on the other side.

She did not regret the closing of that door, but she was very surprised to find that the door existed and more surprised still to discover that, in her mind, it bore the label *Home*.

She was leaving it behind, possibly forever.

And those who had traveled with her, who had inhabited that home with her and left it in her company, were now lost to her, vanished. She might never see them again.

At last she turned uphill to continue her journey. But before she re-entered the forest, the sparrow on her left suddenly ceased its song. Rowan stopped short. She listened.

A far-off, high-pitched piping.

From the south, a flute, blown hard and shrill to carry the distance. Janus's wood and silver flute—and Janus, unseen, squeaking out a little jig compressed into the upper register: a tune utterly silly, completely merry. Rowan smiled.

And in her mind's eye, as if sprung into existence from nowhere, suddenly there was Ingrud: stopping short, listening, catching the idea, throwing off her pack. An instant later—yes! A *blat!*, a *squeee!*, a continual, distant roar as Ingrud yanked the bellows of her squeeze-box, all its buttons depressed. Not music at all but the loudest noise possible, and the combination of roaring and twittering was too foolish to be borne, and Rowan was laughing helplessly.

She wished she and the fourth traveler had some way of joining in; but young Zenna had found her own solution. A sustained hoot echoed off the hilltops, then a series of yips, and then wild yelps and howls like a hunting hound. A dog, a bird, and—what was the squeeze-box? a bull moose!—all serenading the green forest. Rowan wanted to contribute, somehow, but she must first stop laughing, and she could not. The cacophony was impossible. She was gasping, and she fell to a seat on the stones, leaning back against her pack, wiping at her eyes ineffectually.

At last the noise began to die down. Ingrud and Zenna vied for the honor of making the last and loudest noise, with longer and longer pauses between. But it was Janus who ended it with a final, emphatic, almost admonishing *peep!*

Then the moment was past. The last echo died. Rowan sat on the ground, hugging her knees, catching her breath. At last she rose and walked away.

Her friends were not vanished, but only out of sight, traveling to adventures of their own.

Many miles later, it occurred to Rowan that the wind had been at her back, that quite possibly her laughter had been carried on it, and that perhaps she had been heard.

She decided that she liked that very much: that the last thing her friends might ever hear of her would be her laughter.

And there was laughter again, immediately outside the tavern door.

Among Rowan's people, when two people walked together, it was the woman's place to offer her arm to the man; among Janus's people, the identical offer was the man's duty. They both stood a moment, elbows ridiculously cocked at each other, then broke into long laughter.

It was a very old joke between them. At the Academy, they had come to use the gesture in place of a greeting.

Janus recovered first and solved the dilemma by throwing one arm across Rowan's shoulder; she slipped her arm about his waist, and they proceeded down the street in that fashion. And that, too, was very familiar.

Except that the streets were not in Wulfshaven, and the man at her side was not a handsome eighteen-year-old. She studied him sidelong. He was her age, to the month, but there was the gray in his beard, and he had a new, wiry gauntness. He caught her scrutiny and returned it. "You look very much the perfect steerswoman."

"Despite my haircut?"

"Possibly because of it."

He smelled of old dust and new sawdust. "You've been working at the cooper's warehouse."

"I'm impressed."

"It's the only current construction I've noticed in town."

They reached the corner. Rowan had thought they would go right, to the Annex; but, perhaps out of habit, Janus turned them left and they went down Old High Street.

"I'm waiting for that explanation."

"Yes. Give me a moment."

She could feel how uncomfortable he was, and how abruptly he became so. She found it made her sad. "All I heard," she said, "was that the ship you were taking to Southport was lost at sea; we assumed you dead. But two years later Ingrud ran into you, playing flute in a tinker's band."

"I wandered, for a while . . ."

She waited for him to go on; he did not. "Ingrud said," she prompted, "that you told her you'd resigned, and that you refused to explain why. She had to place you under the Steerswomen's ban."

They continued walking. He remained silent. She grew disturbed. "Are you refusing to answer me?"

His reply was quick. "No, I'm not refusing. I'm . . . organizing myself."

Old High Street descended toward the harbor. The drizzle had ceased, and the sun, on the horizon, had escaped the overhang to wash the harbor with gold light, made richer by the gray above. Janus twice drew a breath as if to speak, did not, then at last sighed. "It's not easy to tell . . . partly because it's not really a tale. I could lay the events out to you, one by one . . . all the way to now, but that won't tell it. It's more . . . internal. Plenty of things did happen—and none of them pleasant . . . but really, I just discovered that I'd gone wrong.

"A steerswoman's life isn't for everyone, Rowan, we always knew that. The Academy is designed to sort out those who aren't suited, one way or another, but the process isn't perfect—it can't be."

Rowan reminded herself that the sorting out continued after graduation, and that process was by far the worse.

Janus's voice was quiet, his body tense. "The simple explanation," he said in a voice of obviously forced nonchalance, "is that I found that I just wasn't up to it."

Information this scant constituted no explanation whatsoever. "Janus, you were up to it. You showed that, over and over, during our training."

"I'm sure it seemed that way. But it's one thing to train, another matter altogether to *do*. And I suppose I did do well enough, when it came down to it . . ." He relaxed somewhat, although his voice was bitter. "When the ship came apart in the storm, I did get myself to shore, I did keep myself alive in the wild lands, I did get back to civilization . . ." He grew quiet, then went on, more uncomfortably. "It's a question of heart, Rowan. I could do what was needed . . . but it was just . . . I found it terrible. I found I never wanted to pass through any such thing again."

Rowan found the statement so obvious as to be meaningless. "Of course you don't," she said. "No one does. That's why we learn, and plan, so that when we encounter difficult situations, or dangerous ones, we can survive them and go on."

"That's a very glib response," he said, almost sarcastically, then seemed to regret his tone. "Sorry." He was quiet for a space. "Rowan, the first time I came into any real danger—well, you were there, actually."

She was a moment recalling. "And Ingrud, and Zenna," she reminded him. A starless night, a dim campfire, more than a half dozen wolves. It was not a pleasant memory.

"I got the impression that you weren't frightened at all," he said.

This so surprised Rowan that she laughed out loud. "Nothing of the sort! I was terrified!"

"Well, you didn't show it."

"I suppose I was too busy to show it."

"But it affected Zenna badly."

It had indeed; Zenna, the youngest of them, had been nearly hysterical with fear. But—"Only after the fact." During the attack itself, Zenna had been a small whirlwind of action and had collapsed into tears only when it became safe to do so. In retrospect, Rowan found herself admiring Zenna's strength and control. "And you and Ingrud cheered her out of it."

"Yes. But it affected me as well. I didn't say so at the time. I thought it would pass. I thought I'd get used to it. The shipwreck was worse . . . I had no one to help me." He could not meet her eye. "Rowan, I'm a coward."

"Impossible."

"No." He spoke heavily. "It's true."

She expected him to elaborate, but he did not. "If you were a coward, you'd never have joined at all," Rowan said.

"No. I didn't understand. Now I do."

"What didn't you understand?"

He was so long in replying that she wondered if he would answer at all. "I thought it would be an adventure," he said at last. "I never thought— I never really understood how much danger there is in adventure."

"Janus, admittedly, you had a rather bad experience—"

He made a noise of frustration. "You don't understand—"

She broke away from him, stepped into his path to face him; he stopped short, stepped back. "No," Rowan said to him, "I don't understand. And you're doing nothing to help me. *Make* me understand."

"I don't know if I can."

"That's nonsense. Anything known can be communicated."

He blinked, then smiled. "Known by whom? And by what means? Communicated to whom? And in what fashion?"

The questions were purely rhetorical; he was directly quoting a lesson from their training. The tactic annoyed Rowan. "Janus, I was merely stating the principle, as you know well—"

"Yes, but you mustn't state a principle in a way that makes it seem like a description of the immediate circumstance." He was suddenly enjoying himself. "That's a form of equivocation. And an invitation to misconstruction. Not to mention manipulative." He put his arm about her shoulder again. "And now let's discuss the ethics of the various degrees of manipulation; I can't recall when I last had a chance to talk on this level."

But she slipped from his reach. "You've changed the subject."

"Yes. Unsuccessfully." He sighed. "But there is a truth in there." They had reached the first wharves of the harbor; he took her hand and led her to a seat on one of a group of water barrels, with her back to the harbor. The last light of the sun made him squint as he studied her face, seeming to search for something. "Rowan," he said, "I don't know you." He put up a hand to forestall her protest. "No, it's true. As students we spent four years almost living in each others' pockets, and if you'd asked me at the end of that time, I would have said that I knew you, perhaps better than I knew my own family.

"But I don't know you now. I don't know what you've done, and I don't know what the world has done to you.

"You know how dependent understanding is upon context. But the context needed to understand this is *me*: what *I've* done, what the world has done to me—the me that was before, the me that was during, and the me I am now. And I can't make you be me.

"The young woman I knew at Academy . . . I don't think there's any way I could make her understand what I feel." The last full light of the sun slipped away, and she saw him take a moment to note its passing. "Any more than I could convince the Janus of that time, I suppose," he continued. "And that's too bad. Because I could have saved myself a lot of . . . unhappiness, if I'd known then what I know now."

"But what is it that you know now?"

"I've told you." He said it again, now lightly. "I'm a coward. You can't be a steersman and a coward at the same time, Rowan; it doesn't work. Trust me."

There was something peculiar in that voice: it was at odds with his body. Even in the gathering gloom, Rowan could see how tightly he held himself. His stance contradicted his tone. He was trying too hard to convince her. He wished her to believe him and to let the matter pass.

There was more to know here. "Janus, I don't believe that you're a coward."

"All I can do is tell you that it's so—"

"But why do you think it's so? Because you felt fear? Everyone does, at some point, if they're alive and not living in a cocoon."

He made a movement as if to turn away; the tension in his body had grown too great to permit him to do so. He said, "I didn't simply feel fear—"

"Then, what? I don't mean to, to trivialize your experience—but when danger comes, we do feel fear. And then the danger passes, if we survive it. But to look back on fear as if it suddenly constituted your very nature—"

"*Does* it pass?" The words came suddenly, as if by themselves.

She spoke definitely. "It passes. You are not *now* shipwrecked; you are not *now* alone in the wilderness—"

"That passed." Something released in him, and he took a step toward her. "And the next one passed." He spoke close to her face. "And the one that followed, and the one after that—" He straightened, half turned away, flung out one arm. "And every single thing passes, one by one, but Rowan—" and he turned back "—Rowan, when I look out of my window every morning, *I am afraid*—can't you see?

"It didn't *make* me afraid! It made me discover that I *am* afraid; it made me see the reasons to *be* afraid! It made me see what was always there, that I'd never noticed; and once I'd seen it I couldn't stop seeing it. It's always there, Rowan; it's always right there behind my eyes!" He jabbed his fingers against his own forehead forcefully; and although it was a small gesture, it startled her with its tiny violence. She reached up instinctively to pull his hand away; but he caught her arm suddenly. "No, look!"

He grabbed her shoulders, forced her around roughly. "Look—there, over there." Two fishers, securing their boat for the night. "That man, pulling the hawser. He could scrape his hand, catch an infection, and lie for days in agony, wishing he would die. And his crewmate, that woman— she could fall in the water, bump her head, and drown, and then where would her children be? She has six, and no husband, no other family. Four boys and two girls, and it takes every waking breath of every day to feed them and house them, and in one stroke of chance she'd be gone and they'd be alone. Would they starve? Perhaps not, perhaps people here wouldn't let them starve, but—" His grip on her shoulders was tight, hard, his voice half choked. "—*but can you imagine their pain?* One instant all is fine, and the next . . . the world is in ruins." He released her abruptly, and she slid off the barrel to stand facing him, the imprint of each of his fingers still felt on her body.

Light from the fishing boat caught his dark eyes; but he was not looking at her or the harbor. His voice was strange, eerily inflectionless. "Every single thing can fall," he said. "Swiftly or slowly. In pain, or in silence. Nothing lasts, nothing is safe. Safety is imaginary.

"The whole world is arranged against us. And we make our little accommodations, draw a circle around them, and think: well, that's nice, that works, we can live like this. And we pretend that our little circle is the whole world, or all of the world that matters." He closed his eyes and reached out slowly, fingers spread, like a blind man. His voice became more human. "And we live in that circle, Rowan, huddled together, holding hands in the firelight, and all these little events—the love affairs, the marriages, the waking and sleeping, and all our daily work—they all seem so large to us in the smallness of our scope. But anything, anything could stop it, steal our breath, break our bodies, give our hearts more pain than we were built to endure."

And now he did look at her, or in her direction; but in that gaze she felt herself strangely without identity. "Sometimes," he said, "I think that stupidity is a blessing. Because, what is there to do except live? And we have to live, we *want* to live, but how can we live without pain, without fear, without so anticipating every disaster that terror turns us to stones?

"So, we act. We act because we have to. We protect each other when we can. We do all we're able to; and if we're just stupid enough, we can believe that it's sufficient. Until . . . until we find out that it isn't. With luck, we die at that point. But up until then, with just enough stupidity, it is possible to be happy."

Silence between them. Then: "All this from a shipwreck and being lost in the wilderness?"

"All this," he replied in hardly more than a whisper, "from dreaming one night that I was drowning and waking up to find it was true; from being trapped in the small darkness, with the cabin tumbling, water falling on me, and on me, every time the ship rolled; from the single, solid *sound* of it, a sound made of—of thunder and shattering wood and screams, and then wind, too, suddenly wind, and the flickering light; from what I saw in that light; from what I felt in the dark; from clutching at a piece of wreckage, hoping to float, and finding it was a human body . . ."

His voice stopped. On the boat, the fishers extinguished the lamp and stepped onto the wharf, their footsteps thumping softly and wearily as they passed by, away into the night.

She hoped Janus was finished speaking. He was not.

"From the hunger," he said. "From the cold. From the dark. From the voices in the dark."

And then there was quiet. The steerswoman felt she could not move from the weight of silence; and she found herself trying, as a steerswoman will, to survey the country in which Janus lived.

She almost understood.

Darkness all around, shapes in the darkness: terrible things moving in the dark. Things sensed, not by sight or sound, but by immanence, the knowledge that at any moment one of them might reach out to touch her—

Rowan felt that if she tried very hard, she would be able to see those shapes clearly, but she would first have to do something: make some movement, turn in some specific direction, *twist.*

She could not make herself turn in that direction; it seemed to her that the movement required was one that only a broken body could make.

Eventually she said slowly, "The things you say . . . they're nothing that I don't already know." She was surprised to discover how true this was.

From the shadows: "I know."

"But you're wrong about . . . about stupidity being a blessing." The idea disgusted her; even to entertain it made her feel unclean. "There's something else. There's something you're missing."

"Of course there is. The world is as it is, Rowan, and there are three ways to exist gladly in it: You can be ignorant, knowing nothing of its nature; you can be stupid, and know of it but never truly understand; . . . or you can be brave.

"I have, in me," Janus said, "just enough of that daily courage to do what I need to do, and live as I do. To live as a steersman, too . . . it would take too much. It would hurt all the time. I can't do it."

"I'm sorry." Blindly, she reached out to place one hand on his shoulder. The sensation shocked her. He had seemed, for a while, to be only a voice, a voice out of darkness, speaking darkness. But touch made him real.

He was human. He was Janus. He was her old and dear friend, and he was in pain. This much, at least, she could understand.

"I'm sorry I made you speak of it," she said. "I suppose I can see why you didn't want to tell anyone, even Ingrud . . ."

And he reached up to clasp the hand that rested on his shoulder. "Yes," he said, "and I'm sorry I told it to you. You're too intelligent. Try not to think too much about what I said. I wouldn't want you to understand it too well. I wouldn't want you to become like me."

"I won't," she said immediately, without thought; and only noticed after that there was a sort of cruelty implied by the statement.

"Of course you won't."

They sat down together on the barrels, facing the harbor, and remained so for a long time. Lights from the harborside shops cast a hundred gold coins on the water; small waves chuckled against the wharves; rigging rattled quietly in the darkness.

Somewhat later, a portion of what Janus had said returned to Rowan. "And," she said without preamble, "I don't feel particularly brave, myself."

"Of course not," he replied, invisible in the dark. "That's the beauty of it."

6

*T*he steerswoman leaned back in the sunshine. "I'm hiding from the conclave of gossips," she said.

Brilliant light poured down from the sky, as clean and fresh as new wine. Rowan sat, arms around her knees, leaning up against the aft railing of a small sailboat, which was tethered to a broken piling at the more ramshackle end of the harbor. The ship itself was tidy, but showed years, perhaps decades, of general neglect. The steerswoman decided that her sense of seamanship ought to be affronted, but the day was too fine, too bright and cheery to allow any such feeling to last.

Janus was on hands and knees with a crowbar, prying up one of three deck planks that had worn from sheer age into hazardous nests of splinters. Their replacements stood nearby, good new oak, not yet stained.

Out in the daylight, the previous night's conversation seemed an unpleasant dream, of the dark and murky sort that were the most disturbing, and the most easily dispersed by sunshine and sea air.

Janus laughed, the old bright laugh, now framed strangely by the gray-peppered beard. His skin, naturally brown, had been darkened near black by sunlight, and he wore a threadbare but clean muslin shirt of bright yellow, green canvas trousers, and gray gloves. Rowan considered the overall effect pleasantly decorative. " 'Conclave of gossips,' " he said. "That's a good term." A nail squealed protest as his prying lifted one plank edge. "They used to have something similar in the town where I grew up, and I always thought it was the most miserable, mundane way of passing time imaginable. Now, I actually enjoy it. Especially in winter, with a fire, and the wind rattling in the dark outside." The image was near enough to one he had mentioned the previous night that Rowan felt a quick, small shiver that vanished immediately. Janus seemed not to notice. "There are some very good people in this town, Rowan," he went on. A final tug delivered the plank into his gloved hands. "You just have to learn to appreciate them." He set it noisily aside and began on the next.

Rowan made no attempt to assist him, feeling even more smugly lazy by contrast. "Quite possibly. But I'm afraid I can't yet face the interrogation that will certainly come after our little public scene at Brewer's. They're all agog, I'm sure."

"No doubt. But unless you leave town immediately, you'll have to find some way to deal with them."

She closed her eyes and tilted her face up to the wonderful light. "I'm strategizing," she said.

"So I see." She heard the second plank surrender. "And what do you—" He caught himself. "I mean to say, how—damn." She opened her eyes to find him scowling to himself. "This," he said, "is not the most natural way of carrying on a conversation. I need to get used to talking without asking a single question. Perhaps I should practice in front of a mirror. But first I'll need to buy a mirror . . ."

"I suppose that you've gotten out of practice since Mira died. Or did you not associate with her at all?"

A glance away, a glance back; and he was suddenly giving the problem of the third plank far more concentration than it might reasonably warrant. The steerswoman said cautiously, "What?"

He sighed, stopped working, settled back to sit. "Actually, we associated quite a bit. I was a regular member of the conclave. However," and he winced, "I neglected to mention to her that I was under the Steerswomen's ban." He had, at least, the grace to look ashamed.

"Surely she must have known." Even though word of a person being placed under ban by a traveling steerswoman might take a year or more to make its way back to the Archives, and longer still to double back out to the other steerswomen on the road, eventually the news did manage to become general. And any steerswoman at a permanent posting, such as the Annex, would have the opportunity to maintain regular communication with the Archives. "The Prime certainly would have included the fact in one of her letters to Mira."

"You're assuming that Mira was a person who read her letters." He returned to his work, rather more desultorily. "Or cared about their contents. Possibly she did know. But if she did, she must not have cared."

Rowan suppressed a derisive snort. "That would be typical."

"Mm. Don't be too hard on Mira."

"There's no excuse for her neglecting the Annex as she did."

"No . . . nevertheless."

"Would you have done the same in her place?"

"Of course not. I would have been a model of rectitude. My analects would blaze with brilliance and stun with conciseness. Total strangers would come for miles merely to browse my catalogs. Literate persons everywhere would worship me as a god." Rowan laughed; Janus shifted to deal more seriously with the last plank. "In fact," and he paused as it clattered free, "I was more than a little envious of Mira. Sometimes I think that I wouldn't mind having a job like hers myself." He considered the plank thoughtfully, then held the board with one of the protruding nails tip down on a bit of scrap iron. He picked up a hammer and banged at the surrounding wood.

He had extracted three nails in this fashion before he glanced at Rowan again. She could not tell what he saw in her expression, but it caused him to set his tool aside and watch her curiously.

At last she said, "Would you actually like a job like Mira's?"

The question puzzled him. He made a vague gesture with one hand. "Hundreds of books, information immediately to hand with no effort, a chance to create and maintain order, total safety—not to mention money to live on and a rather nice house . . . of course I would—" He stopped. The steerswoman waited patiently while he passed through several abortive attempts to speak without using questions. At last he settled on: "I've resigned from the Steerswomen."

"True."

"And I'm under ban, as you no doubt have noticed."

"Also true. Now, do you remember the circumstances under which the Steerswomen's ban can be lifted?"

"There are none."

"Think."

He thought. He shook his head, spread his hands, tilted back to sit, regarding her.

"Very well. Consider this." She took a moment to put it together. "Imagine you're me. And I'm . . . oh, some local fisher—"

"Young Dionne," he supplied.

"Young Dionne it is. And you say to me, 'Young Dionne'—not to be confused with Old Dionne, I suppose—'Young Dionne, I've heard that you have a special location you go to get the best catch,' and I reply, 'Well, yes, indeed, that's a fact, and well known it is, my catch being the best to be had in town, and I'm pleased to admit it. Now, I've just gone and hit a nice little run of smelt—' " He laughed out loud at her exaggerated imitation of the Alemeth accent. "And then you say," Rowan went on, " 'Where is this special place?' " She paused to give him opportunity to anticipate her direction. "And I say, 'Oh, there's many'd like to know that, have to keep it to myself, now, don't I, sorry, lady, but there you are.' " She paused again, purely for effect. "And you say, 'I'm sorry to tell you, Dionne, but you're now under the Steerswomen's ban.' And then I say, 'No, never mind, I take it all back, here's how you get there—' and proceed to tell you exactly where to go." She paused a third time. "Now, Dionne is not under ban, correct?"

Hesitantly, "Correct."

"The question becomes: Was she ever under ban?"

He was even longer replying. "I'd say, no, not technically . . ."

"Really? I'd say yes . . . technically. For a few moments. The ban was placed, briefly, and then, as I see it, lifted—and here's the significant part— when Dionne provided the answer to the question she had previously refused." He made a protesting gesture; she forestalled any accompanying comment. "Janus, perhaps you weren't an active steersman long enough for something like that to happen to you, but it has to me, more than once. I thought nothing of it at the time. But I'm thinking of it now, and it seems to me that the principle has been established: the Steerswomen's ban can be lifted—and by a very specific action."

"Rowan—" and he made a frustrated noise—"as we say in Alemeth: I'm not buying this."

"What an interesting turn of phrase. And why not?"

He made to speak, stopped, began again. "I thought it was traditional to offer the person three chances to answer the question."

"It is. I've shortened the story. Assume that the three chances were offered. The principle remains."

He made to scratch his head in frustration, but found himself foiled by his gloves. Instead of removing them, he abstractedly readjusted their fit, finger by finger; it seemed a habitual action. "And I suppose that as you see it, my telling you everything last night now entitles you to single-handedly remove the ban from me."

"Well, no. Interpreting things strictly, you'd have to provide Ingrud herself with the answers that you previously refused."

" 'Interpreting things strictly?' " He threw up both hands. "Rowan, your analysis lacks rigor from beginning to end! You've taken a borderline situation, extracted a spontaneous detail from it, arbitrarily declared the detail a principle; which so-called principle you now, in all steerswomanly assiduousness, decide to apply strictly—and what are you grinning at?"

She was forbidden to reply, but the grin remained. Eventually, Janus provided the answer himself. "Marrane will be thumping the ceiling any moment now."

" 'Keep it down, please, people are trying to sleep,' " Rowan quoted.

" 'The argument will still be there in the morning.' " He leaned forward, elbows on knees, hands folded. "Rowan, I won't go traipsing off cross-country to find Ingrud, just to simplify conversation with you."

"Of course not. You might take years to find her. What I suggest is that we put the matter to the Prime. If she agrees that the principle is sound, she might also allow a substitute for Ingrud. Herself, possibly, for formality's sake. You provide the Prime the same information you refused Ingrud. A letter would do, I suppose." After two years in the Outskirts, it seemed to Rowan strange, marvelous, and immensely civilized that such ease of communication with the distant Archives could exist. The entire matter might be resolved in less than six months.

"Even if Henra concedes that your, shall we say, extremely dubious idea is valid, that doesn't set me in Mira's place. The Annex is tended by a steerswoman."

"No problem there; once the ban is lifted, I see no reason you can't rejoin."

"That isn't done."

"Of course it is. Not often. But I've done it myself."

He was stunned. "Rejoined? You resigned and rejoined? When? Why?"

She thumped the deck with her fist in frustration, setting the salvaged nails rattling; one of them gave a lively jump and disappeared down the gap left by the old boards. It clinked twice on its way down and rolled to a stop far below.

Janus looked after it. "Damn. I really must learn to watch what I say." He looked up at her. "I'll never know now. I'm sure there's a story there, and now I'll never hear it."

"Unless we can get the ban lifted."

He thought a moment. "I can live without the story." He forced the last nail from its home, moved it and its mates far away from the gap.

He reached for the next loose plank, but Rowan planted her foot on it. "Where's the harm in trying? Where's the harm in at least asking the Prime if it can be done?"

"Even if the ban were lifted," he said slowly, his expression held so carefully neutral it pained her to see it, "I can't live as a steersman."

"No, that's not the problem—" He made to rise and turn away; she leaned forward, caught one of his arms. "No, hear me out. You can't live on the road. You can't—" She briefly sought a gentler way to phrase it, failed, and stated mere fact: "You can't live in danger. You're unable to bear hardship and fear. You need safety, stability . . .

"But, Janus, the Annexes aren't merely tended by elderly steers-women; the custodians are chosen from among the steerswomen who can't travel. Age is the usual reason for that, but there are many others—"

"Deficiency of character is not on the list."

It stopped her. She attempted to reorganize her argument, found it difficult to hold, difficult to delineate. She spoke with less certainty. "I . . . can't view it as a deficiency . . . It's . . . just a fact, a discovery. Like finding that you have a trick knee or that you're going blind. It's nothing you have a choice in."

"It's not comparable."

Rowan released him, leaned back, rubbed her forehead. "I think it is. If you had known beforehand, or found out during training and tried to keep it from our teachers, it would have been different." She sighed, spread her hands. "But I'm not certain, one way or the other, yet. The idea needs more analysis, and perhaps by better heads than mine. And that's precisely why it needs to be put to the Prime."

This time he did rise and stepped to the port railing, there to stare out at the open sea.

She rose and went to him. "Janus, the only thing you did wrong was not telling Ingrud about it immediately." She was sorry to upset him so; but it might prove worth it in the end. "And I think, I *do* think that I understand, at least, why you couldn't. Perhaps the Prime will understand as well. But we won't know unless we ask. She may decide it's accurate to regard your . . . inability in the same way as any steerswoman's at the Archives; like Sarah or Hugo or Berry—"

"Berry?" He spun. "Something's happened to Berry?"

Berry was their own age, and had lived and studied beside them for four years of training. Berry was dear to them both.

But with Janus under ban, Rowan was forbidden to answer even this simple question.

And he knew it; but still, he asked again, helplessly, "Rowan, please, what's happened to her?"

He reached for her shoulders as if to shake her; she stepped back, star-tled. But just as quickly he dropped his hands, shook his head. "She's alive," he said to no one. "If she's living at the Archives, she *is* alive." He shut his eyes tightly.

Rowan was disturbed. His reaction seemed too extreme. "Janus—"

"And what happened to *you*?" He opened his eyes, his gaze suddenly wide, wild. "What happened to your hand, to make all those scars? When, when did it happen?" And once started, all the simple, unasked questions came tumbling free, unstoppable. "Where have you been? Where are you going next? What have you been doing? What did you discover?" He wrapped his arms around himself tightly. "Did you see . . ." and he was no longer looking at her but off, away, to some imaginary far horizon ". . . what no one else has ever seen?"

They stood silent for a long time. Water thunked; rigging snapped. Somewhere ashore, three women's voices were raised in noisy argument, as incomprehensible as the conversation of birds.

Eventually, Rowan said cautiously: "It's a good thing you stopped. Had you gone on much longer, I'd be unable to converse with you on any topic whatsoever." And impossible, now, for her to tell him of the wizard Slado, of the urgency of her mission and so, impossible also for her to recruit his assistance.

He stood on the deck in the sunlight, wrapped in his own embrace as if in some great physical pain. Then, slowly, he unwound himself, regarding his own hands as he spread the fingers stiffly.

It came to Rowan that Janus needed her help far more than she needed his.

His anguish was too close to the surface. The strain of masking it was too great. His control was too fragile, and his emotions, when they broke through, too helpless. It was unhealthy; it was dangerous. Something must be done.

"Janus," she said gently, "think of it. You'd live right here, in Alemeth, among people you already know well. You'll have respect, a home, and good work that actually uses your skills, instead of wasting your training on odd jobs. And you'd be host to any steerswoman passing by, and you could talk to her, question her, learn all her adventures as you pour another cup of tea right by your own fireside—"

"Write the Prime." He turned away, carefully placed his hands on the railing, spoke with his back to her. "You write her first. If she agrees to your plan, then I'll see if I can stand to bare my soul a second time."

She felt a rush of gratitude, as if hope were being offered to her instead of him. "Good. Thank you. I wish I'd known this sooner; I could have sent the letter on the *Beria* . . . Have you any idea when the next ship might be coming by?"

"No." He turned back. "Rowan, I'll be going away for a while."

This took her aback. "Away? Why?"

"Sometimes I need to. Once in a while, I become too jumpy, too emotional . . . I reach a point where I can't bear to be around people for a while. When that happens, I go away until I need people again. I always come back."

Good and useful work was what he needed, she told herself. That, more than anything else, would heal his spirit. But it would take time, and he must deal with himself as he saw fit in the interim.

Still, she could not help feeling that her presence, and her insistent questions, were causing his departure. He seemed to guess her thoughts. "It has nothing to do with you," he reassured her. "I've been working up to it for some time now; everyone in town has noticed. I've spent all my money on supplies, the ship is loaded—"

"Ship? This ship? This is yours?"

"Yes, and please don't mock her; she's the best I can do in my reduced circumstances." He stepped past the steerswoman, back to his work. "I'd been planning to go as soon as I fix the deck. I don't care to break my leg the first time I jibe." He stooped, sorted through the waiting new planks.

Surprise rendered her question blunt. "Aren't you afraid of the sea?"

"Of course I am." His voice was weirdly cheerful. "I'm also afraid of falling downstairs every morning. But when it gets this bad, I don't care anymore. If you want to get away from people, it's the sea that's best. There are few things in the world as inhuman as the sea."

She stood looking down at his back as he worked. Something was missing. "What aren't you telling me?"

"How it feels," he said immediately, his tone unchanged. "How it feels to need to do this." He found the new plank he wanted, maneuvered it in place, and banged its side to set the tongue and groove.

She felt she must do something to change the mood. "I think you're just leaving me to deal with the gossips all by myself."

He laughed. "Aha. My strategy has been revealed by the wily steerswoman. By the time I come back the whole matter will have blown over entirely. They'll be nattering about catching Gwen and Steffie in the hayloft, or counting how much money Leonard's spent on the boys and girls at Maysie's house."

"She uses children?"

"No, no; they're just always referred to as boys and girls. I believe, because it lends an air of playfulness."

"That's the solution, then; while you're gone, I'll try to encourage interest in Leonard's debaucheries."

"Just don't ask Maysie to help. She tends to regard her knowledge as a sacred trust. Which is why she never got on with Mira." He returned to extracting nails from the old boards.

Rowan sat on the railing. "Would you consider waiting until I've finished the letter, and putting in at Donner to send it from there?" Donner was a busy port; the letter would move far more quickly than from Alemeth.

"No. There are too many people in Donner. Ow." He had banged a finger. He went to put it in his mouth, and was again foiled by the glove. And again, and oddly, he did not remove it but sat with his teeth gritted, waiting for the pain to pass.

"Is there something wrong with your hands?"

"Mm. Skin condition of some sort. Picked it up in the wildlands." He blew out a breath, shook the hand, and returned to work. "It gets better and worse, but it never quite goes away."

"Perhaps you should let me see."

"The local healer is dealing with it."

"Can you handle a ship with it?"

"I usually wait until it improves. But it's always worse by the time I can come back. And I do believe I'll change the subject now; there's something needs discussion."

She nodded. "Exactly what would you prefer not generally known among the citizens of Alemeth?"

He paused to think. "This whole business about getting the ban lifted. It still might turn out not to be possible."

"I think you're safe. The matter is hardly likely to arise of itself."

"And they don't know I'm under ban at all. And they don't know I was ever a steersman."

"I should be able to maneuver around that one. But if someone manages a wild guess, I won't be able to deny it."

"Well, I suppose I can live with that. And I'd rather they didn't know I was a coward."

"I'm still not convinced that you are."

"Very well, if you insist: I'd rather they not be told that the reason I resigned was that I am convinced that I am unable to fulfill my role, due to what I believe is a lack of simple courage."

"I'll merely say that you discovered that the life did not suit you."

"They'll press for details."

"I'll distract them with all sorts of ancillary information about the life of a steerswoman and the various reasons any one of us might choose to resign."

"That might work for a while. But they'll come back to it."

Rowan thought, then smiled broadly. "I could always use the vindictive approach."

He was a moment remembering to what she referred; then his jaw dropped. "Now, that," he said slowly, "I would like to see. Rowan being nasty: unimaginable!" He caught her expression. "That's a very odd look you've got on your face . . ."

"Actually," she said uncomfortably, "it just occurred to me to try to count the number of people I've killed. I keep losing track somewhere in the middle twenties."

Shock silenced him. Then, "Twenties? Skies above, Rowan, how—" He stopped.

They sat, he on the deck, she on the port railing, the air full of creaks and laps and rattles, with the question and all the unanswered others lying on the deck between them, like a single, mute stone.

At last Rowan stood, made a show of brushing her trouser legs. "I do believe," she said, "that I'll go see to that letter right now."

7

*B*ooks, and books. You'd think there was nothing more important in the world.

The steerswoman was at it every morning, right after her walk and her breakfast. And if Steffie passed by the Annex at night, he could see she was still at it then, too, because there was a light downstairs. And more than once he or Gwen had caught her in the morning with books all spread around, and sometimes maps she'd drawn, too, and you could tell she hadn't slept. On those days she walked after breakfast instead of before, and she did it down by the harbor instead of up by the groves.

She walked by the harbor more and more as the weeks went by. Sometimes she went down of an evening, too, when everyone else was off to Brewer's or the Mizzen, or to their families.

"Looking for her sweetheart," was Gwen's guess. But Rowan had said that Janus wasn't her sweetheart. And she kept on saying it, because people kept on asking it, most every day for a while, when they dropped by of an afternoon. Which they started to do less and less. Not that Steffie blamed them; it just wasn't the same without Mira.

Sometimes Steffie wondered why he kept hanging about himself, and Gwen, too. But after all this time, he sort of felt it was their right. Sooner or later, the real new keeper of the Annex would show up, and maybe things would sort out.

So, Rowan kept to herself, for the most part. After the night she'd run into Janus, the only time Steffie had seen her go to Brewer's was one evening when she'd been up all the night before and all day, and had not stopped at all.

She hadn't been just reading, but writing and drawing, too, and measuring something and covering some pages with numbers. Not numbers in rows, like adding them up, but numbers and letters together in long lines, like they were sentences, like numbers were a language you could talk and say things with. Funny way to think of it.

But, suddenly, in the middle of it, she'd stood up, picked up the page she'd been working on, and stood staring at it. Then she tore it up.

Then she tore up the rest, and the drawings, too. She put them all in the fireplace, strapped on her sword, took money from the jar, and told Steffie that she was going to buy him a drink.

He wanted to ask her what it was all about, but he didn't, because as soon as she sat down in Brewer's, she started talking.

She talked about living in the Outskirts, with all those barbarians, traveling along and fighting with each other; and how funny the goats were; and how noisy the grass was, like rain on the roof, she said, when the wind blew it. She talked about how the air smelled in the morning, sour and spicy; and how Outskirters could talk to each other far away by waving their arms; and how their food was so boring that sometimes they made it taste bad on purpose, just to be different.

She told about a festival, Rendezvous, she called it, when the tribes didn't fight but told stories and had contests. She told two of the stories, one about a dead warrior who wanted his funeral done over right and another one, a funny one, about a girl who took a fancy to the old man who led the tribe.

Pretty soon, people in the tavern started quieting, like a circle spreading out from around her. Rowan looked like she didn't even notice, like it was the Outskirts she was seeing instead.

There were songs, too, Rowan said, and she sang one. She had no voice to speak of, sort of plain and thin; but the song was the strangest one that Steffie had ever heard, with a twisty melody and words that only made sense if you didn't try to understand them.

By then she had everyone in Brewer's gathered around, none of them speaking at all, not even when the song made Maysie cry. It was Brewer took Maysie's hand and gave her his towel; but the steerswoman just went on.

She told about rescuing a man from a whole troop of goblins, her and this friend of hers, fighting a long time, all in the night by a great bright fire; then straightaway told how she saw, at that Rendezvous, a mandolin made out of a dead goblin's head. And a duel she fought with an Outskirter, and how the other person shook her hand after, each of them saying how good the other fought.

She didn't talk like she was talking to a lot of people, not checking how they took things, seeing if they were bored, changing direction to suit the crowd—not the way old Mira used to. Rowan talked like she was talking to herself, or as if it was her own thoughts, the things inside her, that were doing the speaking, and she was just listening to what they said.

She told about things tall as trees that weren't trees but had deadly sharp spines running all through them, and how little Outskirter children would cut them down and laugh when they fell crashing. And how it got so cold last winter they brought all the goats in the tents at night, and she woke up to find a fat doe cuddled up right under her blanket.

And a river, the oldest river in the world, so far below a cliff that the water was just a tiny ribbon, and way off east, up where all the green-colored grass ran out and all the red-colored grass was almost gone, other people living there, who were such barbarians that the *barbarians* called them barbarians.

And when the time came for the tribe to move, they'd just pack up and walk, homes and goats and all, all off across the landscape together, far away . . .

It made Steffie think of what it would be like to be an Outskirter, always moving, always defending, and how it wasn't so barbaric at all but brave, really, hard and brave and good.

Steffie thought about it for a long time before he noticed that Rowan had stopped talking; and it was because she'd fallen asleep right in her chair, her beer, which she hadn't touched once, still on the table beside her.

It was Steffie and Gwen who packed her up, got her home, and helped her unstrap her sword and fall into bed. She wasn't up until noon the next day.

She didn't talk all during lunch, and neither did Steffie. Because if he said anything, it would be about what she'd said last night, and somehow he didn't want to do that. It had been like he'd gone to a strange land without quite knowing how he'd done it; like it was special, maybe magical, and touching it with new words would make it all go away.

Gwen didn't speak either, except for "pass the sauce." She was thinking, too, but whatever she was thinking made her look at Rowan sideways.

And right after lunch, Rowan got out a stack of new empty paper, trimmed up her pens, mixed new ink, gathered a batch of those books, and got back to work.

Gwen left, because a whole group of people were going to be doing laundry together, and she couldn't get out of it. And Steffie ought to have gone, too, doing that or something else at home, but he stayed.

He watched Rowan for a minute or so, going through the pages of a book. Then he said, "What are you asking them?"

She looked up. "Pardon me?"

"All those dead steerswomen. You said you were asking them something. I'm wondering, what is it you're asking?"

She closed the book, and thought a bit. "I'm asking them if they've seen anything magical."

"Magic?" he said, surprised. "Well, it's wizards do magic." Which he knew only from being told, because no wizard ever came to Alemeth that he'd heard of. Plenty of stories about wizards: wild and wonderful tales, with flying houses, magic swords, treasures, and princes or princesses to be rescued. Stories you didn't take as true, but you wanted to hear anyway.

But there were also true things said about wizards: like how the people living around them had to give them food and goods and land, and sometimes be their servants, with nothing in return except not having a bad spell put on you. And those wars—nobody knew why the wizards sometimes would get a war going, but you had to fight anyway, leave your family and all, and even die for your side, not ever knowing why.

"Wizards do magic, yes," Rowan said. "But I want to know about magic that has happened when no known wizard seemed to have been present."

That stumped him. Then: "But if there's magic, got to be a wizard doing it."

"That's what I believe."

The wizard would still have to be around, even if no one saw him. " 'How do you find a man?' "

"What?"

"Well . . . I heard you say that once. Sort of to yourself." He felt embarrassed, like he'd been eavesdropping on her thoughts.

Her eyes narrowed but not at him: at what was going on in her own head, he guessed. "His name is Slado," she said.

"You know his name, but you don't know where he is?"

"That's right."

Have you tried asking around? he wanted to say, but stopped himself just in time, because she'd have done that already, first thing. "I thought steerswomen and wizards left each other alone." Mira had told him: The wizards mostly paid no attention to steerswomen at all, which was sort of insulting; but the steerswomen all *hated* the wizards, because they would never answer any question about magic. Not that Steffie could blame the wizards; if you had a lot of secrets that gave you power, you wouldn't want to just give it all away. If Steffie knew magic himself—

Well, no, come to think of it. If Steffie knew anything that was worth knowing, he was pretty sure he'd pass it around. He'd tell it to whoever wanted to know.

"That's true," Rowan said. "We let each other be. Generally."

"Then, why do you want to find him?"

And she thought some more, and it came to Steffie that the answer was going to be complicated and she was probably trying to figure how to parcel it out in pieces a regular person could understand. So, when she spoke, he expected her to say something simple, sort of step-by-step.

But instead she said, "I want to find him because of a magic spell that the wizards call Routine Bioform Clearance."

Which were a bunch of words Steffie didn't know what they meant— except, now that he thought of it, he did know what "routine" was, at least. It was when things happened over and over, the same way each time, like pretty much everything did in Alemeth. And "clearance" was obvious, too, so that narrowed things down a bit. So: "What's 'bioform'?"

" 'Form' is shape, or type; and I'm assuming that 'bio' refers to living things."

That added up to clearing away things that were alive. Which sounded like a strange thing to do, at first. But actually, it sort of made sense— with trees, say, and maybe wild animals, if you wanted to make a new farm or build a house somewhere for someone to live in.

But imagine that, using a magic spell to clear off the land instead of an axe. And doing it over and over, routinely. "Is that something that Slado wizard does? He makes new places for people to live?"

Rowan turned her chair a bit, so she could look at him straight on. And she was looking at him differently, somehow, he couldn't say how, except maybe that she looked like she found him interesting all of a sudden. "As a matter of fact," she said, "that *is* the correct use of Routine Bioform Clearance. When the spell is permitted to operate as it ought to."

"Meaning, it's not anymore?"

"That's right."

"So, what about the people? The ones who're expecting new places to live."

She leaned back, still watching him. "You mean the Outskirters."

"Outskirters?" But they didn't live in houses at all, they used tents. Still, all those things Rowan had mentioned—the dangerous plants, the creatures and insects and such—be handy for the Outskirters if all that was gone. "Can't the Outskirters clear out those bioform things themselves?"

"They can. They do. Everything the Outskirters do, every aspect of their way of life, serves to destroy the plants and animals native to the Outskirts and aid the spread of those native to the Inner Lands. But the Outskirters can only do that at all because the worst of the dangerous life-forms have already been eliminated."

It was hard to imagine things more dangerous than what Rowan had talked about last night. "Cleared out by that magic spell?"

"Yes."

"But . . . not anymore?"

"No. Not anymore."

Steffie thought about the Outskirters and how even the best of times were tough for them. "Then," he said, "that's bad."

"It's worse than bad." Rowan looked at the papers in front of her on the table and laid one hand down on them. "Routine Bioform Clearance takes the form of an invisible heat that comes down from the Eastern Guidestar onto the land below. It can be directed. It ought to be directed to the east, into the wildest lands, past where what we call the Outskirts ends." She looked up. "At least once, its direction was changed. The heat was brought down upon the Outskirters themselves."

Magic heat from the sky? Steffie felt himself sort of grind to a halt, like a mill with rocks in it. He pushed hard to get himself going again. "Those Outskirters got burned?"

"Not with any flame. But it did—" And she was looking past him all of a sudden, to something far away; and from the look on her face it had to be the most awful thing she'd ever seen. It only lasted a moment, but Steffie saw it clear; then she came back. "Everything in its path was killed," she said, "yes. And I believe that Slado is responsible."

And that's when the whole thing was suddenly just too much.

Steffie had only just got used to the Outskirters existing at all, even though he'd heard about them before—but they'd never been real, only some stories told by the old folks. But Rowan, she'd made them be real by the things she'd said last night: stories, too, but different stories, stories about being there and seeing it all herself. Outskirters were real, and interesting to think about, and Steffie liked them . . .

But now that there was magic in the story—and invisible fire and wizards—he felt like he couldn't make it all hang together right.

Steffie felt for a moment like there was some place really high that he had to jump up to, to see it clear all at once. But he was here with both his feet right on the ground, in the Annex, in Alemeth, and he couldn't figure how to jump.

And then he realized, all of a sudden, that while he'd been thinking all that, he'd been just standing here, staring off into space, not saying anything, probably looking like some kind of dolt, and he didn't know how long he'd been doing it. Which was a thing that happened sometimes. "Stuck in the mud," was what old Galer called it; even though "stuck" wasn't right, because there were lots of things moving, just not on the outside. Still, people laughed when Galer said it.

Thinking of that made Steffie go red in the face; and then he wasn't just standing around saying nothing, he was standing around saying nothing red in the face, and for who knows how long. So he said, just to get himself going again, "Well," but he couldn't find anything else to say after that.

But Rowan said, "Well," herself, stopped being interested in him, and turned back to her papers.

"Well," Steffie said again, because he thought of something to ask, "what are you going to do when you find Slado?"

"That," Rowan said, not looking up, "remains to be determined."

Which was when Gwen came to get Steffie, because there was more work than people working, so to speak. Steffie hated laundry, but he went, because if he didn't he'd never hear the end of it.

The whole bathhouse had been given over to laundry, which never struck Steffie as a good idea, what with who knows who having been in there after having been who knows where and having been in he didn't want to think what. But that was what hot water and soap were for, he'd been told the first time he complained. Still, made him itchy to think of it.

It was all winter's clothes needing to be cleaned before being put away, and that was nasty enough, because not much laundry gets done in winter. But it had to get done sooner or later.

The bathhouse was noisy. Belinda had brought the twins, and Ivy had brought Tarlie, who was too young to be much good, but old enough to complain in words. Old Galer had brought little Anna, and she was all right, quiet and hardworking, but *he* was a chore, always grumping how people had it soft now, not like in his day. Which you wouldn't think should be a complaint, rightly speaking, but he made it one.

So Steffie thought fast and moved sly, and got himself right by a whole tub of blue, which no one liked to do, because the dye stayed on your hands; but that left Galer with one of the tubs of underlinens, which was worse. He spent half an hour complaining about how nice they were.

"Right," Steffie said when he'd had enough. "And in your day people made their knickers out of tree bark."

"And used it for kindling after!" Gwen declared from the other side of the room.

"Think of the stink!"

" 'Cause they didn't have chimneys in those days. They'd open the window to let the smoke out."

"You could hang your hams from the ceiling and cure 'em right then. What with that, and no laundry, you'd have plenty of free time."

"No free time!" Galer said. "We worked hard!" Everyone groaned, and someone threw a wet shirt at him; but it missed and fell into Steffie's tub. "Who's that's?" Steffie called. "Because it's blue now."

Galer went on, but mumbling, which was quieter, at least. But Steffie picked up "steerswoman" in it, so he couldn't help asking, "What?" A lot of voices complained at him, and someone threw another shirt, which hit him; but it was dry, and already blue, so he just put it in the tub.

"You," Galer said, louder. "Fellow your age, lazing about at the Annex with that steerswoman. Doing nothing all day that I can see."

"What? I do my share! See this?" Steffie pointed to the tub. "See me? This is me doing this, and that's something."

"And you," Galer called over to Gwen. "Just as bad."

"Or just as good," Gwen said back. Trust Gwen to have an answer ready. "Because you're supposed to help a steerswoman, and that's what me and Steffie have always done. No reason to stop now."

"Young thing like that Rowan doesn't need your help."

"Think so? You seen how Mira kept her house. We've been setting it straight, and if you think that's easy, come by and try it yourself." Except that they were mostly done setting it straight by now, except for the books. Still, it shut Galer up for a bit, which was good.

Then Maysie and a couple of her boys came in with three big baskets full of nothing but sheets, and that made everyone find plenty of rude and funny things to say; but it set Steffie to thinking about the Outskirters again, because how did they wash their sheets, and did they even have any? And the talk went on all around him while he wondered about that until something got his attention.

It was Maysie, laughing at something someone had said. She laughed loud, and for a long time, like he'd never seen her do before; and everyone else was just as surprised as Steffie was.

When she was done laughing, she said, "Seems to me you've got it backward, Choley. Rowan is a *nicer* person than Mira ever was."

"You just say that because you didn't like answering Mira's questions."

"Questions she had no business asking. My customers have the right not to have their private doings talked all over town. Mira was just a nosy old woman who used being a steerswoman to collect gossip. I think it's clever, how Rowan put you off without breaking her own rules."

But Steffie had missed the start of all that, so he asked Alyssa, who was working just behind him. "He wanted to know what Rowan knew about Janus," Alyssa said, "and Rowan answered, until the questions got too personal. That's when she started asking questions back."

"How'd that stop him?"

"Depends on the questions, don't it?"

And Steffie was going to ask what questions—but then he didn't, because a whole bunch of interesting ones popped into his head, and then he just laughed and laughed.

But Choley was still talking. "Doesn't seem right to me, from a steerswoman. Mira never tried to slip out of answering."

"But that's just what I mean," Maysie said. "Mira ought to have done, if she'd had any respect, considering some of the things she knew about people." She looked down at the tub of sheets, sort of surprised, and then pulled out something, which turned out to be someone's knickers. She balled them up and tossed them over into Galer's tub. "I think I'll start coming by the Annex, of an afternoon. Just to be sociable."

"Well, it'll be you, then, and hardly anyone else. Not much fun, when that steerswoman'd rather we weren't there. Stuck up, that's what she is."

"No," Alyssa said, "she keeps to herself 'cause her heart is broke. It's that Janus, gone sailing away again, and now she's pining after him—"

"He always comes back," Belinda put in, tossing clean nappies to Choley at the wringer.

"She's not pining," Steffie put in. "She's busy, is all."

"Busy with what? She's doing nothing that I can see."

"Looking in the books."

"Never seen no good in that. Toss 'em all out, that's what I say." And that was Galer again, so whatever he said, everyone else was against it.

"Now, it wouldn't be the Annex, would it, if there was no books," Lark said to him. "Got to have the books."

"And got to have someone to look after the books. No books means no steerswoman in Alemeth."

"Who says we need a steerswoman in Alemeth?"

"But then there'd be no one to look after the books!"

"Well, at least she can tell a story, when she wants," Belinda said. "Last night, that was better than anything Mira ever told. Rowan should do that more."

"Story about foreigners," Galer grumbled.

"What, you want to hear all over how Choley got drunk and spent the night in the pigpen?" Which was when one of Belinda's babies fell right in the tub, not by accident but meaning to. And when Belinda fished him out, he started crying, because he liked it in there and wanted to go back. And then the other one started crying because his brother'd had some fun that he hadn't.

"What's in all them books, anyway?" Choley asked, talking loud over the fussing.

"Lives," Steffie said straight off, saying just what Rowan had said to Gwen. "Lives of steerswomen, going way back."

"I thought it was maps and things," Ivy said. "How to go places and what's there."

"Well, that, too."

Then Steffie started to explain, about how Rowan was looking for this wizard; and what Routine Bioform Clearance was; and the trouble the Outskirters were having, what with that spell being stopped. It went on for a while, because he wasn't really good at telling.

But halfway through it, Steffie started to notice something.

That high place he'd thought of before—the place he'd have to jump up to, to see it all clear—it seemed to him that he was almost there. Somehow, explaining was making it happen, all by itself.

So now, almost, he could see everything spread out like a landscape—all the things Rowan said, starting to fit together—and almost, too, he could look even farther, out past all that, to what came next—

And that's when he stopped dead in his tracks. Because all of a sudden he was wondering: If the warrior tribes can't get any new places to live in the Outskirts, what will they do? What *can* they do?

Only one thing Steffie could think of. But no . . . no, he had to have that wrong . . .

Then he realized that he'd stopped talking a while ago. And that now he was just standing there, in the middle of the bathhouse, elbow deep in a tub full of blue, saying nothing at all. With everyone looking at him.

After a while, Galer made a noise, which wasn't words, but everyone knew exactly what he meant.

"But—" Steffie started and wanted to say, But it's not *stuck in the mud* at all, it's just my thoughts moving too fast for my words to catch up. But with everyone staring at him, and his whole head hurting from going so red in the face, Steffie couldn't get a single word out.

And then they laughed—like they always did. And everyone went back to work.

After a bit, Steffie managed to say, "You'll have to ask Rowan about it. I'm not telling it right . . ."

"No right to it," Choley said. "Just crazy talk. Got yourself all befuddled, spending too much time with that steerswoman. That's the problem." He started working the wringer crank, so he grunted when he spoke. "House full of books—" *grunt* "—bunch of wild stories—" *grunt* "—fancy words and—" *grunt* "—fancy manners." He stopped wringing. "Too good for us, that's what she's thinking," he said to the whole room, his fists on his hips. "Too bloody high and mighty to associate with us at all."

Someone snorted. "Oh, and what's so wonderful about you, makes you think anyone'd associate with you?" It was Laney, one of Maysie's boys.

"*You're* one to talk!"

"My job's just as good as yours."

"Says you. At least I stand up to do mine."

"When you're not lying down in the pigpen."

"That was just the one time—"

"Couldn't tell that by the smell—"

But then Mowrie and Jane and Acker and Leonard showed up at the door, saying how Lasker's worms had gone up the hill, and everybody stopped talking about Rowan and started talking about that instead.

But Steffie wasn't listening. He was thinking again. And what he was thinking was that the problem wasn't him spending too much time with the steerswoman; it was everyone else not spending enough.

It wasn't until nightfall that Steffie got a chance to stop by the Annex again.

Rowan looked up when he came in, said hello politely enough, and went back to her papers.

Steffie watched her for a while. There she sat, all alone, one hand turning the pages of a book, and her eyes moving fast over the pages.

After a bit, Steffie said, "There's a tent party out at the dell."

"Another celebration?"

That made him stop and count, because there had been a few parties since she'd been here. "Well, a little one. Lasker's worms have gone up the hill, see. Generally that happens later in the year, when the work stops, and before it starts up again. But with Lasker's spring silk, his worms are spinning right now. So there's some people ready to celebrate, and the rest of us thought, well, why not?"

The steerswoman *hmm*'d. "Why not, indeed? Have a nice time, Steffie. Please don't feel you have to come in at any particular time tonight, or tomorrow, for that matter. I'm perfectly capable of feeding myself, you know." And she kept paging through that book.

Then Steffie said, "You know, it'd be good if you came, too."

She looked up at him. "What?"

"You should come along."

"My work—"

"You keep yourself too much apart," he told her. It felt odd, telling a steerswoman what she ought to be doing; but someone should, and it had to be him, because it surely wasn't going to be anyone else. "I don't know how long you're figuring to stay in Alemeth, lady," he went on, more formal, "but I think it'll be better all around if you can get along with people."

She leaned back in her chair. "I have no problem getting along with people," she said, a little stiff. "I've managed to get along with, and even like, some of the strangest people you could ever imagine."

"Well." That put him in his place. He almost let it go, but suddenly, he just couldn't. "Well, nobody here is strange at all. Maybe what you need is to learn to get along with people who aren't strange. We're all very common here, and we don't like it being held against us." There.

He'd shocked her, all right; but not the way he thought. "Is that really what people are thinking?"

Tell the truth to a steerswoman—even if it's not good news. "Yes. Some of them."

"But I never—" she started, then stopped. "I certainly didn't intend—" She stopped again. She stared off to one side for a while. And just then it came to Steffie that there were a lot of things about herself that Rowan didn't know or notice—the same as everyone else. "You're right," she said at last. "I had no idea. It wouldn't hurt to be a bit more . . . sociable."

Good. "Well, if it's sociable you want," he told her, "a tent party's just the place."

She looked down at her books again, like she was mad at them. When she looked up, he saw something crinkling her eyes. "Dancing and drinking?" she asked.

"Plenty of both."

"And absolutely nothing important going on?"

"If you try to do something important," he said proudly, "we'll stop you."

She laughed out loud; and it was strange to hear from her, the freest laugh she'd ever made. She pushed her chair back. "Then we're wasting time." But she still took the time to close her book, wipe her pen clean, and put her cup in the kitchen basin. On her way back, she picked up her sword and strapped it on. "Let's go."

Steffie eyed the sword and tried not to wince. One step at a time. She'd put it aside soon as someone asked her to dance, he suspected. "Right, then." And they stepped out into the street.

There were no streetlamps this far from the harbor; a few houses with open windows sent candle-dim shadows out onto the cobbles, and there was starshine. It made the house-shapes look like sleeping bears, quiet but still looming. Steffie knew his way well enough in the dark, from the shape of the shapes, and he was ready to take Rowan's arm to lead her; but she strolled along easy as you please, even a half step ahead of him, like it was her leading him.

When they got to the last houses, and the crest of the little dell, she stopped for some reason or other, and he did too, all by himself at the same moment.

Way up, little clouds moved, dashing across the winking stars and showing one Guidestar, then the other, then neither. The air was exactly the best temperature: cool enough to feel but not any cooler.

From here, the lights of the town looked small—not distant, exactly, but one and one and one, each alone. Down below, among the trees, the lights of torches flickered from their own sputtering and flickered more when people passed in front of them. Everything you could see twinkled, but everything you could feel was solid, like the ground beneath your feet and the cool air on your skin. And flowers, Steffie could smell flowers, and that seemed exactly perfect.

Then he wished that he knew what kinds of flowers they were, but the steerswoman must have been thinking the same, because she said, "Roses . . . rhododendrons . . . honeysuckle . . ."

"Daisies," he added. And it would have been a good time to move on, but neither of them did.

And it came to Steffie what a fine thing it was: not so much to go to the celebration but to *be* going there, to be on the way.

And that was why they had both stopped, so they could go on being on the way, for just a bit longer. So they could stand here in the quiet dark, with the stars all above, the little lights down among the trees, and the happy voices and bits of music floating up, all of it like a present you look at for a long time before opening up.

Then Steffie heard a little noise—a rustle in the bushes behind, another off to the side—and he just managed to hold back laughing, so as not to give it all away. Sideways in the dark, he watched the steerswoman.

She'd heard it, too, he could tell. She had moved her head just a little bit, but she didn't say anything. Maybe she was going to play along.

But all of a sudden Steffie couldn't breathe; it was like all the air had been sucked up to the stars, because there was something about the way she had cocked her head . . .

And then there was this shout inside his head, which was himself telling himself to shout out loud, to *stop* what was going to happen—

And he did shout, but it was lost in the other shouts, the whoops and squeals—

And then they were all around—shining shapes, little green-glowing hands flapping, eyes and mouths just dark holes in shining green faces, arms and legs just lines of light—and more of them coming, bursting out of the bushes.

And then another noise, a hiss not made by any voice, and a glitter, sweeping back, starting forward; and he half reached, half threw himself across the space between and grabbed Rowan's shoulder and yanked, hard.

He thought she'd fall down, right on top of him, but she did some wild trick in the dark, arms and legs every which way—then she was free, crashing off into the night, with him scrambling to his feet behind her.

The voices had gone to high shrieks; the little shapes were stumbling through the bushes, away, fanning out; and Steffie gasped one big gasp, which was the end of the shout he'd started: that's how fast it all happened.

But the steerswoman was still after them, each one of them like a shining lamp showing the way. She made no sound now, she was silent as death, and that *sword*, she had that sword held up over her head—

And then she'd caught up to the slowest two, and Steffie yelled again, "No!"

And he was right next to her, somehow. He threw both his arms around the one she held high; he pulled back with everything he'd got. "No! Let them go!"

She'd swung half around. "What are you doing?"

"Leave them! Let them go!"

"Those creatures—" But they were gone now, just wails far off. "That light—"

"It's moths!"

The stars made her eyes hard and bright, like her sword. "Moths? Those things? So huge? No—"

Steffie yanked again, talked fast. "No, not moths—it was moth stuff. The children, they catch the moths, see, and squash them; then they paint themselves with the stuff, and run around at night, scaring people. It's a joke, it's fun!"

"Paint themselves . . ." It was like the words made no sense to her.

"Because it glows."

"Glows . . ."

"The moths," he said, "the moth stuff, it glows!"

She looked at him like he'd just now showed up. "Why?"

"I don't know, it just *does*!" He was still holding on to her sword arm. It was loose now, but it wasn't a moment ago; it had been all tense, and ready to kill. He was terrified by the picture in his head. He let go and stepped back fast. "Damn it, woman, you can't swing at everything you see!"

She drew herself up. "I do not swing at everything I see." She sheathed her sword. "But when apparently monstrous creatures seem to attack me, I do make an attempt to defend myself."

"You fool, they were children," he said, and damn all proper form and respect to steerswomen.

All of a sudden she was dead quiet in the dark; and then it was her grabbing at his arm. "Steffie—"

"Too bloody right!"

"If you hadn't been here—"

"Good thing I was!"

They stood there in the dark, her looking off into the brush where the children had run. "I'll . . ." She gathered herself together. "I'll have to do something, explain to the children somehow, apologize . . ."

He started to pull back roughly, then didn't. "Well . . ." She was sorry, and frightened at herself. She was used to danger, and she thought she'd seen it.

Steffie softened. "No likely chance at that, I expect," he told her. "Story'll be all over town in a minute. No child will come within a mile of you."

She dropped her hand. "Then I'll have to explain to the parents . . ."

"Right." Then he remembered where they were on the way to. "Half the town's at the dell now. Good a time as any."

She didn't seem like she much wanted to go, anymore, not that he could blame her. But she drew a big breath and let it out slow. "You're right." And she turned to go on, but then stopped herself. Very slowly, like it was a hard thing to do, she unstrapped her sword belt and stood with the sheathed weapon in her hands. "You go ahead," she told Steffie. "I'll join you shortly." And she began to walk back toward the Annex.

Steffie fell in beside her. "No. I'm going with you."

"Really, it's not necessary . . ."

"Yes, it is," he said. "You're not safe out alone."

She stopped short and looked up at him. "Do you know," she said, "I've been told that before." And she looked down at her sword again. "But never for this reason."

8

"Woman," Dan declared, "you couldn't dance to save your life."

"I," the steerswoman said with cautiously precise enunciation, "sincerely hope it never comes to that."

She wasn't exactly drunk, merely unmoored, drifting a bit. Objects seemed to exist separately from any previous context. The dim dawn light painting the houses seemed to come from inside the surface of the walls, very pale and inexplicable: a pretty sight.

She had thought it would be impossible to make it up to the townspeople after what she had done, or nearly done, to the children; instead, she discovered herself to be the center of a new and treasured anecdote.

She only needed to tell the tale once; after that, it told itself, all around the party. She found she could trace its route by the pockets of laughter bursting out here and there. Apparently, the scare the children received was regarded as their just desserts by many. Rowan had stopped reminding them that the danger had been real, after being cheerfully told, again and again, that no one had been hurt, that all came out well in the end, and why in the world wasn't she dancing?

Everyone asked her to dance, even people she had never met; and it came to her that she had turned some corner in the town's attitude. She was no stranger anymore. She was a local figure with a place and a history, someone at whom, and with whom, one could laugh.

And so she had danced, not caring how foolish she might look. The dances of Alemeth were not the careful, ordered patterns of her home village so far away; and that, she decided, was a virtue. One made it all up as one went along, depending purely upon inspiration.

Unfortunately, she and her various partners had acquired their inspirations from incompatible sources. Toes had suffered.

"Almost as bad as Mira," Gwen declared muzzily. She was walking with Steffie's arm about her, her unbalanced steps now shoving all her weight left against his shoulder, now dragging his weight with her to the right, resulting in a rather interesting two-person stagger. Dan and Rowan walked on either side of the couple, bracketing them to fend off imminent collisions, which somehow never quite occurred.

"I'm not Mira," Rowan said with dignity, "and I shall prove it if I have to become the best dancer in Alemeth."

"I'd teach you," Dan began, "but . . ."

"But he's not much better," Steffie finished.

"True, true." Sadly.

They ambled on through the close, mazy streets. All the houses were quiet, their occupants either home abed, dancing in the dewy dell, or on their way between the two, in either direction. As the group passed the baker's, a sleepy-eyed little girl wandered out, hair in a tangle, bucket in hand. Dan sang at her in a surprisingly tuneful voice: a nursery rhyme about the man in the missing moon. She grinned shyly, and watched the group out of sight.

"Well, ho, here's my turn," Dan said. They paused. "Can you handle those two?"

Steffie and Gwen were practicing coordinating their steps, using the nursery rhyme as a guide. "I think so," Rowan said. "They seem to do remarkably well. The gods protect fools and drunkards, people say."

"Looks like you've got one of each there." And he executed a deep bow. "Good morning to you, lady; and if your head ever recovers, perhaps I'll get you that dinner after all."

She nodded, gracious. "Good morning to you, Dan; and I think that it will, by dinnertime."

He raised a brow. "Dinnertime tonight, that is?"

"I'd expect so."

"Even if," and here he looked at the sky innocently, "your friend Janus should show up?"

"I assure you, it will take a great deal more than Janus to keep me from dinner."

And Dan wandered off around the corner, striding with his hands behind him, a smile on his face.

Rowan turned back to the couple. They had dropped the rhyme as being too complex and were now counting, "One, two, one, two," under their breaths.

"Come on, you two," Rowan said.

Her "two" had come at the wrong point. "There, now, I've lost my count," Gwen protested.

"It's one, and then it's two," Steffie told her.

"One and two. Right." They set off.

Rowan was a moment finding her bearings. Silly, silly; she knew these streets by now. She could draw a map of them. She immediately did so, in her head. But where were they on it? Coming from the southeast . . . ah, there. "Left here," she called out.

"Left here."

"Left, one and two." They moved between close-set houses, dirt instead of cobbles underfoot.

Rowan kept being distracted. Strange; her mind felt reasonably clear. Perhaps she had had a bit too much to drink; her ears were ringing faintly.

Steffie was humming again, now tonelessly, to himself. Gwen thumped him on the stomach. "Change the note."

" 'S not me," he said. "That's the tune. *Hmm, hmm, hmm.*"

"It's boring."

"*Hmm, hmm,*" Rowan went, idly. Odd . . . "Steffie are your ears ringing?"

"*Hmm, hmm.*" The same note that Rowan heard.

Her steps slowed, halted. "Wait, be quiet a bit." She blocked her ears; the hum vanished. Unblocked, and—

Steffie had taken it up again; standing still he had more breath and was holding each note as long as he could. "Be quiet." Rowan said to him. He complied.

A faint, low humming. "Do you hear that?"

"Hear what?" Gwen asked.

"*Hmm,*" went Steffie, once. When he stopped, the tone continued independently, steady, uninterrupted by any human singer's breath.

Suddenly, starkly sober, Rowan remembered where she had heard that exact sound before.

Steffie and Gwen were joking at each other, some coy, boozy quarrel. Rowan turned to them. "You have to be quiet."

"Have to be quiet," Steffie pronounced solemnly; then poked Gwen in the side. She squealed and grabbed at his hand. "Come off it, then," she protested.

"No—" Rowan said.

"Quiet," Steffie told Gwen. "Mustn't wake the sleepies." He made another grab.

"Hey, now!"

Rowan clutched at their shoulders, trying to separate them, trying to shout in a whisper, urgent. "Quiet, be still! It's a creature, a creature from the Outskirts." And Rowan remembered, in the Outskirts: Bel, wordlessly urging her silent; Bel, ever brave, now terrified; then both of them waiting, motionless, for hours, as something distantly heard passed them by.

"Creature? Outskirts?" Steffie disentangled himself, gathered himself up to speak paternally. "Now, lady, now Rowan, can't always be jumping at things—"

"Creatures?" Gwen was uncomprehending.

"They're attracted by sound, by noise; you have to be quiet."

"What, wild animals, right here in town—"

"Stop it!" Rowan hissed through clenched teeth. "Stop it now, or it will find us!" It would follow their sound, would come for them, would kill them.

The hum grew louder.

" 'S a drunkard," Steffie told her, and his perfectly normal tone of voice terrified her. "Singing along, stumbling home, just like us."

"Stumbling home," Gwen sang, like a line from a song.

"Watch you don't stumble," Steffie told her. "I'll just have to . . . *catch* you!"

"Hey, stop, you! Off, then!"

"No!" Rowan shouted; but she mustn't shout; she mustn't speak. She tugged at them again. The hum could be heard over their voices.

"Hah, stop, you say *now*—"

"No poking!"

"No poking, you say *now*—"

"Nasty man! But I know your weak spot . . ."

"Hey, no! Hey, come off it—"

They would not listen. They were not going to be silent. They were going to die.

The steerswoman could do nothing but save herself.

Her gaze helplessly locked on the couple, Rowan began to back away, slowly, carefully, silently.

In the midst of playing at Gwen, Steffie glanced up once at Rowan; looked up again, in surprise that she was so far away; looked up again, puzzled, then caught her expression.

What he saw on her face made him freeze.

The hum continued, louder.

"Aha!" Finding that Steffie had ceased to defend himself, Gwen attacked. He clutched her arms roughly, no game now. "Hey!" He pulled her to the wall, turned her, pinned her against himself, gripped one hand across her mouth. She struggled, her cries muffled. He shook her viciously once, and his eyes never left Rowan's face.

Now frightened, Gwen subsided. Rowan ceased backing away.

They stood motionless. Overhead, a flood of bats streamed home from the sea marshes, northward.

Rowan could not place the hum's direction. The walls of the houses, whitewashed wood on one hand, stone on the other, confused it. The wood seemed to suck in the sound, the stone echo it back. Rowan tilted and wove her head slowly, trying to find a focus.

Across the street, his back against a shuttered window, Steffie silently mouthed at her, What do I do?

Rowan gestured slowly, both hands up, forbidding: Stay perfectly still. Steffie nodded minutely.

She looked up the street, down. They were one house from the corner in one direction, three houses in the other, with the view past it clear for another six.

The hum grew, and perceptibly now continued to grow, acquiring faint overtones that she had not heard in the Outskirts. The creature must be very near.

She tried to gauge its speed by the change in volume. Slower than a man might walk, she thought. It must be up the next street, somewhere around the near corner.

How well could it hear? In the Outskirts it had never been close enough to see, and Bel had still been afraid; but the land there was open. Here among the houses, could the beast locate purely by sound what it could not see?

There were obstacles here, places to flee to, places to hide. If they moved now, could they make it down the street, around the corner? She could tell how fast the creature moved; she could guess its direction; she knew it was near, but not how near.

She cautiously waved to Steffie, beckoning him across the street toward her, moving herself away from the corner, agonizingly soft-footing each step. Steffie began to move carefully, lifting Gwen so that her feet just cleared the ground. Rowan wondered how long he could keep that up.

Gwen was frightened and confused; her feet tried to find purchase. She shifted in Steffie's arms and one shoe hissed against the dirt. Rowan halted and stiffened in fear; seeing her do so, Steffie froze.

The lowest note was abruptly clear, new overtones blooming above it, themselves half heard, like fever noise; and in the narrow street the air became a substance of sound. The creature had cleared the corner.

Her back to the stone wall, Rowan could not see it; in the center of the street, Gwen and Steffie could. They looked.

Terror on Steffie's face as swift and shocking as a blow, and then his expression was utterly blank, as if his fear had gone beyond what his body could express. He stood empty, head tilted back, lips parted; but he did not let go of Gwen.

Above his hand, Gwen's eyes grew wide, and she cringed back into Steffie's arms. Rowan feared that Gwen would scream; she fainted instead. Steffie continued to hold her upright, motionless.

If they made no sound, Rowan thought, if the creature had never seen a human before, if they stayed utterly still, would it think them an object, would it pass them by?

Cold stone against her back, Rowan waited for her first sight of a demon.

And far away, across the houses: a hoot, a whoop, and an odd warble, voices laughing.

Someone was drunkenly singing his way home: Lasker, with his friends in tow. The voice of the demon steadied, then began to fade back. The creature had chosen a new direction.

No! Lasker could not know to stay silent; Rowan could not shout to tell him.

She ran.

Away from the demon, down the street, left at the next corner, two blocks and left again, up toward the demon's street. She stopped at the tailor's shop at the corner, thrust two fingers into her mouth and let out a shrill, piercing whistle.

It echoed, clearly, hollowly. In the pause that followed, only the demon's hum, now distant, but not retreating. Rowan whistled again. The hum began to approach.

The tailor's door banged open. "Here, you—"

She clutched the man's shoulders, shook him. "Get help. People with weapons. There's a monster in the streets."

"What—"

She meant to shake him again, but her hands acted of themselves. They slapped his face, spun him around, beat him on the back, shoved him. "Run! Run that way, run from the sound!"

The overtones returned; the demon was near. Rowan dashed out into its street and across. A shadowy dark shape two blocks away, moving at the edge of her vision, cut into another side street, ran ten feet down, stopped.

She whistled and stood shuddering, sweat cold on her face and back, waiting.

She had to draw it away from town. And away from the dell, without crossing the center of town. East.

Wood houses here, muffling the sound. She could not tell if the demon was moving; it did not seem to be retreating. She whistled again.

The hum grew. Rowan backed away.

She needed to bring the demon toward her, keeping far enough ahead of it; but she did not know the margin of safety. She stepped back softly, mental eyes scanning an imagined map of the streets.

And then, far off, to her left southwest of her a whistle, shriller, stronger than her own. Someone else was drawing the demon.

Rowan had an ally. And now, a plan, if her comrade was a person of intelligence.

They could protect each other, drawing the demon toward them by turns, running ahead of each other down the side streets. They could take it out of town.

And then? They would end up alone with it, in the sea marsh, with no obstacles to dodge behind.

Possibly help would arrive by then. No time to wonder now.

Streets were less regular here. Rowan chose her route, a zigzag toward the east, staying north of the demon's assumed location, hearing her unknown friend call the creature again. When she guessed she was past that person's position, she whistled herself, needing to try twice, out of clumsy fear.

How smart an animal was a demon? she wondered. How stupid? A few times through this pattern, would it grow frustrated and simply choose the last-heard target?

The distant whistle came again, southeast. Her ally understood. Rowan chose a path, moved.

Buildings grew fewer. She kept close to them, sidling, picturing the demon's route and her own. They were coming to the manufactories; there was less chance of an early riser meeting the creature.

Her friend—he or she must be moving toward the warehouses south along the harbor. The fishers rose early.

Rowan whistled.

Across the distance, above and beneath the creature's humming; a strangled wail became a shriek, and then silence.

Rowan wondered who had died. There was a long pause, and only the voice of the demon.

And then: the whistle, nearer to her, and sooner, than it had come before.

Yes. Draw it away from the harbor. She angled down the length of a long shed, down another, paused to check the loudness of the demon's voice, heard that it was approaching. She and her comrade were now nearly in a straight line from each other. They needed more lateral distance between them, to safely cover each other.

No help for it. Get the demon away from the harbor. Rowan whistled, listened, waited for the demon's approach.

The creature's tone stayed steady.

The next whistle should come southeast, just behind a warehouse storing metal scraps, right next to the ropewalk.

No whistle. The demon's voice continued unaltered, then dropped abruptly as it turned some corner.

It had chosen, and it had not chosen Rowan.

She tried to guess her ally's position, tried to visualize his or her options for escape. Long buildings, there, warehouses. An easy retreat by going closer to the harbor, but further in, nearer Rowan, a mere two streets away—

Cul-de-sac. Two huge, angled warehouses with what might seem an alley between but ending in a shared loading dock.

How well did her comrade know these streets? As well as a steerswoman?

Rowan ran toward the voice of the demon.

And behind her, north: distant shouting voices, rattles as of weaponry, footsteps heavy and quick. Help. But they would arrive too late.

She reached the warehouses, the streets broad and sandy. The lemon dawn sky was high and wide above her; the demon's tone, unechoed and erased of overtones, now sounded deceptively distant. But she could hear a series of soft thumps, in quadruple rhythm: the four-footed steps of the creature. Rowan flattened herself against the front of the first building, edged her way to the corner with painful slowness, and looked down the alley.

The creature stood just over five feet tall: a gray-mottled vertical column of flesh, strange muscles shifting beneath the skin as it raised first one, then each other low-kneed, flat-footed leg, its body weaving in a circular motion as it walked. Its four arms splayed out, horizontal from the top of its body, then angling downward at sharp-jointed elbows. It had no head, no visible face or eyes, no apparent difference between front or back or sides. Rowan could not tell in which direction the creature was looking, but the direction it was moving was certain: down the cul-de-sac toward the loading dock.

Up against the dock there stood an empty, tall-wheeled wagon. And backed up against that, with nowhere further to run, Rowan's ally: Steffie.

Rowan whistled.

The demon stopped and threw its arms high; in panicked instinct, Rowan ducked back behind the building's edge. A short, sharp jet of clear fluid barely missed her, spattering far out into the dirt of the street. An instant's terror as she realized how close the spray had come, but she was already thinking, noting the spot where the jet had come to earth: about sixty feet. That was the demon's range.

She scanned the ground at her feet, gathered up a rusted horseshoe, a half brick, a palm-sized clamshell. The voices and running footsteps were nearer, a few streets away, and Rowan called out to them over the demon's humming; but she did not wait. She took a breath, ducked forward, hurled the brick with all her strength.

The creature, some forty feet away from Steffie, was raising its arms. The brick caught it above one rear knee, and it staggered, weird arms flailing. Rowan dodged back before it could recover to spray again.

Nine people pounded into the street behind Rowan, six men and three women, armed with pikes, swords, bows; a contingent of the town's militia. "Here!" Rowan called to them.

"What's this, then?" one man demanded, as his squad milled to a confused halt around him.

"It's a demon, a creature from the Outskirts," Rowan told him quickly. She tried to recall his name and failed. "It's dangerous— No, you, get back!" She clutched the back of one militia woman's shirt, pulling her away from the alley's entrance, eliciting a cursing complaint from the woman. Rowan ignored her, turned back to the leader. "It's in there, it's got Steffie trapped against the loading dock. He has no weapon; we've got to lure it out and kill it." She stopped to catch her breath. "It may be on its way out now. It follows sound."

"How big a beast is this?"

"So high." Rowan demonstrated, and prepared to explain further; but the leader cut her off with, "Right, lady, we'll take it from here." And he gestured his people to advance.

Rowan spun him viciously around. "Wait, you don't know what you're walking into!"

He threw off her hand. "Here, you!"

There came another sound from the alley, at first like a man's voice, then changing to an animal shriek it seemed no living human could possibly emit. The cry ceased, and Rowan said, "No . . ." once, then, "No!" again when the nearest of the militia ran into the alley's mouth, then: "No! Get *back*!"

The three fighters who had advanced fell back, staggering, crying in pain, one of them screaming in full voice as she fell prone, struggling to scrabble away. Someone ran forward to assist, shouted, and stumbled when another jet caught his leg. Limping, he dragged his comrade aside, and Rowan's hands and others' pulled, helped, leaned the woman against a wall.

The woman was now making sounds like a dog being beaten, writhing helplessly. Half her chest was raw flesh and red bone. Her rescuer's left leg was blood from hip to ankle.

Rowan stood. "Sixty feet," she said, "it shoots a corrosive spray—its range is about sixty feet." The words came out more quietly than she had intended, but the squad leader beside her heard.

The street was wide here; and with waves of his arm the leader directed the squad back, up against the rear of a smithy. Then he sidled slowly along the building until he stood directly opposite the alley's entrance, safely out of range.

Rowan was beside him.

There was movement down in the alley. Someone, a person, was staggering blindly, groping along one wall toward a little door that stood open, tucked away in a niche.

Another figure lay on the ground, silently convulsing as the demon leaned above it, spraying over and over.

Back by the wagon, having moved only enough to fall to his knees: Steffie. Rowan saw white eyes beneath his tangled hair.

The wall behind her seemed to rush up to strike her back; she had staggered against it in relief. "Steffie," she shouted, "stay put! Don't move!" The creature had found other targets, was perhaps too busy to remember Steffie's presence.

How did it *see*?

"Come on, you monster, come this way," she said through clenched teeth. She whistled again, shrilly, the iron taste of someone's blood on her fingers.

The squad leader hissed at her, "What are you doing?"

"Calling it out."

He grabbed her arm, half dragged her back to where the squad waited. "Are you mad? It's better off in there."

She looked at him blankly. "Archers," she said. "You need archers."

The leader glanced about, found faces. "Arvin," he said. "Lilly."

One of the injured fighters had been struck in the face. He stood leaning against a comrade, quietly regarding with his remaining eye a tattered, bloody object in his left hand.

His right hand still held his sword. Rowan gently took it from him.

The leader was speaking to his archers. "Get over there, get a clear view down the alley, and send everything you've got at the monster."

Rowan was aghast. "You can't just blindly pour arrows in there. Steffie is still there. He's alive, he might get hit!"

"Bad luck for him."

"But you can't—"

He turned on her. "We're going to stop that beast, whatever it takes, and if only one more person dies, well, I'd say that's good for the rest of us!"

"While it's partly thanks to Steffie that half the town isn't dead already—"

The archers were standing, confused, watching the argument. One spoke up. "I'm a good shot." Arvin. He looked from his leader to the steerswoman and back again. "Let me try alone. I can put six shafts right in it, and no danger to Steffie, I know I can."

The leader studied him with a narrow gaze, then jerked his head, acquiesence and command.

Arvin pulled six arrows from his quiver, his eyes on the opening to the alley, already gauging his shots. "Sixty feet?" he asked Rowan.

"From what I just saw, yes."

He nodded. "How fast can it move?"

"I saw it move only about as fast as a man might stroll along. Perhaps it can move faster if it wants to."

"Taking its time right now," he observed. The hum was neither rising nor falling; Rowan sensed that the creature was waiting. "Where should I place my shot on it?" Arvin asked.

"I have no idea."

The archer drew and expelled two long, calming breaths, then paced away from her, along the back of the smithy to a central position. Then he took one step forward away from the wall and, gazing warily down the alley, thrust five of his arrows point down into the dirt.

There were voices at the back of the squad: townspeople had arisen and begun to arrive, and were being directed away. The wounded woman had fallen silent; she was dead. The man who had been struck in the face was making small, querulous noises in the back of his throat. Other than these sounds, other than the demon's humming, the squad and the world were silent.

Arvin set his feet carefully, sunlight angling into the street, the long shadows of the buildings dividing the ground before him into fractured shapes of black and yellow.

"Corey," Rowan said abruptly.

The leader turned to her. "What?"

"Nothing. I just now remembered your name."

Arvin nocked his arrow, raised his bow, and let fly; and with fantastic speed he sent two more off immediately. There was a sudden increase in the uppermost overtones of the demon's voice; then the creature was out of the alley at a loping run.

It had all three shafts in it, vertically down its body; it had turned the wounds away from Arvin, and was spraying toward him as it ran.

But Arvin had dodged to the side, opposite the squad, and he sent two more arrows into the creature.

Beside Corey, the second archer cried out and let fly one, two—one arrow striking directly between two of the demon's arms, while the squad fell back again. The creature sprayed left toward the archer without turning its body, but the jet was diffuse; then it sprayed right, to where Arvin had run, and barely missed. Arvin put two more arrows into it, one of them striking between two arms on that side; and instead of a jet the creature sent out an unfocused spray in that direction, with no effective range. It began to turn again.

Spray vents between the arms, Rowan realized. Fourfold symmetry. Two vents were wounded. "That's it," she heard herself say; then she ran toward the creature.

Close by, the demon smelled of salt and musk, and the air around it was chill. One injured vent was still toward Rowan, and just as she passed, she swung the sword back, striking deep between two more arms, then dashed on. The demon's body swayed, bending like a willow, and it sprayed at her, but without force or focus, and Rowan passed unharmed. "There's one vent left!" she shouted to the fighters, as she hurried on. The creature was turning again, trying to bring its uninjured side toward her.

Corey shouted, signaled, but did not wait for his own fighters. He rushed forward, swung his weapon down on the top of the demon, slicing deep. The arms flailed and clutched; a gout of yellow fluid fountained up. The demon's taloned hands grasped at Corey, and he cried out and dropped back; but his squad was with him now, slashing and stabbing. The demon thrust its arms forward, trying to clutch at the blades, trying to turn its remaining vent toward them.

Rowan circled and came up again among the fighters. Corey was now at the rear, on his knees, a ragged, bloody gash across his scalp; but it was his chest he clutched. "Fall back!" he shouted, and spat blood. "Archers again!" But as he was speaking, someone drove a pike deep into the demon.

Rowan thought she had gone deaf, then understood: the voice of the demon had ceased. She felt dizzy in the silence.

The quiet was at odds with the action; the demon still lived, still struggled. The man with the pike was having trouble. Rowan heard ominous cracks from the weapon.

Then the pike shattered, and the creature came forward flailing blindly and silently, and seemingly more by chance than intent, clutched the pikeman. The man cried out, thrashed once, and then sagged, even as the other fighters attacked. The creature tossed the pikeman away, tried to rotate again.

Corey pulled himself to his feet, grabbed the broken end of the pike, and thrust it into the demon near its last vent. He was not accurate, and the demon sprayed; but it seemed to have lost its aim. The fighters backed away in fear, but none were struck; and they advanced again in a mob. Someone hacked viciously at another arm, and Rowan finished Corey's attempt with the blade.

The creature now had two arms shattered, and all its vents uselessly leaked fluid. It flailed out with its remaining arms, but wildly. One fighter, with an overhand axe blow, severed one of the arms; someone else severed another; and Rowan hacked across its midsection, over and over. The creature slowly slid down the wall and at last lay prone, its legs trembling, then relaxing as it died.

The fighters stood, kneeled, leaned against the wall, some gasping for breath, some breathlessly stunned in the sudden stillness. Arvin cautiously prodded the demon once with his foot, eliciting no response.

Eventually, Corey said in a small voice, "That's it, then." Rowan looked around.

Far down the street, a half dozen spectators had gathered: warehouse workers, the smith and his apprentice. In the other direction, someone was peering cautiously through a half-opened door.

Two of the militia were dead, five others wounded. One of these was huddled, trying to protect his blood-soaked chest without touching it. Another, a woman, had removed her shirt and was with great concentration wrapping it around the raw bone of her upper arm.

Corey stood, weaving, regarding the blood on his right hand. There was a puncture in the lower left side of his chest, as if from a spear thrust. He looked up at Rowan. "The wounded need help," he said, as if that number did not include himself. Rowan gestured to Arvin, who called to the spectators and began giving instructions.

Then Rowan walked down the alley to where Steffie was crouched by the corpse of the first person the demon had killed.

The demon had done exactly as Bel had described. Flesh had dissolved under the creature's spray. The victim seemed only half a person; untouched below, raw muscle and bone above. Abdominal organs were visible.

Steffie was quietly regarding the corpse. He himself was uninjured.

Rowan stooped down beside him, put a hand on his shoulder. "Who was it?" He did not reply until she pulled him up, away from the body. She asked again.

"Leonard." His voice was small, distant, abstracted. "Him and Maysie had come out the warehouse." He looked to where the little door still stood open, made a move in that direction. "Someone should see to her, she's hurt . . ."

Rowan stopped him, and waved over some of the people now helping the militia, spoke quietly to them. They cautiously entered the warehouse, calling out Maysie's name.

Rowan led Steffie away. "Where's Gwen?" she asked him.

"Don't know," he said. His voice seemed stronger now; his steps grew more sure. "Maybe run home by now. Maybe still out cold in Carter's Street." They paused by the dead demon; Steffie stared down at it in fascination. "I figured . . ." He swallowed. "You said stay still, and Gwen was doing that all right, so I figured she'd be safe enough." He was speaking quietly, as if to himself. "But you were out there," he went on, "whistling the monster to you. So I thought: she's stopping it getting Lasker, but who's to stop it getting her? And then I thought, Well . . . that would be me."

"That was good thinking, Steffie," she told him.

He looked up and regarded her blankly a moment. Then his mouth twitched. "Funny how good you can think when you're scared to death," he said.

"I know I've found that to be true," she said with sincerity. She considered the demon again. "Does someone have a barrow?" She called out. "I want to bring this back to the Annex."

9

Rowan was hard put to persuade the militia and townsfolk to permit her to take possession of the demon. "What do you want it for?" was asked by many, at different points during the organization of assistance and clearing. Rowan's reply, "to examine," brought only the further question, voiced in tones of incomprehension, "Why?"

"Because I've never seen anything like it." This statement brought blank gazes from most, as if her words held no meaning whatsoever.

But a tiny, gnarled old woman, who seemed to be in charge of the relief efforts, spared an instant to study the dead creature with a squinting, disapproving gaze. "Ugly damn thing," she said. "What's it good for?"

The oddness of the question drew Rowan's attention away from her adamant defense of the demon's corpse against two longshoremen, who wished to drag the thing down to the sea. "I don't know," the steerswoman replied; then in retrospect pieced together the woman's actions and understood that she was the local healer. "Perhaps a tincture of its spray can be used to burn away warts and skin tumors," she hazarded. "If I discover anything useful, I'll let you know about it."

The woman nodded and returned to other work; Rowan returned to arguing with the longshoremen. But shortly thereafter a man drove up with a shabby little pony cart: the town's honey wagon, arriving at the healer's relayed request. Rowan and Steffie cautiously shoved the corpse and its severed arms onto a pair of empty burlap sacks, dragged and hauled them up into the cart, then followed the load and its odorous conveyance back to the Annex.

They deposited the carcass in the weedy yard behind the building, and Rowan entered to fetch paper, charcoal, pens, and a kitchen knife.

Gwen was slouched in the armchair. She glared at Rowan. "You left me in the street!"

With a job at hand, Rowan was disinclined to spare time for Gwen's complaints. "I'm sorry. There were other things going on . . ."

"That monster—it could have got me!"

"Actually, that wasn't likely . . ." Rowan rattled among the tarnished collection of knives.

"Me in the road like a sack of meal, and you two hightailing off like rabbits—"

"Shut up." Steffie had entered and was leaning wearily against the doorjamb. He spoke without force. "Shut up, shut up, and shut up."

His posture caught Rowan's attention. "Steffie, are you all right?" Gwen left her mouth open on an unspoken statement.

Steffie nodded weakly, then jerked his head toward the backyard. "Careful where you step out there, lady. I left last night's dinner in the middle of the path." He turned a pale face and a bright gaze toward Gwen. "Now listen, you," he said, and began quietly to recount the morning's events. Rowan eased herself past him and into the yard.

Within the open wounds in the gray, battered skin, the demon's flesh was a yellowish gray, looking like no flesh or matter that the steerswoman had seen before. Blood like glue, yellow and translucent, had congealed across most of the body, standing on the skin, peeling and flaking.

The steerswoman considered the carcass. Symmetrical . . . She prodded the corpse with her foot, and rolled it. There was no identifiable front or back, as she had noticed before, but despite its cylindrical shape, the creature could be thought of as having four sides. Each arm at the top was aligned with a matching leg at the bottom, defining a quarter of the form. Each spray vent—she leaned closer—was located between two arms, between the shoulder joints, as Rowan came to think of them.

Using the point of the sword she had taken from the injured militiaman, she pushed one of the severed arms clear and away from the body. A bucket of water from the rain barrel sluiced away any of the corrosive spray that might have gotten on it.

She knelt beside the arm and touched it. It was cold, its gray skin the texture of oiled leather. Among the new slices and abrasions, there were a number of old, small scars, of the sort that any creature might acquire in the course of its life; Rowan had more than a few such herself.

The arm possessed an identifiable elbow, which surprisingly bent in both directions, and another joint further along, which Rowan decided to refer to as a wrist, from which directly sprouted three slender fingers. Each finger ended in a talon.

While she was comparing the hand to the foot, she became aware that someone was standing nearby—for how long, Rowan had no idea. "Look at this," she said to the person. "The structure isn't parallel. In other handed animals, the foot will resemble the hand, in general. Raccoons, for instance. And wood gnomes certainly, not to mention humans."

"Is Steffie about?" the person asked.

"Inside," she began, then became aware of the tone of the voices coming from within the house. "Arguing with Gwen," she added. "This foot no more resembles this hand than a bird's foot resembles its wing. Less, in fact." The foot was broad and somewhat flat; it did not seem to possess toes so much as a final division of the five longitudinal supports within.

"Three fingers," Rowan said aloud, "five toes. How odd."

"Huh?"

Rowan looked up; the person previously present had left, and now there were two little girls standing in the yard: one by the edge of the house, apparently eager to leave, the other nearer, regarding the corpse gape-mouthed. Rowan said, "Please don't come any closer. There are parts of this animal that might hurt your skin." Having said this, she recalled a child in the Outskirts who had discovered something Rowan had thought might be a demon's egg. The child's palms had itched slightly the following day.

Rowan picked up the bucket to fetch more water. The children fled shrieking at her approach, as if the steerswoman were herself a demon. They vanished around the corner.

The kitchen knife scored the skin of the arm with difficulty; Rowan had to make two passes to cut deep enough. She peeled back the skin and exposed the muscle beneath.

She regarded it silently; after a moment, she plied the knife again, searching for the bones that would give logic to the muscles' organization.

She did not at first know the bone when she found it. It did not stop her knife immediately, and she assumed that she was cutting into cartilage, until it was impossible to go farther.

She sat back on her heels, thinking. Then she carefully sliced away all the muscle.

If it was bone, it was unlike any bone she had seen before. Its outer surface did resemble cartilage, thickening as one moved inward. Eventually, within, the substance became as hard as bone, although black in color. Rowan rinsed her hands, her knife, and poured the rest of the bucket over one of the creature's legs.

As in the arm, the organization of the muscles resembled that of no other animal Rowan had seen before. She ceased to attempt to relate the demon to her knowledge of other animals and was immediately rewarded.

"Physics," she said. "Levers, struts, supports. Pulleys. The arrangement works."

"How can you do that?" Rowan looked up to find a woman of about her own age standing in the open doorway. The woman's face showed a horror that the steerswoman considered inappropriate to the situation: the demon, after all, was dead.

"I want to see how it works," Rowan said. She grasped the ankle of one undamaged leg and pulled. The leg extended. "Look at this—it seems to be a natural move." She tapped the dissected leg with her knife. "It looks like the animal is designed to jump; but none of the muscles seem to be large enough to make that possible. And it never did so while we were watching . . ."

The bang of the door told her that the woman had departed, quickly.

Rowan considered the severed arm again, then moved to the top of the carcass to see how the shoulder joint worked—and to her amazement discovered the creature's mouth, at the top of its body, nestled among the bases of the arms. "That's interesting . . ." No one replied; she was alone.

Mouth in the center, arms growing out from around it. Rowan took the sword and slid it down the creature's throat, hearing a brittle rasping within. She levered the blade, flat up, and peered beneath it into the maw; the cross slashes inflicted during the fight made the mouth gape obscenely wide. Inside: a series of serrated, overlapping plates that ringed the throat down its length.

Rowan removed the blade and stood regarding the animal, thinking.

She set down the sword and rearranged the demon's two attached arms, extending them over the demon's top, then bending the elbows. The double joints easily brought the hands to the mouth. "It works, but it's not very efficient . . ."

Under what altered circumstances would it be efficient?

In eating, the demon must first pick up its food, then lift it toward its mouth. But it would be best for any animal's mouth to be at the front of the body, so that the animal might move toward its food to eat it.

With an abrupt change of mental perspective, Rowan saw the demon's mouth as being at the front of its body; its arms efficiently gathering in food; its legs, kicking, thrusting behind, propelling it.

"Water," the steerswoman said.

"Right here," Steffie said. He was seated at the bottom of the back steps, a full bucket at his feet, two full pots on the steps behind him. He picked one up. "Where do you want it?"

She gestured him near. "Pour it over my hands." He did so, and with the remainder and the contents of the bucket, they rinsed the demon from top to bottom.

Rowan took up the knife again. "I don't suppose there are any gloves about?"

"No gloves. Mira liked mittens."

Rowan knelt by the carcass. Remembering the woman who had fled into the house, she said, "I hope you're not squeamish." She began slicing down the body.

"No." He had returned to his seat. "I like watching," he said. "Sort of a shame the thing's not alive while you're doing that."

Rowan paused and looked up. Steffie was sitting more quietly, more subdued than was usual for him. His face was still, his eyes dark.

Rowan said, "How well did you know the people who died?"

"Knew them all," he said softly, "since I was a tyke."

Silence.

"Would you like to help me?"

They found two sticks among the rubbish in the yard; Steffie used them to hold the skin open as Rowan sliced down the center of one of the demon's quarters.

Rowan had expected to find muscle directly beneath the skin; instead, from just below the spray vent to just above another pair of orifices between the hips, there was a fine membrane, turgid from fluid within. "Stand back." Using the sword, Rowan cautiously punctured the membrane. It emitted a quiet, sick *pop*.

An oval depression, about six inches long, appeared around the puncture. The rest of the membrane remained taut. Rowan made another puncture, creating another depression. Both leaked a colorless fluid. The steerswoman became methodical, and soon the entire area was honeycombed with depressions. She carefully peeled the membrane from one depression, revealing a little chamber, its back surface striated blue, its edges weirdly yellow-veined.

Rowan rested on her heels, elbows on her knees, hands loose in front of her. She said, "I have no idea what that is."

Steffie tilted his head. "People don't have that?"

"No. People don't have that. Nor do animals."

"Buy my meat from the butcher. Never seen inside a person. Until today." The memory brought shock to his face. He paled, rose, turned away, and succumbed to a fit of dry retching. Rowan watched silently.

When it was over he rinsed his hands, wiped his mouth, refilled the bucket and pots from the rain barrel, and brought them over. "What next?"

"We see what's under this."

They sluiced the corpse again, the knife, and their hands. Rowan cut in at the bottom edge of the lowest chambers, along the edges toward the demon's top, and she and Steffie began pulling the entire area away.

It was difficult. Hundreds of tiny fibrous strands, wound into dozens of slim cables, led from the chambers into the demon's body, passing through cartilaginous openings between adjacent muscle groups. Eventually, Steffie was using both hands to pull the chamber mass away and upward, as Rowan followed with the knife, cutting strands and cables as she went.

It was a long job, and they grew hot. Rowan wiped her forehead on her shoulder, not wishing to bring her gory hands close to her face. Movement at the edge of her vision caught her attention.

A half dozen persons were standing by the corner of the Annex, in the building's shadow. "May I help you?" she called. They left, one by one, some quickly, some reluctantly. None spoke.

"They're wondering," Steffie said, shifting his grip on the oozy flesh. "Heard the story by now, see. Curious."

"So am I," Rowan said distractedly. In the heat and sunlight, the corpse was emitting a rank stench, like rotted fish and spoiled eggs, with a heavy coppery tang that hung cloying in the back of Rowan's throat. "That's enough—leave the top." Rowan examined the muscles on the newly revealed surface.

"Ribs." She pointed. "See how the muscles angle?" There were a lot of them. With the sword, she split the rib cage, and she and Steffie gripped opposite edges and pulled.

Inside, nothing that Rowan could immediately recognize.

She located the cut ends of the chamber cables and followed them inward to where they terminated at a large bluish mass, its surface striated and deeply creviced, shot through with veins. The substance seemed to comprise a central inner cylinder, running nearly the length of the demon's body. Rowan's knife entered it with eerie ease, segments of the matter splitting off, fracturing wetly away from the blade. At the very center, she found a backbone of gnarled black cylinders.

Rowan sat back on her heels again; Steffie waited, silent beside her, puzzled and grim.

Even the smallest animals possessed, after some fashion, ears, eyes, a brain; but Rowan could find nothing resembling these in the demon.

She sighed, washed her hands again, and continued her work.

By sheer logic she identified what must be four lungs, four hearts, and the complicated digestive tract, which she laboriously follwed to a single eliminative oriface.

Between each hip joint she found four more orifaces. She dissected one, discovering its inner surface completely covered by a multitude of short, muscular tendrils. "I cannot even guess what these are for."

Tracing inward from this, she located a large sac whose contents shifted under her probings. She slit it open. Within: a multitude of gelatinous nodes, each with a tiny, twisted, translucent object at its center.

Rowan's interest became intense. "These are eggs."

She maneuvered a few onto the flat of her knife, angled it to the sun, and used a grass reed to probe one egg. Tiny arms uncurled at one end of the embryo, four frail fins spread at the other. A white line defined the future backbone.

"So, that's a lady demon," Steffie said.

"Female, yes . . ."

Rowan knew nothing of the life cycle of demons. But she was certain that special conditions were needed for the creature to survive—conditions found in the Outskirts and the lands beyond.

Of all animals that might wander far from their natural environment, a female carrying fertile eggs seemed the least likely.

Something had driven this demon far from its home. If Rowan could not determine what, she must at least learn all she could about the nature of demons.

She rose. "Ready for more?"

"I am."

"Good. Help me turn this thing . . ."

It was darkness that finally forced them to stop.

When Rowan entered the Annex, the day's work, and the previous night's, suddenly caught up with her. She stood in the middle of the kitchen, stupid with exhaustion.

The battle with the monster now seemed distant, and possibly imaginary. The day that had followed seemed wholly abstract, devoted entirely to thought. It seemed odd to Rowan, at that moment, that so intellectual an exercise could have such an effect on her body.

Steffie had lit a lamp and now stood leaning against the kitchen table, apparently unable or unwilling to move. They both remained still for some time.

"We should eat," Rowan managed to say.

"Right."

Neither stirred.

Standing in the homely kitchen, surrounded by the accoutrements of human life, Rowan recalled that there had been other humans about during the day; many had come and gone while she and Steffie worked. She could clearly remember the first few; the rest existed in her mind as brief, vague presences.

Rowan also recalled, now quite clearly, that the first person who had arrived that morning had been Arvin, the archer; that the woman who arrived somewhat later, with dark eyes and wild-curled hair, had strongly resembled Steffie; and that the two little girls had resembled both the woman and Arvin.

The steerswoman said, "I hope you were able to reassure your family."

Steffie's mouth twitched once. "Sort of," he said heavily, then stirred himself to speak further. "Gwen and Alyssa joined up to ride me. They do that." He looked up at the cupboard before him as if it were an unknown object. He opened it, removed two plates, and set them on the table. "Ends up, I'm to stay away from monsters from now on. Like I don't plan to."

"Words to live by." Rowan gathered her strength, stepped into the pantry, and brought out the first food that came to hand: a plateful of ham slices and half a loaf of soft black bread. The bread smelled wonderful.

Steffie had found a knife; Rowan passed the bread to him. "Funny thing about Arvin," he continued as he sliced bread. "Never much liked him." He was rambling in exhaustion. "Seemed like, well, he's got no prospects, and what with the children, and all, I'd like him to do better." He passed Rowan a plate with bread. "And him always practicing with that archery; militia doesn't pay, except for the commanders. But he'd rather shoot than do most everything else. Never could figure that out." His puzzlement seemed weak, and childlike.

Rowan placed ham on both plates. "He does it for the joy of the skill."

It was a simple statement, which Rowan had made without needing to think; but the phrase seemed to strike Steffie as an odd one, and new to him. "Joy of the skill?" He puzzled it over; then placed bread on the plates, still thinking. "Well," he said vaguely, "quite like him now."

Perhaps it was Rowan's exhaustion, but it struck the steerswoman as inexpressibly funny that one should say of a man who had just saved one's life: "quite like him." And she was unable to speak further but simply sat with her arms on the table, laughing helplessly, a laugh more breath than sound. Steffie had a moment of understanding, then he laughed.

They set to their dinners; but the first bite brought another memory, and Rowan stopped short. "Dan," she said around the mouthful. "I was supposed to have dinner with Dan tonight." She set down the slice of ham, looked at the window to check the time. It was full night. "I suppose I ought to find him and explain . . ." She rose.

Steffie waved a hand to stop her. "Don't need to. He was by here earlier to get you."

"To get me?"

Steffie nodded. "Came out the back door, saw what you was up to, and bolted." His eyes were blank a moment, as weariness overtook his thoughts. He visibly forced himself to recover. "What do we do with that thing out there, then?"

Rowan resumed eating. "Leave it for now. There's more I need to do." Sketches, and recording her observations.

"It's started to smell. Better waste no time, or we'll have the neighbors on us."

At first light Rowan rose, dressed, and hurried downstairs.

When she opened the back door, the smell struck her, magnified by hours passed, weighted heavily with the morning dew. She paused on the stoop, gasping until she adjusted.

"Don't half stink," a gravelly voice commented. An old woman was seated on the back steps, viewing the weird carcass. She had a sausage in one hand and a hunk of bread in the other, and alternated bites between the two.

Rowan suppressed an urge to retch. "How can you eat with that smell about?"

"I've smelled worse." It was the old healer. "Plenty of bad smells in my work." She nodded thoughtfully, then indicated the demon with her sausage-holding hand. "No flies," she observed.

Rowan had noted this already. "It's from the Outskirts," she said, taking a seat beside the healer. "For the most part, Outskirts life and Inner Lands life aren't compatible." In the thin morning sunlight, the carcass looked even more peculiar. Flayed flesh, a tangle of shattered limbs, organs spread out on the dirt and grass: Rowan's careful dissection now looked more like some uncanny disaster visited upon a creature too ruined to be identifiable.

The steerswoman and the healer had never been introduced. "Jilly," the old woman provided when Rowan asked. It seemed more a child's name. Jilly finished her meal, brushed crumbs from her skirts, and heaved herself to her feet. "Right. How's it burn people, then?"

Rowan led her to the carcass, indicated a dissected venom sac, then rolled the corpse with her foot to display the same on a less mutilated quarter. Jilly nodded, and became interested in the talons. "That's what killed Gregory, see?" She pointed. "Shoved that whole paw right into him, almost clear out the back."

Rowan recalled the pike bearer. "Yes."

"Got Corey as well . . ."

Rowan felt herself back in the Outskirts, in the aftermath of a battle—counting, as one did at such times. "How many of the injured will live?"

Jilly shook her head, hobbled back to the steps. "Had to take off Sada's arm," she began. "If she lasts till tomorrow, she'll make it. Sewed up Corey's face, but he's got that hole in his side, see; we have to wait a day to know. Sarton got a bad burn down his leg, but not down to the bone. He'll limp forever, but he'll live." She seated herself again. "Bran, now, he died an hour or so ago—didn't think he'd last that long." She peered up at the cool, empty sky; birds called invisibly from the harbor. "Couldn't do a damn thing," she continued, "but listen to him while he went along, slowly figuring out he hadn't got a face anymore and was going to die."

It had been Bran's sword Rowan had taken. "And what about Maysie?"

"Don't know yet."

Rowan could think of nothing to say, and stood quietly in the sun-bright sour-smelling morning air. "Well."

Jilly nodded. "Hell of a thing."

The steerswoman turned back to the flayed creature in the yard. "This beast has traveled a long way," she said. "I'd better finish my work. I doubt I'll have another opportunity."

The second demon arrived three weeks later.

10

"But what did you do with it?"

"Flung it into the sea, didn't we?" Corey was clearly exhausted, and winced periodically, although apparently more in annoyance than pain. He increased his pace along the dusty road. He had been on his feet two weeks, but dealing with the new demon the previous night had clearly worn hard on him.

Rowan fell in step beside him. "Someone ought to have called me."

"For what? We know how to deal with them now. Get the people off the street and shoot it. This one hardly put up any fight at all."

"And putting it into the sea might not have been a good idea. If the tide doesn't take it far enough away, it could poison the shoreline."

"Makes no sense, that, seeing as it came from the sea in the first place, you said."

"Demons do need a body of water nearby; but it's not the Inland Sea. I have reason to suspect a sort of salt marsh, with a type of salt different from—"

"Lady." He stopped and turned on her. "All this is not so interesting to me as it is to you. I don't care where they come from. If they come here, we kill them, and that's all I want to know about them. Now, does this talk have any point other than you giving me a piece of your mind? Because nobody gives me my food for free, not forever, anyway. And if I want to eat, then Karin's worms have to eat, too. It's everybody's worms out all at once, now, and none of us has time to waste."

They had arrived at Karin's mulberry groves: stunted trees, shoulder high, row upon row, their branches crowded with palm-sized leaves. There were already more than a dozen workers in place, staggered across the low hillside under an utterly cloudless sky. West, past a dividing path, Lasker's own hirelings were hard at work, displaying, Rowan considered, admirable speed and energy.

"Actually," she said, "there is a point. But I'll not delay you any longer. Good day."

She left the groves and workers behind, and went down the path back to town.

Two demons were two too many. *It takes three to know*, was the steerswomen's saying. One might be a random event. Two could be coincidence.

But that operated for facts in isolation. What Rowan had was two creatures not normally seen in the Inner Lands, at a time when she knew that the Outskirts had already been damaged once. Considered as a whole, the information was ominous.

More creatures from the wildlands—goblins, swarmers, snip-beetles, fool-yous, even mud-lions—might be wandering into civilized country. Slado might even have struck at the Outskirters again—with Bel herself still somewhere among them.

Fletcher had given warning last time. There would be no such help next time.

Rowan wished she could take up her pack and charts and search the wilderness for Bel—or at the least, locate Kammeryn's tribe, assure herself that the seyoh and his people had not been harmed.

She found she had stopped in the street, so great was her urge to turn around, go out, and leave Alemeth and its gossipy, mundane inhabitants behind.

Steffie had been right. She was far more comfortable among unusual people. They were easier for her to love.

She continued on her way.

But she was being unkind. Janus recognized the virtues of these people, and cared for them. Rowan loved strange people, she realized, because she loved strangeness itself, newness, and discovery. Janus had moved to the opposite extreme.

He would do well here, in Mira's old job.

She reached the Annex, and paused outside, trying to view it as if coming across it new. It was a pleasant house, with a high ground floor and a small gabled second storey crouched under the roof. Three tall and satisfyingly clean windows of rare glass panes faced the street, the one to the right of the door affording a clear view all the way to the worktable. The other windows presented passersby with two segments of the first bookcase, volumes filling the windows completely, as if in a shop display.

She imagined a steerswoman arriving here after hard travel, finding sanctuary, a warm hearth, a welcoming and trustworthy custodian, someone who would cherish the knowledge she brought, order and protect it . . .

A pleasant thought, especially with Janus in that role—if the Prime allowed it.

It had been three weeks before a ship had been able to take the letter concerning Janus to the port city of Donner. From there, it might have been further delayed.

Still, it was possible, with enough luck and speed, and just barely possible that a reply would arrive soon.

She decided to check again at the harbor.

Alemeth during worm feeding seemed a city of ghosts and children. Old High Street was completely deserted. Someone had left a bucket of dirt and a garden fork under a window box half filled with earth. Rowan had seen the same bucket and fork in the same place the previous morning. At the bakery where she stopped to acquire rolls for her breakfast, the ovens were cold, and only a girl of about nine years old was present, nervously tending the till. Rowan selected three of the least ancient egg buns, waited patiently while the girl laboriously figured change for the coin Rowan offered. She got it wrong, and Rowan was about to demonstrate the correct sum—but the girl shied back when the steerswoman neared.

Possibly she had been one of the pranksters on the night before the first demon had come. Rowan had grown accustomed to such treatment by now; the easy attitude of the parents was not shared by the children. Rowan had sent the word around town that any child bringing the steerswoman a live specimen of the glowing moths would receive a reward, hoping that greed would break the barrier, but to no effect.

She sighed, informed the girl that a fourth bun would even the score, took it, and took herself back outside.

A woman was seated on the sturdy bench by the bakery door, in a head-dropped posture of weariness. Rowan at first took her to be a grannie not strong enough to work the groves—then realized that it was Maysie. The steerswoman sat down beside her, and wished her a good morning.

Maysie returned the greeting, with a quick sidelong glance from under her hair. She had taken to wearing it loose—not an attractive style for hair of her texture, interspersed as it was with grizzling gray. But it was clean, as was her clothing, typical home-quality Alemeth silk worn with typical Alemeth disregard for color combination.

"I suppose your 'boys and girls' are off to the mulberry groves." This elicited a mute nod. "Steffie and Gwen have gone, as well. I was beginning to wonder if Alemeth worked at all, other than the shopkeepers and fishers. And now if I were to find my roof leaking, I suppose I'd have to either climb up there myself or keep a pot under the drips until the worms go up the hill."

Maysie continued to gaze at the ground. Rowan felt sorry. She missed Maysie's wryness, her perspective, her commonsense wisdom. She had been one of the pleasanter aspects of Alemeth, before the demon attack.

Now she sat, head down, hands on her knees, basket at her feet, toying with a handful of coins.

Abruptly, Rowan understood. "Would you like me to go into the shop for you?"

A quick glance up, a brief, twisted smile. "Thank you."

Rowan took the coins and basket, learned Maysie's requirements, and startled the child by returning so inexplicably. She collected loaves of bread, a dozen biscuits, and this time did not leave until the jittering girl submitted to a forced lesson in simple math.

Back outside, she handed the goods to Maysie, then reclaimed her seat. She sat seething, and cast about for something to say to Maysie, but found difficulty broaching the subject without including a comment that might be hurtful. Unable to remain silent, she at last settled on: "That's a remarkably stupid little girl in there."

"I can't blame Anna. She's just a child."

"She ought to be able to handle simple decimal arithmetic by now."

"It's with the adults that I can't bear it. Guess I'll just have to get used to it . . ."

"Nonsense." Rowan spoke with feeling. "It's they who should get used to it—which they would all the sooner if they exercised the simple courtesy of looking you in the eye."

Her vehemence caused Maysie to do exactly that herself.

Rowan had not had the opportunity to survey the damage previously, and was relieved to see that Maysie's right eye had not been blinded. It would require care in the future, however, as evidently the eyelid could no longer completely close. But the mouth could, fortunately, and although the healer's repairs had of necessity drawn what remained of Maysie's nose toward the damaged side of her face, it was still recognizably a nose. The skin on her cheek, forehead, and chin showed the twists and ridges typical of healing burns, tight and stiff.

"You look at me like Jilly does."

"For much the same reason, I suppose."

"It doesn't bother you." The expression on the left side of Maysie's face was one of puzzlement.

Rowan repressed an urge to push Maysie's hair back, behind her shoulders, into some neater and more dignified arrangement. Such an act would be intrusive. "I'd be far more bothered if you had died."

Maysie looked away, and made no comment.

"Well." Rowan rose, gathered three buns in one hand, one in the other. "Can manage that basket by yourself? I'm off to the harbor."

Maysie's voice betrayed a tinge of amusement. "Still waiting for Janus?"

Rowan almost said, out of sheer habit, He's not my sweetheart. She was becoming predictable. But honesty compelled her to admit, "Actually, yes. But I'm also hoping for the *Beria*. I'd heard that she was coming in for Lasker's spring silk."

The two women parted, and Rowan continued to the water, munching one of the egg buns as she walked.

No sight of Janus at the harbor, but there was sail on the horizon. Rowan recognized the *Beria*, but the ship was having difficulty. The wind was not favorable for an approach to the harbor.

Rowan stood at the end of the biggest wharf, finishing her breakfast and studying the wind and the amount of canvas *Beria* showed. A full dozen swooping and hovering seagulls divided their attention between Rowan's buns and a crab boat unloading its catch nearby, unable to decide which presented better prospects. The steerswoman delighted them by splitting her last bun and tossing the pieces high in the air.

The *Beria* began bringing in sail; the captain had decided to stand off until evening. There was plenty to occupy Rowan until then.

As she passed the crab boat on her way back down the wharf, two of the crabbers began a wry conversation, concerning delayed sailors and the constancy of lovelorn women, carefully pitched to be audible as Rowan passed. She gritted her teeth and forebore to comment.

The steerswoman spent the day following a false trail through the works of two different steerswomen, gave it up, found more books from her selected period of time, and laboriously studied the entries.

It was around supper time that Gwen and Steffie showed up. Rowan was surprised that they had stopped by at all, so clearly were they exhausted. When she said so, Gwen dropped herself into the wicker chair, saying, "If I go home, my dad'll have me doing dinner for the whole family. Like he can't cook himself. Like I haven't been working as hard as him."

Steffie had been about to settle himself on the bench; but at this comment he stood again, obviously on his way to the pantry. Rowan, a bit guiltily, jumped to her feet and took the job from him. "I hope you don't mind cold; I didn't think." The pantry was nearly bare; she would see about fixing that tomorrow. But she was able to assemble cured ham, cheese, and some nearly stale but edible bread. She wished to do better than just water to drink, then remembered Brewer's daily contribution. She had not thought to bring it in; it would still be by the door.

It was. And so were two other things.

She brought them all in, and set the bucket on the table.

"What's that?" Steffie asked, as Gwen dipped mugs.

"A letter." The *Beria* must have come in, and someone from the ship or the docks had completed the delivery. Rowan suspected a child; an adult would have knocked on the door. "And a package."

The letter was satisfyingly fat, with *Rowan, Steerswoman, The Annex, Alemeth* written large and round and neat. Rowan recognized the Prime's handwriting, and had the letter open even before she settled into Mira's old chair.

After the opening greeting, Rowan found an acknowledgement of Rowan's report on her travels in the Outskirts and the Guidestar fragments Rowan's package had contained; a description of the systematic search being conducted by the residents of the Archives for any clue of Slado's whereabouts; confirmation that Rowan should stay in Alemeth to continue independent researches, at least until such time as Mira's replacement could be selected.

Rowan nodded satisfaction at the details of the search. There were seven members of the Steerswomen living at the Archives, and the records there were already precisely organized and cross-referenced. Rowan felt certain that significant progress would be made soon.

But it was clear that this was a reply to Rowan's first communication only. At the time it was written, her news and suggestion about Janus had not been received.

The letter continued in a more personal tone, with surprise at the state of the Annex, sympathy for Rowan's predicament, and regret at Mira's passing. The words were formal, but Rowan thought to detect a sort of plaintive perplexity on Henra's part that Mira would conduct herself in so irresponsible a fashion. Reading the passage again, Rowan understood that Mira had once been a dear friend of Henra's.

It gave Rowan pause. Henra would never have befriended the Mira Alemeth had known. Mira had changed.

Reading on, Rowan found news of the residents—Berry's eyesight continued to deteriorate, but old Hugo was thrilled with the new project and was displaying more energy than he had in years—and comments on the state of the gardens.

Tucked in among these, and stated in an offhand matter, was the fact that the next Academy, which ought to have taken place while Rowan was in the Outskirts, had been postponed, due to a period of ill health that the Prime had suffered. A new date, five years from the planned one, had been set.

This was unprecedented; Henra must have been very ill indeed. Rowan studied the handwriting and the tone of the entire letter; but the Prime seemed now merely herself, as ever, and Rowan assumed that she had recovered. Still, it was disturbing news.

Eventually, the letter devolved into reports on the recent antics of the wood gnomes. The Prime ended with the wry observation that when one starts gossiping about the animals, one really has run out of things to say.

Signature and date followed—but there was an addendum, apparently written in haste.

The Prime had selected Mira's replacement. The person would follow as soon as arrangements could be made. Henra was pleased with her own choice, as, she commented mysteriously, it used one problem to solve another.

That was all. Rowan checked the back of the sheets for further information, found none.

Trust the Prime to tease her with a mystery.

But this was not good news. With an official custodian already selected, it was unlikely that the person would be removed to make a place for Janus. But, at the least, perhaps the ban could still be lifted.

"You going to open that package?"

Rowan looked up.

"Unless it's personal," Gwen added. Supper was finished, and both of them had remained in place, watching her curiously.

Rowan could hardly blame them. Packages from faraway places are rare and fascinating. Only the Prime's handwriting had sent her to the letter first.

"I can't think of any reason why it should be." The address was merely: *The Annex, Alemeth*. Most likely, it was intended for Mira. "Here." Rowan brought it to the table, set it down. "You do it; I'll clear these dishes." As she turned away, she already heard the rustling of wrapping paper.

She was at the basin when she heard the yelp.

"What's it?" Steffie was asking. "Something sharp?"

"It *bit* me!"

Rowan glanced back: a small object on the table, dark wood, bright copper—

She abandoned the dishes. "Wait, don't touch it again!"

Gwen was shaking one hand as if from a bee sting; Steffie stood protectively in front of her, eyeing the package with suspicion.

It was a small box, about four inches square. It still lay on its wrapping: layers of oilcloth, paper, and a second cloth, grayish in color. This last seemed to have an odd texture, which Rowan confirmed with her fingers; somehow dry and slick at the same time.

"Booby-trapped?" Steffie hazarded. "That's a bad trick to play on someone."

"I'm sorry; I hadn't expected it would be anything like this." The box was carved decoratively, with copper lines inlaid on the highlights of the pattern. Rowan had seen that unique style before. "I think this box may be magic."

Gwen and Steffie stood dumbfounded. "What you felt may have been a protective spell," Rowan went on. She flattened the paper surrounding the box. "Fortunately—" And she touched the lid—

A *snap*, and a sting.

Rowan jumped back, shaking her hand sharply. "That shouldn't happen—"

"Happened to me," Gwen pointed out.

"But it shouldn't to me." The stinging tingle had vanished almost immediately, as had a quick, sharp scent. The eeriness of the sensation remained. "I should be immune . . ." Puzzled, Rowan stooped to bring the box to eye level. "It does seem to be a guard spell . . . but Steerswomen are immune to the usual sort. Steerswomen, and sometimes sailors, especially officers."

She had twice in her life circumvented guard spells, once without knowing beforehand that the spell was there at all. So dependable had been her immunity then, that now, although with immense caution, she reached out with one extended finger to lightly touch the box again.

Rowan discovered that Steffie and Gwen were helping her to her feet; she did not recall falling. "I'm all right," she said, and in saying so discovered that she was not. Her words were slurred, her thoughts were slowed, and she had the disturbing feeling that if she did not breathe consciously, she would cease to do so at all.

Gwen pulled a chair over, and Rowan sat. "That really shouldn't happen," Rowan repeated stupidly.

"A steerswoman should be able to open that box?" Gwen asked.

"Yes."

Gwen opened her mouth to say more—then stopped short, blinked, closed it again.

"Let's get a sailor," Steffie said.

"What?"

"A sailor. You said, steerswomen and sailors. Maybe a sailor can open it."

"No . . ." Her head began to clear. "It must be different from the usual sort of guard spell."

"Something to get you no matter who you are?"

"But then, why have a guard spell at all? Why not something that immediately kills?" She stood again, approached the box, but made no attempt to touch it.

It was, in fact, a lovely little thing.

The carving was intricate, with decorative trellises along the sides. On the top: a depiction of a woman striding through forest. The woman had short hair, touseled by an unseen wind, her cloak streamed behind her, and the end of a tube protruded from the top of the pack she carried. Her boots were plain and high.

"A steerswoman." The intention could hardly be made plainer.

"I'll bet Mira could open it," Gwen said.

"Possibly," Rowan replied, distractedly. How had she lost her own immunity? What had changed?

"What do we do with it?"

A good question: it certainly was not convenient to have it sitting in the center of the table, where any passerby would naturally investigate it.

"Well, it managed to get here safely enough." The box was still resting on its wrappings. She touched the inner wrapping again: no effect. Holding the edges, she picked it up, with the box resting in its center. Still no effect. She glanced about, and carried it back between two aisles of shelves, where the low stepladder rested against the back wall.

She stooped beside it, regarding it with distaste in the gloom.

"Does that Slado wizard know you're here?"

She looked up; Steffie had followed her into the aisle. He had spoken quietly.

"I don't know," she replied. "That's an interesting possibility."

Possibilities were two—no, three: It was meant for Rowan; it was meant for whichever steerswoman was custodian of the Annex; it was meant for Mira.

Could a guard spell be made so specific that only one person could get past it? "I don't suppose you heard of Mira's having any dealings with wizards?"

"No. She hated 'em."

"That's usual."

But if Slado knew Rowan was at the Annex, and knew enough to consider her a threat, certainly some more direct and dependable means of eliminating her could be used. "I think," she said slowly, "that I've simply lost my immunity. Somehow." She made a noise of frustration. "And I don't even know why steerswomen should be safe from guard spells in the first place. We simply are. Or ought to be."

Gwen appeared at the end of the aisle. "I'm off," she said, then added, "and thanks for making the dinner."

"You're welcome. In fact, come by tomorrow, and I'll do better, since I'll know to expect it."

This left Gwen with such an ambivalent expression on her face that Rowan and Steffie exchanged a quick wry glance; then the two departed for their homes.

Rowan dreamed that Tyson, ship's navigator from the *Morgan's Chance*, unexpectedly appeared at the door of the Annex and that they two had a long and detailed conversation concerning the nature of guard spells. Interestingly, both of them seemed well-informed on the subject. The Rowan who observed the dream tried desperately to listen to what the Rowan who participated in the dream was saying. But, as is so often the case with dreams, the conversation proved to have no content whatsoever when examined closely.

Rowan woke to Mira's lumpy bed and dim light filtering through the slats of the shutters.

No surprise that Rowan should dream of Tyson: it had been he who first demonstrated their mutual immunity to guard spells.

She tried to return to sleep, but was frustrated by the fact that the sheets had become so tangled that she would have to rise and remake the bed to get them right. After half an hour of attempting different postures, she gave it up and rose for the day.

She stubbornly ignored the box until she had prepared and eaten a makeshift breakfast, dealt with the dishes, planned what provisions to acquire for the evening, set out papers, ink, pens, and her logbook. Only then did she fetch the box.

She brought it back to the worktable, carrying it again by its wrappings, and set it down. Then she moved about it like a dog investigating a scorpion, crouching to view it from every possible angle, staying well back.

It clearly was meant for a steerswoman; the depiction on the lid left no question.

How had Rowan lost her immunity?

The woman on the lid was shown in typical steerswoman's garb, with typical accoutrements: hooded cloak, trousers, high leather boots, pack with protruding tubular map case, and a sheathed sword hanging at her waist. It came to Rowan that it was only these details that enabled her to recognize the subject of the picture as a steerswoman.

She looked down at herself. She was wearing clothing salvaged from Mira's wardrobe: a faded blue blouse of age-softened silk; moss-green canvas trousers, stiff from being stored unused for decades—and she was barefoot. Not at all the traditional appearance for a steerswoman. And how had she been dressed when she touched the box the previous day? Much the same.

Rowan brought her pack down from the storeroom and placed her map case inside; the protruding end of the case she carefully arranged to precisely the same angle as that shown on the box lid. She strapped on her sword, and arranged it with the same care. She took Mira's cloak from its hook, swung it around her shoulders; her own she had discarded in the Outskirts, when the constant abrasion against the rough-edged redgrass had worn it down to the lining.

Then she shouldered the pack, readjusted her gear, and considered herself again. Anyone seeing her would instantly know her as a steerswoman. All she lacked were her gum-soled, gray leather steerswoman's boots, which had suffered the same fate as her cloak; but if, as she guessed, the box was able to recognize a steerswoman, Rowan had certainly provided sufficient clues by which to be recognized—

By any person of average intelligence. Rowan found very disturbing the idea of an object like a box possessing intelligence, or an inhabiting spirit.

Perhaps it was merely that certain conditions were necessary for the spell to work. Three years ago, when she had watched the boy Willam prepare to execute his particular kind of destructive magic, she had been impressed by the total concentration and utter precision of action he displayed. Exactitude had been required, exactitude in every detail. Willam's spell had not been intelligent; the intelligence had been Willam's, in the precise re-creation of the proper conditions.

Rowan considered her own bare feet. She ought to search the house for Mira's boots.

She sighed in impatience and doffed pack and cloak, wondering where to begin—then recalled the old boots sitting on the back stairs.

They were dank with damp, crusted with mud. Rowan spent some minutes sitting on the steps, scraping the mud with a broken broom haft. The boots were ancient and had not been well cared for even in their youth. The gum soles were worn to the leather, and apparently Mira had continued to use them in that condition, as the leather itself was also worn, nearly to the insole.

Rowan had no idea if the box's requirements might include the soles of her feet. Still, the lack would be easy to remedy. The gum, distilled from the sap of certain trees, was available on any ship and in all seaports; sailors routinely used it to coat the soles of their boots and shoes, in order to improve their traction on wooden decks.

Rowan stopped short.

Gum-soled boots were used by steerswomen and by sailors—and by almost no one else. Those sailors most likely to wear footgear were those whose income enabled them to afford the expense: that is to say, officers. Like Tyson.

Rowan abandoned the boots, swept back into the house, scrabbled inside the cash jar on the mantel, extracted a small number of coins, and hurried out into the street.

At a harbor shop she found a secondhand pair of brown sailor's boots with soles in good repair; the shopkeeper, knowing she was a steerswoman, offered them free.

Back at the Annex, she immediately donned the boots and turned to the table where the box still rested.

She wore no cloak, no pack, no sword. She made no attempt to make herself visibly a steerswoman. She reached out her hand and touched the lid of the box.

No effect. The steerswoman's mouth twitched once in satisfaction and she pulled up the lid to examine the contents.

It was empty.

"*Rowan*—"

And she was on the opposite side of the room, her drawn sword at the ready in her hands, her back toward the now-open door. She stood, tense, shuddering with fear, equally prepared to strike or escape. Her breath came harsh through clenched teeth.

The box sat on the table, closed; she had slammed it shut when she fled.

It had spoken to her.

She sensed a presence behind her, spun.

A little boy with a stack of kindling balanced on his head stood in the center of the street, gape mouthed in terror. Rowan considered the sight she must present: a madwoman in a fighting stance, weapon fearsomely wielded, wild-eyed with panic.

Rowan blinked and relaxed her posture. "Excuse me," she said, and shut the door.

There was no one else in the room; Rowan was alone with the box. She cautiously approached it again, with her sword in her right hand, and reached out slowly to open it with her left.

The box continued: "I hope you will forgive me for choosing to communicate with you in such a startling fashion." The voice was identical to that of Corvus, the wizard in Wulfshaven. "You certainly chose to startle me with the contents of your message. I'm sure you had your reasons. And I have mine."

Rowan found she was clenching her teeth painfully. She forced her jaw to relax, made herself take one step closer.

Corvus would hardly be likely to have magically reduced his size and traveled in a little box in the cargo hold of a ship for weeks on end, purely in order to speak to Rowan. The wizard was not present. The box contained only his voice.

Did it contain his hearing, as well? "Corvus . . ." she said hesitantly; but the voice spoke over hers, oblivious.

"I'm sure you know that I was startled," it continued, "not to say shocked, to hear that you knew of the existence of the links. You neglected to tell me how you found out about them, and of course"—the voice acquired a wry tone—"I cannot ask." It had been Fletcher who had

told Rowan of the magical devices carried by the wizards' servants stationed in the Outskirts. He had destroyed his own link before changing
his loyalties.

"But I did as you suggested," the box said in Corvus's voice, "and you
are correct. Until fifty years ago Routine Bioform Clearance was a regularly scheduled event, repeating in a twenty-year cycle. By comparing
old traces and maps, it's clear that the beam was always directed at areas
just beyond the Outskirts, and the result each time was an increase in
the rate of expansion of human-supporting life-forms. We can only assume that its original purpose was to destroy the . . . the inimical life, so
that the Outskirts could move eastward—and the Inner Lands grow behind it."

Inimical life, such as demons. This was why demons did not exist in
the Inner Lands: destroyed by magic, just beyond the ever-shifting edge of
the Outskirts. And now—what would prevent the strange animals at the
edge of the world from moving inward?

Corvus continued. "I still have not determined why the Clearance
stopped, or whether Slado actually had anything to do with that; but you
can be certain that I was concerned to hear that he had directed the
beam into inhabited lands.

"I could not use my own link to communicate directly with the field
agents currently working in the Outskirts, as you had requested. The action would require my messages to . . . shall we say, to take a route where
there would be watchers. The messages might be intercepted; questions
would be asked. And that's particularly unfortunate, because some of our
people did die. As you suspected, the record of the actual event had been
erased, but I learned a great deal by replaying surveillance taken before
and after it, paying particular attention to the flags." Rowan wondered
again how something as small as a link could possibly carry a flag large
enough to be visible from the watching eye of a Guidestar and how that
flag could be invisible to human eyes.

"There were four flags," Corvus said, "in or near the affected areas.
One nearby ceased to move after the gap in the records." That wizard's
minion, Rowan understood, must have died in the bizarre weather that
occurred after the heat. "Two flags directly in the path of the beam had
vanished entirely after the event." Two wizard's servants, suffering the
horrible fate of death by the magical heat; Rowan thought of the corpses
she had seen, burst wide and turned hard as rock, and found herself dislik-
ing Corvus for referring to the minions themselves as flags, impersonally,
instead of as people.

The voice acquired an affected innocence. "One flag, oddly, vanished more than a day before the Clearance"—Fletcher's, Rowan thought—"and the heat track of the tribe that it was originally with showed a rather interesting pattern of motion. Due east. Very quickly. It looked"—and the voice became ironic—"like a difficult journey." Three tribe members had died from the physical strain of that flight and more than a dozen others in the tempests and tornadoes that followed. Rowan felt her dislike begin to transform into positive hatred of Corvus for his callous manner; but abruptly, he dropped his tone and spoke simply. "Slado is not the only one who can erase a record, Rowan. The gap in the record is now two days longer than it was originally. No other wizard will know that one tribe had warning. They're safe."

By now Rowan was sitting on the edge of the table, sword hilt slack in her hands, absorbed in the words. "There's no more that I can tell you—safely or wisely, I should say. But if the Outskirts are not allowed to continue to move, as is their nature, the results will be—troublesome.

"However, I still do not know why this is being done, nor whether or not some useful purpose is being served. When we last spoke, you told me that a time would come when I must choose for myself which side I will stand with. I can only tell you now that that time is not yet."

Silence.

Corvus would provide no help. Not even so simple a fact as Slado's location.

Still, he had not yet aligned himself with the master wizard's purposes. Perhaps there was reason to hope.

Rowan reached out to close the box; but the spell had not run its course.

She heard the wizard's voice again but quietly, as if from a distance: "Willam, say hello to your friend." And then a sound, like a breath in her ear and different voice, close and loud, young and deep. "Um, hello, Rowan. I hope you're well." Willam, whom Rowan and Bel had befriended, now serving Corvus as apprentice. "Hello, Willam," Rowan could not help replying, despite knowing that the young man could not hear her. Rowan understood that the message had been spoken in the past and that somehow she was magically listening across the intervening weeks.

There was silence again. Rowan smiled to herself. In her experience of magic she had seen, for the most part, horror and evil. But this charmed her, like the tiny dancing statue she had once seen, spinning with single-minded innocence. Pleasant to hear the voice of a friend across so many miles—

Then a third voice spoke; and at the sound of it, Rowan froze, her hand suddenly tight on her weapon. The voice was thin, colorless as stone, and utterly expressionless: the sort of voice a corpse might use.

It said, "This message will not repeat."

11

*I*t was nice to think of dinner waiting. It made the whole day go better.

They spent the morning stripping leaves, him and Gwen and Arvin and Alyssa, and Gwen's dad, and Ivy, and a couple of Maysie's girls, all in one group, each close enough to the next to talk if they wanted, which meant anything interesting had to be sort of relayed back and forth along the line. They could just see each other's straw hats over the tops of the short trees, until they cut the leaves, with face after face popping up out of the green suddenly, then the whole line moving up into more green to start over again.

It was Gwen in the middle, and they'd managed it so her dad was at one end and the girls on the other. Steffie was right next to him, which was good, because when the talk got saucy Steffie could choose what got passed down to him.

Gwen picked the least and worked the slowest; but Lasker knew well enough that any group she got put in made up for it by working lots faster, and happier, with her carrying on in the middle. Sometimes you'd see hats bobbing up all across the groves, people trying to see what was so funny.

The girls were saying that they couldn't stand being around Maysie anymore, seeing that face every day, so they were giving up the work. They were looking for husbands, now, and everyone should get the word out for them.

Gwen made like she and Steffie were going to take their places, and Steffie played along. Which was fun and interesting, too, because he had to say things that sounded normal to Gwen's dad but had a whole other meaning when they got sent up the other way.

After lunch, they chopped for a couple hours, then spent the rest of the day in the sheds, while the people in the sheds took a turn at the groves. It was not so much fun inside, because you had to be quiet and not spook the worms.

Also, Steffie didn't like the worms much. When they first hatched out, they always made him think of maggots. Until they got this size. Then they made him think of *big* maggots. And sometimes when you pulled out a rack, a couple of them had died, and then you had to get them out with your fingers. Why big maggots dead should be worse than big maggots alive, he couldn't figure, but there it was. He always tried to get Gwen to pick them out for him, when he could, or one of the other women. The worms never bothered the women.

And there was the noise. Thousands of worms eating sounded like nothing else in the world. All those little mouths, munching away like there was no tomorrow. The sound never stopped, and it got right down inside your head, or at least it did Steffie's.

But the thing was, today, when it was over, everything that had anything to do with busy-ness was all done with, and that's what was nice about dinner waiting. So it was him and Gwen, not a care in the world, just swinging along home, except not home, really: the Annex. Which was starting to feel like home. Which it had when Mira was there, too, but in a different way.

The first thing Rowan said when they got in was, "I hope you don't mind eating by the hearth; I don't really want to disturb this." Her voice was sort of faraway, even though she was right there.

The "this" she meant was the magic box, except not any more. "I guess you got mad at it," Steffie said. It looked like it had been dropped from a height, or had something dropped on it from a height, or had maybe been pounded a few times. It was all in pieces, spread out across the table, along with lots of papers with writing on them.

Steffie wouldn't have minded a better look at it, but he remembered how it had stung people before, so he thought, Better Not. Gwen stood, half in the door, gaping, until he nudged her.

Dinner was in a pot on the hearth, and Rowan had pulled out the bench to hold bowls and spoons and plates and butter. There was bread, too, and fresh, but it was funny and flat, and not risen at all. Steffie figured Rowan made it herself, which was just as well, since no one was baking lately.

The steerswoman was in one of her states again, and Steffie was getting used to them; but she always answered if you asked her. "What happened to the box?" he asked. Gwen sat in the wicker chair and started dishing out, one eye on Rowan.

"I dismantled it," the steerswoman said. Gwen shot Steffie a glance, one of those glances that people give to each other when they're both

thinking the same thing. But Steffie wasn't this time, and was still puzzling over it when she handed him a bowl. "Didn't it sting you?" Gwen
asked Rowan. There was something funny in her voice, too, but Steffie
couldn't put his finger on it.

"The guard spell stopped working after I opened it."

That was interesting. "You opened it? How'd you manage that?"
Steffie couldn't use the bench to sit, so he ended up in Mira's big chair.
He had to squirm to make it fit decently.

"It was the boots," Rowan said, which was just like her when she was
like this, answering exactly what was asked and no more. Steffie wouldn't
have minded hearing a better explanation, but there she was, all wrapped
up in writing things, and thinking hard, so he figured he'd wait.

Dinner was chicken stew; not fancy, but it smelled wonderful. He had
the first spoonful halfway to his mouth, when Gwen took it right out of
his hand, and the bowl, too, and took his elbow and dragged him straight
out the front door.

It was a little chilly outside, the houses across the street making shade,
with the sun so far down. Steffie opened his mouth to say something to
Gwen, like Hold up or What do you think you're doing?—but the time to
say that was when she was dragging him out, and that was over, so it was
too late. So he closed his mouth again.

Gwen leaned up against the wall of the Annex, and crossed her arms
over her chest. "That's it, then."

"What's it, then? What do you mean?"

"What do you think I mean?"

"Well, that's what I'm asking, isn't it? Wouldn't ask if I knew."

Gwen twisted her mouth. "What do you think she's doing in there?"

Which made no sense, because you only had to look to see what
Rowan was doing. "Studying it. Like she studied the demon, and her
books. Magic box, and all—you don't think she'd want to study it?"

Gwen reached out and pinched him on the arm, sort of to make her
point. "But she couldn't touch it before."

"Ow."

"And now she can?"

"Well, yes. Seems like."

"But how?"

This was starting to feel bad. "Something about the boots, she said,"
he said carefully.

"Makes no sense."

"It might if you asked her. Go on; you know she's got to answer."

"And you think she'll tell the truth?"

It took Steffie a moment or so to grab hold of that—and once he got it, he didn't like it at all. "You're thinking that she maybe *wouldn't*?"

"Steffie, you're dense. When'd I last tell you you were dense?"

"You want time of day, or day of week?"

Gwen knit her brows, thinking hard. Usually Steffie liked it when he saw her think like that, because it meant something interesting was about to happen. But this time he had the feeling that he wasn't going to like where she was headed.

And he was right, because the next thing Gwen said was, "She says she's a steerswoman, but who's to say otherwise? Mira's gone. Who else would know?"

Steffie had never heard of such a thing in his life. "Of course Rowan's a steerswoman. Who's being dense now? She opened that box, didn't she?"

"Says you. And says her. But you and me, we didn't see it happen, did we? We just saw a box that bit and then a busted box that didn't."

"She took it apart after."

"She says."

"But—" This was just mad. "Why would she say she was a steerswoman if she wasn't?"

"Well, there's a free place to live, isn't there? And people giving her things without her paying? And you and me doing her cooking and cleaning—"

"She does it, too, herself—"

"—but it's mostly just you and me, isn't it?"

"Well, yes, but she's working, see—"

"And what's that all about, then? Mira never done that."

"But that was wrong!" And he was going to go on, but they were talking pretty loud, which he suddenly noticed. The neighbors were all busy with their own dinners, but it wouldn't do to let some late passerby get an earful of this nonsense.

So he took her elbow himself, and got them both around the corner to the blind side of the house. "That's just foolish," he said to her, but quiet-like. "You shouldn't go saying bad things about a person unless you know for sure." But it did start him wondering, not about Rowan, but about other people, and wouldn't it be easy for just anyone to say she was a steerswoman? "Is this talk doing anything? Because I don't see any reason for it. Sounds to me like trouble for trouble's sake, and what's the good of that?"

She poked him on the chest. "*I* don't like being made a fool of," she said, as if he did, which made him mad.

"Well, no one's making a fool out of me, and you'd know that if you spent more time paying attention to what Rowan was doing, instead of what she's not doing, which is everything Mira did, which she ought not to have done anyway!"

"Mira treated us better than Rowan does!"

"Didn't she just make us dinner? Twice? Mira never done that even once! And have we lifted a finger at the Annex since the worms came out? Mira'd still have you dragging her out of bed in the morning and tucking her in at night."

"But it's all *wrong*. She's not acting normal!"

He couldn't think what to say back. "Well," he started, then didn't know where to go. "Well," he tried again; but it was basically true, so what could you say to that? "Well, so what? Not everyone's normal, and what's wrong with that?"

Gwen talked right into his face. "She's fake. She's using us. That's just like stealing, and it's *wrong*."

And it would be, if Rowan wasn't a steerswoman. He tried to set it up that way in his head, just to see how it stood.

And it did stand, in a way, but only if you left out a lot of things, things Gwen didn't know, or didn't pay attention to, or maybe didn't matter to her. And it was funny, because all those things were still there to see or find out, if you tried, but Gwen just hadn't, and he couldn't figure why.

He was going to tell her that, but the whole idea was sort of slippery and kept oozing away. And it was hard to find a nice way to say it, because as soon as he was about to try, he could see it was going to come out that there was nothing wrong with Rowan, but there was something wrong with Gwen.

So he hemmed and hawed and ummed, until Gwen got tired of waiting and took herself back into the Annex.

When he got in himself, she was already in her chair, tucking into that stew, watching Rowan sharp-like. Steffie didn't much feel like sitting by her, not right then.

So he took his own spoon and bowl, put one of those flat breads in it, then stood there with no place to go.

The steerswoman looked like she hadn't even noticed that they'd gone and come back, like she hadn't once stopped what she was doing.

She'd set each piece of the box on its own bit of paper, and each one
had some word or sentence written by it. She had her own logbook open,
too, and a separate paper, and was writing on them both in turns like she
was writing the same thing on each.

Steffie wandered over. "What was in the box?"

"A message."

Everything there looked like it was written by her. "What, from a wizard?" And what wizard would send her messages?

"Yes."

"Steerswomen don't deal with wizards," Gwen put in from the hearth.
"Everyone knows that. Wizards are all under the ban."

"Groups can't be put under ban, only individual persons." He could
see that the answer-making part of Rowan was talking all on its own,
while the figuring-out part kept busy with the box bits. Steffie wondered
what that was like from the inside—to have two parts of you both knowing what to do and doing them at the same time.

"Never heard of that," Gwen said.

"It's true." Rowan picked up a round thing, like a fat coin, and shifted
it to catch the light better. "But as it happens," her answering-part went
on, "the only wizard not currently under ban is Olin." She put the coin
down and picked up a bit of string, except maybe it wasn't string, because
it looked too stiff. "The last I heard, that is."

"What about Slado?" Steffie asked.

Rowan looked up at him, surprised; and he could see the two parts
come right together, making all of her be in one place. The difference between her in two parts and her in one was sort of shocking. It came to
Steffie that when Rowan was all there, she was more *there* than anyone he
ever saw. "That's very interesting," she said. "It never occurred to me. If
Slado happens never to have met a steerswoman, then he can't have lied
or withheld information from one. So, no, he would not be under ban."
She looked like the idea didn't please her much.

"Then who is the message from?" Gwen asked casually, but it was easy
to tell it was a fake casual.

Maybe it was because Rowan was all in one place again, but she noticed it; Steffie could tell right away. She looked at Gwen with a this-is-
odd look on her face. "From Corvus, the wizard in Wulfshaven," she said,
and it seemed like she was watching to see how Gwen would act next.

Gwen was putting butter on her bread and pretending she was only
paying attention to that. "Then he's one of the ones under ban. And you

can't talk to him, and he can't talk to you. I guess that means messages, too." She bit the bread.

"No," Rowan began, talking slow and careful, "it means that I can't answer any question he might ask. It's perfectly possible to have a conversation with someone under ban, if both parties are willing. The person under ban would simply not ask questions, and the steerswoman would simply not reply to any question asked."

"Never heard of that," Gwen said; and Steffie had to admit it sounded strange. It'd make for a pretty odd conversation—

And it was a funny thing, because right then he heard in his own head a conversation exactly like that, and he tried to remember where and when he'd heard it, because it must have been a while ago; then he sort of looked around to see where it was going on, and he saw that it had been right in the middle of Brewer's Tavern—

Rowan was saying something to Gwen, but Steffie spoke right up anyway, because the sentence was in his head, and if he didn't say it, there wouldn't be room for anything else. "Is Janus under ban?"

Rowan stopped talking to look at him, and Gwen sat there with her jaw dropped. "As a matter of fact," the steerswoman said, "he is."

Gwen got hold of herself again. "Never!"

"It's true."

"Janus was up here all the time when Mira was alive, and they talked back and forth, with questions and everything, and if he was under ban she couldn't *do* that, could she?"

"You're assuming that she knew he was under ban—"

Sort of all by themselves, Steffie's legs took him over to the mantelpiece, and his hand reached up, and his legs brought him back again; and he said, even though both the women were still talking, "Are there men steerswomen?"

And they both stopped again. Gwen got over it first. "That again? Steffie, don't be foolish—"

But Rowan made her go quiet, and did it by just raising one finger at her, not even looking at her. It was Steffie who had all of Rowan's attention. "Yes," she said, and watched him, like there was something else he might say and she was waiting for it.

"Can you be a man steerswoman and be under ban at the same time?"

"We call them 'steersmen.' And, no, you can't."

Steffie set down what he'd brought from the mantel. "I guess you only looked in there and never took them out." It was Mira's old trinket box, sitting on the table among the broken bits of the wizard's magical box. "But they're not Mira's. The ring's too big."

Rowan lifted up the lid of the trinket box—and a shabby old thing it looked, lying next to the beautiful carved top of the wizard's box—and looked inside.

Gwen found something to complain about again. "Of course they're not. Mira wouldn't do a thing like that, put aside her own ring and chain, and we buried her with them—" And she stopped in the middle, probably because she got what Steffie was about to say next—so he didn't bother saying it.

Rowan had poured the gold and silver into her palm and was sitting there just looking at them.

She kept quiet for a long time. When she spoke again, what she said was, "He *did* tell her."

12

The boat moved awkwardly.

It was not the best-sized vessel for single-handed sailing, and it required a lot of activity from its sailor. Today, the wind was light but steady from the east, not perfect for entry into Alemeth harbor but simple enough for a lively seaman. Nevertheless, the boat was making too much leeway, and tacks were too long, executed sloppily and clumsily.

As the steerswoman watched the approach, she considered that a tow by rowers might be needed. But a clever and risky last-minute jibe placed the boat in a more favorable position; and at the last it gently slid up to its dock, sails luffing.

Rowan walked down the shabby wharf as the boat was being secured. She stopped two thirds of the way, where the stable boards ran out and splintery gaps appeared, and waited.

Janus noticed her as he finished tying off the stern line, glancing up twice, the second time with a tired smile of recognition. "I hadn't hoped to have someone actually on hand to welcome me." When he used a boat hook to snag the piling, she saw that his soft gray gloves had been replaced by a bulkier canvas pair. Walking sideways along the starboard side, he pulled the bow closer in. "You know, I could use some help with this." She neither replied nor moved. His next two glances were curious, then speculative. He finished his work, then stood in the bow, watching her, unable to ask a question.

The steerswoman held out one fist before her, then opened it. The silver ring fell, to hang dangling from the end of the gold chain wound around her fingers.

He blinked but showed no great surprise. "I see you found them."

"Mira had them." He did not reply, but began making his way back to the stern. "Did you give them to her?" Rowan asked.

"Yes. It seemed like a good idea at the time."

"You told me she didn't know that you used to be a steersman."

"I told you that I'd never told her so. Whatever she reasoned out by herself, she never discussed with me. Excuse me." He reached the companionway hatch, and clambered down into the hold.

Rowan waited. Presently he returned, clumsily hauling up a canvas duffel bag, its strap looped around one elbow. Once on deck, he shifted the bag, managing to maneuver the strap over one shoulder without using his hands.

Rowan had not moved. Janus studied her. "That's not a proper knot at the end of the chain. If you wiggle it too hard, the ring will slip right off." She gathered them up with her other hand; he made the jump to the wharf. "Oof."

"Janus, are you telling me that you actually handed Mira a steerswoman's ring and chain and she never asked you how you had come by them?"

"I didn't hand her a ring and a chain." He was a moment regaining his balance. "I handed her a silk handkerchief with something tied up inside. I asked her to keep it safe for me."

"She didn't open it?"

"Not that I saw."

"And she never asked what was inside or why you gave it to her?"

"No." He thought, taking rather a long time about it. "Mira did get a sly look on her face. I'd thought that she planned to open it later, and I kept expecting questions. But they never came." He shifted the duffel bag on his shoulder uncomfortably. "Eventually I assumed that she'd set it aside somewhere in that junk pile of a house, and forgotten about it." He weaved a bit in place. "Rowan, I'm sorry I didn't mention it before, and I hope you don't think I was hiding anything from you. I know the facts don't sound very likely, but that's just the way Mira was—and I was not about to volunteer information she didn't ask for. Now I need to get my bag back to my room"—and it slid from his shoulder, to thump on the wharf—"and frankly, I could use a little help."

The steerswoman considered; then she put the ring and chain into her pocket, then picked up the bag. She found it not particularly heavy. "Where is your room?"

"Dan's been letting me use an old storeroom above his shop. Cold in winter, hot in summer, breezy when the wind blows, and stuffy when it doesn't. All the comforts of home, assuming you were raised in a shipping crate."

She made a noise, a half-laugh in the back of her throat, and saw the bright smile flash in his dark face. "That's better."

They made their way up the wharf and to Harbor Road. Janus paused when they reached it. "I ought to pay Jilly a visit." Rowan was a moment recalling that this was the healer. "And out of courtesy to her, if not to you, I really ought to bathe first."

"Perhaps if you used your hands less hard, they'd have a chance to get better."

"Well. Try making a living at unskilled labor without using your hands; it can't be done." He raised one hand to forestall a possible comment by her. "I know; sitting in the Annex and working with pen and paper would solve the whole problem. And I can't ask you if you've received a reply to your proposal, but I assume you'd have told me right away if you had." He sighed. "Rowan, if I could impose on you further, it would help a lot if you'd be so kind as to haul that bag up to my room—just leave it on the landing outside. I'm afraid that if I have to climb all those stairs just now, I'll just fall flat on the floor when I reach the top and sleep for the rest of the day. And never make it to the bathhouse."

"Of course. You go ahead."

"Thank you." He had gone a few steps away before he stopped and turned, to stand regarding her with a trace of puzzlement.

It must be, she thought, the very stillness of her demeanor that he was noticing. She never was able to feign emotions, and was very bad at keeping them concealed. Blankness was the best she could manage.

"Rowan, I'm sorry you thought I'd been dishonest—although why I ever would be to you, I can't imagine."

She managed a smile. "Never mind. Consider the subject closed. I won't mention it again. In fact, let me feed you lunch. Or better, buy you dinner, if you need to sleep until then. At the Mizzen. Sunset."

He grinned again, standing wearily slack-limbed in the middle of Harbor Road. "The Mizzen? Rowan, everyone will think that I'm your fancy boy! All right, the Mizzen. I'll see you then." And he trudged off, whistling a bit to himself as he went.

Rowan watched him go, then turned away, lest he glance back and catch her scrutiny.

The stairs were daunting indeed, the mere skeleton of a staircase, three storeys up to the little landing under the overhang of the roof.

She set the duffel bag down outside the padlocked door, then turned.

Janus had, at the least, a very nice view.

The cooper's shop was one of the highest buildings on the street, and the view swept cleanly east and west over the rooftops of the harborside shops and businesses, blocked only once by the equal height of the building that housed the ropewalk. Fast scudding clouds cast quick shadows onto the tiles and shingles and gables. The low hill that carried Old and New High streets north toward the mulberry groves rose gently up behind the backyard, houses peeking out from between the sycamores.

Crab and clam boats stood in the shallows east and west of the deepest part of the harbor; Rowan could just discern the small, distant figures hauling and raking. Other than these, no persons were in sight.

The steerswoman sat down on the top step, elbows on knees, gazing at the scene, alternately cooled and warmed by cloud and sun.

She had first found Mira's trinket box sitting on the nightstand beside the bed: dusty, as was everything else but in no way lost in the junk pile of a house. When Steffie had brought it out again, the conclusion seemed obvious.

But Rowan had failed to take into account Mira's peculiarities. The entire matter was easily explained.

Then, what was this feeling she could not shake?

Mira was a wild card; Mira could be used to cover any deception. How extremely convenient.

Nonsense. This was Janus.

Rowan shut her eyes against a passing moment of particularly bright sunlight. Sounds rose from the courtyard below: a woman's voice speaking softly, the slap of harness, the thud of hooves on earth as a pair of horses were led out into the street. A few moments later, the warm animal scent reached Janus's high landing briefly and was gone.

Inertia, Rowan thought, habit.

She had spent the better part of the week weighted by shock, anger, and a deep sense of personal betrayal. She had, in fact, been able to think of little else.

A strong, entrenched emotion would sometimes resist change in the face of new information. Rowan's training had warned her of this. When emotion and fact were at odds, follow fact. Eventually, with some effort, emotion would alter.

Still, she was rather surprised to see the phenomenon so strongly expressed in herself; she had rarely suffered from it in the past.

But how very peculiar that Mira had not asked such a simple question of Janus . . .

The steerswoman hissed annoyance at herself, rose, and made her way down the rickety staircase, blinking against the sunlight.

She was making too large a matter of this. She had merely reached an incorrect conclusion, misinterpreted evidence. Easy enough to do.

As, for example, Gwen had done.

It was, in a way, interesting to watch the progress of Gwen's little rumor, like an object passed secretly, hand to hand, possession of which caused random persons to eye Rowan askance, to pause infinitesimally before speaking to her, to pause longer before politely refusing payment for supplies or goods she requested.

Rowan had no intention of going about town vocally defending her own authenticity. The very idea was demeaning. Let the people reason it out for themselves.

Truth eventually declares itself. Always.

At the Mizzen, Rowan stepped inside to secure a table for the evening and discuss the menu.

While she and the owner were conversing, she noticed the higher level counterpart to Mira's conclave of gossips. Taking their midday meal together at one table: silk farmers Lasker and Karin; the cooper Dan; Michael, who owned a large ships' supplies shop; the woman who ran the only bank in town; two men, brothers of nearly identical appearance, who owned competing weaving manufactories; and a dark-haired woman, thin as a blade, who single-handedly produced small amounts of the most extraordinary fabric in the world, woven by some closely guarded process from pure spider silk.

This group routinely took their midday meal together at the Mizzen. Save the spider-wife, as she was called, they represented the most influential employers in the area. The spider-wife was included out of deference to her immense wealth.

The townsfolk collectively referred to them as "the Bosses." Maysie was generally considered to be one of their number. She was not present.

As if Rowan's thought of her had invoked her, Maysie entered the Mizzen. Conversation at the Bosses' table ceased at a noise from the spider-wife, who was the person best situated to notice Maysie's arrival.

Maysie stood uncertainly in the open doorway, harbor sounds coming in over her shoulder: fresh sounds of water and gull calls and rigging. She had brushed her hair in a different style, swept back from the uninjured left side of her face, falling straight down close to her cheek on the right, where it was gathered in thick braid worn down her breast. Her clothing had improved as well: a deep-yellow shirt of home-quality silk; an indigo cotton skirt with a pattern of small red figures, worn knee length in the Alemeth style; and high brown boots laced up the front.

Prompted by the spider-wife, the rest of the Bosses looked up. Maysie shut the door and walked toward their table. Immediately, each of them found some other part of the room intensely interesting, except the spider-wife, who watched Maysie's entire approach with an unpleasantly avid curiosity.

At their table, Maysie spoke; Rowan could not from a distance hear what was said. A simple greeting, perhaps. From the Bosses quick glances up, then glances turned away, and some brief words spoken in reply. A pause, which grew long.

Then Karin pointedly addressed one of the weaver brothers; he replied. A general conversation began, clearly on some subject other than Maysie's arrival and clearly not including her. Only the spider-wife did not participate but tilted her head a bit as her gaze continued to explore Maysie's face.

Rowan saw Maysie stiffen, then turn and begin to walk away.

At the very moment when Rowan was prepared to despise every one of them, Dan looked about the table in disbelief, looked after Maysie, then half rose, reaching back to pull a chair from another table, his mouth open and about to call to Maysie—but the owner of the bank caught his arm and pulled him down to direct some vehement whispered comment to his ear. He protested; she persisted. The second weaver brother leaned across the table to speak to Dan. And under their urgings the cooper subsided into his seat, retaining, at least, enough conscience to look ashamed.

Maysie had reached the door. Rowan rose to call to her; but of herself Maysie paused. She looked right, then left, then with awkward dignity walked across the room to a small table and sat down, alone.

It came to Rowan that this was one of the bravest acts she had ever witnessed.

There was enough trouble in the world without people making things difficult for each other, she said to herself. There were wild animals, enemies who would come at you with a sword to steal your flocks, snow and cold in winter, drought in summer, falls that would break your bones, disease, wizards to blast you with magic—all things beyond one's control.

In the face of all this, one would think that those things within one's control ought not be so directed as to cause misery without reason. One would think, at the very least, that human beings would recognize a sort of camaraderie of survival.

"Excuse me, lady?" Rowan had forgotten the proprietor. "I think we're done here, am I right?"

"Of course," she said distractedly; then she remembered. "And here." She pulled a number of coins from her pocket, pushed them into his hands. "No, really. Since I'll be bringing a guest, please let me pay for the entire meal. Everyone's been very generous, but—"

A bang. Rowan turned. The door had been slammed open against the wall.

Janus stood in a wild pose, arms thrown out, breathless.

Puzzled, Rowan made to wave him over, but his gaze swept past her and straight to the Bosses' table. He took a half step toward it—they were staring at him, gape mouthed—then he stopped and scanned the room, seeing and ignoring Rowan.

Maysie had turned when everyone else had. When Janus sighted her, hurried toward her, she turned away again quickly.

He reached her side. Rowan saw but did not hear him speak to her; she could not tell if Maysie replied. He leaned down, spoke again urgently, took Maysie's shoulder and turned her to face him. She ducked her head to the right and down; but stooping to be level with her Janus reached out and pushed the braid back.

The shock on Janus's face was unlike anything Rowan had ever seen.

It was so complete, so overpowering, that it seemed to drive everything else from him. His face showed no fear, no disgust, no revulsion, not even any visible pity. He did not draw back. He did not so much as wince.

Instead, after a long and painful moment, he went to one knee beside Maysie's chair and gently folded her into his arms.

She resisted briefly, then surrendered and laid her head on his shoulder and wept. And they remained so, oblivious of everything else.

Across the room, the steerswoman stood stunned.

While Janus had been at sea, monsters had come to town, killing and destroying the lives of people he loved—

And the steerswoman had neglected even to mention the fact.

She could not believe that anyone could be so self-centered, so consumed by personal affairs as to not warn Janus, not tell him, as soon as he arrived, what had happened in his absence. She could not imagine how any person could be so cruel, so unthinking, so lacking in simple human compassion.

But that person existed. That person was herself. It seemed impossible to grasp.

Rowan discovered in herself a sudden, urgent desire to flee and hide in some dark place.

Instead, she crossed the room.

Janus was stroking Maysie's hair, speaking softly to her. His own hair sparkled with water droplets, his skin was damp, his shirt tucked in sloppily. He had run from the bathhouse as soon as he had heard.

Rowan felt she ought to speak. She could think of nothing to say. She stood, mute, beside them, then reached to pull another chair close for Janus.

He took it blindly, one-handed, the other hand still holding Maysie close. He sat on its edge. Maysie's weeping was nearly silent. His voice was a gentle whisper, repeating, "I know, I know." He rocked her slightly in his arms.

Just when Rowan understood that there was nothing she could do but go, he looked up at her. His face was blank with pain.

Rowan said, "Demons. From the wild lands." At the back of her mind, all her information ordered itself into a clear and logical explication of the events and the nature of the monsters.

She did not deliver it. Janus knew all that he needed at this moment. She said instead, "I'm sorry—"

"Go away." And he closed his eyes.

She left them.

13

At the east end of the harbor a short expanse of open water lay between the wharves and the shallows. Beyond, the shoreline rustled with sea oats; beyond this, scrub blended into forest. There, the land narrowed, becoming a woody spit that terminated in a single, angled crag: a long outstretched arm indicating the unseen, unknown southern shore of the Inland Sea.

Rowan sat on the last wharf with her legs folded beneath her, gazing at the spit. By sitting exactly here, looking in precisely this direction, the town of Alemeth behind her, she could almost feel herself back in the Outskirts. A clean, uncomplicated place, where she knew how to act, knew what to do. A place where whatever errors she might make would cause pain to no other person than herself.

She wished Bel were here. Bel was like the wilderness, in her own way . . .

Three days had passed since Janus's arrival. Rowan had spoken to no one of the events in the Mizzen, and no one had asked her about it. But with Janus so vigorously shunning her, and Rowan so obviously distressed, unable even to work, there was surely no lack of fodder for gossip.

Let them speculate. Let them have their entertainment. She did not care.

She had wounded an already fragile soul, and lost Janus's friendship, probably forever.

She felt footsteps on the wharf, rocking it a bit. She did not recognize the steps and did not turn, but of itself her mind passed through a list of possibilities and settled on one as most likely.

Steffie paused behind her, then sat down nearby, just outside of her range of vision.

Rowan continued gazing at the water and the woods beyond; perhaps Steffie was doing the same.

After many minutes, the steerswoman spoke. "Do you know how many kinds of stupidity there are?"

She sensed him thinking. The question was rhetorical, but he treated it as real. "No. But I bet you do."

Of course. She was a steerswoman. She was supposed to provide answers to all questions. Rowan said, "Infinite." And then, because she could not know for certain if this was absolutely accurate, she amended: "To the best of my ability to discern at this time." Her voice sounded toneless.

They returned to silence. She did not need to turn to see his puzzled regard; but he did not break the silence nor try to fill it with idle chatter. In this, Rowan thought, he was being very kind.

She spoke again. "I'm extremely intelligent."

Surprise that she would state this. "Well . . . yes."

"But what I lack is wisdom."

He pondered. "Not the same thing?"

"Oh," she said with sincerity, "no."

Wind ruffled the water toward them, tiny ripples from no visible source, as if a minuscule unseen ship were approaching. "Steffie, do you think that Mira was wise?"

His reply was not immediate. "Don't know. Sometimes, maybe. Or maybe she was all the time but only showed it sometimes. But, you know, come to think of it, she could be mean, once in a while. Seems to me, if someone was wise, they'd also be kind."

She sighed, but the intake of breath was more forceful than she expected, and it surprised her—almost a quiet gasp. "Oh," she said, "that's true. To the best of my ability to discern. At this time."

Out of the corner of her eye, she saw him lean forward to study her face. Eventually, she returned his gaze. "You're not mean," he informed her.

"Not intentionally. I have that much, I suppose."

"Well, that's a lot. 'Cause some people *are* mean, on purpose."

"I've noticed . . ."

"So, what you do when you've done something bad by mistake is go and say you're sorry."

"I've tried. If he sees me coming, he walks off before I can reach him. If I manage to approach him, he jumps when he sees me, then leaves." She sighed. "If I corner him, he stands staring as if he were afraid of me. If I address him, he says nothing. If I persist, he says . . ."—and she turned back to the water—" 'Go away.' "

Silence for a time. "Well . . . if it helps any, Janus has been acting funny all around. To everybody."

"It doesn't help."

"And Michael says he's been trying to buy ship's supplies on credit. Stocking his boat again already."

"Even worse." Janus was being driven back to the sea, away from humanity.

Long silence from Steffie. Then: "Funny."

"What's funny?"

"Well, makes no sense, does it?"

"On the contrary, it makes a great deal of sense. Unfortunately, I can't sail away from myself."

"No . . . no, I mean"—and his voice was puzzled—"it's got to be not just you, doesn't it?"

"True." It was, in fact, everything Janus feared—pain, danger, horror—all of it coming true, coming to Alemeth. And Maysie—Rowan had not known that Maysie was so dear a friend to Janus, but it must be so. And Rowan had given him no warning, allowed it to strike him like a blow, drive him to his knees—

But Steffie was still speaking. " 'Cause it's too big, isn't it? It just doesn't fit. There's nothing you could do just by mistake, on your own, to make Janus go all spooky like this . . ."

She turned around to regard him. "Steffie," she said, "do you even know what it is that I did?"

His mouth was set in a determined line, chin forward, his dark gaze stubborn. "No," he said. "And I don't need to. Unless you want to say. But it can't be just you, because you'd have to have done something big— really bad and big and on purpose. And you don't do things like that. Not you."

His certainty was absolute. He was ready to challenge her, on her own behalf. With slow amazement, Rowan realized that somehow, while she had not been watching and without even trying to, she had acquired a friend.

The rush of gratitude she felt was so sudden as to be almost painful . . . but welcome, nonetheless. "Oh, Steffie," she said, "you're right. It's not just me. It's—" It would be unkind of her to betray Janus's confidence. "It's a complicated matter."

He nodded, definite. "That's what I mean. There's got to be more to it. There's something else going on—"

Suddenly, Rowan found that she was no longer listening; and Steffie had stopped speaking. For no reason she could identify, the steerswoman felt an urgent need to scan the entire visible area.

She did so, puzzled: harbor, forest, Harbor Road, hill. Houses, boats . . . nothing untoward . . .

She climbed to her feet; Steffie did the same. He said, "Something just spooked me, and I don't know what."

"Yes . . . Do you hear anything?"

"No . . ."

In fact there was much to hear: wind in the trees; water; the pounding of hammers and distant voices from the repair crew at the cooper's shop; two children, kneeling in the mud on the water's edge, squealing as they tortured an unfortunate crab; gulls calling.

Hammers. She had also been hearing the very distant ring of the blacksmith's hammer. That had stopped.

And birds—a mob of starlings somewhere had been making their typical ruckus. But they had abruptly ceased.

Two crab men nearby had been arguing about boat repairs; they had stopped and now stood looking about in puzzlement, exactly as Rowan and Steffie were. As Rowan watched, they shrugged, then returned to their work, although more quietly.

"I don't hear any demon," Steffie said.

"Neither do I." Where were those starlings? She scanned the treetops for them.

"I don't know . . . We're just jumpy, I guess," he said, coming around from behind her.

"Perfectly understandable." The leaves were too full for her to spot the starlings.

"Still, can't jump at everything," he commented, coming around from behind her again—at which point she realized that she was attempting instinctively to stand back-to-back with him, like two warriors waiting for the enemy. The move only confused him, and she stopped trying.

"We have every reason to be overcautious." She sheathed her sword. She did not recall having drawn it.

Then she turned, startled, when as one the starlings took to the air, rising in a dense cloud from a tall elm north across town. Near the smithy. And, so distant that she would not have heard it if she had not been listening, a shout.

But only one. It might have been caused by anything. As clues went, these were rather subtle, and she did not want to alarm the town without cause.

Nevertheless, in unspoken agreement, Rowan and Steffie slowly made their way back up the wharf, listening, glancing about suspiciously.

When they reached Harbor Road, Rowan turned left, but was stopped by Steffie's hand on her arm. "No, that yell was this way." He pointed. East by northeast. "There's a couple houses back there. Faster to cut across the rise. I know a path."

"Wait." Starlings near the smithy, a shout from somewhere else: two separate events.

Probably not connected. She calmed. "I think it's all right. Still . . . let's just check things out quietly."

"Right. Which way?"

The houses were closer than the smithy. Rowan pointed up the brushy rise. "Show me the path."

They weaved through a maze of chest-high blueberries. As they climbed the hill, more and more of the harborside came into view, and Rowan began including it in a widening circle of surveillance. Her senses heightened, acquiring a thrilling clarity.

They both froze at an inhuman shriek. Steffie clutched her arm. "What's that? Say it's not a person!"

"It's a horse." Again, and more. "At least two. The smithy."

"Then we're going the wrong way. Can't get there from here." He started back down the rise, half skidding.

They had enough evidence. She called after him. "Don't go to the smithy. Go straight for Corey and the militia."

"What about you?"

She looked back; the path they had been following was now more clearly visible. "Something doesn't feel right." That isolated shout and then silence . . . "I'll go on this way. Just to check."

He was appalled. "There can't be two at once!"

"I hope not."

He started scrambling back up. "Then I'll go, too."

"No. Get to Corey—you might be the first to reach him."

"You can't take on a monster alone!"

"I don't plan to. I'll go close enough to hear if it's a demon, then I'll come back and let the militia know."

He did not like it. Nevertheless: "Right." And he was off.

The path wound through the brush and dove into a wooded section: young oak, old oak, and laurels. Rowan moved slowly and cautiously from light into shadow. The sun, now close to the horizon somewhere behind her, cast jittering spots of light ahead against the low, close leaves and tree trunks.

It would grow darker yet, soon. But she dared not hurry. She went on, deeper, listening.

Eventually, underbrush began to thin. Color up ahead through it: red, blue. Houses.

Also ahead: the sound of a demon-voice.

But no sign or sound of people. Hiding, or sensible enough to stay still and silent. Rowan backed away slowly.

Sounds behind her: not a demon but the small snaps and rustles of a person moving cautiously. Ahead, animal sounds, suddenly. Chickens, making brief complaints, then quieting; curious grunts from some pigs.

Rowan backed further away, nearly silent, and the person behind made a noise of startlement as he suddenly came on her. She turned, motioning for quiet.

Arvin, bow in hand, arrow nocked but bowstring not pulled. He nodded greeting, mouthed silently: *Steffie sent me.* She nodded back.

He eyed the sword in her hand. Then he caught and held her gaze, gave a wicked smile, and indicated the demon's direction with a lift of his chin.

A bow to disable its vents, a sword to kill it. Arvin knew where to strike the demon and was possibly the only archer good enough to make a two-person attack feasible. With enough objects to hide behind . . . Rowan weighed the advantages of a mass attack by crowd of armed men and women against the precision and stealth she and Arvin could execute.

At that moment, the pigs began voicing panic, then terror and pain.

The perfect diversion to cover the sound and motion of Rowan's and Arvin's approach. A chance too good to lose. She nodded to Arvin, and they moved toward the buildings.

They emerged from the woods into the backyard of a two-story blue house. No demon was visible, but its unending voice declared its presence somewhere out of sight. They crossed the yard, past the trash piles and outhouse. As they neared the house, the back door opened and a gray-haired woman slipped out, ushering two children forward, all wide-eyed in fear. They meant to make a break for the trees. Rowan and Arvin waved urgently, gestured them back in the house. The three saw them, retreated.

Rowan and Arvin separated to sidle up to opposite corners of the house. The steerswoman paused, watching Arvin as he peered around the corner. He turned back, shook his head.

She edged up to her corner, looked out; she waved Arvin over.

A big front yard, a barn directly opposite, pigsty to the left. The pigs were in a squealing panic, crowding back against what fence remained, climbing over one another, the back fence about to collapse under their weight.

At the shattered front of the sty: the demon. It was taller than the first Rowan had seen, thinner, colored mottled gray and black. It was tearing at the bloody carcass of one of the pigs.

She felt Arvin move up beside her, sensed him about to aim and let fly. She held up one hand, watching.

The demon was lifting chunks of flesh in its hands, pushing them down into its maw, the muscles of its torso working to the action of the grinding plates within. With no warning, the motion ceased; and, apparently involuntarily, the creature vomited, sending gobs of bloody meat up into the air. Then it dropped to sit on the ground in a weird demon pose—feet flat, knees high all around.

It could not eat Inner Lands animals, as she had suspected. Perhaps it had had no food of the correct sort for many days. It would be weak, ill.

Something must have drawn or driven it from its native lands, some force irresistible.

The creature brought all four arms up, elbows bent inwards, fingers curled tight. It sat, its arms knotted above its maw, perhaps contemplating the sorry state of its digestion.

Its spray vents were neatly exposed.

Arvin stepped away from the house and, swift, powerful, let fly.

A perfect shot. One vent gone.

The demon jumped straight up onto its feet, spread its arms in attack stance, took a rotating step toward them, and brought another vent into position. Arvin placed another arrow, disabling the second vent.

Now it ran directly at them. Rowan took a step back; but Arvin took one forward, shot again. A miss, too low. The creature sprayed, but they were not in range. With terrifying calmness, Arvin took one more step forward, nocking and letting fly.

A strike, but not perfect. The demon shot its spray; Arvin dodged right. Rowan ducked back behind the corner.

She could not see him. She shouted, "I'm going around!" And she dashed to the other side of the house, came out to the front.

The demon was still running; it took another arrow, turned again as it ran.

A disabled quarter was facing Rowan. She made straight for it.

The demon slowed, with two targets now. Another arrow, and another, not near the vents—but pain made it focus on Arvin.

Rowan reached it. A high sweeping slash severed one arm, broke another. It tried to turn; she turned with it, flaying a third arm. In a new and startling move, it reached over its own top to slash down at Rowan with its fourth arm. She felt its talons barely brush her hair; she dropped to one knee, thrust her weapon deep into its body, twisting and slicing.

The demon writhed; her sword was wrenched from her grasp. It kicked; the splayed foot caught her in the center of her chest, thrust her back and away.

She rolled, found her feet, fled.

To the barn, inside the open door, there to duck to one side and peer out.

The demon had fallen and lay flailing, each movement levering the sword that impaled it, causing more and more injury.

Rowan sighted Arvin, tucked behind a collection of barrels. He raised a hand in recognition. The demon's voice ceased; pig squeals were suddenly audible again and the gasping rasp of Rowan's own breathing.

The monster continued to writhe; Rowan and Arvin watched as it slowly killed itself.

When it had stopped trembling, she went to retrieve her sword. She stood, eyeing the monster, trying to decide whether the visible differences between it and the first demon represented a normal range between individuals or difference in type.

She was startled by an arm about her shoulder, a voice both shocked and solicitous saying, "Here. Here."

"What?" She pulled away.

"You're hurt," Arvin said.

"No." She looked down. "Yes. But . . ." She was in no great pain. Shorter talons on the feet. "I'm all right. It's not deep." Three long scratches, straight down her chest. There was blood, but not a great deal. "Really. It's not serious."

His gaze was dubious. "If you say so." He set down his bow, unslung his quiver, and pulled his shirt off over his head. He handed it to her.

"What? Oh." Her shirt was in tatters. She found herself more amused by his propriety than embarrassed by her exposure. "Thank you." She removed her shirt, put on his, and used the rags of hers to wipe her sword. "Let's go up to the smithy. Was it another demon there after all, do you know?"

"I don't. Came straight after you. Steffie said."

"It was a good idea. I think we make an excellent team." She thumped his shoulder. "Let's go."

They jogged. She led. When they reached the brushy slope, he spared enough breath to say, "Town could use more like you."

"Thank you." Later, as they climbed New High Street, she said, "Can you teach me to use a bow?"

"You don't know how?"

It had been part of her training, but since then she had used one only briefly. "I want to be good at it."

"I'm your man."

They did not reach the smithy; they met Corey, and a few of the militia, returning from it. The rest had gone back to their homes. "Was it a demon?"

"It was. We took care of it." One of the militia had been injured and was walking with the assistance of another member. There was blood down her back, and one shoulder was raw from burns.

"Anyone else hurt?" Arvin asked.

"We lost young Dionne. It'd already got the smith and his girl." Corey glared at him. "And where were you?"

"Me and the steerswoman did in another. Over at Choley's place."

"What, two of them in town?"

"Looks like."

"Where's Steffie?" Rowan asked.

"With the monster. He says you'll want to see it." He noticed the blood now soaking through her borrowed shirt. "You two took on that other one alone?"

"That's right."

"You should've seen us," Arvin said. "Fast and smart."

A handful of people were straggling up New High Street, cautious and curious. Corey called to them. "All over! Taken care of! Go on home!" He waved them off. "Let's get Lark over to Jilly's."

Most of those he had called to hesitated, turned back; one did not. A single figure continued up New High Street at a dead run. Rowan recognized Janus.

He arrived, breathless. "Where was it? Is anyone hurt?" He had one hand pressed against his side, as if at a stitch; the other held a naked sword. Irrelevantly, Rowan remembered where and when he had acquired that weapon during their training, remembered sparring against him under the eye of the sword master.

Corey planted the butt of his pike against the ground, set a fist on his hip, shouted up into Janus's face. "Can't have everyone running every which way! Leave things to those as know what to do, and that's the militia! You want to join, fine—we practice once a week, show up if you like, but . . ."

Janus was not listening. His gaze went past Corey's shoulder.

The guard leader noticed, stopped with his mouth still open. And then, with the greatest reluctance, he slowly turned to look behind.

In the far distance, one person, moving fast, coming from the area of Lasker's plantation. As the figure grew nearer, Rowan recognized her: one of the evening feeders from Lasker's sheds.

Abandoning Janus, Corey began walking toward the approaching woman, slowly, almost as if against his will.

Arvin glanced at the shuttered houses, stepped up to one, yanked open the door. A woman and two men were startled: they had been peering out through a crack. "You, you and you; take Lark down to Jilly's house." The injured fighter was transferred to their care.

Arvin came back to stand at Rowan's side. They traded a glance; then all present waited for Corey and the woman to meet.

They did not need to hear the words. The woman fell against Corey, clutched at him, gestured frantically. "Three," Rowan breathed. "That makes three."

"No . . ." someone said, in a voice that cracked.

"Come on!" Arvin led the fighters forward at a jog in a straggling line that rapidly formed into a close group. Rowan was among them, toward the rear.

Abruptly, someone pushed past her, broke through the militia, passing Arvin: Janus. Arvin noticed at the last moment, reached to pull him back, missed, then increased his own pace to catch up.

Janus got there first. "Where?" Rowan heard him shout, "where is it?" She could not hear the answer.

He tried to go on, ahead, alone, but Corey spun him around, shouted at him. The militia reached them. Corey did not release his grip on Janus. "It's in the fields," he told the fighters, "coming this way from where Loho creek has that bunch of crab apples. Land's open and the field is cut between us and it. Nothing for us to dodge behind, but nothing for it to, either—"

"Let go of me," Janus spat at him, struggling.

"I want an arc, about a third of a circle, facing the monster, and we'll just pour arrows at it—" A wordless noise from one of the militia; Corey needed no interpretation. "How are we fixed for shafts?"

Archers spoke up. "Two." "Three." "None." "Two." "Five."

"Four," Arvin said.

"I said, let *go!*"

With casual brutality, Corey fisted Janus full in the face. Janus fell, sprawling to a seat in the dirt, his sword beside him. Corey turned away. "Marga, you give three to Arvin, two to Bert. Then get back to the monster we killed, grab all the arrows you can, bring them here. Watch out for the burn-juice. Go." His glance found Rowan and flicked once, down to her bloody shirt, back to her face. "How about it, lady? Ready for more?"

"Yes."

He nodded. "Good. Stick by Arvin. You just might have to show us how one bow and one sword can kill a demon." He found the shed worker, who had quieted but was still gasping in pure panic. "Get to town. Spread the word. Some of the militia's gone home—I want them back out. Go." She fled.

He looked about at the road, the fields, the darkening sky. "We can't wait for Marga. We need to move. Light'll fail soon. Can't fight it in the dark."

"Torches," someone said.

"What, so it can see us better?"

"Maybe it hates fire."

"And maybe it loves it. Goblins do." The look on Corey's face told of past experience with goblins. "But if we can't finish it off by full dark, we'll set the field on fire. Burn it to death."

"Lasker'll kill you."

"He's welcome to try."

The troop moved, passing around Janus as if he were a stone. Only Rowan paused when she reached him.

He still sat, half stunned. His dark face was streaked with blood, a red weirdly bright in the pale light of the falling sun. "Janus, don't be stupid. We know what to do. You don't. Go away." And she left him behind.

They were halfway across Lasker's eastmost field when they heard the demon-voice. The demon itself was difficult to see against the backdrop of the twisted crab apple trees—until it moved. Then Rowan found the sight strangely shocking, as if one of the trees had moved, the demon's own body so much like a smooth gray trunk, its arms like low-hanging bare branches, all, impossibly, in motion.

The militia stopped well out of range of the demon's spray. Now silent, using gestures only, Corey directed his archers into position. The men and women hurried to their posts, each moving in an awkward stoop along and across the rows of mulberries, trying to gain as much coverage as possible from the trees. But this field had been stripped of leaves, and the trunks and branches were trimmed waist high.

Rowan found that she could tell when the demon noticed a person; its arms lifted suddenly each time, almost to attack stance, then dropped. But it did not approach, nor try to spray. Perhaps it could not decide on one target.

Corey kept Rowan and Arvin beside him, along with the pike bearers, all in the center section of the curve of archers. Rowan analyzed this strategy, comparing it to one where each pike bearer stood by one archer, and found Corey's choice to be better.

Especially if Corey did exactly what he did next.

Leaning the shaft of his pike against one shoulder, he cupped his hands about his mouth. "*Hey!* Hey, you, monster! Over here, damn you! Come *this* way!" Rowan thrust two fingers in her mouth, whistling loud and shrill. Behind her, someone drew a deep breath and let out long, earsplitting ululations. The other pike bearers joined with hoots and yells.

The demon noted the sounds, lifting and dropping its arms, over and over. But it did not approach. "Maybe this one's smarter!" Arvin shouted to Rowan over the noise.

"Or weaker! Starving! There's no food for it here!" She returned to whistling.

Left and right, Corey gestured broadly. The entire line moved forward— still well out of range of demon spray but also still out of accurate bow shot. They closed the distance slowly.

When Arvin lifted his bow, Rowan knew the demon was within at least his range of accuracy; and as the line moved near, the other four archers, one by one, nocked and lifted.

Corey stopped shouting; the fighters in the center silenced. In the sudden quiet, the demon's voice seemed loud and near.

"Go!" Five archers let fly. Two of the shafts struck home. And the demon ran.

Straight for the center. "Go!" Corey called again. Four arrows struck, one missed. The demon came on, rotating a quarter turn.

"Someone got a vent," Rowan commented.

"Lilly," a woman said in fierce glee. Then she shouted, "That's for Dionne!"

Rowan glanced right, left, to see three archers drop back, their arrows gone.

"Go!" Lilly and Arvin both struck. Demon spray, but it fell far short. Only Arvin had arrows remaining. "At will," Corey told him; then, to the pikes, "Spread. To the right." The disabled vent was to the right. Rowan and the pike bearers ran.

Corey and Arvin remained in place. Corey readied his pike, yelping to bring the demon to them. Arvin shot; the creature turned again as it moved. "Another vent," Rowan said.

"What's that?" The fighter spoke in quiet tones.

"What?"

"There." He pointed. Past Corey and Arvin.

"Marga?"

"No . . ."

Rowan cursed in a whisper: "Oh, gods below . . ."

She knew him by his height, his shape, by how he ran, by the bright sword in his hand. "He's on the wrong side."

"He's a dead man." And then they were too far to speak.

Corey spotted Janus, shouted his name. Janus continued, angling right—and then he was squarely between Arvin and the demon and, an instant later, in range of the spray.

Corey silenced, placed a hand on Arvin's shoulder to stop the next shot. Not protecting Janus from Arvin's arrows, but logically if cold-bloodedly, using Janus, allowing the creature to take him for its target.

Rowan stood, swaying helplessly, agonizingly, from the pain of holding every muscle locked against the wild need to move, to run, to attack the monster herself before Janus was hurt.

No. Useless. Too far. Too late.

Incredibly, Janus slowed to a walk, then stopped. Even more incredibly, the demon did the same.

They both stood, some forty feet apart, Janus perfectly still, the demon with arms raised and waving.

Then Janus continued forward, at a slow and deliberate walk, his sword held wide to one side. Rowan could not see his other hand. "Use both hands," she said, her voice choked behind clenched teeth.

The demon moved again—but slowly, to the left. Janus angled to intercept it.

It stopped once more. It dropped its arms from attack stance. Then, slightly faster, it headed right.

Janus broke into a run.

He crossed the gap, reached the demon, swung one-handed, struck once, twice.

The creature pulled away in staggering steps. Janus closed in, stabbed hard.

Abrupt and utter silence.

Voiceless, waving its arms wildly, the demon took another step away. Janus swung once more, slicing deep into its body. It dropped, flailed, trembled to motionlessness.

All was still.

Rowan's body unlocked so suddenly and completely that she fell, sprawling back into the sharp, cut branches of the waist-high mulberries. She thrashed stupidly, then regained her feet.

No one else had moved. Then a pike bearer began to laugh—the odd, weak laugh of one amazed and still disbelieving. Then another laughed, brighter, triumphant—and all broke into shouts and hurrahs.

Rowan found the noises unreal. She could not integrate these events. This made no sense.

The pike bearers scrambled across the field toward Janus and the demon, the archers doing the same. Janus stood silent. His sword, point on the ground, shone red in the last rays of the sun, as if painted with human blood.

Rowan found herself not by Janus but beside Corey and Arvin, who had not joined the others. Both stood dumbfounded. Finally, Corey spoke. "Stupidest thing I ever saw. Taking a chance like that."

"It never sprayed," Arvin said.

"Damn lucky for him."

"That," Rowan said, "is exactly what it was." And she pushed her way through the mulberries toward the crowd.

The fighters were gathered around Janus, slapping him on the shoulder, making laughing comments. He stumbled a bit under one particularly strong thump, but otherwise seemed unaware of their presence. They began to quiet as they noticed this, and silenced when, without even one comment to them, Janus turned and walked away down the row of bushes.

Rowan intercepted him. He stopped, only because she planted herself directly in his path. "You were *lucky*," she said with unexpected vehemence.

He seemed only at that point to recognize her. He took a breath to speak.

She flung out both arms. "Yes! I know! 'Go away!' But you're going to listen to me, you incredible fool!" She stepped close, spoke up into his face. "You were *lucky*. Those animals can't eat Inner Lands food, and that one was starving, or sick, or out of whatever mind it had. It didn't have the sense, or the strength, to kill you—and that was a stroke of fortune you can't depend on next time." He tried to pass around her; she did not permit it. "If you ever try anything so stupid again, I think you'll find it's a very good way to kill yourself!"

She heard herself say these words, and then stopped, stunned.

Perhaps he had been trying to do exactly that.

She found she could not speak; and in the rapidly gathering dark, she could not read his face.

But now she saw his stance: one hand loosely holding his sword, the other arm wrapped tight around his body. Words came by themselves. "Are you hurt?"

"No." Then: "You are."

She looked down. In the failing light, her own blood looked black against Arvin's pale shirt. "A bit."

"Have Jilly see to it." He brushed past her.

She watched him go; and all around, in the darkening field, people were moving, calling out. Family, comrades, friends, looking for each other, finding each other, laughing relief, and already telling the tale of Janus's mad attack. Some people were carrying lamps, like small searching stars.

"Rowan."

"Steffie." He was beside her, and had a small star of his own.

"Oh—"

She recovered her wits. "No, I'm all right. For the most part. Merely some bad scratches."

"Oh. Right. Let's get you to Jilly's." And he walked beside her, lighting her way.

14

*H*e thought he'd just check.

The steerswoman didn't strike Steffie as the kind of person who'd take it easy after being hurt. Not that she was hurt bad, not like Lark. But still.

He put his lunch pail down by the door of the Annex and sort of slipped in, not wanting to make a noise in case Rowan was sleeping.

But she was up, eating breakfast, though she already had a whole big stack of books beside her on the floor, tall as her chair, and three more open and spread on the table all around her. Which you did have to expect, he supposed.

When he saw her, she was moving her hand away from her sword, hung at the back of her chair, as usual. Which meant that when the door opened, her hand had gone near her sword, same as it always did, until she saw it was just him.

That used to bother him. Didn't anymore.

"I hadn't expected to see you. Aren't Lasker's worms still hungry?" She looked tired, dog tired. And she held herself sort of stiff.

"I expect they are," he said. "Hungrier than usual, I guess, 'cause when that demon was in the field, all the shed workers got so scared they hid behind the racks." He came over and sat. "I'll bet a bunch of them died waiting for their suppers. The worms, I mean. And some probably got so thrown off, they won't go up the hill at all, when the time comes."

She pushed a plate of gummy-looking rolls toward him. "That will be soon, won't it?"

"Any day. Don't mind if I do." But he minded after he took a bite, because it was the worst roll he ever ate. It needed to be baked a lot longer. "Anyway, thought I'd stop by. You know." He tried to think of a polite way to get rid of the roll, but he couldn't, so he kept eating it.

"Thank you, Steffie. But I'm doing well, really. Although, I did get no sleep." Up close, she didn't look just tired; she looked dark, somehow, like she'd been far away, to somewhere not very nice, and was going back there soon.

"Me neither. Not much." He'd kept hearing demons in his dreams. "But it's over now." All of a sudden, Rowan's face changed, as if that dark place she was thinking of was a lot closer than she liked. He went cold. "Isn't it?"

"I hope so. But four demons is far too many."

Four? He counted them up: three yesterday, one before, and the first one—the one she'd cut up. "No, that's five, all together."

She didn't answer straight off. "I mean," she said, "four yesterday."

He dropped the roll. "Where was the fourth one? When? Was anyone hurt?"

She put up one hand. "No, no one was hurt—unless you count the fourth demon itself. I found it, what was left of it, residing in the stomach of demon number three."

He calmed down. "It got ate up?"

"Apparently."

"And when did you find that out?"

"Last night. I took a lantern, sometime before dawn. Since I couldn't sleep, I thought I'd do something useful."

Well. He was right about her not resting when she ought to. Still . . . "Just for something to do, or did you have some idea in mind?"

"I had an idea." She ate a few bites of her eggs. "There are two places that I've heard of demons living. One is in the salt bog, hundreds of miles north of here—but the stories about them are old, and no demon has been seen there in living memory." She put down her fork. "The other place is the Outskirts—where they are so exceedingly rare that the arrival of even one will inspire people to write a song to mark the occasion.

"But life native to the Outskirts and to the lands beyond is very different from Inner Lands life. The two types don't coexist easily. And the largest reason is that most living things of one type cannot eat living things of the other type. It made me wonder how demons coming in from the Outskirts could survive long enough to reach Alemeth."

"So, they did it by eating each other?"

"One of them did." She went back to her eggs.

"Well," he said, "I guess that makes sense. If you're going someplace where there's nothing to eat . . . bring friends."

The steerswoman laughed so suddenly and so hard that she spit egg straight across the table at Steffie, which made him laugh, too; and seeing him laugh made her laugh more. Then she got some egg down her windpipe, which made her cough, and up her nose, which made her sneeze four times in a row, just like a cat—which made Steffie laugh even harder. And then they both had to hurry to get the egg bits off the pages of the books on the table, so they wouldn't be there for the next person to find, maybe years later. Which, when Steffie pointed it out, made them both laugh all over again; and the steerswoman said that maybe she ought to label the stains, so that the next person wouldn't be confused and spend years trying to figure them out. Then she described something called a catalog entry and cross-reference for the egg bits, of which Steffie didn't understand a single word; but just the way she said it, so serious and formal, made them both laugh so hard that they had to sit back down and wait until they were done.

And when they were, Steffie said, "I think I should stay by the Annex today. Just to do this and that for you, 'cause you've been hurt and you're tired, and I'm not, not so much."

"Lasker won't give you the sack if you miss a day?"

"No. It's not so strict. Whoever shows up gets to work, and since almost everybody does, he's almost never short. He won't miss me."

And that's what he did. She went back to her books and writing, and he got going on the dishes from breakfast. And then he thought maybe he could give those rolls another chance in the oven, but they were low on wood. So he left the steerswoman pulling books off some shelves and putting other books up on others, and went and got some logs. And when he got back, she'd fallen asleep in Mira's chair.

So instead of moving around the house, where he might wake her up, he took the two smallest logs out back, to split into kindling.

Which was what he was doing when she came out later and sat on the back steps, looking sort of bleary and stubborn, too, both at the same time.

She sat there, thinking for a while, before she said anything, and she was smart enough to wait until after one chop and before the next. "Steffie?"

"Hm?" He was down to taking one piece and making it into two, and taking one of them and making that into two, over and over, which he always found sort of interesting.

"Can you read?"

"More or less . . ."

"That's rather vague. Can you be more specific?"

"Well . . ." And he put down the axe. "I suppose I can puzzle out words, with enough time. If they're written clear." He started gathering up the kindling. "Anyway"—and he turned to Rowan—"I don't get much practice."

She was looking at him just like his words made no sense at all. He was suddenly ashamed, knowing what she was thinking, clear as if she said it: *How can you spend all your time in a house full of books and not read them?*

But she sighed. "Well, come and take a look at this."

He brought half the kindling to the stove and put the other half by the hearth. Rowan was at the table, pulling out a clean sheet of paper. He went over.

She picked up her pen, dipped it, and started writing something. "Now, I don't need you to read these words, exactly—I just want you to be able to recognize them. You can hold them in your head like pictures, if that works for you."

His ears went hot, but she didn't really mean it as an insult, so he didn't say anything and just watched her write. "Demon," he said when she finished the first word.

Her quick smile was back. "Very good." She did another. "But I know that name for them because it was told to me; someone else might not call them that . . ."

He sounded out the second word. "Mmm, mm, mon, monster."

The third word was a long one. Steffie was at sea, with no idea at all how to even begin. "That's a *q*," the steerswoman said, "and that's a *u* after it. Together they sound like *kw* . . ."

"Qua," Steffie said. He felt like an idiot. "Quad, quade, quadey—"

"Quadrilateral," Rowan said. "That's the most important one. Demons have quadrilateral symmetry, meaning that they have four sides, each the same as the others. Very few living things are quadrilaterally symmetrical, so any steerswoman who saw a demon, or heard one described, would be certain to include the fact in her notes."

A bad suspicion started to grow in him. "What notes?" And her glance told him. He turned around.

And there they were, five big aisles of shelves, up to the ceiling, back twenty, thirty feet to the end of the long room. "Oh, no."

"You don't have to read everything," she said in a rush. "Just look at each page, and bring me any book or piece of paper that has any of those words on it. Too many demons have come to Alemeth; I don't like it. We need to know more about them—their habits, their life cycle, migrations.

Perhaps . . . somewhere, at some time, some other steerswoman has seen a
demon, or spoken to someone who has—and she put it in her logbook.
We might learn something we can use."

He wanted to help, but: "Every single page . . ."

"It'll go faster than you think, if you just look for those words."

Demons.

He *hated* demons. And he couldn't fight them with a sword, like
Rowan, or with a bow, like Arvin. Maybe he wasn't any better with words
than he was with a sword or a bow, but he wouldn't die if he tried and
failed at it. Which he might, with a sword or a bow. "Right."

She clapped him on the shoulder, like he'd seen the militia do with
each other. "Good man. You start on one end, I'll start on the other."

"And we meet in the middle?"

She stopped short, opened her mouth, then closed it again. "I sincerely hope," she said, "that it won't take *that* long."

She gave him the front aisle, where light from the windows made
it easier; she lit a lamp for herself and went off to the other side, the
darker one.

Steffie just stood there dumb, with three words on a paper in one
hand, and the books all lined up on the shelf, just like little faces looking
at him. Then he shook his head, took one deep breath, and dove in.

He thought he'd been at it all day, but the sun out in the street said it
wasn't even one hour. Not this page, not this page, not this . . . At last he
was done with the one book, and he put it back.

Then another book. Every page.

It was hard.

But the thing to do when you have to do something hard is just dig in
and do it. After a while, it being hard doesn't matter anymore. It's just
what you're doing, and you keep on doing it.

He dug in. Another book, every page, one by one, checking to see if
any words matched the ones on the paper.

And then another book—and he did find *monster*, but he didn't want
to waste the steerswoman's time, so he stopped to figure out the whole
page, and it was just some steerswoman saying how rotten some local guard
captain was. Then later, in another, he found *quadrilateral* and even *symmetry*, which took some figuring; but it turned out the writer was talking
about a tree that some wood carvers were forcing to grow into a special
shape for a special room in a special house, and that was interesting, think

how long that'd take, your father would have to start the work for your son to finish . . .

He made himself go back to his job. Another book. And then another; but instead of going faster, he was going slower, or he seemed to be, because he wasn't turning each page over so quickly anymore . . .

Rowan came and got him around noon, and he was surprised to see her; he had got to feeling like he was all alone, sitting on the dusty floor by the sunshiny windows.

They brought out cold food for lunch, and when they sat down to eat it, Steffie said, "You didn't tell me."

"Tell you what?" She was prying the cooked chicken apart with her hands, in a hurry to get done.

He'd brought the book with him, and he held it up. "You didn't tell me there were stories in here."

"I suppose there are some—" and she licked her fingers "—but for the most part, it's purely facts. Information."

"No, no," he said, "it's *full* of stories. Look here." He opened the book where his finger was holding the place. "Here, this woman Henra is walking along in this place and she's thirsty and not finding any water for a long time. But there are all these big trees growing around, all green and leafy, so she thinks there's water underground. She decides to find it. And then she finds a cave, and she wants to go in to see if it leads to a river under the ground,"—and think of that, a whole river running forever in the dark—"but a bear lives in the cave, and she has a terrible fight with it, and kills it . . ." And he looked down again at the page he had puzzled out.

Funny.

There was the description of the trees, all right, but now that he looked close again, it was all just measurements, numbers. And there . . . there were Henra's guesses about the river, and where she figured it was and why—just a list of reasons. And then the cave and what it looked like, and then: "The bear attacked me, and I had to kill it." And that was all she'd said about the bear.

It wasn't laid out like a story people tell by a fireside, not step-by-step the way it happened. But you could put all the pieces together, and they went together easy, they all fit so smooth, and when you did that, it was just like you were right there in that steerswoman's own head, doing what she did, seeing just as clear as she had done.

"It is a story," he said again. A far, far part of the world, and struggles and danger, and winning out in the end—"It doesn't say so, but it is really, when you put it together. It's . . . it's an adventure!"

She was grinning at him like he had found out a happy secret. "Are they all," he started to ask, but then he answered himself: Yes, they were all of them, every single book, filled with adventures.

True adventures that people really lived. Think of that.

The steerswoman wiped her mouth, went to wash her hands in the kitchen basin. "Finish your food, and then let's see if anyone's adventure will help us with our own."

Much later, all of a sudden, he found it; but not by the words in the books. It was a picture.

There was a leather folder, rolled and tied with ribbon, lying in a box full of blank paper. When he untied and unrolled it, loose pages popped out, jumping like little animals, rolling themselves up again, crowding around his feet on the floor. He knelt down and pushed them together, and it was the first one he picked up, the first he laid flat to see.

It wasn't drawn by Rowan; that was the first thing that hit him. It made it seem more real, somehow, as if the monster were something he and the steerswoman had dreamed up together; but seeing it in this stranger's hand made it all new.

The demon stood just like he'd seen the first one, arms up and ready to shoot its spray. The person who drew it was better at it than Rowan, because there was a kind of feeling to it, like something about to happen—and a kind of magic that froze that about-to-happen, so that the monster stood still for Steffie to stare and stare at. It made it look like forever, from the beginning of the world until the end, and it made him afraid.

After a while he noticed the writing. 5 *feet tall,* said words running along the side of the demon. Well, that was about right. Steffie had a good feel for numbers. And two feet thick, he said to himself, and he found the words that said that right away. A line like a curved arrow pointed at the demon's top, and words beside it said, *mouth on top.* There was another drawing next to the first, a view from the top like a bird looking down—and there was the monster's throat, wide open, with the grinders showing inside, and Steffie saw more words, which when he sorted them out turned out to say, *grinding plates.*

A demon would never let you look down its throat; this person had seen live demons and dead ones both.

Quadrilateral, was on the page, and so was *symmetry. Quadrilateral* had a line drawn under it and an exclamation mark after.

Bring it to the steerswoman, came into Steffie's head, and he got up to do it; but then he knew what she would ask next, so he stopped to look at all the other papers in the folder and in another that lay beside it; and he riffled through the blank pages in the trunk. He found nothing else about demons.

He said nothing when he brought the drawing to Rowan, just handed it to her and waited.

She looked at it a long time. "Was there anything else?"

"Just that." She went silent again, and as he stood looking at her looking at it, Steffie noticed that the paper was crinkled in hard ridges and splotched. Dunked in water, he thought, then remembered that the ink would go fuzzy in water, and so the drawing was made after the paper had got wet and then dried. The left edge of the paper wasn't smooth like the others. Torn, he thought.

A steerswoman's log, dropped in water, come apart at the seams—then the steerswoman had gathered up the insides, dried the paper, and some time after that saw the demon, and drew it.

But—"I guess it doesn't tell you anything you don't already know."

Rowan said quietly, "You're wrong." Steffie waited. After a while, she said, "It shows me exactly how blind I have been."

He waited some more. It took a long time.

Then: "I recognize the handwriting."

15

Janus was not in Lasker's sheds nor in Karin's. He was not at the harbor, working on his boat. Nor was he at Brewer's nor at Maysie's house. He was not at the Mizzen, where, she had learned, he had found employment hauling trash and tending the few horses in the stables.

She went to the cooper's and began to climb the rickety staircase that led to Janus's room high under the eaves. But halfway up, the height afforded her a view of the yard behind the building. Janus was down by the holding well. Rowan descended and approached.

His battered gray gloves were on the stones of the well's edge, beside a damp, rough towel. A tangle of soiled bandages lay in a dented tin pot. Beside it, a clay jar, its lid off, held a yellowish substance smelling sweetly of herbs.

Janus was winding a fresh linen bandage onto his left hand, wrapping it down to his wrist. He stopped when he saw her, did not speak when she greeted him; then he silently returned to his work.

He fumbled tying off the bandage end one-handed, using teeth and fingers. He must have done it alone any number of times, but now he struggled, clumsy. The steerswoman watched for a time, then stepped forward and held out her own hand.

He stopped. They stood regarding each other, her face carefully neutral, his expressionless.

He held out the bandaged hand. Rowan tied it off, using an efficient slipknot that would undo with a pull on one end. When she finished, she released his hand and looked up.

He was watching her. He was thinking something—she could not tell what—but it seemed to her not to be a thought that moved. The thought stood motionless, directly behind his eyes. She could not tell what was looking at her from behind Janus's face: Janus himself, or that thought.

They both stood so for a moment. Then Rowan picked up the second
bandage and with a small lift of her chin, indicated Janus's right hand. He
looked down at it, as if it did not belong to him, then moved the fingers
stiffly as if discovering that it did. Then he held it out to her.

She worked in silence, taking her cue from the bandaging on his
other hand. A single strip of linen ran up the outside and down the inside
of two fingers, held in place by windings. It was necessary; otherwise, raw
places would adhere to each other, perhaps permanently. On the thumb
and first two fingers, the nails were mere stubs that ended directly at the
cuticles. The last two fingers were nearly normal.

The condition was worst on the fingertips and palm, diminishing toward
the back of the hand. Healed patches of pink against the dark brown of his
skin made his hands seem painted.

When she finished, he stepped back and began pulling on his gloves.

Rowan said, "That didn't happen to me." He stopped, looked up at
her. "Nor to Steffie," she continued. "After dissecting the demon, our
hands itched the first day, peeled the second, and were healing on the
third. Even people the creature wounded directly—the injuries are scar-
ring and healing. For everyone except you."

His head jerked back slightly, a mere tightening of muscle in his neck.

She reached into her shirt, pulled out the sketch. "Where were you
when you saw this demon, Janus?"

He looked at the page, showing no recognition whatsoever.

He turned. He walked away.

Rowan stood a moment, stunned with disbelief, then hurried to catch
up, stepped in front of him. "That shipwreck—where did you end up? Was
it near here? Are there now demons around Alemeth, right here in the
Inner Lands?" He moved to go around her; she blocked him. "The demon
in Lasker's field was not sick, was not injured, and was better fed than the
others—and you killed it easily, so easily. Why didn't it spray you or slash
you? How did you know it would not?"

He began to back away; she followed him, step for step. "If you know
something, Janus, you have to tell! When demons come, people *die*!" He
stopped; she pushed the point. "Leonard." Whom the first demon had
sprayed to flesh and bones. "Bran." Who had died from his injuries after
the demon burnt away his face. "The smith and his girl. Young Dionne."
A militia member and, Rowan recalled, a fisher. "Janus, you know something, and if you won't talk to me, talk to someone. Tell Corey or Arvin—
gods below, Janus, tell *Brewer* if you must, but tell someone!"

But he stood before her, utterly silent, utterly still, his face utterly blank. He was not looking at her at all. His eyes were focused somewhere far, far through and past her.

Rowan stared at that empty face and wondered if he might be insane.

Then she remembered that look. She had seen it before.

Fletcher. In the Outskirts.

Fletcher, in the moments when a particular memory came to him: a memory of a sight so horrific, an event so terrible, and a guilt so great that it closed all the doors of his thought and his heart, and he could do nothing but stand motionless and merely breathe.

That look was on Janus's face.

Rowan heard herself say quietly, "What have you done?"

He did not reply. He stepped around her. He reached the foot of the stairs, began ascending.

Rowan stood back to watch him climb. She shouted up to him, "Is it you? Did those demons come because of you?" No response. "Do you at least know why they came?" He continued up. "Will there be more?"

He stopped. She held her breath. She thought: That means yes.

He said, "No."

But was it answer or protest—truth or denial?

She could not tell.

Then he continued to his door, entered, and was gone.

16

Rowan said quietly, "I think that more demons will come."

"Let 'em. We're getting even better at killing them." Corey's voice was just audible. The continuous crunching of the worms as they fed sounded to Rowan like a thousand footsteps on fine gravel.

She leaned closer; loud voices were not welcome here. "And Janus knows more about them than he is telling."

"Makes no sense, that." He continued trickling chopped leaves from between his fingers. "If he did, he wouldn't have gone running at that last one. Wouldn't take him in the militia now, not if he begged. He's risky." He spared a glance at her. "Not like you. When the worms go up the hill, I want you and Arvin to show us how you did in that one you took alone."

Their success had hinged on Arvin's skill, and Rowan doubted that any other archer in town could equal it. "Yes, of course—"

"And come to think of it, let's get the whole militia—and maybe the townfolk, too—and you can lay out for everyone what you know about demons. Just in case."

"Yes, of course," she said again. "But you already know what I know about the demons themselves. And I don't know the important things. I don't know their habits, their preferences—" Corey slotted the tray, pulled out the next. Rowan stooped to stay near him. "But listen," she continued. "I think Janus does know more. I don't believe he succeeded by luck. I think he knew that the demon wouldn't injure him. Now, wouldn't that be even more useful than anything I could show you?"

"How could he know a thing like that?"

"I don't know. He won't tell me."

"Huh." He blew gently across the top of the tray; dried leaves flew. "Won't talk to you at all, that's what I hear. And got no good to say about you, either." Three of the worms were shriveled and brown; he flicked them out, one by one, slanted the tray to study the living worms suspiciously.

The steerswoman passed a hand through her hair, resisting an impulse to tear at it in frustration. "He hates me. I thought I knew why, but now . . . But, Corey, if Janus cares at all for the town, he must share what he knows. Perhaps if the questions came from the leader of the town's defense, he'd see that. You might get through to him."

"If he said nothing, then nothing's what he knows."

"He's hiding something. I think—" she hesitated to suggest this "—it's just possible that something he's doing is actually bringing the demons here."

Corey straightened and stood regarding her; and Rowan noted that his expression was not one of surprise but of disgust. "Now, that's not a good thing to be going around saying. Janus been here for years, now. Never had any demons come till lately. Only new thing in town is you. Might as well say that you're the one bringing them." He pushed the tray back with perhaps more force than was wise; the stack rocked, earning him a sharp glance from Karin, patrolling along the end of the aisles.

"Corey, where does he go when he sails away? Everyone knows he goes; has he told no one where?"

"He keeps mum. Lots of rumors. He doesn't say yes or no about them."

"What about his hands? Handling dead demons irritates the skin—"

"That's his and Jilly's business. Now, look." He turned back to her. "Whatever trouble you and Janus got between you is yours. People turning on other people for spite, that's no good."

She was stunned. "Is that what you think I'm doing?"

"Wouldn't be the first time sweethearts quarreling tried to stab each other in the back—"

"He has never been my sweetheart—"

"But when I see you pulling things out of the air—"

"Steerswomen do not pull things out of the air!"

He glanced past her; Karin was making her way down the aisle. Corey leaned close, spoke quickly. "So I hear. Rowan, you want to fight alongside us, you're welcome. Anything else, I'm not interested. Now, let me work. I just don't want to hear this."

"And why do you feel we need to hear this?"

The steerswoman took a breath. "You're the most influential people in town. The decisions you make affect everyone. If people of your importance took interest in this, it might cause Janus to stop being so—so secretive."

They were gathered by the fireside at the Mizzen, mugs in hand, a deferential serving woman watching sharply from across the room.

Rowan noted that the silence had continued to an uncomfortable duration. Lasker took a breath. "If what you're saying is true—"

She said immediately, "Of course it's true."

"Sounds like a lot of guesses to me." One of the weaver brothers.

The bank proprietress lifted her free hand. "Even so, we can't force him to answer to you. Do you expect us to have it beaten out of him?"

Rowan found that her left hand had tightened to a fist on her knee. "He's endangering the entire town."

"Sounds to me like he's done just the opposite," Lasker said. "And took a big risk to do it. Town owes him a lot—"

Dan spoke up quickly. "No less than we owe you, Rowan." A sidewise glance betrayed that this statement was not only for her benefit.

"Of course," Karin said. "We're lucky to have such brave people among us—"

"Have you heard that Janus used to be a steersman?"

A pause, but no great astonishment. "That rumor seems to be going around, yes . . ."

"He resigned. And he would not explain why." Rowan set her own mug on the floor, leaned forward. "He gave me an explanation, but I don't believe it anymore. I think it was because he has been doing something, something he won't admit to, that he feels he must keep secret. I think it has to do with demons."

Another lengthy pause, with many glances among the Bosses. "Janus has always been a good citizen."

"Right. Ever since he come here, done nothing but help."

"Besides, nothing says any more demons will come by . . ."

"These are wild ideas you have." This from the spider-wife.

"Well, I wouldn't put it so, so baldly, myself." Karin suddenly found her beer fascinating.

"It's sheer speculation!" The second weaving brother declared; and both nodded stubbornly in unison.

"I assure you," Rowan said, "a steerswoman does not go about making accusations based on sheer speculation."

The pause occurred but seemed to get cut short before its natural span. "Even a steerswoman can be mistaken," Dan said.

"See? That's true."

"Nobody's perfect . . ."

"We won't interrogate Janus on your behalf," Karin said. "We need more than this. We can't help you."

*   *   *

"Why do you need my help?"

The steerswoman organized her thoughts, took a breath. "Maysie, I know that Janus knows something about demons, something important—but he won't tell me. He won't speak to me at all. I thought that if it was you who spoke to him, if *you* asked him to at least share what he knows, he might listen. Because he cares for you. Because you're such close friends."

Maysie sat back on her heels, a conical sun hat, such as the field-workers wore, shading her face. "Yes . . ." She mused, her voice faintly puzzled. "Yes, he does seem to be a friend . . . now."

Rowan's planned speech vanished. "Now? You mean—" She knelt on the grass beside Maysie. "Do you mean recently? Since—"

"Since," Maysie said. As if by itself, her right hand came up to lie against her scarred, twisted cheek. "That's right. Only since." She dropped her hand, glanced away, then returned her attention to the flower bed before her. "We knew each other, of course," she said, plying the hand spade. "Everyone in Alemeth knows each other. And he's always been very charming, but he's like that with everyone. But, no, we were never close . . ."

"But," Rowan began, wanting to ask: But then why did he rush to your side as soon as he heard? Why did he hold you, comfort you, treat you as dear? But she could not ask it. Because, if nothing else, it had been a kind act, and Maysie did deserve kindness.

"He's good to me . . ." Maysie went on. "He runs my errands on the days I can't face the world. And he comes out with me on the days that I can. It helps." She set a daffodil bulb into the ground, pushed the earth over it with her hands. "And it helps with the townsfolk, too. I think that seeing Janus treat me well puts a bit of shame in them. Though, I don't believe that's his intention . . ."

"What *is* his intention?" Rowan immediately realized that the question, so bluntly stated, could not help but imply that Janus's motives were suspect.

If Maysie noticed the implication, she chose to ignore it. She answered simply, "I don't know. And I'm usually good at understanding things unspoken. One learns it, to be successful in my sort of work. I can recognize kindness when I see it, and pity, and it's neither of those." Maysie noticed an invading weed, pulled it from the bed with an almost apologetic gentleness. "But all I can tell is that, somehow, now, I've become . . . important to him. Precious. Cherished." She regarded the clods left by the weed, and then carefully patted them back into place. "I know it's strange. I don't ask him why. I don't want to ask. I'm just grateful."

The steerswoman thought a long time before speaking again. "Can it be guilt?" Maysie turned toward her in surprise. Rowan hurried on. "Maysie, I think this isn't over, I think more demons will come to Alemeth, and if Janus knows how to help but doesn't do it—"

"But he *did* help. I heard how he went after that last one, all on his own—it was so brave, it terrified me!" Maysie sat up, looked at the steerswoman directly, the undamaged side of her face in shade, the ruined side in light. She composed herself and spoke more formally. "He's a *good* man, lady, a kind one, and a brave one. I'm sure that if he knew anything that would make a difference, he would tell us."

Rowan sat silent. At last she sighed and rose. "Just ask him, Maysie. Please. That's all."

"I'll ask, lady. But I don't think it will help you."

"What makes you think I can help?"

The steerswoman sighed. "Actually, I don't know what you could do. Other than mention it to other people. The more people who know, the better. I think I've come to you because I must speak to someone, and you're someone I respect."

Sitting beside her on his front steps, Arvin made an amused noise, gazed out at his grubby front yard. Happy sounds tumbled out of the open door behind him: Alyssa and the girls, preparing for dinner. "That happens. People fight together, they think good of each other. So, tell me, lady, are you really sure about all this?"

Perhaps because he presented the question in the formal mode, she took the time to calmly review her evidence. Arvin waited with a patience so complete that it reminded her of Bel. "Yes. I'm certain."

He took some moments himself, perhaps reviewing his own array of facts. "Steerswomen are good at figuring things out. Trained to do it, they are."

"That's true."

He twisted his mouth at his own thoughts. "So, tell me lady, are you a steerswoman?"

She stopped short, speechless. Then: "Yes. Yes, I am."

"Makes a little puzzle, that does," he said, not meeting her eye. "If you are, then you can't lie; if you're not, then you would. Either way, you'd say the same thing. Too deep for me." He slapped his knees, sat straighter, turned to her. "Well. I believe you."

"Thank you. On what are you basing that?"

He shrugged. "Feel, mostly. Nothing else sits right."

She rubbed her forehead with the heel of her hand. "No wonder people seem so reluctant to take my word. I suppose I can thank Gwen for that."

"Gwen and Janus."

"What?"

"That's right. Last few days." She stared at him, gape mouthed, as he went on. "I didn't hear it from him, but I hear it from people who did. He says he used to live in Wulfshaven, and he met you there, and you weren't a steerswoman then. Then he meets you here, and you say you are. But there's something about that big training session, I forget what it's called—"

"The Academy," she provided, sheer habit overcoming her astonishment.

"Right. There wasn't one between now and then. So, he sort of wonders, just thinking out loud, so I hear, how it is you got to be trained. And people are just adding it up."

"But this is *insane!*" She was on her feet, pacing the dirt in Arvin's front yard. "Why lie, why lie about me, why lie about *this?*" Her fury was too large to be personal; she felt she was witnessing a crime, a crime against the very concept of the Steerswomen. Rowan's own membership in that group was irrelevant; it was the concept, the principles, the acts, and the hopes that she loved and believed in.

Nothing equaled her love for that ideal. She thought that, if she had a personality only slightly different, she might even pray to it. And this was like sacrilege.

"What generally happens?"

"What?" It was difficult to draw herself from her outrage.

"When someone says she's a steerswoman when she's not. Got to happen sometimes. What do the steerswomen do?"

"Very little." The specifics ordered themselves and required themselves to be communicated. "If we know it's happening, we expose the false steerswoman. But how often it happens, we don't know; unless a steerswoman witnesses it, or hears about it, no report will reach the Prime."

"But if you do know, all you do is say so? You don't punish her?"

And she found, quite suddenly, that she was calm again. "All we have is knowledge," she said simply. "All we have is truth. That's what we provide."

He nodded slowly. "Then, it's up to the locals to deal with her."

"That's right. And local situations vary widely." She had read of a false steerswoman in The Crags being executed; of one in Donner thrown in prison under a law against confidence artists; others being beaten . . . "At the very least, the woman is run out of town by the authorities."

Quite suddenly she recalled that the subject of this conversation was herself.

Arvin had apparently not lost the thread. He was watching her closely. "And how long was it you planned to stay in Alemeth?"

She would not run. She would not. "At least until Mira's replacement arrives," she said slowly. And the new steerswoman could verify Rowan's authority. "But, Arvin, with this demon business going on, I have to stay. I have to help, I have to try to find out—"

You're too intelligent. Janus, on the docks, that very first night.

She said out loud, "That's it. He wants me to leave."

Try not to think too much about what I said, Janus had said. *I wouldn't want you to understand it too well.*

"He knows that I won't stop until I understand. Telling me to go away doesn't work, so he'll *make* me go away."

"Would that be so bad?" Arvin put up a hand. "Just for a while. Let the stories run their course and get boring. Let Janus get all comfortable, drop his guard. And when's this new steerswoman due?"

She counted the weeks since the Prime's letter. "I suppose we could expect her any time now."

"Well, no. Unless she hires her own ship. Shipping here goes with the worms. If the worms went up the hill tomorrow, it's two, three weeks till there's enough thread worth coming for. So one ship's already scheduled, for about a month from now. After that, cloth starts coming out, and two months or so to build up, then it's a ship a week."

Rowan could not see the Prime releasing enough funds to hire an entire ship merely to hurry Mira's replacement. "And . . . your suggestion is that I find something to occupy myself away from town for the next few weeks?"

"Right. That's my advice exactly."

She found herself looking at her own two hands. "It's hard for me to do nothing. And suppose more demons come?"

"Well, we got two of 'em without you. We'll get the next ones. And, as for this Janus business . . . maybe you haven't noticed, Rowan, but there really isn't much you can do, is there?"

It certainly seemed not.

But by the time she reached Carter Street, she realized that she might be wrong. There might be a way to learn more.

The steerswoman threaded her way westward along the docks, each in worse condition than the next, finally reaching the point where she had to step widely to avoid gaps in the planking. Water gurgled and plashed below, seaweed swirling deep green and murky to the movement of small waves.

Janus's boat had been shifted, and was now stern-tied to the splintering wharf, bow-tied to a broken piling. The contrast between ancient neglect and recent small repairs made it a shabby and motley vessel. Sometime long in the past some proud owner had embellished the transom with a name, now evident only from the blistering beneath layers of old paint: a name long and ornate, beginning with an E, ending with DRA, and otherwise illegible. A more recent owner, a simpler soul, had painted it over and replaced it with a single, short word; but even this was now unreadable, mere shadow lettering. Janus's boat had no name.

Rowan glanced about. This end of the harbor was deserted. Even Harbor Road was empty of everyone but Steffie, whom Rowan had shamelessly recruited to guard her back.

It was one long step from the last plank to the boat. Arrived, Rowan found her feet immediately steadier.

Too steady. The boat was riding heavier than its construction suggested. She was disturbed; there must be stores already aboard. And that meant that Janus planned to leave soon.

A hatch from the cockpit led below. Rowan descended the steep ladder to find herself in a short companionway open to a tiny portside galley. Aft, a door led to a simple cabin, with a bunk, a cabinet, a small stern window, a tilted chart table bolted to the flooring.

No charts were in evidence. The cabinet was empty, as were the storage drawers beneath the bunk.

A small room adjacent to the galley was also empty: used, Rowan guessed from lingering food scents, as a pantry. Apparently Janus had yet to stock it from his main stores.

From the companionway, the forward door led to what was clearly designed to be a second cabin. Scratches on the floor indicated that heavy objects were sometimes brought there; perhaps it was also used for storage, but now it stood empty. A small door forward of the room opened to the sail locker, with its hatch leading up to the deck, now dogged tight.

Back in the companionway, Rowan clambered further down the ladder to the hold, and paused to give her eyes time to adjust to the gloom.

Empty.

Impossible: there must be stores aboard or some kind of cargo. Disbelieving, Rowan paced the length of the hold, ducking under the beams. Nothing.

She leaned on one leg, then the other; the boat's response was slow.

Odd. Save the anchor, the steerswoman herself was the heaviest single object on board. The boat ought to have reacted more to the displacement of her weight.

She ran her hands across the inside of the hull. Good solid oak, despite its age and neglect; but not heavy enough to explain the boat's behavior. She pulled up the free floorboards; perhaps something was hidden below. But the bilge held only six inches of water.

Perhaps the hull itself was thicker than she had assumed. She walked the hold again, measuring in her mind, then climbed back above and studied the visible size of the vessel.

The hold matched the deck.

Rowan walked to starboard, back to port, back again. The boat did respond by rocking, but not as easily or quickly as it ought.

"Something lashed to the keel?" she wondered aloud.

This time she did look about; no one was visible nearby. She stripped, then eased herself over the gunwale and into the water. She took a breath and dove.

She came up almost immediately, gasping, deeply regretting her action. The salt water was like fire pouring into the three long scratches the demon had left. Clutching a porthole cowling with her fingers, she waited, jaws clenched, until the pain subsided.

When it did, she dove again. She resurfaced, steadied herself with one hand on the cowling, used the other to confirm what she had seen.

The hull was not bare wood. There were strips, like tin—but tin would quickly corrode in seawater. Tacks held the strips in place. No gleam of metal showed through the water. Rowan's delicately searching fingers found the place underwater where the black paint of the hull ended, leaving metal bare further down, out of view of the casual eye.

The paint continued above the waterline, for about a foot. Rowan scraped at it with her fingernail.

Copper. The hull was sheathed in copper.

The steerswoman clambered back aboard awkwardly, and lay in the sunlight beside the tiller to dry and to think.

So much copper must have been expensive. It seemed an extravagance. But Janus lived on the edge of poverty. Therefore, it was a necessity. Rowan felt eyes on her. She sat up, turned.

A boy, perhaps four years old, sat on the edge of an adjacent houseboat, studying her with deep curiosity and a degree of astonishment. Rowan felt it rather misplaced: he was as naked as she, and as wet. Possibly he was startled by the appearance of the demon scratches. "Have you been swimming?" she asked him casually. "It's a lovely day for it." She squeezed water from her hair, shook her fingers.

"Yes," he replied, and watched as she stood to dress. He knit his brows. "I think you lost something."

Rowan stopped to consider. "No," she informed him, "that's how I'm constructed." She resumed dressing. "Does your mother never swim naked?"

"My mother never does anything naked."

He was not at all intimidated by her; perhaps he was too young to have been among the tricksters she had frightened. "Do you know the man who owns this boat?" Rowan left her sandals off, and found a seat on the gunwale, opposite the boy.

He scanned her, seeming to compare her previous appearance with her present. "Janus. He's nice. But he likes that scary woman. He brings her here sometimes."

"Scary woman?"

He demonstrated by screwing up one side of his mouth and using his fingers to push his nose toward his ear, and making noises of disgust.

"That's not fair," Rowan said. "Maysie can't help how she looks. How would you feel if something bad happened to you and people didn't like you anymore, even though it wasn't your fault?"

The issue was too complex for him. He gave up the effort and set to winding his bare legs in a complex configuration in and around the gap-spaced uprights of his boat's railing, one leg in each direction. "I can do this," he said, half surprised himself.

"So I see," Rowan replied. An interesting possibility came to her. "Does Janus talk to you very much?"

"Sometimes." He was suddenly caught by a happy memory. "Oh, oh!" he exclaimed, unwinding his legs. "One time we flew kites, Janus and me, they went way, way up!"

She smiled. "They must have been very good kites."

"We flew them from that hill." He leaned far over the railing to indicate. "I was going to let mine fly loose and fly away, but Janus said, he said a kite can't fly without a string, it'll just fall right down. He told me all about it."

Apparently some steerswomen's impulses had not left Janus. "That's very true," Rowan said. "What other things has he told you?"

The boy missed the change of direction. "And then he cried," he said nonchalantly and began to amuse himself peeling splinters from the railing.

Rowan was taken aback, uncertain that she had heard correctly. "Did you say that he cried?"

"Yes." Peeling splinters became a deeply absorbing occupation.

"While you were flying kites?" The event made no sense to her.

Exasperation. "Yes. I *said*. We flew the kites, and they went way up, and we were laughing, and then he cried."

"Did he tell you why? Did you ask him?"

Another nod. "He gave me a big hug, like my dad does when he's been away." He squirmed a bit, uncomfortable at the memory; perhaps he found it as confusing as she. Then he brightened. "Then we went and got some biscuits. There were a lot of them. I ate the most." He began to eye her with sudden speculation.

"But didn't he say why he was crying?"

"He wasn't anymore. When we got the biscuits."

"But earlier, when he was crying, didn't he explain?"

"He said it was nice. Everything was nice. Are you going by the baker? I could go put on my clothes now."

Rowan persisted. "What exactly was nice?" And she added, "I think I might go by the baker's in a little while. What kind of things did Janus say were nice?"

Gluttony spurred his memory. "He said, 'Look how beautiful. See how pretty the town is?' Something about all the people, how good it is here. And he liked the boats, they were all sailing away to places, and that was—that was—Janus said it was brave and good. And he said I was a good boy, and I should grow up and get married and have lots of babies and play with them. Belinda has two babies, but she's not married."

This last was his own contribution. "Perhaps she hasn't met a good boy."

"She's met me. But I won't marry her. I don't like *those* babies." He undraped himself from the railing. "Let's just go and see about those biscuits, then, shall we?" The statement was incongruously serious and precise, and was obviously copied from some adult, perhaps Janus himself.

She could not help laughing. "That's a good idea." And he thumped off to get dressed.

She rose and slipped on her sandals. The falling sun glaring on the water made her shade her eyes, to view the world through her slitted fingers. She sighted Steffie at the foot of New High Street; he waved at her once, then ambled off.

This was the signal that he had spotted the day workers returning to their homes; Rowan jumped back to the wharf and strolled toward Harbor Road. The little boy, clad and shod, stamped up to join her and took her hand with utter trust.

She did owe him biscuits.

17

At the bakery, young Anna dealt with her fear of the terrible steerswoman by fleeing out the back door the instant Rowan and the boy entered. Rowan collected a dozen assorted biscuits, counted out the precise amount of change from the abandoned till, and sent the boy on his way with biscuits in both fists and more bulging his pockets.

She had managed to hold on to two. She handed one to Steffie, and they sat on the bench by the door. "Don't know about boats," Steffie said, after she had described her findings on Janus's vessel.

"A copper-sheathed hull is not usual."

"Wouldn't it last longer, just generally? I thought salt water makes things rot." He bit the biscuit, made a face; they were not the freshest.

"Yes. That's why we paint boats. With maintenance, paint is sufficient. Perhaps . . ." But no. "That wouldn't work."

"What?"

They waited as a small group of people passed by on their way home to dinner. "Demons require water with a different kind of salt than is found in the Inland Sea," Rowan said when they had gone. "Perhaps that sort of salt would cause more damage to a hull—but if Janus is using his boat to sail to wherever he goes, then it must be someplace contiguous to the Inland Sea. It's not possible for seawater to maintain a different composition in only one place."

"Why not? Oh. Waves and things. It'd all mix up."

"That's right. If the demons need different water, then that water must somehow be separated from the sea. And Janus could not sail there."

"And he can't haul his boat across land to some lake or other."

"No. Not by himself. Not by any normal means." A part of her mind had been taking note of a series of quiet crunches and rustles; it now found reason to direct her full attention to the little noises. Rowan combined the audible clues with a little simple reasoning.

She pitched her voice slightly louder. "If you want to take part in this conversation, you'll find it much easier if you come to the front of the building, Gwen."

Gwen emerged from behind the corner. Her grin showed no trace of embarrassment. "You're hard to sneak up on."

Rowan said coolly, "It's generally not wise to make the attempt."

"Well." Gwen shrugged, tossed her head. "Just did it for a lark, really. Needed to find you, anyway. Corey wants you."

"It's not a demon?" Steffie was already on his feet.

"No," Gwen replied. "But if it was, what you should do is go the other way!"

"It's not like I go looking for 'em."

"Oh, yes, it is—"

Rowan interposed herself. "What," she said, "does Corey want with me?"

Gwen looked her up and down. "There's someone asking for the steerswoman. Corey figures that means either you or Mira, so he sent me to get you."

"Why you?" Steffie wondered.

" 'Cause I saw the stranger first. We were out in Lasker's north field, hard at work, and I spotted her across Sandy's Dell. And where were you all day?"

"Helping the steerswoman. She got hurt, if you remember, killing a demon, if you haven't forgot, saving your neck and everybody else's, just thought I'd remind you—"

"The stranger is a woman?" Rowan asked.

"From a distance, seems to be," Gwen said. "Barbarian, by her outfit. Militia won't let her pass, and she won't let them near her—"

By the time Rowan reached the dell, Steffie had nearly caught up to her.

She found Corey and three of the militia grouped together in rather an admirable array: two pike bearers, weapons braced against the ground, down on one knee; standing tall above them, with bow raised and arrow nocked above their heads, the archer Lilly; and Corey to one side, his own pike held at the center and balanced. A small, efficient configuration.

The focus of all this defensive might was a single figure, standing knee-deep in timothy at the far end of the dell, her back against the forest. Her sword was ready in her hand, her legs were planted wide, and she seemed prepared to fight all comers. She wore high, shaggy boots, leather leggings, a rough woolen vest, a cloak patchworked in goatskin: the garments of an Outskirter—

But it was not Bel.

Rowan recognized the fact immediately, from the woman's stance, her height, her color. The steerswoman's disappointment was so deep that for a moment she could do nothing but stand and wait for it to pass.

Steffie arrived at her side, noted her expression, made no comment.

Corey backed up to join them, keeping a sharp eye on the Outskirter. "Wants to get to the harbor, she says. And something about a steerswoman. Hard to talk clear, at this distance. I won't let her near with her weapon out."

"She won't sheathe it." Some shift in the warrior's stance made her sword flash, once, in the light. "I can't imagine Mira having contact with the Outskirters. If she wants a steerswoman, it must be me."

Corey regarded her with a trace of skepticism; then seemed to reach a decision and nodded. "Right. What do we do?"

"You might lower the pikes to a less threatening angle . . . other than that, nothing. I have to do it." And she walked past the defenders, out into the dell, wading through the timothy.

Some fifteen feet away from the warrior, Rowan stopped. Blue eyes under a tangle of blond hair watched her warily. With careful slowness, the steerswoman drew her sword and stood with its flat resting on her left forearm.

The warrior's gaze narrowed, but she remained in battle stance. This was proper neither for a friendly warrior approaching an Inner Lands village, nor for an Outskirter approaching a strange tribe. Rowan suspected that the woman had attempted both methods already, and had been met with only incomprehension and hostility. The steerswoman hoped to reassure her with purely Outskirter protocol.

Etiquette required that Rowan warn of any possible threat nearby. The steerswoman gave a small smile. "Five very nervous townfolk, at twelve by you," she said, using Outskirter orientation.

The narrowed gaze relaxed a bit toward amusement. "Warrior at ten by you." The woman had a comrade nearby, watching from the forest.

"You mentioned a steerswoman. Could that be me?"

The woman shifted a bit, a thoughtful weaving motion not much different from Bel's own habit. Then she reached a decision, relaxed her stance, stooped once to place her sword on the ground before her feet, and stood before the steerswoman unarmed and trusting. "I was given something and told to take it to the harbor here. I was to find a sailing ship going to a place called Southport, and the people on the ship would bring the object to a steerswoman there, named Rowan."

"I am Rowan."

The Outskirter's mouth twitched. "This isn't Southport."

"I was on my way there and got delayed. You can give what you have to me, in person."

"Can you prove who you are?"

"I can give you three names," Rowan replied, "three names I believe are known to you."

The warrior nodded. "And the first of those names will be 'Bel.' "

"Yes. I'll give you the others, but I'd like to step closer." Outskirters guarded their second and third names carefully. Knowledge of a warrior's three names was confirmation of connection, and that person's tribe would be duty bound to render assistance.

But Bel's own names meant far more. They would soon become a password among all the Outskirter tribes. And the time was not right to give that password to the Inner Lands folk.

Instead of waiting for a reply, Rowan placed her own sword on the ground and stepped over it to approach the woman: also not strictly according to form, but the level of trust implied was so great that the warrior immediately stepped forward herself. The two women met in the center, both their weapons completely out of reach.

Rowan said quietly, "Bel, Margasdotter, Chanly."

"This is yours." The object was already in the warrior's hand, and she passed it to Rowan.

A rolled goatskin, bound with thongs. Rowan untied the thongs immediately. The skin fell open. She held it spread and found on its smoother side a message, written with blue ink in letters childishly large:

> Ive don what I can and things wil move with out me for a wile. Im coming to meet you in South Port. Stay wher you are or I wont find you.

Then, lest there be some confusion on the point:

> This is from Bel.

A final line was added at the bottom of the skin, apparently a last-minute recognition of contingency:

> Or leve a message.

Rowan discovered that she was laughing out loud, and managed to restrain herself from embracing the messenger. "It's from Bel!" she said fool-
ishly, waving the goatskin at the woman. After so long apart, even this
symbolic contact with her long-time traveling companion filled Rowan
with relief and joy. She could hear Bel's voice in the words; the letters
were written in Bel's own hand . . .

The messenger watched her with the sort of fond amusement that
showed she had herself, at some time in the past, experienced a similar
emotion. "Have you seen Bel?" Rowan asked her. "Is she well?"

The woman's eyes widened slightly. "I've never seen her. This thing
has been passed from tribe to tribe, the way Bel's tale is being passed."
She went on, a shade hesitantly. "And you're the steerswoman in the
tale."

Rowan detected a trace of incipient awe in her tone. Bel was apparently on her way to acquiring mythic proportions among the Outskirters
and, by association, so was Rowan. She grinned uncomfortably; spoke as
casually as possible. "That's me."

The woman glanced past Rowan's shoulder at the pikes and the
nocked arrow. "Bel says that the wizard Slado will force my people to fight
yours and that what we need to do instead is all of us join to fight Slado
and his wizards, together."

"That's right."

"But you don't trust your own people."

Rowan winced. "No. Not yet. They don't yet understand." She rolled
the goatskin.

"If Bel comes to speak to them, they will." Utter confidence.

Bel's tale was cast as an epic poem, set in a form Outskirters used only
for true tales. The truth of it, the language and form used, and the specific
emotions addressed combined to stirring, compelling effect—to other
Outskirters. Rowan doubted that it would similarly move Inner Landers.
"I think that that job may fall to the Steerswomen."

After further conversation, the warrior declined Rowan's offer of shelter
for the night; and the two women parted, one to the forest, one to the
groves.

"A message from a friend," Rowan called out as she neared the militia.
She held up the goatskin.

Steffie was intensely interested. "From that one you mentioned, that
Bel?" he asked when she arrived.

"Yes." She passed him the skin; he opened it, peered at the words. "She's on her way here," Rowan informed Corey. "Let's try to be a little more hospitable when she arrives, shall we? I wouldn't like Alemeth to gain a bad reputation among travelers."

"When will she get here?" Steffie asked.

"Well. That's the problem," Rowan said. "Travel through the Outskirts doesn't have regular shipping routes or times, as sea travel does. And there are any number of possible events that could delay her. From what the warrior told me, Bel could show up tomorrow; she could arrive a month from now. All I know is that she is coming."

"What, another barbarian?" This from one of the pike bearers.

"Yes," Rowan said carefully, "I do have friends among the Outskirters . . ."

"They're killers, all of them."

"They live in a dangerous country. If you need to use violence to survive, then you use it. As perhaps you have noticed lately."

The pikeman looked off to one side. "Well, never did need it much, until you came along—"

"Here!" Corey stopped him. "All of you off and back to work, now. Whole thing's over."

They dispersed with reluctance. Lilly paused before leaving. "Shouldn't we set some sort of guard?" she asked Corey. "That one might come back and kill us in our sleep."

Rowan spoke up. "Had she wanted to do that, she would have done it last night and not given you even this much warning. She merely came to deliver the message."

"Outskirters attacked the town once," Lilly said, turning a flat gaze on her. "My gran said."

"Not the same sort of Outskirter," was all Rowan said.

"Oh?" The syllable spoke volumes.

"Yes."

Corey stepped between them. "Rowan knows about Outskirters—she just showed us that. Now, she's been helping us with these demons, so I'm ready to take her word on this, too. And if you're not, then your memory's not so good, is it?"

Lilly shifted her glare to Corey. "You're only my boss when there's trouble. Rest of the time, you just work with the worms, same as me."

"Well, that's good. 'Cause it's when there's trouble that you need someone doing your thinking for you. So go take care of Lasker's worms, and I'll go take care of Karin's, and we'll both be doing what we should."

Lilly departed with ill grace. The steerswoman watched her out of sight.

"Rowan." She turned back. Corey managed to look both determined and uncomfortable. "All I need to know about you," he said, "I already seen. You protect. That's the thing I care about. Wouldn't have this job if I didn't; the extra pay's not big enough to matter.

"But it's the *only* thing I care about. Now, I'll keep an eye out for your barbarian friend, and no one'll shoot her soon as they see her. But if I should find out that you've invited trouble in for dinner, then you can be sure that it's trouble you'll get on your own self. Just thought I'd say that. Just in case."

"Perhaps you should be saying that to Janus."

"Well, maybe I'll do exactly that. 'Cause it's something everybody ought to keep in mind." And he left them.

"Didn't like that much," Steffie commented, when Corey was out of earshot.

"Nor did I." They went down the dusty path between Karin's and Lasker's fields. "But I can't blame Corey . . . although I rather wish I could. Just for someone to be mad at."

He made an amused noise. "Not fair, is that? Everybody else gets to be mad for whatever reason they like, but a steerswoman's stuck with just the truth. But I didn't mean Corey. Nor Lilly—she's a good shot, but she's not what you'd call clever. I meant Kylan."

She thought. "Do you mean that pike bearer who spoke?"

"That's him. What he said, it sounded like . . . like he was just about to go down a road, so to speak, that would get him to a wrong place."

As usual, she found Steffie's use of language both awkward and apt. "Yes. One more step and he would have been blaming me for the demons."

They reached the end of the path, where it joined Old High Street. It was past dinnertime, and the day was dimming; light from Karin's second shed leaked out in stripes from gaps in the siding.

No one was in sight. Rowan stopped and turned to Steffie. "You've lived here all your life, Steffie, so you tell me: How likely is it that the general populace will rise up in a group and run me out of town?"

The question did not inspire immediate protest; but his face scrunched into an immense wince, and he stood shifting his shoulders in frustration. "Rowan, *I* don't know. Everyone's different. I'd have to add up everybody in town, and everything I know about every one of them . . ."

"Well, go ahead and do that. I'm in no particular hurry."

His head moved as if he were literally adding figures. "No," he said at last. "No, they wouldn't. They'd have to be all thinking the same wrong thing, all at the same time. See, one by one, none of them's smart as a steerswoman; but if you put them all together, then the really stupid ideas sort of fall out the bottom, and the ideas that make sense sort of clump in the middle where everyone can look at 'em. So, the wrong thing would have to look like the right thing to most of the people doing the looking, and it can't, because it's the wrong thing. So, they wouldn't. Run you out of town. Unless more things happened to make the wrong thing look right. To most of the people. Or if the people with the stupid ideas made a lot of noise and kept putting the stupid ideas back at the top, 'cause it takes a while for them to fall out the bottom—it doesn't happen straight off, and in the meantime . . ." He stopped, a pained look on his face. "That's as far as I can go with that. Right there in the middle of me talking, the whole thing fell right apart. I guess it didn't make any sense . . ."

"On the contrary," Rowan said, bemused. "It made perfect sense. I'm very impressed."

"Well . . ." They continued down the path. "It's a good thing I stopped when I did. My head was going to bust like a chestnut."

"We wouldn't want that to happen. I'd hate to have your demise on my hands. It might be the very thing that tips the scales."

"Oh, sure." He scuffed the dirt a bit as he walked. "Everybody loves Steffie."

As they were about to part ways, she to the Annex and he to his home, he spoke again.

"That Outskirter friend of yours . . . if you know she's coming, and she's not too far away, maybe it'd make sense for you to go out and meet her halfway? Bring her right into town yourself?"

She recalled that not so long ago, this was exactly what she had most wanted to do. "And while I'm gone, all the stupid ideas would have time to fall out of the bottom?"

It embarrassed him to be seen through so easily. "Well, yes."

"No, Steffie, I won't run away."

He nodded. "Right. Didn't really think so."

18

Searching for information on demons was far easier than searching for clues of Slado's whereabouts. With *quadrilateral*, *demon*,
and *monster* held in her mind, the steerswoman moved through volume
after volume, in whatever order they came to her hand, stopping only
when her eyes and mind required rest from the dizzying speed at which
she scanned.

She soon found an entry, from over six hundred years earlier: a steerswoman, recording the experiences of two women who hunted in an area
east of Lake Cerlew. The hunters had been keeping a sharp eye out for
goblins, which were not uncommon in that area in those days, had from a
distance sighted a goblin jack guarding an egg cache, and had watched from
hiding while the jack was attacked and consumed by a group of eight creatures: headless, eyeless, and quadrilaterally symmetrical.

From this, Rowan learned that demons, which the Outskirters
knew as solitary animals, could move in packs. She wondered if Janus
knew this.

When she heard the door open, she recognized Steffie immediately by
the sound of the latch. She did not turn. "I'm beginning to think you're
using me as an excuse to avoid the worms."

"Not expecting another package, are you?"

Then she did turn. He stood holding the door ajar behind him. "No,"
she said. He opened the door wide.

A brown and gray bundle lay on the doorstep. "What is that?" She approached, book still in her hand.

"Not *what*, I reckon, but *who*?"

It was a child: ragged, filthy, damp with dew, and fast asleep. "Do you
recognize—" Rowan could not determine the gender—"it?"

Steffie pursed his lips, shook his head. "New to me."

Rowan thought to wake it, but found herself reluctant to approach
close enough to do so, due to a truly astonishing stench that surrounded

the child. Wrinkling his nose, Steffie stretched one leg to cautiously prod the ragged backside with his foot.

The child stirred in annoyance, mumbled a series of syllables consisting largely of "yar," "gar," and "er," pulled into a tight knot, continued to sleep.

"What's that it's got, then?"

"It looks like a jar." Plain brown fired clay with a lid; the child lay curled around it.

Holding her breath, Rowan leaned down to shake the child's shoulder, eliciting the same response as Steffie's attempt. Noting the position in which the child slept, the steerswoman gently nudged the jar.

"Gerroff!" The child came instantly awake, snarling, arms and knees wrapped protectively around the object; then glared up at Rowan and Steffie in turn, settled on Rowan. "Where's the money?"

Rowan lifted her brows. "Excuse me?"

"You that one, that steerswoman?"

"Yes . . ."

The child raised the jar at her. "I heard. You said. It's alive and all. I want my money."

Rowan searched her memory, and eventually recovered the information. "Of course!" It had been so long ago, and the event so minor, with too much else occupying her attention since. "You have one of those green moths!" Steffie's face was a knot of confusion. "I promised a coin to whichever child brought me one first, alive," Rowan reminded him. She turned back to the child. "Thank you. I'll just take it and fetch you that coin . . ." She reached out for the jar.

It was snatched back, and its owner turned a squinting glare on her. "I want the pot back."

"Very well." And because she could see no way around it: "Come inside."

The child followed them in, carrying its remarkable odor with it. Steffie glanced about the room with a pained expression, as if fearing that the smell would leave a visible coating on the walls and furniture.

Rowan took a coin from the dwindling supply in Mira's money jar, and hesitated before handing it over, eyeing the child.

Far too thin. "Would you like some food?"

Hope, and suspicion. "I still need the pot back."

"Of course."

Rowan passed the coin over, then brought smoked eel and bread from the pantry. The child set on the food with speed and concentration, as if expecting it to be snatched away again. "I assume you have a name," Rowan said.

"Gebby." Spoken through a greasy mouthful.

No clue there as to gender. Steffie was less tactful. "Are you a boy or a girl?"

"Girl." Gebby grinned gappy eel-flecked teeth at him. "Wanna try me?" The idea set Steffie sputtering incoherently, causing the girl to emit a series of harsh, barking laughs.

The sound was both unpleasant and oddly familiar; Rowan puzzled. "How old are you?"

"Fourteen." A glower. "I'm scrawny."

Rowan was taken aback. "So you are." A more accurate term would have been *stunted*: Rowan had assumed her to be around nine. "Try not to choke on a bone, please." Gebby apparently intended to let not a scrap of food escape her, and was already sucking industriously at a segment of backbone.

"Nar," she said. Although decipherable in context, this was not a negative that Rowan had ever heard used in actual conversation.

The steerswoman picked up the jar, inspiring a quick glance of suspicion. "I'll just take this outside for a moment," Rowan said. "I'll bring it back."

A grunt, and increased concentration on the food.

Rowan carried the jar out the back door, leaving Steffie torn between following to watch or remaining to guard the Annex against their unpleasant visitor. The steerswoman assisted him by leaving the door open. She sat down on the steps, studied the heft and size of the jar; then, holding the lid in place with one hand, she inverted it.

Steffie came to stand just inside the door. "You going to take it apart, like the demon?"

"I'd like to examine it alive first." Rowan shook the jar vigorously, then let the lid drop into her lap, swiftly replacing it with her left hand. She inverted the jar again, her hand now on top, covering the opening.

"Now, it should come up . . ." The light leaking between her fingers would attract it. Rowan waited, and presently felt tickling grips on her palm. "Good." With one hand on top and the other on the bottom, she began moving the jar in tight, quick circles.

Steffie's expression at this peculiar behavior made her laugh out loud. "I'm making it dizzy," she explained.

"Dizzy?"

"Yes." She continued the circling. "If you were dizzy, what would you do?"

"Nothing much. Until I stopped being dizzy." He caught the idea, was impressed. "Steerswomen teach you that?"

"Actually," Rowan said, remembering a moment of youthful pride, "I taught it to them. Apparently, in eight hundred years of recorded history, no one else had ever thought of it." After sufficient time, she inverted the whole arrangement once again, her left hand on the bottom, and smoothly lifted the jar with her right.

"Oh . . ."

The little creature stood desperately clutching her fingers, showing no interest whatsoever in escape. Tall wings were held vertically in a curious crossing configuration; slowly and experimentally, the insect spread them flat.

But all anticipation of pleasant study had already vanished from Rowan's thoughts. "I don't like this . . ."

"But it's so beautiful!"

It certainly was. Wingspan was nearly four inches across; wings and body were both a vivid, rich green, veined with blue. The abdomen featured horizontal stripes, of a green so pale as to be translucent. Two rows of eyes glittered ruby red.

"Have you never seen one before?"

"No. Not close up."

"You never painted yourself with moth juice when you were young?"

He shook his head. "Didn't have 'em back then."

"They're recent? That is very interesting." The steerswoman raised her hand to peer under the wings. "Four legs."

"Lost a couple?"

"No." Most insects had six legs attached to the thorax; this one's thorax was in two distinct segments, two legs and two wing sections to each.

The moth began to roam, and Rowan turned her hand to watch its progress, noting the jointing and the action of its legs. When it clambered over her fingertips, she was suddenly face-to-face with it, some five inches apart.

Six eyes in a double row down its head; mouth at the end of a pointed chin, with four tiny rasps at each corner—the face of a goblin, in miniature, so nearly perfect that Rowan jerked back reflexively. At the action the moth sprang away from her hand, fluttered about her head three times, then flew away over the roof.

Rowan watched it go, deeply disturbed. Then she gathered up jar and lid, rose, and quickly brushed past a startled Steffie and back into the Annex.

Gebby was using her teeth to scrape the fat from the inside of the eel skin. Rowan slowly sat down across from her and watched.

Small stature; dull, rough skin; brittle-looking hair; so thin and wiry as to seem almost wizened. Gebby noticed her scrutiny, spared her a sneer. Rowan said, "Do this," and bared her teeth at the girl. Gebby did so, with a will. Rowan noted the spacing, the unevenness.

"Guess you'll rec'nize me next time," the girl grumbled, tearing fistfuls of bread to sop up the grease on her plate.

Rowan leaned back. "I believe I recognize you already."

"Never seen you before."

"Nor I you. But I think I know your type. Where did you come from?"

"Har. Out a' the dark, same's you. Out a' the dark, inta the dark, here we come, there we go."

"Very colorful. I mean, where did you come from recently? Where do you live?"

The girl stopped short, eyes wide. "I gotta go." She stuffed the heel of the bread down her shirt, rose, reached. "Gimme the pot." When Rowan did not relinquish it immediately, she became outraged. "You said!"

"It's a very simple question."

"That's a steerswoman," Steffie said sternly. "You should answer a steerswoman. Or she won't ever answer your own questions."

"Only question I got, if I bring another them bugs, I get more money?"

"No. But I'm very interested in other information that I think you have."

"Bet you are. Be my hide if I tell."

"Really? Merely for telling me where you live? And who exactly is it who would take it out of your hide?"

"My boss. Pro'ly kill me straight off. Easier."

"Well." Rowan folded her hands. "We certainly wouldn't want that to happen, would we?"

"Har. No skin off your arse. Keep the pot." Gebby made for the door, but Steffie was faster. Finding her escape blocked, the girl spun, threw a wild glance at the back door, seemed to decide it was too far to make a break, and turned back to the steerswoman with a face of such absolute terror that Rowan was instantly, deeply regretful.

"No one here is going to hurt you," Rowan said, shocked.

Barely audible: "Says you." Gebby stood huddled into herself.

Steffie's puzzled glance requested instruction. Rowan indicated that he should stay in place; then she returned to the pantry, found some scraps of smoked beef, the last of the bread, nearly stale, some butter and jam. She brought all out and laid them on the table.

Gebby watched, her expression altering only subtly; but she swallowed several times.

While not stupid, the girl was certainly deeply ignorant, despite the age she claimed. Rowan was convinced that she did not properly understand the nature of the steerswomen's ban. The principles allowed leeway in such situations, and Rowan declined to apply the ban for Gebby's earlier refusal to answer.

Instead, she sat down, cut a slice of bread, began buttering it. "I definitely do not want to get you in trouble with your boss." Especially as Gebby's appearance and behavior implied harsh treatment in the past. "So I'm going to ask my questions very carefully." She added a thick layer of raspberry jam to the bread. "When I think that what I'm about to ask is something you won't want to answer, I'll say it differently or try a different question."

Whether Gebby followed the logic of this was unclear, but she watched each of Rowan's actions with a deepening interest, swallowing more and more frequently. "But you still won't let me go . . ."

"On the contrary." Rowan waved one hand; Steffie stepped away from the door. "You're perfectly free to leave any time you like." She crunched into the bread. Jam dripped on her fingers; she licked it off.

Gebby was instantly back at the table; Rowan passed her the bread. "I think you don't get enough to eat," she commented.

"Never."

The slice was gone. Rowan prepared another. "And I'll bet the food isn't very good, either. And no fresh vegetables."

"Nothing's fresh. Dried and smoked. Gotta last."

Rowan handed over the slice. "And rationed." Gebby's glance told that the word was not familiar to her. "Counted out, bit by bit."

"Got to. Run out if I don't." But this would only account for Gebby's thinness and not the other signs Rowan noted.

The steerswoman found paper and charcoal, brought them over, began sketching. Steffie came near to watch. "If I were to ask you if you've ever seen this plant, would you worry about answering me?"

The girl looked, shook her head. "Never seen it."

Rowan tried again. "This?"

"That's twister-grass. Can I have more?" Steffie took over the serving duties.

"We call it blackgrass," Rowan told the girl. She drew another. "And this? It's blue."

"Grows along under the twister-grass."

Interesting. "All along or just here and there?"

"All under. Dig a hole, find even more, deep down."

Another sketch. "What about this?"

"Huh. That's a rock."

"With this inside it . . ."

Recognition. "Them's bad. Step on 'em, they break and slice you up. See?" She thumped her right foot up onto the table top; caked grime crumbled. Steffie huffed a stifled protest and stepped back, driven by outrage and stink.

The steerswoman found the smell irrelevant. She leaned forward to examine the instep, which was the cleanest part of the foot; then she nodded slowly and laid her own left hand beside it. Foot and hand bore nearly identical collections of small, white scars.

Gebby gaped a mouthful of half-chewed bread and jam. "You *been* there!"

"I believe I've been some place very much like it." Rowan sat back. "Steffie, you were interested in my Outskirts tales. Well, take a good look. We're talking to a Face Person."

Gebby did not recognize the term; Steffie had to think long to recover it. "Face People . . . Those ones that live far out, way past the Outskirters?"

"That's right. Most of the plant life out on the Face is poisonous to humans. Not immediately but cumulatively. Daily contact, year after year"—and she gestured at Gebby—"results in this."

Steffie stared at the girl in frank amazement. "How'd she come so far by herself?" Gebby returned his regard with squinting hostility.

"Unfortunately, I suspect she did not have to travel far at all." The girl's pronunciation and speech patterns were degenerated alterations on the typical Alemeth accent. "She's lived nearby for most of her life."

Plant life native to the Outskirts and the Face was more vigorous and aggressive than Inner Lands forms, and typically would overcome it; but Gebby's condition spoke of years of contact. If Outskirts life-forms did exist so near Alemeth, all green life should have been completely driven out by now, unless— "An island," Rowan said. Gebby stopped chewing. "Off the shipping lanes," or it would have been sighted and charted long ago, "due south or southeast of Alemeth. And probably quite small," or passing fishing boats would have come across it at some point, and Gebby's concern about protecting the location would be meaningless.

Gebby regarded Rowan as if the process used to discover this information had been wholly magical. "I din't tell you," she said, slowly. "Din't tell nothing 'bout no island."

Rowan pushed the plate of beef across to her. The girl picked one slice up cautiously but did not eat. "Of course not," Rowan said. "You can tell your employer that with perfect honesty." She phrased her next statements carefully, again, more interested in reaction than answer. "I'm very interested in the comings and goings of a man named Janus. Anything you can tell me would be helpful."

"Don't know him."

The reply was immediate and casually delivered; the girl was telling the truth. Very well. "I assume you arrived here in a boat of some kind . . ." She could not come up with a useful circumlocution, so she asked outright, "Does the boat have a copper hull?"

"Huh?"

"Under the waterline. Is the boat plain wood below, or is there something covering the hull?"

"Dunno what you mean."

"Very well. One more picture." This time Rowan took her logbook, flipped to the appropriate page. "Look at this."

Gebby tilted her head. "Wossit, a tree?"

"No, it's an animal."

"Huh. Where's its head?"

"It hasn't got one."

"Never seen it." Gebby began on the beef slice, chewing thoughtfully.

Disappointing—but still, a pocket of Outskirts life, right on the Inland Sea . . . and the fact that Gebby did not know Janus did not rule out his visiting the island in secret . . .

The steerswoman needed to see for herself. She must visit Gebby's island.

If Rowan left now, the entire town would assume that she had been a false steerswoman, a trickster and confidence artist.

But the demons were coming from somewhere. The fact that Gebby did not recognize the drawing meant little. The creatures might breed in a secluded part of the island, in a pocket of the proper salt water; they might not be dangerous until grown; they might be instinctively impelled to leave when they matured—they might be able to survive immersion in the waters of the Inland Sea long enough to reach Alemeth.

And if Gebby's island was the only source of demons, then it could be possible to eliminate the creatures entirely. It would be a hazardous affair, certainly, but with enough help, depending upon what Rowan found . . .

She really did need to go there.

Rowan gritted her teeth. People would assume that she had run—

But, she thought, but—she had refused to allow their misconceptions to drive her from Alemeth; was it any more legitimate to allow them to keep her from leaving when she ought?

She was abruptly ashamed, and angry at herself for even considering the matter. She was a steerswoman; she would do exactly as steerswomen do, nothing more nor less.

But she did need Gebby's cooperation. And the girl was protecting something.

What, in Alemeth, required secrecy?

"Gebby, listen carefully." The steerswoman stressed the next words. "I am not in the least bit interested in spiders."

Steffie missed the connection. "What?" But Gebby sat slack, gaping astonishment.

"As far as I'm concerned," Rowan continued, "the spider-wife is welcome to keep her methods secret. But I do need to go to the island."

"You can't!"

"I think we should let—" Rowan tried to recall the spider-wife's name, realized that she had never heard it used—"your employer decide. Where is she now, do you know?"

"At the island. I got the boat. I get stuff, and go back."

"Then you'll just have to take me back with you."

"You show up, she'll kill you!"

Rowan wondered if this was literally true. No matter. "She won't be able to," she said simply.

"Then she'll kill me."

"I won't permit it."

"Then she'll throw me out."

"Considering the treatment you get, I don't understand why you stay with her at all."

" 'Cause I'm next. When she goes, *I'll* be the spider-wife." The scrawny girl's eyes glittered. "*I'll* have all the money and the soft clothes and the pretty house in town. People, they'll want to be nice to me, and they'll listen all polite when I talk. 'Cause I'll be the one does what nobody knows how. And—and anyone in the whole world, they want the spider cloth, it's *me* sells it to 'em. And they'll pay lots. And I'll brush my hair in a twist, and wear blue silk every day, and if I grow up ugly, it don't matter, 'cause all the boys will come calling anyway. Maybe you, even." This to Steffie.

He snorted. "Not me."

"I'll be rich."

"Then it's Maysie's boys'll be after you."

"Good. I like 'em pretty."

"Hope you plan to take a bath before then."

"I see you have your future all mapped out," Rowan said. "And I don't intend to jeopardize it. I'll stay away from the area where you work. I will not ask you about the methods you use." And this was hard for her to say—because now she *did* want to know: how such a thing as a spider could be coaxed to give up its silk, how the adhesiveness of the strands was neutralized, how anything so fine as spider silk could be handled and woven into cloth . . .

More urgent matters were at hand. She could forgo inquiries about spiders.

"All I plan to do," the steerswoman continued, "is examine the island itself, study the plants and animals, and see what sort of creatures other than spiders might live there. I'll stay out of your way. I'll bring my own food. If the island is very small, I may only need to stay for a few days." She neglected to mention that if demons were found, she would need to return with help.

Gebby remained stubborn. The girl shook her head. "You can't."

"At the very least, take me there and let me talk to— Gebby, what is the spider-wife's name?"

"Luwa." The girl pushed the plate away. "I won't." She rose.

"Haven't you heard what's been happening in town?" Rowan half rose, pushed the logbook toward the girl again, stabbed at the picture with her finger. "These animals, these demons, have been coming into Alemeth and hurting people and killing them—"

"Din't hear nothing. Don't talk to people. Luwa don't like me to."

"It's possible the creatures may come from your island—"

"I never *seen* 'em—"

"They may be hard to find when they're small, and they might not make any noise until they grow—"

"*Won't* do it, *won't* take you—"

"Don't you *care?*" Steffie said. The girl and the steerswoman both turned to him. "People hurt and dying—don't you care at all?"

Gebby thrust her chin forward. "Don't none of 'em ever care about me. Animals eat 'em, so what, I say."

By this statement, Gebby lost whatever right she had to Rowan's sympathy. "Very well." The steerswoman sat. "Since I know that the island exists, and the general area where it must be located, I'll simply have to mount my own search. With so much area to cover, I'll probably need assistance. Perhaps a number of the fishers might be willing to help."

Steffie caught the idea. "Oh, sure. 'Specially if you mention it's the spider-wife's place you're looking for. Bet you could get a whole fleet going."

"Yes, that would be efficient. Unfortunately, I doubt the fishers would be as considerate as I am, nor as able to control their curiosity. They'd likely be clambering over everything, poking everywhere."

"Maybe that wouldn't be so bad. Lot of people making spider cloth, spreading the money around. Might just try to go there myself."

"You can't!" Gebby was desperate. "That's *bad*. The spiders is *Luwa's* work, and *her* money, and we work hard, and you'd be taking it away, and that's not fair!"

"True. Under normal circumstances, it would be wrong of me. These are not normal circumstances."

Rowan closed her logbook, began gathering her pens and blank paper. "You have exactly two options," she went on. "Either dozens of people scour the seas, stumble on your island, and pry into every aspect of your work—or you take me there, I look for demons, and if I do not find them, I leave quietly. There are no other choices."

"And if lots of people go looking, who do you think Luwa will blame?" Steffie pointed out.

"She'll blame me either way."

"Then," the steerswoman said, "which would you rather have her blame you for?"

Gebby half grumbled, "Luwa was right. Talk to nobody you don't got to, she said. See where it got me? All for a bug."

"I need an answer."

The girl's entire body radiated hatred. "I'll take you. Let Luwa sort it out."

"Then I'll just get my pack."

Upstairs she loaded appropriate clothing into her pack, brought it back downstairs. In the main room, she retrieved her map case, rolled a collection of sea charts. "I'll need to get some provisions. I don't want to throw off your rationing. Where do you get your food?" The maps went into their case.

"Michael's. He's the only one knows about me and the island. He told me 'bout the bugs—look what that got me . . ."

"Then I'll use someone else; it's best no one connect us. Also, we shouldn't be seen together. I'll meet you at your boat. How will I know it?"

"Har. By the smell."

"Very well," Rowan said, bemused. "I'll go ahead now, and try to get myself aboard your boat without being observed. You come later."

Gebby seemed to be turning over in her mind various methods by which to circumvent Rowan's wishes. Apparently, nothing suited, and she gave up the effort. "You got a long wait. I got to buy things."

"Even better. A delay will help. People will be less likely to connect our departures." The steerswoman slid the map case down into her pack, tied down the flap.

"What should I tell people?" Steffie asked. "They'll ask where you've gone. I won't want to say about this island."

"That's true." Rowan considered. "Just say that I've gone looking for the source of the demons."

"You know what they'll think."

"I do." She shouldered her pack. "I'll deal with their misconceptions when I return."

"And when will that be?"

"Gebby, how long will it take to reach the island?" An inarticulate grumble from the girl. Rowan sighed. "I'll know the distance as soon as I arrive, there's no reason to hide it from me now."

"*He* don't need to know."

"Oh, very well. I'll get two weeks's worth of supplies. If I'm gone any longer, you'll just have to split your own rations with me." She turned back to Steffie. "I'm afraid I don't know how long it will be before you see me again . . ."

"Right." He stood before her, uncomfortable; then, to her surprise, he took her hand and shook it formally. "I'll keep an eye on the Annex for you, lady. And look out for that Outskirter friend of yours, too."

"Thank you." She laughed a bit. "Steffie, I *will* be coming back."

"Right." He released her hand, stepped back. "Of course you will. In a while. We just don't know when."

19

There were three kinds of books in the Annex, Steffie found out.

First, there were the ones that Rowan had mostly worked with; and those were the ones all bound alike, in dark red leather. They were all the same shape and mostly the same thickness, too. Except some of them were bound in green instead of red, and they were taller than the red ones. But he thought of them as the same as the red ones, because the green ones were like all the other green ones in the same way the red ones were like all the other red ones.

This stopped making sense when he thought about it too hard, but seemed to make a lot of sense when he didn't.

The second kind were all different sizes, and no one of them looked anything like any other one. Some were plain; but some were beautiful, bound in the kind of leather that your hand wanted to keep holding, all worked in with little twists and sometimes colors. He decided that they were all the same kind, being books-that-no-one-tried-to-make-look-like-each-other.

Basically, he just wanted to clear the stacks of books off the floor by the table, the ones he knew Rowan was done with. And the ones on the floor in the aisles. And as long as he was doing it, he'd like to do it in some kind of sensible way. Someone else could fix them right later.

So at first he figured that he'd put the either red or green ones all to-gether, and set aside all the really different ones. It seemed like a good place to start, since there were more red or greens than the other kind. And they also had names written on the spines, so he could put all the ones with the same name together, too.

And once he'd finished with the books on the floor, it seemed kind of natural to just keep going. Just putting all the names together and all the really different ones separate from the other kind.

Gave him something to do. Other than keep an eye on the Annex and an ear out for anything Janus was up to. Rowan had asked Steffie to sleep at the Annex, too, while she was gone. In case Bel came by.

But there he was, all night at the Annex, and no one to talk to, with Gwen still mad at him for siding with Rowan. So, he picked up a couple of books, put them on the shelves—and once he was doing it, no reason to stop, really.

It was funny. He could tell where Rowan had been before him: here and there, up and down, back and forth, there were places where all the red and greens with the same names were together already. He kept coming across them. It was like Rowan was a ghost, and he was following her footsteps.

He was doing that when he found the third kind of book, in one of the big boxes pushed back down at the end of the third and fourth aisles.

These books were even *more* different.

They were light in his hand, most of them. They were in rough shape, battered and dirty. Each of them had some kind of strap or string that tied them closed. The edges of the covers went far past the paper and even curled over, so that when the book was closed there were no paper edges showing anywhere. On a couple of them, the covers weren't stiff at all, so that the books drooped and tried to wrap themselves around his hand when he held them up.

The paper was thinner than what the other kinds of books used, and the writing was smaller—a lot smaller sometimes, especially toward the back of the book. It made the pages crowded and harder to read. One was even written through twice—once the normal way and once turned around sideways, with the words going across the other writing. It sent him cross-eyed to even try reading it.

He held one of them in his hand, trying to think where to put them, other than just off by themselves somewhere. And he'd have to lay them on their sides, because some of them looked like they wouldn't stand up too well.

And, sort of by itself, his hand put the one book up on a shelf, next to one of the green ones; and sure enough, it flopped right over. *Not made to stand up*, he thought.

His other hand picked up a green book. He looked at it. *Made to stand up. Made to sit on a shelf*.

Fair enough. Made sense. He put it back. He picked up the floppy book again—

And all of a sudden he'd sat himself right down on the floor, and he was looking at that book with his jaw dropped.

It shouldn't be here.

The Annex was not the place for books like this one.

All the red or green books were copies. That was why they were so all alike—so they would fit easy on shelves. And why they were written so neat—so they'd be easy to read. And why they were sturdy—so they could last a long time, hundreds of years, maybe. They could be all that because they happened *afterward*.

These other ones—he stopped to count them: nine of them—these were the *real* ones, the first ones, the ones other copies were made from. These were the very books steerswomen carried themselves, out on the road. So they were dirty and battered from being dragged around the world; and they were made light, to carry easy; and when the steerswomen got close to the end and they saw they had just a few pages left, they wrote smaller, to fit in more.

And they shouldn't be here. The Annex was a place you stored extra copies of things. These books were not extra anythings. They were one-and-onlys.

They should be in the Archives. The women there would make copies, and send those copies to keep here in the Annex.

They shouldn't be *here*! They just shouldn't, and there was no excuse for it—

—and somewhere out in the main room a woman's voice said, "*Who's a bloody stupid old cow?*"

Steffie sat still. Not Gwen's voice. He got up and looked around the end of the aisle.

Two people were there, one being Dan the cooper. He was shifting some things from a handbarrow that was stopped right outside the front door, to a place inside, next to the coat hooks.

And the other was a woman, standing in the middle of the room, looking at Steffie sort of tilt headed and sidelong. She was young and smallish and thin, with long black hair. Her skirt was long, all the way to the floor, which was longer than most people wore them in Alemeth, and she was using crutches to stand.

"What?" he asked her. If that was Bel, she didn't look much like Rowan said.

"You said that somebody was a bloody stupid old cow. I can't help wondering who? Not Gwen, I hope."

And how did she know Gwen? "No . . ." He came out of the aisle, feeling awkward and sort of shy with a stranger standing in the middle of a house he knew so well. He tried to figure how to explain why he'd said what he'd said, without it taking forever and a day to go through it all.

To start it off, he just held the old logbook up, and tilted his head toward the back of the aisle. "Found it back there . . ."

And he stopped right then, because she did, too, standing in the middle of the room with her eyes wide and her mouth open. And when she got past that, she said, like she really did mean it, "The bloody stupid old *cow*!" She swung herself at him, taking six thump and swings to get there. She put out her hand for the book; and when she took it, Steffie saw that her left hand had the twisty silver ring and there was a little gold chain around her throat—and there she was, another steerswoman.

Mira's replacement, he thought straight off—but no. She was young, a couple years older than him, maybe. "There's nine of them," he told her, "that I found so far, that is."

"Nine? That's insane. What can Mira have been thinking?" She riffled through the pages. "Where are the others? I'll have to pack them straight up and off to the Archives—" Then she stopped short and looked off into the air all of a sudden, like she'd heard something no one else could hear. "Dan!" she said—to Steffie, which made no sense that he could see. But then she did a neat little spin in place that brought her around the other way, crutches and all.

The cooper was still standing by the door, watching like he'd had a hod of bricks dropped on him. "It was really very kind of you to help me bring all my gear from the ship," the woman said to him, "and as soon as I can figure out where we keep the fixings, I'd be happy to get us some tea. Unless there's something better around." She looked at Steffie over her shoulder, needing to look up as she did it, being so small. "Is there anything better around?" Close up, her eyes were as black as her hair.

"The beer's from yesterday."

"Dan, the beer's from yesterday. Will tea do?"

Dan looked like he was having trouble keeping up with her. "Um, thank you all the same, lady, but I need to be getting back. It's gone pretty late, now; I need to close up things for the night." He got a little easier. "I was glad to help, lady, and I hope to see you again soon." He nodded a good-bye to Steffie and went out the door.

The steerswoman was nodding to herself. "Dinner," she said.

There was a little pause, and then Dan came back. "Excuse me?"

"You mentioned dinner. What was the name of that place, the Mizzen? Perhaps not tonight—I'm really too tired—but tomorrow night? I'll see you there?" And Steffie had to smile: *One step ahead of you.*

Dan was taken aback. "Yes, but . . . I'm thinking, Brewer's is just around the corner, and that'd be easier for you to get to, if you take my meaning."

She smiled a long smile. "Of course. Tomorrow, then."

Dan left, and the woman pegged herself over to the chairs by the hearth. "I am exhausted." She dropped into the wicker chair, then gave the room a once-over. "This is nowhere near as bad as I thought it would be." She set her crutches aside.

"Lot of work been done." And he figured he had the right to ask: "Do I get to know who you are?"

And she laughed. "I'm sorry. I'm Zenna. And you're Steffie, and Gwen is probably around here somewhere."

"Well, no." Gwen was still acting all huffy with him. But she was starting to get over it, with Rowan two days gone. Probably get huffy again when Rowan got back. Everyone was thinking Rowan had gone for good, and he wasn't telling them different. "Are you looking for Rowan? 'Cause she's not here."

"Dan mentioned something about it. I'm not surprised."

"Right." He felt a bit funny, her showing up here with him in charge, in a way. But she'd just got into town, and she already knew his name and Gwen's. Maybe Dan told her—or maybe she'd read Rowan's letters? "Were you at the Archives?"

"Months ago. Then I got stranded in Donner." The chair set up a riot of creaks, her shifting in it while she tried to use one crutch to pull the short stool closer to her.

It was too far, really. Steffie came around the table and hurried over to help, so she wouldn't have to get up. "How long was it you were thinking of staying?"

She pulled one side of her mouth back, not a happy look at all. "Well, I wasn't thinking of coming here ever; but it looks like I'll be staying here, oh, for the rest of my life."

By now he had the stool, and he'd put it right in front of her. Which put him eye to eye with her about three feet apart when she'd said that, and when she said the next thing, which was: "I'm Mira's replacement." She thumped one foot up onto the stool.

Funny. "You mean," he said, "just for a while? Until your leg gets better?"

"My leg," she said, "may it rest in peace, has done all the getting better it plans to do."

Which was when, all of a sudden, he realized that the foot on the stool was the only foot she'd got. And that her other leg, the right one, ended someplace between the hip and the knee. He could see that now by how her skirt lay.

It hit him with that sort of thump and twist inside that people get when they see something like that. And that twist made him want to turn away and look at something else and not stare like a clod; but then he remembered what Rowan had said about people not looking at Maysie, and how that made things worse instead of better. So he tried to do as Rowan said and just look at Zenna the way she was, instead of as something people thought she was supposed to be.

It didn't exactly work. So he ended up just going red-faced, and her looking at him staring at her; and he figured he ought to say something or other, but all he could think of was: "Could be worse. You could be dead." Which was true, because that was a bad place to lose a leg from. Most people just died from it.

She put her eyebrows up and said, "Oh, yes."

He backed off. "I guess you'll want to know where Rowan went, and why."

"I already have a good idea. But I'd be interested in how she managed to figure it out. Did she happen to leave any notes behind?"

He thought. "No, took her logbook and all with her. But there's a sketch around here someplace." Janus's sketch of that cut-up demon. Now, where was it . . .

Rowan had told him not to tell the townfolk much; but she couldn't have meant for him to keep it from another steerswoman. He figured the only reason she hadn't mentioned Mira's replacement was because it was too soon for her to come.

Come to think of it, how *did* Zenna get here?

And he must have said it out loud, because Zenna said, "Hired a ship."

"All for yourself? That must have cost a lot."

"Not that much. I pulled a few strings. I still have connections." She settled back a bit and watched Steffie poke around the room, looking for that sketch. "It's too bad I couldn't catch Rowan before she left," she said. "But it's just like her, getting the jump on us all. Do you know if she's going through Southport or through The Crags?"

That came out of the blue. "She didn't say anything about either of those places." He'd heard of both before, but he didn't know where they were. Far away, anyway.

"Well. What a steerswoman tells you can depend on what you happen to ask her. Still, I'm sorry I missed her."

"But she'll be coming back . . ."

"Oh, I hardly think so."

He knit his brows. "But she is. She said so."

"It's a long way to Southport, and longer to The Crags. And plenty to occupy Rowan after that. I'm sorry, but it's not likely you'll ever see her again."

That's when he stopped looking for that drawing, and walked right over and sat down in the big chair across from Zenna. And he put his hands on his knees and said to her, "Lady, what's happening here is you and me are talking about two different things. It's you talking about what you think is going on, and me talking about what really is. Seems to me, if you come to a place where you've never been before, it's the people who are already there stand the best chance of knowing what's up."

She looked at him like you look at a kitten that's done something especially clever. "Very well, then . . . What is up?"

And right then he remembered exactly where that sketch was; and he went and got it, and handed it to her. "Things like that are up, to start with. Rowan says they're called demons." And he sat back down.

She looked at it; and it was funny, because he could see her look at it three different ways, one right after the other. The first was a sort of What is that? and that made her sit right up; and the second was a happy Oh, I see—this is amazing!; and the last one was No, hold on a minute . . .

And that one went on for a long time. And the reason came into Steffie's head, all by itself.

Handwriting. "I guess you know Janus," he said.

"You guess right." She put the drawing down on her lap and looked at him again, but different this time. She looked like she had thought that he was someone else, but he turned out to be himself. "And I guess it's a long story."

"Well, you guess right, too."

"Then before you start—yesterday's beer is fine by me."

20

*I*t took a long time to tell.

Steffie kept missing bits, backing up, filling in, going on. He got it all out in the end, but it did take a while—all through dinner, in fact.

When he was finally done, they were by the hearth. Zenna sat in the wicker chair with Janus's demon drawing in her lap, thinking about the whole thing and sipping beer. Steffie sat on his heels, with his back to the fire, just for the change. He watched her think.

Zenna thinking was different from Rowan thinking. Rowan would look far off in the distance with her brows a bit knit and her eyes moving like she was looking at some hard country up ahead that she'd have to travel through—or was maybe already traveling through; and sometimes she'd pace back and forth.

Zenna thinking stayed still and leaned back, and was quiet; and she tilted her head and held her eyes half closed, like a cat with some plan on its mind. She stayed that way all the while she was figuring. "Rowan was right to go," she said after she'd thought for a while.

"I think so, too." And as soon as he said it he was suddenly embarrassed, because the way he said it made it sound like he had some say in the matter—and who was he to be agreeing or disagreeing about what a steerswoman ought to do? But it was the truth, and it wasn't like he knew nothing.

"I hope the island is *full* of demons." That surprised him, and he saw her notice, so she went on. "Because I don't like the other explanation. It's much better that demons be living close by and stumbling blindly into the nearest large town than that demons have suddenly got it in their heads to travel hundreds of miles, specifically picking out Alemeth as their target."

"But it's got something to do with Janus, either way. Right?"

She twitched her mouth. "Possibilities are two: Either it's got something to do with Janus, or Janus has got something to do with it."

3

Steffie had to stop and sort that out, because it sounded like she'd just said the same thing twice—but she hadn't, not really, not if you thought about it. "But it's just as well Rowan's out of the way, because one thing he's definitely got something to do with is making people feel funny about Rowan." And he did some explaining about that, how Janus was spreading bad stories, and Rowan saying exactly the opposite, and no one knew who to believe. "They're mostly putting it down to a lover's quarrel. People figure she's an old sweetheart of his."

Zenna was thinking hard, and her face didn't change at all when she said the next thing, which was, "No. That would be me."

"Oh."

She nodded slowly. She'd gone all quiet, not just her voice but everything about her; and it made Steffie sorry to see that. "I was already on my way here when Rowan's letter about him reached the Archives," she said. "When the Prime read it, she wrote to me and to Rowan. The letters caught up to me in Donner. I read them both. I dropped everything. I hired the ship."

"Oh."

She stirred herself, then she looked at her beer like she'd forgotten she'd had it and was glad to see it again. She took a big drink. "How much did Rowan tell you about Janus's history?" She sounded more normal.

"Well . . ." Steffie began, then he stopped again, trying to think how to say things nice, now that he knew Janus was her old lover. "Well . . . she just said he used to be a steerswoman—I mean a steersman. He got in a shipwreck, had a rough time, and took it bad. Figured he didn't want to be a steersman anymore, and quit. Oh, and some steerswoman asked him why, and he didn't want to talk about it, so he got put under the ban."

"That's it, that's the thing," she said. "He wouldn't say why."

"But . . ." There were some things a person might not want to talk about; and things that hurt you or scared you were right at the top of Steffie's own list. He'd still tell, himself, if it was a steerswoman who asked. But it wasn't hard to see that someone else might feel different.

Before he could say all that, Zenna went on. "Over a year later."

"What?"

"If Ingrud had asked Janus right after it happened, and Janus couldn't answer, that would be one thing. Or a month later or even three months—but nearly a year and a half later? No. He'd be able to talk about it, at least in general terms, by then."

"So, you don't buy it?"

" 'Buy it'?" She smiled a bit, which he was glad to see. "What an interesting turn of phrase. Must be local. No. I don't buy it. And the Prime didn't buy it, and neither did Arian—" She saw him start to ask, so she answered before he could. "One of our teachers. He's the only other steersman we have, at the moment, now that Hugo's passed on. Arian took a special interest in Janus during our training, as you might guess. And Arian definitely did not buy it."

Steffie hadn't known that, about it being a year and a half later that Janus got asked about quitting. Made things different. He chewed his lip. "How come Rowan bought it? At first, I mean." Because it seemed to Steffie now that he wouldn't even have bought it himself.

"He must have given her some explanation. Including an explanation of the delay. And it must have been a very, very good explanation." Her face said, clear as if she spoke, that she couldn't think of any explanation that good. "Well." That look on her face went away. "Either whatever Janus said was enough to convince her, or it was enough for her to give him the benefit of the doubt."

"Well, doubting's all she gives him now. Don't think she'd trust him as far as she could toss him with one arm."

"Hm." She leaned back in a slouch, with her mug held on her one knee.

And that brought Zenna up to date, Steffie figured. So, it was her turn. "Tell me, lady," he said in the formal way, and he was about to go on and say, Why is it you thought Rowan was gone off to those places you mentioned?—but all of a sudden he saw that he already knew, because there was just one thing that would make Rowan stop worrying about demons, stop looking in the books in the Annex, and go running straight off somewhere else. So instead, he asked, "Where's Slado hiding? And how did the steerswomen figure it out?"

Zenna sat right up and raised her eyebrows and blinked a couple of times. "Steffie, has anyone ever told you that you're a very surprising person?"

"Well, no," he said. "Mostly they tell me exactly the opposite."

"Hm. Well, in answer to your question, we figured it out by looking very far into the past. Actually, I say 'we' but that's not entirely accurate. 'We,' the steerswomen living at the Archives, yes; but we had split ourselves into two groups, each following a separate line of investigation. And it was the other group that found the clue." She put on a frown. "Damn them." But she said it in a friendly way, the way you say it about people you're jealous of but really like, so you're happy they did good, but you still wish it was you instead.

"You see," she went on, "up until quite recently, we didn't even know there was any one wizard with authority over them all. That's something Rowan discovered herself. When it became urgent that we find that wizard, we all just delved in and started looking for clues."

"Signs of magic," Steffie said, "with no other wizard around." That was what Rowan had said to him.

"That's how we began, yes. We found one hundred and eighteen books covering the ten-year span around the time the Guidestar fell. And other than a few false leads, the only interesting thing we found was some peculiarities in the weather. But then," Zenna went on, "one of us came up with a very interesting question: How long has this been going on?"

"How long has Slado been causing trouble?"

"No. How long has there been a master wizard?"

"I don't get you."

"Possibilities, as we like to say, are three." She ticked them off on her fingers. "Either Slado is the first wizard to gain authority over all wizards; or at some point in the past one wizard gained that power so that Slado is the latest in a line; or there has always been a master-wizard. And if master-wizard is a position that gets passed on to another—"

"Maybe the place he lives gets passed on, too!"

"Exactly. And that's when we split into two groups. One looking for unattributed magic in recent times and one looking for it anywhere in all the rest of recorded history."

She stopped, so Steffie could let that sink in. "But," he said, "wouldn't that take forever? You'd have to look in every single book."

"So you would. But then one member of that group—and come to think of it, it was Arian—suggested that if there has always been a master-wizard, we might try looking for one single, inexplicable thing, which has persisted, or repeated, since our records first began."

Still seemed like it would take forever. But Steffie said, "Right," meaning he understood it.

"And then"—and Zenna smiled—"Berry pointed out that if we're looking for where Slado is, we're really looking for a place." She folded her hands on her lap. "Now, if you're looking for a place, what do you do?"

Steffie winced, because the answer to her question seemed just too easy. But he said it anyway. "Look at a map?"

Her smile got tighter. "Will you fetch my map case for me?"

He did, and she opened it and pulled out the charts. She picked one and set the others aside.

The map was big. Too big to hold in your lap. She looked at it like it had done something mean on purpose, then shrugged and slid herself down to sit on the floor. She spread the map right on the floor in front of her, and Steffie moved the big chair back so he could sit down there, too. "I suspect you've seen a map of the Inner Lands before."

It took him a while to answer. "Not one that big," was what he said in the end. You wouldn't think any map would ever need to be so big. But then he saw that there was more on it than the other maps he'd seen. It made it seem realer, somehow, more like the real world.

"It allows for more detail."

"There's Alemeth," he said, happy that he found it. It was just a little thing, off to the side of the great big everything else.

"Very good. Now, the interesting thing about maps is they *are* history. The more we learn about the world, the more we add to our maps. So every map contains information dating from the very first time any map was ever made, all the way up to the present day.

"And that's exactly what Arian and Berry's group had wanted to do: look at all of our history, all at once."

Zenna pointed. "Here's the oldest city in the world." THE CRAGS, Steffie read; but it was only easy because he had the name in his head already, her having said it before. "And this is one of the youngest towns in the world." SOUTHPORT.

There was something written between them, right on the water. "Um." It wasn't easy. "Ships var, ships . . . ships vanish?" There was more, but he couldn't make it out at all.

Zenna was looking at that place like she was mad at it. "Any ship that passes through that area is never seen again. Unless—and isn't this interesting?—you have a wizard on board. And it's been that way from the days of the first steerswomen.

"It didn't strike us as odd because—well, because very early on everything seemed odd, really, and there wasn't much we knew about the lay of the land or what was in it at all. The fact that there was a part of the world that we knew nothing about didn't seem important; after all, the part of the world that we do know anything about is actually still very small.

"But now, hundreds of years later, look: Everything to the immediate north and northeast is well mapped. And recently people have reached the southern shore of the Inland Sea and started living there. But they did it by crossing the entire sea from the north. Because, in that one area, ships still vanish.

"It didn't seem important. We were used to it; we didn't question it; and there was plenty else to keep us busy . . ." She was quiet a few moments before Steffie noticed that she'd stopped. He looked up at her.

Her brows were down, and one eye sort of squinted at him. "Are you listening to me?"

"Um . . ." Silly of him to ask, and then not pay good attention to what she said. "Sorry. I was just looking for the other one."

The eyebrows went further down, and the squint went away. "What?"

"The other place where ships vanish." He looked back down at the map. "There's Alemeth here, see—" But he got lost after that.

Zenna said—and she said it sort of carefully, like it'd turned out he wasn't as smart as she'd thought at first—"This chart can't show every place where a ship went without ever returning; there are too many reasons why a ship might be lost. But the interesting thing about that one area is that no ship entering it has returned."

"I know. But—" Alemeth, and some shore off to the right, which was east. But then the lines stopped. "Well, I guess it doesn't matter . . . So, the steerswomen think that Slado might be hiding out in that ships-vanish place?"

"We don't know that he's there. In fact, we don't know if he has a single residence at all—but most wizards do. If you're looking for someone who's hard to find, and you notice someplace nearby no one can get to— wait. Steffie, are you saying that some ships leaving Alemeth never return?" She had all her attention on him.

"Well, no." And he relaxed a bit. "Not any more," he went on. "Because no one goes that way anymore. Not meaning to, anyway."

She turned around so that she was sitting facing him directly. "Tell me about it."

Not much to tell. "Well, just what the fishers say—you can go east, but only so far. 'Cause otherwise, you don't come back . . ." And all of a sudden this sounded very bad to him. "Um . . ." He tried to put together what he'd heard, but he never paid much attention to the fishers' stories. They were all how big a catch, how winds blew, what currents to watch out for—not all that interesting. "I could be wrong." But what if he wasn't?

A place by The Crags, where ships never came back. Another one east of Alemeth? And funny things going on in Alemeth, strange things. All of a sudden, Steffie started feeling cold.

He was thinking, and shivering, a long time; Zenna was thinking, too. "Why have we never heard of this?"

"Don't know. The only steerswoman hereabouts was Mira."

"Damn her."

And, well, it hadn't seemed important. Not like it was new or anything. Why would Mira even wonder? "What are the steerswomen going to do about that place by The Crags?"

And she answered like she was thinking of something else but could answer anyway, just like Rowan would sometimes. "Arian is going to walk into it. It can't be all water. He and Berry, and Berry's husband, have gone to The Crags. Berry and Josef are going to set themselves up as far south of the city as seems safe. Arian will work his way further south from there."

They both sat, looking at the map; it flickered and jumped in the fire-light, with the whole room around it dark. "Maybe," Steffie said, "Arian should try sailing there . . ."

"In a copper-bottomed boat," Zenna finished.

21

Steffie went straight to the Annex first thing in the morning. When he got there, there was no one downstairs, but the room smelled like food, even though there were no dirty dishes. Eggs, smoked fish, and toasted bread—and not so long ago.

Too late. Zenna must've gone down to the harbor to talk to the fishers by herself.

Maybe she didn't want him tagging along. Might as well work for the day. He could ask her about it later. He got himself a heel of bread from the pantry and ate it while he went up the street to Lasker's.

But when he got to the mulberry groves, he could see way off past them somebody all alone, moving in a way different from how people usually move. That had to be Zenna, walking with her two crutches, so he jogged along the path to catch up to her.

She waved when he got near and called to him. "I'm glad you're here! I'm counting on you to introduce me to the fishers."

He reached her, and fell in beside her. "I'll be glad to do that, lady, but you're going exactly the wrong way."

She made a noise. "I don't mean right now. Right now, I'm just getting a little morning exercise. You're welcome to come along, if you can keep up."

"Well, guess I can." Rowan used to get out and walk every morning, too; but it must be harder for Zenna. He wondered why she was doing it.

"What I need," she said, and she pushed herself along a little faster, "is some flat ground, as long a stretch of it as I can find." He noticed that her crutches had loops on them, made of leather, one down over the back of her hands, another further up. Looked like a smart idea.

"Well, Harbor Road is long and flat. Even got paving stones for a piece." He had to walk a little faster now, but it was still slower than he'd go by himself.

"I'd prefer a place where there aren't a lot of spectators."

Steffie looked around. "Then you're going the right way. Big meadow, just past Karin's last field. Been fallow for a while—she used to use it for beans. So there's no tree stumps."

They went along, him strolling, her swinging. He was still wondering about the ships vanishing, wondering and worrying, too. He was about to bring it up, but she spoke before he could. "How do you think people would feel if I worked with the worms sometimes?" she asked.

He almost stopped dead in his tracks. "Well, they'd be surprised, that's for sure. Do you really need the money?" There was that ship she'd hired to get her here. "People will give you food and things, if they know you need it or if you ask. You're supposed to help a steerswoman."

"No, I don't need the money. I think."

"Then, why work? I mean, other than at the Annex, on the books and things? Mira never did."

"Mira was an old woman. I'm not. I can't sit still all the time. I'll rust." She sped up a bit more.

"Well, I guess people would get used to it. In the end." By now she was going as fast as she could, and Steffie could see it was hard work for her. She was getting sweaty, and there was this funny twist showing up as she moved, like she was shoving one shoulder before the other sometimes. It looked hard, and it looked clumsy.

He could see why she didn't want people gawking at her. Maybe he shouldn't be around, himself, staring at her and all.

No, that was wrong: he wasn't staring, he was just going along with her, and that was just the way she moved. If that was the only way she could do it, then that made it her way of doing it, her own right way.

"Well, if I'm going to"—and it was getting hard for her to talk, getting out of breath—"live here . . . for the rest . . . of my life . . . they'll get used to me . . . one way or the other—"

And she was off.

Then Steffie stopped dead so sudden he almost fell right over, and now he *was* gawking.

Zenna was already halfway across the field, and she was *running*. Steffie said in a little voice, "Bloody hell!" And he took off after her.

He couldn't see how she was doing it—he couldn't figure it out at all; but there she was, moving smooth and fast, practically flying across that field. It wasn't two-sticks-then-swing-the-foot-through-the-middle, but how else could someone go on crutches?

He caught up, which was harder than he'd thought it would be, though once he was there he could keep up. "How do you *do* that?" he yelled across. There was something about how she worked her arms, not together but each one separate, one forward, one way back, and her leg doing something in the middle. It made Steffie think of the way a bird moves along in the middle of its beating wings, if a bird could fly putting one wing forward and the other back.

"I have to build up momentum first," she called back at him. And she talked easier moving this way than the other. The whole thing was easier. It looked like she could keep it up for a long time. "And I get my weight moving just right; then I start it by skipping one crutch . . . It's harder to explain than it is to do."

"It's beautiful!" And it was. It was smoother than a two-legged person running; there wasn't any up and down to it, nothing bumpy or jumpy. Zenna just flowed along—strong, fast, easy.

And her black hair blew out behind her in the wind, and the hem of her dress, too, which was yellow silk, that made a fluttery noise like feathers. It was the prettiest thing he'd ever seen, and it made him feel good and happy just looking at it.

So for a while he forgot all about Slado and Janus, and he just ran. Right beside her, all across the field and back again—her like a little bird, going so fast and smooth, and him more like a dog would go, keeping up and not going any faster, because it's happy and wants to stay around.

After that, they did go down to the harbor, except that Lasker's foreman spotted Steffie and asked him to come and work, because she was short-handed. He promised to come after lunch. Then he had to introduce Zenna, and all that took some time. But they got to the harbor in the end.

Most of the fishers were out fishing already. But Zenna looked around, spied some oldsters, and struck up a conversation. The oldsters knew some old fishers, and there were a couple other sailors around, too.

Pretty soon Zenna had a whole troop of people around her, and they were talking over each other, and she took it all down. She had her charts on a crate, and she drew and listened and asked, all at the same time. They talked winds and currents and seasons and weather, and a lot of sailing things Steffie didn't know anything about; but at the end of it *ships vanish* got written down, with a lot of numbers around it, on three or four different-sized charts of the same part of the water.

When they were done and the sailors and fishers wandered off, Zenna rolled the maps and put them in that leather tube steerswomen carried. She'd tied a strap to it, so she could carry it slung across her back, the way Rowan sometimes carried her sword.

"Do you have a sword?" Steffie asked. He hadn't seen her with a sword yet.

"In my trunk. Why? Someone you want me to do in for you?"

"Well, no. But Rowan, she never sets her sword aside. Except once. And she was sorry after that."

"I'm not Rowan," Zenna said.

"I guess." And Rowan wasn't Mira. Looked like no steerswoman was like any other steerswoman. Not even Janus. Especially Janus, come to think of it, him even being a man and all.

But the reason Janus came to mind was that right then Steffie was looking at him.

He was over at the cooper's, where there was a cart and a line of people loading empty crates into it; and Janus was in the line, toward the middle. It was a ways away, but Steffie could still tell it was him.

Zenna had her back to it all, closing her map case. "Janus is over there, on shore," Steffie told her.

She didn't turn; she just went ahead and slung on her map case and slipped into those straps on her crutches. "How close?"

"At the cooper's. That's Harbor Road, three buildings down from New High."

"Can he see me?"

"His back's turned. And he's busy."

That's when she turned around herself and watched the people loading. There wasn't any expression on her face, none at all. "I see him. I suppose he must know I'm in town by now . . ."

"Maybe not. Keeps to himself a lot, these days. Talks to no one."

She was quiet for a bit. "Steffie, are you up for a little subterfuge?"

"Might be, if I knew what that was."

"In this case, it's this: You and I are going to walk down the wharf together as if we're heading for New High, but when we get to the corner, you turn left and stroll along casually past the cooper's."

"And what'll you be doing then?"

"I'll be right behind you. But ignore me."

He shrugged. "I'm game."

And that's what they did; and when he turned left at the corner, he couldn't see her anymore, because she was walking in that place right behind you where you can't see if anyone's there. Except he could hear her. The way she walked gave her a sound all her own. Which was when he figured out that she was keeping him right between herself and Janus. If

Janus looked this way, he might see some of her, but he wouldn't see all of her with Steffie in the way.

So Steffie ignored her, strolled right up to the cooper's, nodded hello to Dan, and strolled right past. A few steps on, he didn't hear Zenna behind him anymore. Then, he couldn't help it; he stopped and looked behind.

Zenna was in that can't-see-you place again, but now it wasn't Steffie's, it was Janus's. A couple of the other workers looked at her sidelong, and Dan saw her and made a move to go and talk to her; but Steffie got to him and pulled him aside.

And it was right then, with Janus having just let go of one crate and about to get another, that Zenna tapped him on the shoulder.

Steffie couldn't see all of Janus's face, and he wished he could, because he wondered what it was doing right now.

But what Zenna did was look right up at Janus and say, loud enough for everyone else to hear, "What do you know about demons?"

Janus tried to take a step forward, but he stopped, because that was when he saw that Zenna was on crutches. But Zenna swung one step forward herself, which made her tilt her head back further to look him in the eye, and she said, "Why did you resign from the Steerswomen?" And she didn't stop there. "Why didn't you explain yourself to Ingrud? Why are you spreading lies about Rowan? What happened to you when you were shipwrecked? Where did you end up? What did you see? Where do you sail when you sail away? Why does your boat have a copper bottom? What are you *hiding*?" Then she did stop, except she said one extra thing, in a casual-sounding voice. "Answer the questions in any order you like."

But Janus didn't answer them. He stood there with his bones hanging funny in his body, like maybe they would all let go at once. And then he twisted sort of sideways, like he wanted to leave and he wanted to stay, both at the same time. And Steffie wouldn't have been surprised if Janus had split right in half, because the hand on the staying side actually started to reach out to Zenna.

Then he got himself all together at once, and he turned, and he shoved right through the other workers, who were all gathered around, and he ran, just like it was a demon behind him instead of Zenna. When Janus ran by him, Steffie got one good look at his face, and that's exactly how he looked.

When he was gone, Zenna swung herself around and went off in the opposite direction back toward New High. Leaving everyone standing there looking at each other. Not saying anything.

Except they would soon, and Steffie didn't really want to hear any of it, so he left them all behind, and Dan, too, who was huffing out his cheeks and building up to saying something.

Zenna wasn't running, but she was moving pretty fast and in a jerky way. Steffie caught up to her. "I guess that didn't do much good."

"It's too soon to tell." And she stopped all of a sudden. "Is there a place nearby to sit down?"

Steffie looked around for a barrel or a crate or something; but then he saw her face.

He got her into the Mizzen, which was empty, it being early still; and as soon as they were in the door, Zenna sat right down on the first chair she came to, put her face in her hands, and cried. Steffie just stood there.

Young Acker was on the other side of the room, starting to lay out the tables for lunch, and when he saw them he started to come over and see what they'd like. Steffie waved him away; but he saw what was up and came anyway, not to take their orders but to slip a nice linen napkin into Steffie's hand; and then he left the room.

Steffie looked at the napkin; then he sat down next to Zenna and handed it to her. She took it and held it against her eyes; and when she'd got enough voice back to speak, she said, "That was not easy."

Steffie tried to think of something to say, but he couldn't, because no words came into his head, none at all. But words came out of his mouth anyway. "I guess you still love him."

"I love the boy I knew in Wulfshaven. I'll always love the boy I knew in Wulfshaven. But I don't know if Janus is still him." And saying that got her crying all over again right from the start.

Steffie wished he knew her well enough to give her someone to hang onto while she cried, but he didn't, so he couldn't. But he sat by her, quiet and not hurrying her, until she was all done, which sometimes is the only thing you can do.

At last she wiped her eyes in a way that said she was just about finished, and she looked at the napkin. "I really hate to blow my nose in anything so nice." Then she went ahead and did exactly that.

"Do steerswomen always have to make things hard on themselves?"

"It depends on what they're trying to accomplish." She set to folding the napkin and unfolding it, over and over. Her eyes were shiny and dark at the same time; and suddenly Steffie wondered how old she was, because she looked very young right then. "I wanted to shock him."

"I guess you did that."

She took a few deep breaths and went on folding the napkin. "When people are really, really shocked, they either start thinking very clearly— or they stop thinking altogether."

He started getting it. "And you want him to think clearer than he's been."

She nodded, not at him, it seemed, but at the napkin. "That would be best. The other would do. With any luck, Janus will soon either do something intelligent or something very stupid."

Owning up and getting it all in the open would be the something intelligent. "What's the good of him doing something stupid?"

She looked up at him; and all of a sudden she stopped looking small and young and hurt and started looking small and sharp and angry. "He'll slip. He'll give himself away. And then Rowan and I will figure the whole thing out for ourselves."

That's when people started coming in for their lunches, the ones who could afford to eat at the Mizzen just for a lunch. Steffie and Zenna went back to the Annex, where they ate their own lunch, not talking much.

But Steffie talked a lot later, up in the fields, because everyone'd heard that a new steerswoman showed up yesterday.

He had to tell everything he knew about Zenna, which, when he thought about it, wasn't really all that much—not most of the things they all wanted to know, like where did she grow up, who was her family, how old was she. But he did tell how her leg got broke so bad it had to come off, because that was the one thing he'd asked her over lunch. The only reason he told it was because he knew someone would ask her later, and he didn't want her having to say it again, ever.

When he'd finished telling it everyone went dead quiet, and all the women looked at all the men hard, like they hated them, and all the men looked at nothing at all, hard, for a long time.

Then, more or less to change the mood, Steffie told about Zenna being interested in the ships vanish place.

And he told about how she knew Rowan, them being old friends who had taken their steerswoman training together.

And he told about Zenna cornering Janus with all those questions; but he didn't tell how she cried after nor why.

Later they went into the sheds and couldn't talk any more. And even later, everybody got more interested in something else, because Auni stopped working and went and got Lasker, and they both came back and stood looking at one of Auni's racks. Then Lasker made everybody stop and told them to start making the reed hills.

Which is what they did; and when Steffie put the little hills among the worms in his racks, most of them didn't seem interested. But a couple of them reared up on their hindquarters and waved their heads at the hills, with a hello-what's-this-then? look about them. So maybe it wouldn't be long.

Then the night workers came in, and Steffie and the day workers started walking home. Gwen was there, and she ran and caught up with Steffie. She'd been working in the opposite order from him, and hadn't heard what he'd told the others, so he told it all over again, to her and everyone else nearby. Gwen didn't even bat an eye when Steffie said again about Zenna and Rowan knowing each other. She just laughed, tossed her head, and said that with a new permanent keeper at the Annex, maybe everything would get set right again, and about time. She acted nice toward Steffie, funny and flirty and sassy, just like old times; and he thought, well, maybe she's right about that.

So they stopped by the Annex on the way home, but Zenna wasn't there.

It wasn't until a lot later, in the middle of his own dinner, which he was eating with the family, that Steffie remembered about Dan and Zenna having dinner at Brewer's. So he told everyone; and they all hurried to get done, and went up to Brewer's themselves, except Steffie went to Gwen's home and got her first.

When they got inside Brewer's, they found out that the whole town had the same idea, and the room was filled up with people who looked like they planned to stay a long time, just like nobody had to work the next day. If Dan had been hoping to have Zenna all to himself, he was right and wrong at the same time. Because even though they had a little table all to themselves, and no one else was talking to them, everyone was paying attention to nothing except Dan and Zenna. Although they all pretended they weren't.

There were no free seats. But Gwen went up to young Acker, who was at a table right next to Zenna and Dan, and she started talking to him; and then she started teasing and flirting with him, while Steffie stood not far off, looking the other way, because he knew this trick.

Then all of a sudden Gwen tickled Acker, then dashed back, and Acker was up out of his chair to snatch at her—and Steffie got right behind him and sat down. And Gwen slid around, and sat in Steffie's lap and he put his arms around her. And they both sat looking up at Acker, smiling, and everybody laughed. But they kept the chair.

They were close enough to hear whatever Dan and Zenna were going to say; but Zenna was waving at Brewer across the room. Brewer saw and waved to one of the servers to go over there. But then Zenna waved bigger, meaning she wanted Brewer in particular, so he edged over.

When he got there, Zenna said, "I'm going to be inviting a few people over to the Annex for an evening, and I suspect that in Alemeth you're the person to hire to provide food and drink. Am I right?"

"Well, if it's not fancy fare, you're looking for, I'm your man. But, you being a steerswoman and all—"

She put up her hand to stop him. "No, I won't hear of it. It's one thing for the whole town to feed me, and another to expect them to feed my guests. I'll pay you for the job, just like anyone else would. Although, if you really insist, you're welcome to charge nothing for the portion that I'll eat myself. But I will pay for my own guests."

Which was nice of her, Steffie thought, and Brewer thought so, too. "Well, that's fair, I say. Now, how many people are we talking about?"

"That's a very good question. Give me a moment while I find out."

Then Zenna stood right up, looked around the room, and let out a two-toned whistle—sharp and loud. Everyone got to stop pretending they were doing something else and looked at her.

She called out to the whole room. "I have a question for everyone. How many people here can read?" She put up her own hand to show them what she wanted them to do.

Then they stopped looking at her, because they were all looking at each other, confused. Steffie did, too, looked at Gwen, who just shrugged. But Steffie put his hand up, and then a few other people did, slowly.

"Six. Thank you. Now, who can tell me how many people who *aren't* here can read?" That took a little longer. "There's Michael," someone said. Steffie said, "All the Bosses, really. Michael and Maysie and Karin and Lasker and the brothers. The spider-wife. And Sulin. And Dan."

"I already counted Dan. Any more?"

"Can Janus read?" Gwen asked Steffie.

"Janus isn't welcome at the Annex," Zenna said, sounding offhand about it. "Who else?"

It took some talking, but Sulin and Michael's clerks got named, and one of Maysie's girls. And Steffie's Ma, once he thought of it, even though she hadn't thought of it herself. Then Corey put up his own hand and counted himself, which he'd forgotten to do earlier.

"Nineteen. And myself, that's twenty." She turned back to Brewer. "Twenty people exactly."

"Um, right." Brewer was flustered. "And when would that be for?"

"Tomorrow night. Food and drink for twenty. Oh, and what sort of entertainment is available in Alemeth?"

"Well," Brewer said, "there's the little band plays sometimes down at the Mizzen. But they're dear. But Belinda, she's got a fiddle."

"Perhaps I can afford Belinda."

But Belinda called out herself, from across the room. "If you feed me, I'll come for nothing and play all night." A couple of people clapped at that, happy, until they remembered they weren't invited.

"Thank you, Belinda. And that's twenty-one. Brewer, can you manage that for tomorrow night? Do you need more notice?"

The old man blew out his cheeks while he figured. "No, no, I can manage." Then they set to working out the cost, which Brewer ended up setting too low, but Zenna just smiled bigger and said thank you. Still, the little sack of coins she pulled from a pocket in her skirt jingled when she brought it out and didn't jingle at all when she put it back, only went *clink, clink* a couple times.

And when she was done with Brewer, Zenna started to sit again; but she stopped herself, looking around like she'd just noticed the whole room staring at her, dead quiet.

She let it stay quiet for a long time; then she put her fists on her hips, just like a mother chiding a flock of children. "Oh . . . all right. Everyone else can come, too. But if you can't read"—and she put on a pretend-mean face—"you have to bring food!"

Then she sat back down across from Dan. The whole room set to buzzing, everyone trying to guess what was up, even though Zenna was right there to ask. But sometimes it's more fun to guess, and then see how close your guess came.

Gwen couldn't wait. She leaned across the space between and asked Zenna, "What's the party for?"

"Books," Zenna said cheerfully, then set to spooning up her stew.

"Books?"

"Specifically, five books."

That was interesting. "Which five?" Steffie couldn't help asking.

"Any five. Five per person who can read." And she just went on eating.

"What do they do with the five?" It was Dan who asked, looking half at sea and half wondering if it might be fun to swim.

"Place them in order. Alphabetically." She put down her spoon. "Every person who can read will be asked to take five books, look at the names, and place them in order. Then we eat, and drink and dance until Belinda falls asleep."

"You're going to make people fuss with those books?" Gwen didn't think much of the idea.

Dan glanced at her, then back to Zenna. "Just put the five in order?"

"That's right."

"But that's easy. Five'd take no time at all." And Steffie was about to say, But there's *thousands* of books; but Dan went on. "I can do better than five."

"Ten?" Zenna asked.

"Ten's nothing. Bet I could do twenty."

And all of a sudden Steffie saw how it would go. Zenna would ask just for five, and people would do the five, because it was a new thing to do, and they'd go along, if only once; and after all, there'd be a party right after. But for a good reader, five would feel like nothing, so they'd go ahead and do another five. Then some of the others, like Dan, would think ten's not so many and would do even more. Then some really smart person would want to show everyone up and do twenty-five or more, and someone else wouldn't let them get away with that and would match 'em, at least.

Twenty fives are a hundred. Twenty tens are two hundred. With some doing five, some doing more—

Well, he lost track there, figuring who would do what. But by feel and guess—"Could be four hundred at a go," he said.

"That's what I'm hoping," Zenna said.

Still—"Plenty left."

She gave him a look. "Steffie," she said, "I'm going to be here for *the rest of my life*. This won't be the last sorting party."

"You just spent a lot of money," Gwen pointed out. "Can't keep that up."

Dan looked around at them all. "But," he said, "Zenna, you don't have to feed me. If you do this again, I mean. I know you don't have money."

And that would happen, too, Steffie saw. If the party was a lot of fun, people would want to do it again just for some excuse to get together and celebrate, even if they had to bring their own food. Then it would turn into a special thing, a tradition, an Alemeth thing to do.

It was a smart idea, really smart. "How come Rowan never thought of this?"

Zenna threw her head right back and laughed and laughed. "Oh, Steffie, Rowan would *never*, not in a hundred years, ask someone else to do her work for her!"

Dan grinned. "But you would?"

"Absolutely!" She grabbed her mug and held it up. "At every possible opportunity!" And she finished it off with a big gulp. "Did you ever hear of a ship called *Graceful Days*?" No one had. "Well, I shouldn't be surprised; we never made it to Alemeth."

"Who's 'we'?" Dan asked.

" 'We' is me and my family." And now she was talking to everyone nearby. "It was our ship, and we were her officers and most of her crew. My grannie was captain, until she started losing her faculties. Then my dad took over. I grew up on the water, working side by side with aunts and uncles and cousins, not to mention the hirelings, most of whom got to be just like family. And not a few of whom married in.

"Now, the thing that I learned—" and she took a moment to thank the server for another beer "—the thing that I lived and breathed every day is: you work together. Someone organizes it, someone is in charge— but everyone pitches in. The more people, the less effort per person. I can't set all those books in order by myself in any reasonable amount of time, so—I organize."

"Organize a party!" Dan laughed.

"Absolutely."

Gwen clapped her hands and laughed, too. "Well, one thing's sure— you're better at this than Rowan was."

"Better at throwing a party? Oh, yes. The only party Rowan ever organized, we spent the entire evening discussing natural manifestations of the Fibonacci series." She stopped short. "Actually, that was a lot of fun. For steerswomen. But it's not for everyone."

"No, I mean, better at being a steerswoman."

And even though Zenna didn't do a thing, not a thing different, and her face didn't change at all—even so, Steffie heard this voice in his head go: *Watch out!* And it looked like Dan heard that same voice, too, because he sat right up and even moved his chair back a couple of inches.

"Gwen," Zenna said with a friendly smile on her face, "count my legs." Gwen didn't answer straight off. "Go ahead. Count them."

And looking like she was cornered, Gwen said, "One . . ."

"Now count Rowan's."

And because he knew she wouldn't, Steffie said, "Two."

Zenna slowly folded her hands on the table. "Rowan has spent her entire career traveling hard roads, threatened by the weather and animals and bandits; having, at one point, every wizard in the world scouring the Inner Lands, trying to find her and kill her; wandering the Outskirts, fighting hordes of warriors, being attacked by goblins and monsters; and *surviving blasts of magic coming down from the sky at her*—and she strolls into Alemeth on her own two feet. I," she went on, "spent five years cheerfully ambling along the Shore Road, on one of the easiest routes a steerswoman can get, and I get sent home on a stretcher and end up here, doing work intended for an old woman. Now, tell me: Who's the better steerswoman?"

Gwen didn't want to answer, but she had to. "Well . . . I still think it's you."

"Really? How interesting." Zenna picked up her mug. "Gwen, I'm going to have to assume that your own personal definition of *steerswoman* is: the lady who lives at the Annex, who's so much fun to be with." She twitched her mouth. "I suppose I can manage to live up to that much, at least."

Funny thing was, that really had been Steffie's own personal definition of a steerswoman, too. Until he met Rowan.

And Steffie was exactly right about how the party went.

Five books went so fast that everyone did ten, even Corey, who took a long time to do them; but he wasn't alone, because a bunch of people went right on to twenty. Then the food came out, and everyone stopped; but some went back after. When the music started, everyone stopped again. But every now and then, all through the night, someone would wander back into the aisles and do a few more.

Zenna had tacked up papers with letters on them on the ends of the aisles, so you could tell which names went where. Steffie went back himself, between dances, and he took all the names that he'd done days before and set them in the right aisles. And Evanna', one of Maysie's girls, saw him do that; she put her beer right down and dove back in, pulling and putting books, moving so fast that everyone stopped and gawked. Then they cheered her on. Then Belinda made up a special new tune to help her move, and everyone clapped along; and Evanna' did fifty books in maybe a quarter of an hour all by herself. After which Zenna sat her down in Mira's big chair, and made everyone wait on her just like she was a queen.

In the end there was more party outside than inside, because the Annex couldn't hold all the people who showed up with food and drink. And the band from the Mizzen came by, not officially, so to speak; but they brought the drum and banjo and squeeze-box anyway.

Gwen flirted with all the men, but she did it looking sideways at Steffie, which made him feel good, like it always did. And the night was fine, and the lights were warm, and the food was good, until it ran out; but the drink kept on being good after that.

Toward the end, with it all going quiet, and people drifting off, laughing down the streets, Steffie noticed that Gwen was missing. He wondered about that, until he turned onto First Baker's Street to go home and a hand came out of the shadows to snag him.

He let himself be snagged. He didn't know what was going to happen next, but he had a pretty good idea of what was going to happen in the end.

So he was happy to go along, with his arm around Gwen, all the way down New High in the whispery dark and left at the harbor, toward where the houses ran out. The stars were out so bright that it looked like there was more light up there than down here. One of the Guidestars had gone dark, the Western one, that's how late it was; but the other looked twice as bright, like a little door in the sky that someone had left wide open.

His feet knew the street, and when they got to it, the twisty path up the hill. And as they climbed, higher and higher, he felt like all of Alemeth—streets and fields, ships and shoreline, people born before him and the ones not here yet—all of it wasn't really outside him at all but right inside his own head. That's how well he knew it. And it hardly ever changed; so, in a way, he really knew it forever.

Zenna was new, but she'd already found her place, and everything would fall into order. Rowan was new, but she'd be going away one day; and those demons, they'd get stopped, one way or another. And things would be safe again, and all the old patterns would come back.

That wasn't a bad thing, not really. In a way, it made Steffie glad, to think that Alemeth would go on forever, more or less the same—

But it came to him right then that this was what he liked about Gwen: You never knew.

You never knew what she was thinking or what she was going to do. She might be sweet, or she might go all spiteful; she could say funny things or even mean things; but the thing was, you never knew which it was going to be. You had to stay on your toes, stay sharp, keep up. In the middle of Alemeth, which was mostly always the same, there was this one person who was always different. And if you have to be stuck living out your days in one town, in the middle of all these tame town patterns, then the thing to do—and all of a sudden this made a whole lot of sense to him—the thing to do is to keep one wild thing right by your side.

That's when, halfway up the hill, he stopped in his tracks, pulled Gwen in, and kissed her, the best way he knew how. She kissed him right back, just as good, then pulled away, taking his hand, leading him, and they went on.

And just when they got to the top, a sentence came into his head, and it was: She runs because she has to. He didn't know where that came from; in fact, it took him a minute to realize that the "she" wasn't Gwen.

It was Zenna, running across the field.

Running, because she's made to move free, so she's *got* to do it, any way that she can.

And where anyone else would have given up, or wouldn't even have tried, Zenna went right ahead—and taught herself practically to fly.

22

*R*owan found no demon hatchery on Spider Island.

Three days of hard sailing against unfavorable winds and currents had brought Gebby's garbage-filled catboat to the rocky shores of the island. Luwa, after an initial vicious and vehement argument, had eventually resigned herself to necessity, and the steerswoman was permitted to conduct her investigations.

Rowan stayed well away from the sheds that housed the spiders and the manufactory, as she had promised. Nevertheless, Luwa enforced the promise by escorting the steerswoman personally: a constant, silent presence, neither hindering nor assisting but only watching, with a gaze sharp and narrowed.

Rowan worked systematically, painstakingly, tediously. She paused often to make notes, each time causing an increase in Luwa's annoyance. After failing repeatedly to enlist the spider-wife's help, Rowan ignored her.

The steerswoman quickly discovered several types of life-forms usually found only in the Outskirts and beyond: all those Gebby had mentioned and a few others. But there seemed to be nothing larger than the green moths.

The handful of standing pools of water interested Rowan at first, but these were small; and when she very cautiously tasted them, they proved merely to be collected pools of sea spray and one small marsh of murky freshwater, home to a multitude of mosquitoes. Green and blue dragonflies flitted merrily across its surface, glinting in the sunlight.

It was not until close to nightfall that Rowan noticed a distinctive odor, brought to her by a change in the wind: the unmistakable stench of dead demon flesh. She followed it, Luwa trailing behind.

In the lee of a small rise was bare earth, loose soil. Prodding the ground with the tip of her sword, Rowan felt first the crunch of sandy dirt, then something quite different. Scraping, Rowan exposed a few inches of what lay beneath.

She looked up at Luwa. "Dead demons can hardly bury themselves. I assume you did this?"

The spider-wife indicated an affirmative, watching the steerswoman intently.

Rowan said, "When I asked you if you had seen demons on the island, you said that you hadn't. I doubt that you buried this thing blindfolded. Surely you realize that I must place you under the Steerswomen's ban."

A sharp shrug communicated Luwa's uninterest in the fact.

"How did you manage to kill this demon?"

Luwa declined to reply.

Rowan threw out her hands. "This has nothing to do with your secret techniques," she said vehemently, "and everything to do with learning as much about these monsters as I possibly can! The more we know about them, the safer we are from them. Surely you want that!" Still no reply. "Luwa, may I point out that you live in Alemeth yourself? You're as vulnerable as anyone."

Luwa thought, seemed to reach a decision. She tilted her head. "It was dead when I found it."

"Could you tell how it had died?"

"No."

"And *where* did you find it?"

She indicated, past the rise. "Washed up on shore."

"Now we're getting somewhere," Rowan muttered. Possibly the Inland Sea itself had killed the creature. This could be instructive. "Some sort of shovel seems called for," Rowan pointed out. The spider-wife made no comment.

Rowan strode away from her, back to the shabby shack where Gebby lived, and searched the nearby grounds in the failing light. No shovel was in evidence. She turned to Luwa, now back at her side. "I have every intention of keeping my promise, despite your now being under ban. But I do need a shovel, and I'm certain you have one, and if you don't want me exploring the sheds looking for it, could you please," she said between gritted teeth, "*bring* it?"

Gebby fetched it, emerging from the largest shed at Luwa's shout. Through the doorway behind her, a glimpse of the room beyond revealed only a complex lattice of laths.

The steerswoman pointedly turned her back. "Bring a lamp, too," Rowan called over her shoulder, and a nod from Luwa confirmed the request.

Back at the site, Rowan set the lamp on a nearby boulder and set to digging. Luwa watched silently, and eventually found a seat on another boulder.

The creature slowly emerged from the dirt. There were no maggots on it, but by some internal process it was well decomposed. Muscles were nearly liquid, split skin curled away from the subsurface fluid sacs, which seemed to have each burst from the inside. Rowan considered the corpse in the lamplight.

What could possibly impel these creatures to leave their native lands?

She knew nothing whatsoever about a demon's daily life. She had no idea what might motivate it, other than the things that motivated any animal: food, escape from danger, impulse to reproduce. But if any of these applied in this case, why were only demons reaching Alemeth?

Janus knew; she was certain of it.

Rowan noticed the condition of the dirt a few feet away, moved there, dug some more. The shovel immediately encountered something soft. "More than one, so I see."

"Yes."

"You might have told me that immediately."

Silence.

Rowan's exasperation became complete. Straightening, she said to the woman with feeling, "Are you merely naturally uncooperative, or do you actually hope to accomplish something by this?"

The spider-wife made a feral grin, showing teeth as wide spaced and twisted as Gebby's. "A little of both. And also, there's the entertainment of it."

It occurred to Rowan then to wonder how many generations of spider-wives, mistress and apprentice, there had been. The narrow, knob-jointed woman seated before her, half lit in lamplight, seemed a shadowy vision of Gebby's future—in both physical shape and sour spirit.

Rowan stifled her temper. "You don't want people to come here," she said stiffly. "That's understandable. If the demons have merely washed ashore, there's no reason for anyone to do so. So, tell me—how many of these monsters are buried here?"

The spider-wife took time to think. "Eight, I think. And bits of another or so."

"*Eight?*" Rowan stood stunned. Then: "I want to know exactly when each one arrived."

Luwa's squint glinted in lamplight. She drew up her bony knees, rearranging her fine green silk skirt, and wrapped her arms around them.

"One, about a week ago. Two more a day or so later. The rest, and the bits, yesterday."

Rowan tossed the shovel to her in a rough motion. "Show me those," the steerswoman demanded. "The most recent."

These had only begun to decompose. Still, their skin was loose, peeling back, fluid sacs burst. No obvious wounds on the ones most whole. And the various demon bits: rough-edged shreds of muscle, as if torn by talons, and severed limbs. Rowan opened one of the whole demons; its stomach was full. "Eating each other," Rowan muttered, "and dying in our poisonous sea."

Five arriving, all at once.

Rowan slowly rose. All around, sounds: the hiss of waves against the beach beyond the rise, the whistle of wind in blackgrass, crickets. Beyond the pool of lamplight: a shadowed landscape, silver edged in starlight. Far above, one Guidestar, the Western, had entered the shadow of the world, passing into darkness.

Five. "That," Rowan said slowly, "is a lot of demons." And not starving, not weak: dining upon one another, traveling stronger, more easily—and in greater numbers.

And reaching this island yesterday.

Rowan stepped back from her dissection clumsily, quickly—as if the dead creature were living, about to attack.

"I have to get back," she said. She turned to the spider-wife, spoke urgently. "To Alemeth. I have to get back *right now*."

23

*D*amn.

Steffie tried again. Lie back—no, curl up, tucked up against Gwen's back nice and cozy, pull up the blanket, shut the eyes, breathe deep, sort of float along . . .

"Damn." It was just no good. Every time he tried to drift off he got this feeling, like someone was standing over him in the dark, just waiting till he fell asleep so he could pinch him all of a sudden. Or kick him.

It never happened. But it always felt like it was *going* to happen.

He sat up. There was dim light from some of the boats. It was the good side of the harbor down there, which meant that the people staying on the boats had money to light through the night, if they wanted. Seemed that some of them did, tonight. So there was dim silvery light coming down from the stars through the leaves above and dim gold light coming up from the boats. Just enough to see by, if you already knew what was there.

What was there was just the little twisty branches close overhead, the little twisty trunks all around, an old pile of hay added to over years and years, the old tarp, the blanket, and a cushion and Gwen.

It used to seem like a forest to Steffie and Gwen when they were little and came up here to play. But really it was just brambles and bushes, grown over together with the space underneath, if you knew the way in.

It was a nice place. It was their own place, sort of sweet and secret.

Gave him the creeps, tonight.

He sat in the dim, listening to the water splashing at the wharves, and the leaves making soft noises all around. He liked that sound; something like bird feathers, like birds all crowding cozy together for the night, to sleep.

Couldn't sleep. Couldn't, not any way.

"Jumpy," he said out loud. "Nerves." His voice didn't wake Gwen, probably because she'd got hold of the one cushion she'd brought and was sleeping with it over her head. It looked like a good idea to Steffie. He wished they had another one.

Far off, a dog set up a noise. Not exactly a howl. Just one note, held low and steady. It went on for a long time. "You and me both," Steffie muttered when it stopped; then it started up again.

Actually, it was kind of a pretty sound, deep and pure, almost like a person singing. The dog had a good voice, for a dog.

Steffie rustled around in the old leaves and tried to make up something like another pillow under the blanket. Then he lay down and tried again.

After a bit, he sat up and stayed like that, looking down at Gwen in the shadows, her head buried under the cushion and both arms wrapped over it, holding it in place.

She seemed happy enough.

He pulled the cushion out of her arms. She went on sleeping. He went on watching.

She started tossing and turning. Then she came part awake and began to grope around with one hand, grumbling, her eyes still closed. Steffie leaned close over her. "What's bothering you?" he asked her quietly.

"Grmph."

" 'Cause something's bothering me, too. And maybe that dog."

She found the cushion and snatched it away from him, with her eyes still closed. She flopped back down and put it over her head. Then she sighed and went quiet, straight back to sleep.

Steffie stuck his fingers in his ears.

Peaceful. Restful. Like someone'd lifted something heavy, and maybe even itchy, off his shoulders.

He took his fingers out.

And all of a sudden he was shaking Gwen, saying, "Wake up, wake up," only not very loud, because it was hard to get it out. And he was shaking all over himself, and all of a sudden he was freezing cold.

Gwen fought him off in her sleep, until he took away the cushion and grabbed her by both arms. Then she came awake by herself, already mad, already jumpy, and fighting.

He held her hard and steady as he could, and he spoke right into her ear. "It's demons, far off. We're hearing them in our sleep. And so's that dog—he's hearing them better." He couldn't hear that hum they made, but he heard *something*, something like a push on his ears. Part of him remembered that, from the first time. When he stood so close to it. When this noise was a part of that other noise, the part that got under your skin.

His whole mouth and throat went dry; and he swallowed hard, swallowing nothing, and it hurt. "I think there are a lot of them." The dog got itself a good deep breath and started up again.

Then Steffie was getting into his trousers, and he tried to put on his shirt; but Gwen had the other end and she wouldn't let go. "Get dressed," he told her, pulling at it, wrapping it around his hand to tug it hard. "Get dressed and get out."

"No!" A whisper, but with just enough voice in it to make it sound strange and sort of half there. She was hanging on to that shirt like she was in the water and it was a rope. "Stay here. Stay here."

"What? Stay? What do you mean, stay?" Then he knew what she meant.

He could hide. They both could. Until it was all over. It would be easy.

"No." Maybe he was the first to hear, the first one to know, and he had to warn everybody. He pulled harder.

"Don't go." She got louder, and he couldn't see her face under her hair, but he could hear tears in her voice. And then she said, "please," which was a thing she never, ever said.

"Got to." He gave up on the shirt and went for his shoes.

"Why?"

"There's Corey to tell." And Janus, he knew about demons. "There's a whole town to wake up." And then get something—like a pike or a pitchfork, or a stick or some stones, or something, anything.

"Someone else can tell them. Someone else will hear soon. If you go, you won't just tell and stay back. You'll get into it."

"Too right." He got both shoes on. Maybe if some people got on a roof, if the demons came down a street, and maybe dropped things on them—

"No!" She yelled it, and it made the dog shut up. "Let someone else! How come it's *you* got to go after monsters? How come *you* have to do it?"

He took a breath to answer, but before he even finished, he suddenly saw that he couldn't answer her—because the question just made no sense to him, no sense at all.

How come *he* had to do it?

He couldn't find a way to grab hold of that question, somehow. It was like it was just noises, or empty air, or water, or nothing having anything to do with anything. He *wanted* to understand it, he wanted to answer, he really did; but it seemed like there was nothing *there* for him to understand and no way to make there be an answer.

So he figured he'd say nothing; but instead, when he took the rest of that breath, and even with his head empty, words came out all by themselves.

They were: "How come you *don't?*"

He shouted it. It surprised them both. Steffie never shouted at her.

Gwen was pulled back against the branches, with the blanket hugged against her, and all her hair a-tangle. He couldn't see her eyes, just shadows with flicks of light in. She looked like a stranger; she looked stranger than a stranger, because he couldn't guess what she was thinking—and then he could. She was thinking that it was his question that made no sense at all.

They both crouched there, under the leaves, in the dim, looking at each other's shadows; and it was just like they were a couple of animals with no words between them at all, because nothing either one of them said could make any sense to the other.

The dog stopped moaning. Steffie heard something like bad music in the distance, all different notes, all at once.

The demons were closer.

"Stay, then," he said to Gwen; and then he was down the little leafy tunnel, out, and standing up.

He could get to Corey's faster if he cut up the hill through the brush. He could get to Janus faster going straight down.

Then he was moving fast, not running so much as stopping himself from falling down, just. So fast that when he got to the bottom of the hill, he had to grab hold of a tree trunk so he could spin onto the road or he would have gone straight into the water. Then down the road, pounding, past the good end of the harbor, toward the shabby end, right at the cooper's, into the backyard, up the steps.

Then he was slamming his fist on Janus's door and trying the latch, which wouldn't open, and he was yelling, "Wake up, you bloody stupid bastard, get yourself ready to do whatever it was you did the last time, because they're back again, except there's more of them, so you've got to do it again, so *get up!*"

He heard a voice inside, and someone moving; but Steffie didn't wait. "Get up to Corey's place!" he yelled, and then he was back down the stairs, back down the road, and up New High Street. Behind him more voices were calling: the people who'd heard him, yelling it all to the people who hadn't.

By the time he got up to Corey's door, the word wasn't far behind him. He could hear it moving up the street, door to door, and he knew it was going out to other streets, too, people waking their neighbors to tell, all down the line.

Corey didn't have a house, just a room at the side of Karin's, with its own door. Steffie banged it, and then tried it. It wasn't locked, but Corey was there already when Steffie opened it.

"More," Steffie got out, between two gasps.

"Them demons?"

"Right," between two more gasps.

"Where?"

"South. Not up to old Galer's yet. Heard 'em. Didn't see 'em. A bunch. All together." Steffie put his back against the doorway, and coughed and gasped.

"Right." The dark room swallowed Corey, then spit him up again with a bucket in his hand. "Take this." He pointed up across the street. "Hit that." Corey went back in the dark, and Steffie could hear him grabbing things.

The bucket had rocks in it. Steffie took a good-sized one and hurled it at the shutters of the upstairs window across the street. Then another, two good bangs. He was already flinging the third when the street door opened, and Nola came out. She was pulling on a heavy leather vest over her shirt, and she had her spear in one hand and a short sword he'd never seen her with before strapped on. She bolted off, already knowing what to do and where to go.

Corey came out again. He had a lamp in one hand, not lit, and an old bow in the other. Steffie had never seen Corey use a bow. "We've got to fetch more than Nola, don't we?" Steffie said.

"No. She tells two, then those two tell two, and it goes out to the militia like that. They'll all come here."

Steffie looked down the street. "Well, there's more people coming than that," he said. Because there were: a straggle of people coming up Karin's road from New High. And one coming down Hill Path, as well; the news had run itself past Karin's house already and was probably still going strong.

They gathered at Karin's cutting shed. Big, empty space—but they all stood close at the front end. There was the green smell of new-cut leaves on the tables all around and the dusty smell of dead leaves on the floor, like spring and autumn jammed both together by someone mean, who wanted to hurry things.

"We need someone to go out and see where they are now, and how many, and then come back and tell us," Corey said.

"That'd be me," Steffie said; but Belinda said it, too, and faster, so she got it. Good enough. She ran better. She could run all night and not notice.

"What I want," Corey went on—he was standing up on a table so people could see. "What I want is to get at them with nothing behind them, so we can shoot them. I want them where if we miss no one gets hurt, because the way I see it, whoever can hold a bow gets to use it. You don't need to be good, you just need to keep shooting in the right direction."

Someone bumped Steffie's shoulder, and he turned. Arvin was there, with his own good bow and another one, older and smaller. He handed it to Steffie—but Steffie gave it right back. "Got to be someone here can use it better than me," Steffie said. Arvin nodded, and sidled off through the crowd.

"If we can't get the monsters while they've got nothing behind them," Corey went on, "the thing to do is let them come into the streets. If we can get them into the smaller streets, we can stand off down the street from them and try to pick them off. It depends on how many they are, and if they split up, which way each one goes."

One of the militia spoke up. "Then we need more runners, to spot 'em and come tell. So they can split, too."

"Right. So I want about five people, willing to follow that noise the monsters make, and just sight them, and then come running to tell me." And it was about five voices answering, but they were all the wrong ones. "No. You two girls, and you, boy, you go running 'round to all the streets now, and tell everyone who's awake and wants to help that they should come here fast. Right? You, go north; you, northwest; you, southeast. If you hear any demons, just run the other way, as fast as you can. And, you two others, you go home now and hide under the beds—you're too little."

"I'll be a runner, and that's two when Belinda gets back."

"Steffie, good. Who else?" No one spoke up. "I don't want to use my fighters for this; my fighters will need to fight, and some of the rest of you will, too." A couple more voices, not sounding happy about it.

Someone came up and stood just next to Steffie. He thought at first it was Gwen, but when he turned and looked it was Zenna.

"You can't fight," he told her.

"I know."

"Right." He turned back to watch Corey.

Karin had got one of those extra bows, and was looking pretty mean, holding it. She was standing beside the table, not watching Corey, but watching the other people. She was still a boss—but she wasn't Corey's boss, not for tonight.

Corey went on. "When Belinda gets back, we'll have a better idea of where to set up. If the demons haven't reached Harbor Road, I'm thinking we should swing 'round on them from the north, and there'll be just marsh behind them . . ."

Steffie listened close, lining up all the bits in his head, trying to figure where he'd fit in. Plans were good, but you never knew when they'd fall apart . . .

Funny, he thought after a while. Seems he had a clearer view of Corey than before. A clearer view all around the room.

It was because some people had left. He hadn't seen them going, but he saw them gone.

Some people who could help a lot were off and gone; while some people who couldn't help at all, like Zenna, they'd come up here all the same.

All the people like Gwen were gone, or going; all the people like him were here and still coming.

Good. Good both ways.

Across the room, he saw that little boy from down the harbor—Ivy's little boy, Tarlie. He hadn't gone to bed like Corey told him; he was sitting in a corner, looking at the world through people's legs. Couldn't do a thing to help, but there he was.

Ivy's boat was at the bad end of the harbor. Way past the cooper's.

If a little boy from there could make it here by now, so could Janus.

Steffie looked all around. What he saw was no Janus anywhere.

Must've decided to be one of those other people. The ones who don't do things. The ones like Gwen.

But someone who did what Janus did last time wouldn't be like Gwen this time.

And where was Belinda?

"Something's gone wrong. Because Belinda's not back, and she should be." He talked loud, right over Corey, and everyone turned around to look.

Corey didn't like it. "Maybe she's warning more people on the way back," he said, and tried to go on.

"But she wouldn't do that, because you said come right back here. And what about Janus, with him so eager last time? I told him already myself, but he's not here yet."

And all of a sudden it was everyone paying attention to Steffie—him in the middle of all these faces—and it didn't feel natural to him at all. But he pushed on anyway. "So, it looks to me like any plans you're thinking are already gone out the window. Maybe we should just get down there, all of us, and figure what to do, when we see."

"No, I want to have some idea first—"

"But something's up, something's up *right now*, and we don't know a thing about it, so everything you're figuring will be no good, because you don't *know*."

Corey thought a bit. It looked like it was just for show, but he made sense when he talked again. "Then I want you other runners out right now. Just listen for where the demons are, see 'em if you can, but back off. One runner—you, Kenno—you go down New High as far as Jilly's. Wait by the corner there. You others report to him, and he'll come tell me, if we're not already there by then. We'll regroup there as soon as I'm finished here."

"I'll take Harbor Road going east," Steffie said straight off. He didn't wait to hear about the other runners.

He was all the way down Karin's road and at the corner of New High, running steady but not so hard he'd get winded, when he got a picture in his head, and it was of the room full of people just before he'd run out.

Zenna wasn't in that picture.

At the healer's house there were lights in the downstairs windows. Someone had told Jilly, maybe one of the children. She was ready.

He was up to the second baker's house, halfway down the hill in New High, when he passed Zenna. She must have used that three-point run of hers to get there so fast, but she couldn't now, because it was too steep. "Go back!" he shouted as he went by, running fast enough that he said the first word before he reached her and the second when he was past.

She yelled back at him, her words getting littler as he left her behind. "No! You go forward!"

And he did.

Back at the bottom of New High, he started listening hard for the demon hum. He stopped and took off his shoes, and stuck them in the back of his belt with the heels against his back; then he was off at a jog trot again. He didn't know why he'd done that until he wondered; and then he saw that it was because his shoes made noise on the stones and demons came after noise.

Good thinking, Steffie. Now, *listen*.

He slowed. He stopped. He listened, hard.

Demon-voice, east.

There were paths down there through the sea grass, and they all came up to Harbor Road. The demons were down there, but how far down?

Funny how sounds sounded different, depending what they were and where you were. If the noise was a person talking, he'd know straight off how far away he was. But that hum, all those hums together, like all the strings on Belinda's fiddle all at once, only deeper . . .

Then he did hear voices, two of them.

One was that dog, barking instead of moaning, then just growling mean, like: *Burglars, stay back!*

Good dog. Do your job. You're a dead dog, but you're a good one.

Quarter of a mile away, just past the end of Harbor Road. Right.

The other voice was a man's, and it was just one shout. Janus. Steffie could tell. From the same place.

Stupid, stupid bloody idiot Janus, off all by himself, going to get himself killed—and Steffie was supposed to run *back* now, pass the word up to Kenno and get the militia, and *leave* Janus, just leave him on his own—

Steffie, there's not enough time to waste it standing and thinking. Either do what you want, or do what's right, but do it *now*.

He was a third of the way back up the hill on New High when he came to Zenna again, still coming down, swinging herself slow so as not to fall. "Go back," he told her, like before; but if she said anything, he outran it.

Kenno was at the crossroads by Jilly's. Steffie told him where the demons were. "And that Janus, he's doing something, he's right with them, but I didn't get close enough to see. Tell Corey. Don't wait. Something's happening now."

And that was the best he could do—except he thought of one more thing. Kenno had a scythe; Steffie took it.

Like it was enough to help. Like if he got close enough to use it, he wouldn't be already dead from that spray.

At the bottom of the hill, already going down Harbor Road, Zenna was swinging along hard, her shadowy shape making that shoulder twist that said she was about to start running, and she'd almost be as fast as Steffie that way.

And she had no weapon, and no hands free to use one, and she'd only got one leg. Nothing she could do, but she was still going.

So he got right in front of her, and let her crash against him; he dropped the scythe and grabbed at her shoulders to stop her falling. One of the crutches ended up swinging around and hitting the back of his legs, hanging loose from the strap around her left arm. He almost stumbled but got himself right before they both went down. "Stay out of it—you can't help."

"Are they coming?" She was clattering that crutch, trying to get it back right.

"The militia? Yes. The demons? Yes. There'll be spray coming one way and arrows the other. You don't want to be in the middle. What is it you think you're doing?" And in his head, Gwen's voice added: And how come *you* have to do it?

Then he didn't need to wait to know that Zenna wouldn't answer, because there was no answer, not to that question. And no words either one of them might say would change it.

So he did the only thing he could think of, which was to pull that crutch right off Zenna's arm and swing it once over his head and let it go, out into the harbor. He heard it thump, then clatter, then splash. Then he swept up the scythe, and he left her behind.

It was a rotten, *rotten* thing to do to someone like her, and it hurt him like a knife to think he'd done it, and he swore to himself he'd find the crutch later, fish it out for her—but Zenna wouldn't be going on now, and that was what mattered.

Up ahead, just past the end of Harbor Road, there was light, there was something burning. Someone was shouting, but it wasn't Janus, and that dog was making noise again, but not *Burglars*, now; it was more wild, like *Wolves! Evil! I will kill you!*

Of Janus he heard nothing, and Steffie ran silently himself, barefoot sore on stones, then dirt, then grass.

24

Something crashed into him, something grabbing at him, and falling, almost pulling him down. Steffie tried to get the scythe where it would do good, but the thing was too close. Then he knew it was some person—except it didn't sound like a person, making just noises, horrible noises, right in his face.

Steffie grabbed with one hand, and shook, and shouted, "Where? Janus and them monsters, *where?*"

It was a man, and the noises started being words, nearly. "Yes," Steffie told him, "there's help coming, yes, but I'm not help for you, I'm help for Janus." He couldn't see the man in the dark, and he was glad, because there was a lot of wet under his right hand, and shreds of cloth and bits of things shifting that shouldn't ought to, not properly. Steffie tried to break free without hurting him more. He spun him around, and pushed. "That way, go that way, it's Corey and the militia coming, soon—now *go!*"

He shoved him away, and the man stumbled half on the path, half in the bushes, and Steffie didn't stay to watch him go.

The light was up ahead—something burning, something big. Galer's old shed, maybe, Steffie thought, and that must have been Galer himself he was leaving behind.

Farther down the path he tripped over something, and he thought it was that dog—but then the dog set up again, yelping and whining, still ahead. There was the demon noise ahead, too; and Steffie tried to count the voices, but he couldn't. A lot. Just a lot.

Then he thought what he'd tripped over might be Janus, so he put out his hand—and brought the hand back fast. It was demon skin he touched, all sticky with that stuff they used for blood.

Well, good then. That's one down. Steffie wiped his hand on his shirt, and put his shoes back on.

Right then the shed fell in on itself. Steffie couldn't see it, but he heard it: a big sudden noise, and a hot wind pushed at him, hard. A huge spout of sparks went straight up, with the tree branches and leaves all turning away from the wind. Then the gust stopped; and it was just heat and light that Steffie was walking toward. He could feel it right through the trees. He got off the path and sidled along from trunk to trunk, stepping careful, because Galer always threw his trash out into the woods.

When he got to the edge of the trees, the whole yard was lit by that fire. He didn't have to worry about not seeing demons in the dark; and maybe that was what the fire was for, because what could a demon do to a shed that would make it catch fire? So it was Janus who set it.

Janus had to have light, to swing that sword. And he was doing that.

But it was funny, because that was *all* Steffie could see at first. It was like he couldn't put together anything else. Everything looked like nothing he had ever seen, and he could make no sense of it. But he could make sense of a man, a man with a sword in one hand, swinging it hard and slow and hitting something.

Then the thing Janus was cutting at sort of came together at the same time it was coming apart, because something fell off it onto the ground, and Steffie thought, Well, that's a demon arm. Cut right off.

And all at once Steffie's brain caught up with his eyes: the wreck of the shed to the left and the house beyond it; the open yard beside the shed, rutted; broken-down wagon half in the raspberry bushes; Janus stepping over a dead demon to get to a live one beyond it.

Right beyond it. Right there, within sword reach. Just a few feet away, but the demon wasn't spraying. It was just backing off, slow.

And past that demon, there were four—no, *five*—more, and Steffie couldn't tell which way they were facing, because of them having no faces—

But what they all were doing was walking away. Not running, just fading back. With Janus hacking at one still in his reach.

Then off to the right, with their arms pushing back the bushes, two more of the monsters coming out of the woods, crossing into the yard, moving fast—and pretty soon they'd be right behind Janus, where he couldn't see them, and that's when Steffie yelled, *"Look out!"*

They put up their arms to spray—but not the arms toward Janus, the ones toward *Steffie*. And he thought: Sound, they go for sound.

There was a broken bucket at his feet. He grabbed and threw it, past the demons, toward the shed.

Didn't even come close. But it hit the ground, it clattered, and the demons sprayed at it instead of him.

And Steffie ducked back.

Good. Good. Now what?

Stay still. Like in the alley, with that first one. Can't sneak up behind the monsters—they've got no behind to them.

But Janus did. He'd turned when Steffie shouted, and the demons now behind him started coming back. But the others—the ones Janus faced now—*they* were walking away.

Weird. That was weird.

Then the five from behind caught up with Janus and reached out their twiggy hands—and Janus spun back around, sweeping his sword, and demon hands got broken and jerked back.

And the demons *still* didn't spray.

But they moved back. They moved away.

Janus had something in his left hand, maybe a rock—and what a good idea that was. Steffie looked around on the ground nearby. He spotted something: not a rock but half a broken plate. Wait for a chance to use it.

The two from the bushes had started closing in again as soon as Janus's back was toward them; then Janus half turned, stepped to one side, and angled himself out—

And everything stopped.

Everything living just stopped dead still.

Only the fire moved, raging huge and wild in the wreck of the shed; and the light from the fire, flicking, weaving, on the ground, on the trees, on demon arms and demon bodies.

And on Janus, standing like a great dark stone, with the monsters lined up in a half circle before him.

His sword arm was thrown back, his sword point dropped down: not pointing at any demon—no weapon on the demons at all, unless you counted that rock in his left hand.

He stayed like that. And the demons stayed. All, all of them standing still . . .

And then, slowly, not in any hurry, every demon started moving off.

Away. Away from Janus.

And that's when Steffie knew.

That's when it all came clear. It was one thing to hear Rowan say it, a whole other thing to see it himself.

None of those demons were going to hurt Janus. Not while he was facing them. That was the thing.

Then Janus moved, and he moved fast: three long steps, sweeping his sword, and he hit the nearest demon straight in the side, and the sword went in, deep. The demon fell, thrashing. And Janus pulled out his sword, changed his grip, stabbed straight down, and twisted and twisted; and the monster flailed once, and died.

It hadn't tried to fight back at all. The whole thing was brutal and ugly; and it made Steffie feel good to see that demon die.

But going after that demon made Janus put his back to the others, and they started coming in again—

That's when Steffie figured a flying plate might do some good. He stooped, grabbed, threw, and ran to the right, across the path to another tree. The plate shattered on the ground, one demon raised up its arms and sprayed at it; and another shot right where Steffie had been.

Made his stomach twist, to see that.

But maybe the noise did help, because Janus had cut down another demon, and was going after a third one.

And all the rest walking again, just walking away.

Because Janus was facing them. Somehow, somehow something about him made them go. Janus didn't need help.

Steffie didn't need to be here. He could leave. He could run, tell people what was happening.

But . . . they were already coming. Weren't they?

They were supposed to be. And they should be here by now.

Even *Zenna* could be almost here by now.

But they weren't, nobody was. Which meant something was keeping them. Trouble.

How many demons could come at Alemeth all at once?

Plenty, it turned out.

He heard their voices; he turned; he saw two demons break through the bushes running straight toward him. He stood there with the scythe in one hand and he thought: Well, this is where I die. But those two went right by him like he wasn't worth the trouble.

So when another came out the same way, he said, out loud, "Right," and he got both hands on that scythe, and even though the monster spotted him when he moved and put up its arms to spray, Steffie was faster.

He put all his weight into the swing and didn't stop, and that demon was cut right through. Its bottom half took three steps and tumbled, its top half fell on the ground, and the spray it meant to shoot went straight up in the air.

The swing turned Steffie right around, and he saw Janus again and *more* demons, maybe a dozen: a whole ring of them all around Janus.

And Steffie figured, maybe Janus did need help, after all.

Someone to guard his back.

Right.

So when Janus went for one demon, Steffie went for another: just ran out from the trees, straight for the nearest monster, raising that scythe high, swinging it down like an axe.

That move saved his life, because the demon did spray; but it was stupid—it sprayed high at the blade.

Which hit it on the top. And went straight down its gullet. And Steffie yanked back, hard, and the thing's whole body burst toward him, sliced right open from the inside out.

And another demon sprayed, but Steffie was gone—he'd never moved so fast in his life.

Across the yard, toward that wagon wreck, then over it, behind it, then flat on the ground and staying still, just holding still and gasping.

He couldn't believe what he'd just done; he was scared to the bone, and shaking and sweating, and he said to himself, Steffie, you're the stu- pidest man in the world to be here right now. You've got more heart than sense, and what you've got to do is either lose some heart or get some more sense. Run away. Right.

But he didn't. He looked around for his scythe.

Then he remembered: he'd thrown it when he'd made for the wagon—to give the demons something to shoot at instead of him while he ran.

Must have worked. He was alive.

But—bloody *fool*, what good was he now, with no way to kill demons? What was he here for? All he could do was hide and watch.

That's when it came to him that that's exactly what he *was* here for.

To see. And then to tell.

People might not believe what Rowan said about Janus; but Steffie was right here seeing it, and they'd believe him. And if he and Janus lived through this, Janus would tell everyone how he'd done it. He *would*.

Because even if Janus could keep demons off him, there was no way he could keep Steffie off him.

So Steffie wormed along on stomach and elbows behind that wagon, and looked around the edge.

Everything had changed. A demon had Janus.

One big demon, its body spotted like a wildcat's, was right up against him, holding him, all its arms wrapped around him . . . and it had him from the *front*—how did that happen?

But now it was the demons on Janus's left all going away; and demons on his right all coming for him, grabbing at him, cutting their own hands on his sword blade. Then one got it away from him, dropped it. And then the demons on that side were all over Janus, clutching him, pinning him, and Janus fighting, kicking, trying to bash them with that rock in his one free hand.

Which was when Steffie realized that he'd stood right up behind that wagon. And the demons could see him.

So could Janus; he spotted Steffie standing there, and he shouted—for the first time yet, he yelled out loud, "*No!*" And he kept on—struggling, shouting, saying, "*Run! Get away! Go*, damn you!" And he flung that rock at Steffie, like he was chasing off a dog.

It hit the wagon, thumped, and fell—

And every demon there, all of them, went straight for Janus.

They didn't kill him; they didn't spray him. They didn't even slash him. They grabbed him and held him.

They dragged him off.

Away into the woods.

After a while, Steffie noticed that he was standing in the middle of the yard, and he must have walked there, but he couldn't remember doing it.

He just stood; and he felt like it was quiet all around, even though it wasn't. There was the fire roaring behind him; the demon-voices, getting quieter; and Janus, too, yelling, swearing at those demons, his voice getting farther away. But still Steffie felt like there was something like a silence all around; and he couldn't move at all, it was that quiet.

A thought came to him, sort of slowly; and it was that this was the right time for Rowan to show up.

Then he got a picture in his head: himself, years from now, sitting by the fire at Brewer's, telling the tale of the demons. And when he got to this part, he would say, Then Rowan showed up, and she thought of a really clever plan, and we went after them demons, just us two, and killed them all and saved Janus, and that's him sitting right there in the corner.

But Rowan didn't show up. She kept on not showing up.

After a while, other people showed up. But none of them were Rowan, and it was all too late.

25

"I shouldn't have left Alemeth," Rowan said.

Steffie winced, and glanced away. "Don't know. Looked like the thing to do, didn't it? And you got back as fast as you could . . ."

"I wish I'd seen those marks on the beach myself."

"Had to be a boat," Steffie said again, "sure as anything. Marks from some big thing, dragged up on the beach, and the trail them demons left leading right to it."

Rowan was pacing the width of the room. "Animals can't possibly use a boat." She reached the back door, glowered at it, turned. "Nor could they capture a person and spirit him away," she said. "They haven't the wit."

Zenna, seated in the wicker chair, her hands lying loose in her lap, did not even lift her head. She said only one word. "Magic."

"Of course."

"Magic done on animals . . ." Steffie said. "Like those dragons in Donner Zenna mentioned?"

"Yes . . . Jannik, the wizard in Donner, can cause dragons to do his will." Rowan reached the front door. She wished she had more room to pace or the calmness to do so more slowly. "Apparently," and she turned again, forced herself to stand still, "apparently some other wizard can do the same with demons. Some unknown wizard. Magic that cannot be attributed to any known wizard. Here I've been, all this time, looking in book after book—" she found she was halfway across the room again; she stopped by the worktable—"when what I ought to have done"—and she threw out her arms—"is simply look *around*!"

Steffie startled and eyed her warily; Zenna continued to gaze at her hands. Rowan dropped her arms. "It's got to be Slado's doing. It must be."

"And Janus mixed up with him and his demons, somehow," Steffie said. "But if Slado had it in for Janus, why didn't them demons just kill him once they got him?"

There was a long silence before either steerswoman stated the obvious. "If Janus knows something about Slado's doings," Rowan said, "the wizard will want to know how much. How he learned it. Who else he told it to. Janus is going to be interrogated."

Quiet. Outside, rain pattered briefly, then drove sweetly against the high glass windows; a rare sound, and beautiful, Rowan thought, like no other in the world.

"Won't do much good, that," Steffie said eventually. " 'Cause Janus told nobody else."

"Maybe there's a reason."

"What?"

Rowan had not realized she had spoken out loud. She blinked. "Something someone said to me, once. Someone who knew magic." Willam, now apprentice to Corvus, trying to justify keeping his own magic secret.

Maybe it's something people shouldn't know, Willam had said, pleading for her understanding. *Maybe it would be terrible if anyone else knew . . . Maybe it's terrible that I know.*

"And so Janus resigned," Rowan said, half to herself. To protect us? "No. There is no knowledge of that kind."

Steffie was lost. "What? What kind?" Zenna raised her head to study Rowan, her gaze narrowed.

"There is," Rowan said slowly, "no knowledge of which the mere knowing constitutes danger. There is never a need to be protected from knowledge itself. It's action, or inaction, that causes danger. Information is neutral." She took a few pacing steps again, found herself angry at the uselessness of the activity, forced herself instead to lean back against the worktable. "Janus ought to have spoken. The more the common folk know about wizards, the less they can intimidate us."

"He's alive." Zenna had been so long silent that Rowan and Steffie both turned to her in surprise. She was sitting erect; she looked from one to the other defiantly. "We have to help him."

Rowan drew a breath, released it, found that her grip had tightened on the edge of the table behind her. "Yes. If we can. But we don't know where to look—"

But Zenna was already shoving herself up out of her chair in a lurch that brought her to the worktable without using her crutches. She scrabbled among the papers and charts there, found the one she sought, yanked it from among the others, and set it down, oblivious of the smaller sheets that slid to the floor all around. "There." She stabbed at the chart with a pointing finger.

SHIPS VANISH. A new notation. Rowan listened, speechless, as Zenna explained, rapidly and concisely.

When she finished, Rowan stood gazing blindly at the chart very still, the spread fingers of both hands bracketing the notation. "That's where Janus landed after the shipwreck," she said. "It must be. That's where he learned about demons. That's where he's been sailing to"—her hands became fists—"in his copper-bottomed boat."

"And that's where we have to go."

"Not we, Zenna. Me."

Steffie was making abortive attempts at speech; both women ignored him. "We," Zenna said. "I'm a better sailor than you are, Rowan. You know that. I was raised on the sea."

"But—" Steffie managed.

"Zenna, have you seen Janus's boat?"

"From a distance. Sloop-rigged but too broad in the beam. Fully loaded, and with that copper hull, she should wallow like a cow in a swamp. You'll need sharp sailing to keep her right."

"But, but—"

Rowan remained adamant. "It won't be easy. But I can manage."

"It *will* be easy, because there will be two of us."

"Zenna, no."

"Why not?" Then she stopped short, straightened, answered her own question. "All right—I know why not. But you're wrong. Even with one leg, I can be useful. I can hold a tiller. I can chart a course. I can cook. Skies above, Rowan, I know I'm better at *that* than you are!"

"Can you handle the boat alone?"

"There will be two of us—"

"Can you handle it," Rowan asked again, "*alone?*"

Silence. Then, "I won't need to."

Rowan felt a grim smile on her own face. "Possibilities," she said, "are two."

Bracing herself awkwardly against the table, Zenna glared up at her friend. "I'm willing to take that chance," she said forcefully.

Rowan said very quietly, "I am not. It's not your choice. Zenna, Slado is the most powerful wizard in the world. I have no idea what I'll find when I go there. I don't know what I'm getting into, and I don't know if I'll come out of it alive. But I will not allow you to become stranded, alone, on a boat you can't sail—right in Slado's shadow. I go alone."

No steerswoman could hide from the truth. Zenna surrendered. "Then I'll help you here. Come on." She pushed off from the table and took a lurching step toward the hearth and her crutches.

Steffie finally managed to interject, "Hey!"

Both women turned to look at him. The sudden attention flustered him, but after some sputtering he got out, "I've got something to say."

"Say it," Rowan said, and she went to the coat hooks, retrieved Zenna's cloak and her own.

"Well, well, first off, it's this. Janus, and all. I mean"—he turned to Zenna—"I know how you feel about him, lady, and I'm sorry, but"—and he turned to Rowan—"I know how you feel about him, too, and I'm thinking it's a lot like how I feel about him—and if it was Janus being here brought them demons to kill people, and him never warning anyone about it, and a wizard's got him now, then I say serves him right. Why is it you want to go sailing off to rescue him?"

Rowan hardly knew how to begin answering. She stood mute while the reasons ranked and ordered themselves in her mind.

A wizard living perfectly hidden, in a perfectly secret place.

An old friend who had lied to her, lied about her, betrayed her.

Slado. Janus.

Rowan said, "I need to know."

Steffie dropped his jaw. " 'Need to know,' " he said in a small voice. "I guess I can tell I'm talking to a steerswoman. She needs to know."

Rowan swung on her cloak, passed the other to Zenna. "Second off," Zenna said as she donned and clasped it.

"What?"

"You said 'first off.' There ought to be a 'second off.' "

"Second off," Steffie said. Then he turned to the chart on the table. "Second off—I don't know much about maps, ladies, but I'm looking at this one, and what I see is a lot of exactly nothing, exactly where you're meaning to go. Miles of nothing. Wizard's got to be in some one place in all them miles, and you don't know where that is."

"Charts," Zenna said.

"Nautical charts," Rowan amplified. "Any sailor would have them. If Janus kept returning to the same place, he'll have made charts of the course."

"They'll be in his boat," Zenna said, swinging herself toward the door.

Rowan held the door open; rain swept in. "No. I looked there. But he has a room in town, and he keeps it locked; that's where they'll be."

"Good. We should take a lamp."

"I'll get it." Rowan stepped back, brushing past Steffie, snatched the lamp from the mantel, and used a twist of paper to light it from the fire.

"Third off," Steffie said. Rowan looked up. "What about them demons? Janus knew how to keep 'em back, when he was facing them anyways, but you don't."

"Not yet." Rowan adjusted the flame, returned to Zenna's side.

"Steerswomen write things down," Zenna said to Steffie. "It's like an instinct with us. If Janus learned anything at all, he'll have kept notes of some kind—"

"If we find nothing, then you're right, and there's nothing I can do," Rowan said. "And I'll abandon the whole idea. But I believe that we will find *something*. If we find charts, we'll find notes."

"Between Rowan's knowledge and mine, the two of us might just be able to reason out how Janus's spell operated."

"Spell?" Confusion on Steffie's face; then sudden realization.

"It could be something quite simple," Rowan said to Zenna. "If it's an incantation, the entire spell itself might be sitting up in his room, written out."

"With any luck," Zenna said.

"It had better not be!"

Steffie stood in the center of the room, arms flung out, hands in trembling fists. His eyes were huge. "If, if," he said in a voice that cracked, "if you find a magic demon spell that could have kept people safe, sitting *right up there in his room all this time*, then—then, Rowan, I swear I'll knock you on the head and *sit* on you for three weeks straight until I think that wizard has got all his answers and killed Janus dead! I'll do it, Rowan, I swear I will!"

The change in him stunned Rowan, and she was a few moments finding a response. "Steffie," she said, "if I find a spell that simple and that strong . . . then I will go and get Janus and personally deliver him into the justice of the people of Alemeth."

"Good." His eyes told her what he thought the people of Alemeth should do with Janus. Then he drew deep breaths, relaxed his stance, looked away from her, eyes narrowed. "Good."

Zenna spoke. "It's a one-person spell."

Rowan turned to her. Zenna continued, "Possibilities are two: either only Janus himself can work the spell, or only one person at a time can work it. He would have shared it if he could—I know he would have. But he didn't. So he couldn't."

Rowan was not at all convinced of this. Nevertheless: "Let's take that as a working assumption."

"Right," Steffie said. "Let's go and find out." And he pushed past the steerswomen roughly on his way out.

When they did not follow immediately, he turned back to them, standing in the street in his shirtsleeves in the rain. "If that door's locked, you'll be needing someone to knock it down," he said, raising his voice over the hiss of water. "Right now, I feel just like knocking something down."

26

*B*y the time they reached the cooper's shop, rain had cooled Steffie's anger. Nevertheless, Rowan stood back and let him use the hilt of her sword to smash at the rotted, thin wood beside the padlock, which he did with a cold and methodical efficiency.

Down in the courtyard, Zenna's up-tilted face was a spot of paleness in the gray, rain-pattering light. The stairs were too narrow and unsteady for her to negotiate.

The wood gave; Steffie handed back Rowan's sword, pried away the hasp with his fingers, then swung the door open and stood aside to let her enter first. She raised the lamp as he came in behind her. "Hell of a way to live," he commented. He brushed water from his face, shook his head like a dog.

"It's hardly worse than Mira's when I arrived." Piles of used clothing were scattered about; the motion of the lamp gave them moving shadows, like small animals ducking in and out of hiding. "At least there are no dirty dishes."

"Well, here's a place to start." Steffie made for a small chest in the room's far corner. Rowan slipped out of her cloak, allowing it to drop to the floor, then remained where she stood, scanning the room.

If she herself lived here, and she wished to work, to study or write, where would she do it?

There was no table, or desk. A straight-backed chair stood alone against the damp-stained outer wall, but clean clothing stacked on it demonstrated that it was rarely used.

The bed was merely a straw-stuffed canvas mattress lying directly on the floor, strewn with ancient pillows. A small lath crate served as nightstand, with a reflector candleholder resting on it.

Rowan crossed the room, set the lamp beside the candle, and sat on the mattress, finding musty pillows already cradling her back comfortably.

A sweep of bare floor lay before her, illuminated by a wash of lamplight. A perfect work space.

The crate was open on the side toward the bed. "Here," Rowan said.

It had been agreed that the first examination of notes must take place in Janus's room. Rowan had good evidence of magic's dependence on precise conditions; quite possibly the spell could only be worked, or even comprehended, in this one place. As Steffie folded himself to a seat opposite Rowan, she pulled out the contents of the crate and spread them on the floor: a fat folder of stiffened paper, tied with a ribbon; pens, spare quill nibs, and a penknife; a brass ruler and calipers; a stone bottle of ink; a leather roll; a burlap sack.

The sack was unexpected. Rowan loosened the drawstring, upended it. A number of brown and black objects spilled out. "What in the world?"

They were like nothing she had ever seen. She sat regarding them stupidly, entirely unable to integrate their shapes into anything she could name. Presently, she resorted to counting them: nine. The act of enumeration steadied her, oddly, and she found that she could at least see that the objects were designed with a particular orientation. She reached out to begin setting upright those that were lying on their sides.

But the first that she touched, she recognized not by sight but by feel. "I *know* this . . ." She closed her eyes to let her hands remember. "In the Outskirts, we found something near where a demon had been. A sphere . . . we thought it was a demon egg, but it had only water inside. It felt like this . . ." Both sandy and gummy, as if some steerswoman had not waited for the soles of her boots to dry before walking on a beach.

Rowan opened her eyes again. "But it did not look like this." The sphere had been simple and the reddish-brown color of Outskirts earth. The object now in her hands was complicated and mottled brown and black.

It was a canted cone, she saw now, with odd bulbous protrusions and a flat base. She set it down. The next was a rounded ellipsoid section from which rose three curving flutes, their surfaces completely covered with close, shallow depressions. The others were vague blocks, scarred masses, and a number of rough, flattened pyramids.

Cautiously, Steffie touched one. "Be careful," Rowan said. Handling the sphere had caused the Outskirters' hands to itch and peel the next day. "I'm sure these are the cause of Janus's problem with his hands." Steffie drew his finger back, more quickly than was necessary. "The effect is cumulative," she assured him. "If you do handle them, be sure to wash your hands later." She set down the object she was holding.

The leather roll almost certainly contained the charts, and at that thought, Rowan felt a sudden, sharp yearning, as if the maps were almost audibly calling to her. But the spell was more likely in the folder. She opened it, found a collection of loose pages. She sorted through them, seeking the unexpected.

She found first: pages with torn edges and writing spoiled by immersion in water—from Janus's own logbook, Rowan surmised, rescued by him after the shipwreck. Then: sketches in charcoal on dried, damaged paper: a mudwort; the leaves of a tanglebrush; a skinny, four-limbed insect Rowan recognized as a trawler—Outskirts life-forms, with the proper accompanying descriptions and measurements. Among these, executed in lampblack ink, was a diagram of one dissected quarter of a demon's body, nearly exactly as Rowan had drawn her own.

Finally: page after page of drawings, each resembling the others closely. Rowan thumbed through them to confirm the fact, then returned to the first of that series.

Steffie tilted his head, trying to read the notation. "What's that say?"

" 'Talisman,' " Rowan read. She drew a breath. "This must be it."

"Is that a one-person spell?"

"Yes."

The sketches showed a truncated pyramid, with a swirling grooved surface; the notes described it as standing about four inches square at the base, rising to two and a half inches, rounded at the top, colored in blotches and twists of black and brown.

Rowan glanced through the pages. All were views of the talisman: careful, detailed. At first sight they seemed exactly the sort of precise work Rowan would have expected of any good steerswoman, but there were far more sketches than were necessary to convey the information. She went through them again, more slowly.

First: rough sketches. Next: sketches less rough, with measurements more and more specific and precise. Then: one depicting the object with an obsessive, almost hallucinatory clarity but which included no measurements whatsoever, rendering it oddly mute to Rowan's eye, and disturbing.

After that, all the way to the end, the talisman: page after page, view after view, numbered, measured, marked, each executed with dry, detached precision, each page telling the same tale, over and over.

Rowan reached among the strange objects on the floor, pulled out one of the rough pyramids. She compared it to the eerie, voiceless drawing. "Similar . . ." But not exact. It was close in shape, but the colors did not match at all, the surface was uneven, the raised swirls clumsy and notched.

She picked up the penknife, compared its size to the irregularities. "He was trying to make one. And failing." And handling the objects bare-handed—at least for a while. Janus must not have realized, or not realized at first; apparently, with repeated exposure, even washing between times was not enough, and damage to the skin became permanent and self-sustaining. If Janus had learned this, he had learned it too late.

She set aside knife and object, turned the pages to the later drawings. "These specifications are very precise . . ." Decimal divisions of an inch down to four significant places, for the size and height of each swirling groove; degrees of arc for the cross section of a typical groove, and a for-mula for increase and decrease along the groove's length. "I'm not sure this is humanly possible," she told Steffie.

He did not reply. She looked up, and found him sitting loose limbed and slack jawed, stunned, his eyes on Janus's failed creation. "Bloody hell?" he managed to get out, barely audible.

"Steffie?" Rowan felt a sudden twist of fear at the thought that magic might be about to manifest itself, here and now, somehow choosing to de-volve upon Steffie. She put out a hand to touch him, then held back.

Very slowly, he reached out and picked up one of the pyramids. He gazed at it in a breathless puzzlement for a long moment, then carefully placed it in his left hand.

He rose. He stood in the center of the room, holding the object away from his body, slightly to his left—and then, in a movement utterly natu-ral, and so seeming even more bizarre, he hefted it, as if testing its weight.

"Bloody hell!" He flung it down, and was out the door and pounding down the stairs.

Rowan scrambled after him, tripping over her cloak on the way. "Steffie!" She picked it up.

"It's still there!" she heard him call back.

"What?" Zenna shouted the question. Rowan was halfway down the stairs when she discovered that she had somehow snatched up the roll of maps.

In the courtyard, Zenna was trying to restrain Steffie. "What do you mean?" she asked him.

"He tried to *give* it to me!"

"When?" Rowan reached them, swung her cloak on. "How?"

"In the fight!" He blinked rain out of his eyes. "He *threw* it at me! It's still there—it's got to be! Come on!" He pounded off into the street.

With a glance back at Zenna, Rowan ran after him, sighted him, called ahead, "Wait! We don't know where you're going!"

"Galer's place!" But he did pause, jittering with urgency, while Rowan and Zenna caught up. "See, see," he said as they hurried on, "them demons, they only could come up behind him, 'cause that thing, it was always in front or to the side—" he paused to gasp for breath "—and that's why they would come at his sword on the right side, but not on his left—"

"Shut up and run," Zenna said, and then suddenly did so herself, using an astounding, efficient method that Rowan had never before seen. Steffie showed no surprise, but sped up, then fell in beside Zenna as easily and naturally as if he had been doing it all his life.

Rowan followed close behind, clutching the roll of maps under her cloak, ignoring a startled shopkeeper standing in his door and two gossiping, oilskin-clad fishers who called after her.

Harbor Road ended; Steffie led them into a woody path, slower now. They passed a burly woman dragging a burlap bag on which lay a demon corpse, a man with a wheelbarrow that held a demon in two pieces, and then entered a cluttered yard that stank of wet, burned wood. Three women were sifting through a pile of smoking rubble; other workers stood by the open door of a shabby house, conversing.

Steffie ignored them all, went straight to the tilted wreck of a wagon. He knelt. "Here. I was standing behind, Janus threw that thing, it hit here"—he rapped the wood—"and fell." The three of them grubbed among the grass in front of the wagon. The workers left their duties and drifted over.

"I've got it." Rowan's hand knew it immediately. She drew it out carefully, mindful of the rain-driven grass wrapped around it; she did not wish to injure the critical precision of its surface.

She stood; Zenna and Steffie crowded close to see. The object lay in Rowan's hand, wet and streaked with broken grass, otherwise exactly like Janus's drawings. *I'm holding magic,* Rowan thought; but the idea seemed unreal.

"Now that we have it, somebody please tell me what it is," Zenna said. Rowan did so, describing her findings in Janus's room.

"What's a talisman?" someone asked. Rowan discovered that the work crew, Corey among them, had gathered around to listen.

"According to general information, a talisman is a magical object that protects its user from evil," Rowan replied.

"A one-person spell," Zenna amplified. "And Janus was trying to make more of them. He was trying to help."

Rowan did not point out that Janus ought to have reported the finding to the steerswomen; they could have set a dozen people to copying
the spell.

Corey looked extremely uncomfortable as Rowan explained further,
and she could see that he was struggling with ideas beyond his usual
scope. "But he couldn't make another one, so Rowan just said," Corey
stated finally. "So there's only one of them." He glanced around at the
assembled people. "I think it's me that better keep that." Perhaps the
simple pragmatism of his duties overrode any fears of magic; still, he did
not put out his hand for the talisman but only held Rowan's gaze levelly.

She passed the map case to Zenna, not doubting that Corey knew that
the action freed her sword hand. "It's staying with me," she said firmly.
"You won't need it again. No more demons will come to Alemeth."

"And how's that?"

"They were sent by a wizard, to get Janus. They got him. There's no
reason for them to be sent again." It had been Corey himself who, after
dealing with the other attacks, had led a crew of archers along the trail
that ended at the beach.

"Are you sure it's him they wanted and not that talisman thing?"

Steffie spoke up. "When Janus threw it away, it was him they went for,
not this."

"I assure you," Rowan said, clearly enough for the statement to carry
to all listeners, "we have no intention of damaging the talisman." She did
not mention that it, and she, would be leaving town entirely.

Corey studied her determined expression, then considered Zenna's,
and even Steffie's, seeming to give equal weight to all three. "Right," he
said, also pitching his voice to carry. "You lot go ahead and study it all you
like." He turned to the little crowd. "And you—got plenty to do your-
selves, haven't you? More dead demons to clear up, more wood to sal-
vage." He shooed them and followed them but paused to call over his
shoulder. "Rowan, if you don't want us putting demons into the sea, what
should we do with 'em?"

"Find a place very far from town and bury them," she answered. "Plant
nothing nearby that you intend to eat."

"Right." He glanced again at each of them, then turned away quickly;
and from the flicker of speculation in that glance, Rowan suddenly understood that he knew she had some plan involving the talisman. He had
publicly provided her with a reasonable excuse to keep possession of it
and the time to act without interference.

Zenna had arrived at the same conclusion. "Smarter than he looks. Isn't that always the way with the peacekeepers?"

"What next?" Steffie asked.

Rowan looked down at the talisman, feeling the weight of it in her hand, trying to sense the magic it held. She could not. She sensed only the utter strangeness of its design, a thing seeming even more alien to her than the wreck of the fallen Guidestar. She almost felt she was hallucinating it.

She looked up at Steffie. He was bedraggled, soaked to the skin, shivering.

"We get you dry," Rowan said. "We eat. We read the charts. And then we try to find out why it was that the magic failed Janus in the end."

27

"Like this?" Rowan asked.

Steffie looked up from the mug of hot broth he was cradling. "Looks like. Sword in the right hand, talisman in the left." He was shirtless, wrapped in a blanket, ensconced in the seat of honor in Mira's old chair by the flickering fire. His shirt was draped over the wicker chair, drying. "Sometimes his hand was out further than that, and sometimes it was closer in."

"That might be merely for balance." She tested a few moves: a crossing sweep from left to right, a downstroke, two twisting stabs. She found that the talisman hand tended to get thrown to the left. "Still, it's fortunate that I'm not left-handed. And the only demons that did approach him came from behind . . ."

"I think it's an emanation of some sort," Zenna put in, "and Janus's own body blocked the power from affecting the demons behind him. Think of it as a torch, or a lantern, and you can see the shadow your body will cast." She was seated at the worktable, copying Janus's maps; the originals must remain safely behind.

"Mystical emanations . . ." Rowan disliked the idea. And why would the presence of a nonmagical human body have any effect? "It might be most effective held directly overhead. But I couldn't hold it there for long."

"Could you put it on a hat?" Steffie asked.

"I don't know. But the only clue to its use that we have is what we saw Janus doing. I shouldn't risk doing anything differently."

"You'll have to get some gloves," Zenna said. For the present, Rowan had wrapped a kerchief around her left hand as protection against irritation.

"Yes. I hate using a sword with gloves." She set the talisman on the table, returned her weapon to the sheath hanging from the back of one chair, and sat down across from Zenna. "I wish I could be certain that I need merely possess the talisman to be protected." But the notes had contained nothing other than the sketches. "Steffie, you didn't hear Janus say anything, did you? Anything like a chant or an incantation?"

"Nothing." He looked faintly ludicrous, bundled up and bedraggled, the blanket pulled up over his wet hair like a shabby cloak hood. "And that's something, too: Janus didn't say a word at all, never made a sound until them demons already had him."

"Then silence is what I need, as well," Rowan said, unknotting the kerchief. She folded it more carefully than was necessary, patted it flat with a sigh of deep dissatisfaction. "I need more information, I really do. The demons captured Janus despite the talisman."

Zenna said, "Once the first one caught him from behind—"

"No," Steffie said. "First one had him from the front."

"He must have turned in its grip."

"Maybe . . ."

"Or," Rowan said, "the wizard himself was somewhere nearby—"

"Waiting in the boat," Zenna suggested.

"Perhaps," Rowan said. So close. "And he . . . he did something, called forth some counterspell to overpower the talisman . . ."

"But wouldn't he have to be right there?" Steffie said. "To see what those demons were doing?"

"Maybe he used another spell," Zenna speculated, "to see through the demons own eyes."

"Could be . . . or invisible?" Steffie wondered.

"It's possible," Zenna said. "An invisibility spell."

Magic. Spell after spell, upon spell—

Rowan threw up her hands. "This," she said, "*this* is what I hate about magic!" She rose abruptly, knocking over her chair, took two angry steps away, one back, and stood, dithering in frustration. "Every time one talks about magic, it's all ifs and maybes—it's all guesses, and guesses built on other guesses"—she made sharp, agitated gestures—"and hypotheses based purely upon guesses with anything, anything at all, possible—there are no *parameters*!" She flung out both arms, spoke to the world at large. "There *have* to be parameters!"

She leaned on the table, spoke urgently. "Anything that happens," she said—addressing Steffie only because she must address someone, and Zenna already knew these things—"any event, process, initiation, conclusion, any occurrence at all, must take place within a framework of delimited possibility. Reality is not infinitely fluid; if it were, the world would be a very different place than it is.

"Magic does have parameters. It must have. Look at this." Bare-handed, she picked up the talisman, went to Steffie, stooped to hold it before his face. "The construction is very, very precise. That precision isn't merely decorative. It's a result of the delimiting parameters, like the shape of a scythe or the keel of a ship. Those things are the agents of events, and they are shaped by their parameters and they reflect them. So must the talisman." She regarded it herself. "This object embodies its own parameters, and they are all right here, in clear view. It ought to be possible to *read* this thing like a book!"

"You know," Zenna said in a conversational tone, "you're asking rather a lot of yourself."

Rowan looked back at her. Zenna's expression was wry. "Yes," Rowan admitted, relaxing somewhat. "You're right." She turned back to Steffie and realized from his face that he had followed little of what she had said. She ought to have chosen a different vocabulary.

She sighed, straightened. "Well." She set the talisman on the table and then, very sensibly, went to the kitchen basin to rinse her hand. "At the very least, let's try not to stack too many guesses on each other. The whole thing could come crashing down on me in the middle of the wizard's keep."

"All right." Zenna folded her hands. "Looking at this as rigorously as possible, all we have is what Steffie saw and what you saw." Rowan had already described Janus's attack on the lone demon in Lasker's field. "Demons retreat from the talisman unless something else, like a human body, stands directly between them. And that adds up to line of sight."

Rowan sighed, dried her hands. "Demons have no eyes."

Zenna looked at her from under raised brows. "They must have eyes. They do have eyes. You simply didn't recognize them." She started sifting through Janus's notes for his sketch of a demon; but before Rowan could ask him to, Steffie retrieved Rowan's own logbook.

"I'm sure you're right," Rowan said. "I also did not recognize any ears. Nor organs of smell or taste. The only thing I'm certain of is touch." She pulled up the third chair, and the three gathered around as Zenna studied the pages.

She pointed. "What are these?"

"Small pockets of fluid, distributed all over the demon's torso. And the skin is very opaque; I already thought of that."

"Hm." Zenna flipped forward, back. "Where's the brain?"

"I didn't find one."

"No head," Steffie put in.

"Some simple animals do have no brain. But nothing as large and complex as a demon."

Zenna tilted her head back, her eyes half closed, thinking. Rowan found the pose so familiar from their Academy days that she could not help but smile. "Have I mentioned," she said, "how very good it is to see you again?"

Zenna's mouth twitched. "Be quiet, I'm thinking."

"About anything in particular?"

"Edith." She came out of her thinking posture. "Do you remember what she said about the senses?"

"I remember that she had a conjecture, which we discussed endlessly, to no conclusion whatsoever. She suggested that all senses might ultimately translate into touch."

Zenna explained for Steffie's benefit. "Your skin touches an object, and you feel it. Light bounces off everything around you, enters your eye through your pupils, touches the back of your eye, and you see. Sound vibrations travel through the air, enter your ears, touch certain small structures inside, makes them vibrate, and you hear."

Steffie almost visibly floundered in a sea of new concepts, then got his head above water. "How about when you're smelling things?"

"Well, Edith suggested that tiny pieces of objects, so small you can't see them, break off and float, like smoke. You breathe them in, and they touch the inside of your nose."

"The critical point," Rowan said, "is that, other than touch itself, all the other senses require something to actually enter your body to be perceived."

Steffie fingered the bridge of his nose, looking mildly affronted. "Sort of cheeky, that, getting right inside you and all."

"Edith's conjecture is only a conjecture," Rowan said.

"Hm. But for sight and hearing, there still have to be specialized structures." Rowan sat considering; then she emitted a noise of frustration. Zenna gave a weary sigh, and they turned back to the relevant page.

"The fluid pockets are the only things that come close. All the other unidentifiable structures are deep inside the body," Rowan said.

"Touch is attached to the skin; smell must be attached to the respiratory system. Taste would have to be in its mouth. That leaves only sight and hearing."

"Got to be just one or the other, you mean?" Steffie asked.

"If it sees, it can't hear; if it hears, it can't see."

"Huh. Deaf as a post or blind as a bat."

The steerswomen spoke simultaneously, reflexively. "Bats aren't blind."

Perhaps the precision of their performance took Steffie aback; it was a moment before he spoke in a perplexed tone. "They're not?"

But Rowan and Zenna were regarding each other in utter astonishment. Then Rowan made a small noise, and then a huge grin. Zenna threw back her arms. "That's it!"

"Yes, yes, it's perfect!" Rowan laughed out loud.

Steffie was watching them as if they were mad. In a sudden excess of glee, Rowan pulled him out of his chair. "Come here."

"What?"

"Stand up, stand up." She brought him to the center of the room. "Right here. Close your eyes."

"Um."

"Go on." She put her hand over his eyes until he complied. "Now, listen." She clapped her hands: a hollow sound in the big open area.

"Er, right, but—"

"Now come here." She half dragged him down an inner aisle of books. "There. Shut your eyes. Listen." A clap: close, smaller, more intimate. "Can you hear the difference?"

"Well, yes . . . yes, I can."

"You can tell what sort of space you're in from nothing but the sound. You can tell a lot from sound alone." She abandoned him, hurried back to the table. "And, in answer to your question," she called back, "bats can see, although their eyesight is poor—"

"But," Zenna said, "they hear very, very well."

"They emit noises—"

"Very high—"

"And they listen to the echoes—"

"And they can steer themselves in perfect darkness."

Steffie emerged from the aisle and approached, rather cautiously. "Echoes?" He adjusted his blanket.

"Yes. If you block a bat's ears—and we know this, because it's been done—they can't navigate in the dark."

"Exactly, exactly. Zenna, look." Rowan remained standing, too excited to sit. She jabbed at the page. "Sound touches the skin, the skin is in contact with the fluid—"

"And vibrations travel much better in fluid than in air—"

"And these strings from the back of the pockets: they're nerves, they have to be. Dozens of them from each pocket."

"And *thousands* of them, counted all together. Rowan, this animal hears very well indeed."

"Demons emit a *lot* of sound. The fundamental tone is the loudest, but there are overtones all the way up the register. So many different kinds of echoes—their perceptions must be fantastically detailed."

"So, that noise, then. They make it . . . so they can see?" The idea clearly intrigued Steffie.

"Exactly."

"It's not line of sight," Zenna declared. "It's line of sound."

"Yes," Rowan said happily, then laughed. "Amazing."

Zenna looked up at her. "I see one very pleased steerswoman."

"Absolutely. I have a parameter." She held out her hands as if feeling the sounds moving around her with the palms of her hands. "Only one, but it's real. The demon's voice can't pass though a human standing in the way, can't reach the talisman, can't echo. The demon then can't perceive the talisman." In actual effect, this was little different from line of sight. "It's not a guess. It's a fact. It's something I *know*, something I can trust. I feel much better about this."

"Despite that we still have no idea why a demon retreats from the talisman when it does sense it?"

Rowan stopped short. She blinked. She sighed.

She sat.

Zenna set the talisman in the center of the table. The three of them regarded it silently.

"Maybe," Zenna ventured at last, "it's really, really ugly."

They laughed, and they continued laughing, the helpless laughter of persons who had been too long at a difficult job and had spent all they had in them. "Oh, that's got to be it, then," Steffie said. "Demon takes one look—or one listen, that is—and thinks, 'Bloody hell, I'm having none of that thing!' and heads for the hills."

"And," Rowan said, wiping her eyes, "being so extremely stupid, as soon as something blocks the view"—and she put on an exaggerated Alemeth accent—"it's 'Wonder where it's got to now? Oh, well, think I'll just have at this fellow waving the sword at me'—"

Silence. "Oh, dear," Rowan said stupidly. "Zenna, I'm sorry—"

"Never mind. You just bring him back."

A knock on the door: so unexpected that they were all a moment reacting. Steffie rose, but Rowan motioned him back to his seat and answered it herself.

Barely recognizable in billows of oilcloth and a wide-brimmed hat, Corey stood in the rain. "Ought to get curtains for the windows," he said, brushing past Rowan, pulling off the hat, leaving a trail of water.

"I was thinking of it," Zenna said, bemused. "The sun's not good for those books—"

"Not them windows"—pointing at the ones in front of the first aisle—"that one"—to the left of the door. "Person outside can see everything going on in here. Good thing no one's out, night like this. Here." He arrived at the table, extracted from under the oilcloth a small wicker box. "Hope you can keep quiet about it."

Rowan shut the door and approached, as Zenna lifted the lid. "Oh, lovely! Thank you, Corey."

"What is it?" Rowan asked.

Corey shot her a glance. "The steerswoman—Zenna, I mean—she hasn't got a penny to her name, has she, since that party?"

Rowan was lost. "What party?"

"I'll tell you later," Zenna said. "Corey, where did this come from?" The wicker box contained a large number of coins.

"I went around, quiet-like, to a few people. Don't want everyone in on it. Too many people, and not all of 'em sensible—some might get the idea that it's asking for trouble, and try to put a stop to it."

"A stop?" Rowan said.

He looked at her. "Well, you're going to go chase your sweetheart, aren't you?"

"He's not—"

"Right, right, he's not your sweetheart. But you're going, and you'll need supplies, and the steerswoman can't help you, and there it is. If I was you, I'd buy it all tomorrow morning while everyone's at work, and be gone by noon." He brushed past her again on his way to the door.

"Corey—" He paused; she searched for adequate words. "Thank you."

"Don't thank me. It's Dan and Maysie put the most in there. None of my money."

"But they didn't think of it. You did. Thank you."

He nodded curtly. "Try to get back in one piece." And he left.

Rowan shook her head in astonishment. "Imagine that."

The coins clinked as Zenna sifted through them with one finger. "There's much more than you need here."

Steffie tested his shirt by the hearth, found it sufficiently dry, slipped it on. "Well, that's good," he said from inside the shirt, "because"—and his head emerged—"it'll take twice as much, won't it?" He shook out his hair.

"Not quite," Rowan said. "Janus will only need food for the return trip."

"Oh, right, Janus. Forgot about him for a minute. Then, I mean two and a half times." He tucked in the shirt.

"Steffie, I can't let Zenna come—"

"Don't mean Zenna." He came and planted himself solidly in front of her. "I mean me. I'm going with you."

Rowan was beyond words; and when words did come, they were very few. "Oh, Steffie," she said. "No."

His stance was stubborn; his face, less so. But he spoke defiantly. "You'll have to tie me up to keep me from going."

"I'll get the rope," Zenna said.

Rowan took him by the arm, led him to the armchair, made him sit; then found that she was sitting on the floor before him, both his hands in her own. His hands were large and strong and had far fewer calluses than hers did. She remained speechless, unable to combine gratitude, admiration, and unequivocal refusal in one sentence. She wished she did not need to deny so great a spirit.

Zenna spoke. "Changed your mind about Janus?"

He glanced over at her. "Maybe. Sort of. I don't know. But that's not the thing." He looked down at Rowan. "Janus has got two good friends willing to do anything it takes to help him, and one of them going straight ahead and doing it. Maybe that's more than he deserves, maybe it isn't. But seems to me that what I've got is my own good friend, going straight into bad trouble, and I couldn't look myself in the eye if I didn't help her."

From his face, he knew every one of Rowan's objections; and that very fact forced her to voice them. "Can you handle a sailboat?"

"Never done it."

"Use a sword or a bow?"

"You know I can't." His hands shifted in hers. "But I'm strong, and I'm steady, and I'll do any kind of work that's put in front of me for as long as it takes. I've seen enough demons not to freeze up when I spot 'em. I don't give way, I'm smarter than I look, and I'm good at taking orders."

"How good?" Zenna asked.

He turned to her, then back to Rowan. "Real good."

"Complicated orders?"

Something in Zenna's voice gave him pause. "Well, sure. I can keep a list in my head, I do it all the time."

Zenna regarded him sternly. "Can you do what you're told, do it straight away, and save any questions for later? Lift something, push something, haul on a sheet?"

He blinked, sat up straight. "If you tell me to," he said with enthusiasm, "I'll pull a pillowcase right over my head and not ask you why until springtime."

"A sheet is a rope."

"Well, I've seen a rope before."

"Perfect. Rowan, we're *all* going."

"What?" She released Steffie's hands.

Zenna folded her arms. "My brain," she said firmly, "and Steffie's body. Between the two of us, we can sail that boat all the way back to Alemeth, even without you."

"But—"

"Shut up, Rowan, it's settled. Steffie, get over here for your first lesson in seamanship." He leapt to his feet as Zenna reordered Janus's charts; Rowan was left sitting on the floor by an empty chair.

"Now," Zenna said to Steffie with mock seriousness, "this is what we steerswomen like to call a map."

He played along. "Map. Right. Got it."

"Here's Alemeth. And here's where we think the wizard's keep is. Now, as you can see, only the first part of the journey is by sea, and the rest is over land—"

"I guess I know how to walk—"

"You'll be walking nowhere!" Rowan climbed to her feet. "You," she said to Steffie, "will be staying with the boat and with Zenna. You are *never* to leave her on her own."

He smiled at her. "Right. Sure. Makes sense to me. If I'm the body and Zenna's the brain, well, you never see your body walking off and leaving your brain behind, do you?"

"Actually," Zenna put in, "I know a few people who fit that description—"

"And at the first sign of trouble, you will both turn around and sail home!"

Steffie pursed his lips, shook his head. "No, don't think so. Just can't see that happening."

"I think that what we'll do instead," Zenna said, "is turn around at the *last* sign of any trouble that we can't handle ourselves."

"Right." Steffie stepped behind Zenna, rested his hands on her shoulders. "That's the way it's going to be, Rowan," he said, "and you can take it or leave it. In fact, forget about the leaving it part, because you're going to take it, and that's a fact."

Rowan realized then that she had already acquiesced and they were merely hammering out the details. She huffed a small, helpless laugh, and then another. "Oh, very well." Steffie laughed and clapped his hands; Zenna leaned back in her chair, with a broad, catlike smile of satisfaction. "For as far we sail," Rowan said, "we sail together."

She came to the table, turned the chart around. "From Alemeth"— and she indicated it to Steffie—"east and then south"—avoiding a number of islands with treacherous crosscurrents—"east again through the center of this."—THE CHANNEL, Janus's chart read—"past these"— MERMAIDS? the notation wondered and later declared, oddly and emphatically LITTLE SNAILS!—"then to shore and an anchorage . . . here."

Steffie leaned in to see, paused while sorting out the words, then breathed them in a tone of wonderment, " 'The Dolphin Stair' . . ."

"And from there," Rowan said, "I go on alone."

28

OUR, the notation read, nothing else.

And at that point, Janus's chart of the shoreline route beyond the Dolphin Stair ceased. Squinting in the sunlight, the two steerswomen studied the map clipped to the chart stand. It rattled slightly in the breeze.

"That must be it," Rowan said.

Zenna's finger traced the marked path that followed the wavering shoreline. "Something's there, for certain." Her finger passed the numbered sites in turn. "One, two, three, four." Sites one through three were circled, then crossed over. Only four was merely circled.

"Possibilities identified, then eliminated," Rowan stated.

"Only if the crossing means elimination," Zenna said, with obvious reluctance. "For all we know, it might mean something else entirely."

The ship's rise and fall became, briefly, a stutter as the bow met a series of small cross-waves. A startled "Ho, hup!" came from above, and the motion smoothed again.

"Something was found at each of these sites. And the last is different from the other three. That's got to be it: a wizard's keep."

Rowan had once seen a wizard's keep, when she and Bel had infiltrated the fortress owned jointly by the brother and sister wizards, Shammer and Dhree. It had been huge, with towers and chambers, courtyards—in all effect, a village unto itself. The wizard Abremio possessed something similarly impressive, built on a cliff overlooking the city of The Crags.

As a student in Wulfshaven, Rowan had once wandered near the limits of the spawling riverside estate belonging to Corvus; a forester, one of several in Corvus's employ, had kindly warned her back.

Of the other known wizards, Jannik possessed a large and mysterious house in the heart of the city of Donner; and Isara dwelt in a seemingly humble but magically impregnable cottage in the upper Wulf valley. Only

Olin's abode—variously described by perplexed witnesses as a palace; a fortress; a floating house; a cave; and on one occasion, a hollow tree— had never been reliably located but must lie in his holding, somewhere north of Five Corners.

One more wizard, previously unknown, immensely powerful, jealously secretive . . . And a mark on paper, reading FOUR.

"You'd think," Rowan said aggrievedly, "that Janus would at least have had the courtesy to label it 'Wizard's keep here.' "

A few strands of hair had escaped the tight braid Zenna wore; the wind caught them, streamed them across her face. "And since he didn't," she said, capturing and twisting them behind one ear, "is one there at all?"

Rowan was silent a long moment. "It's the easternmost location on the map."

"Yes."

"It's the last place Janus went."

"Yes."

"After which . . . demons came to drag him away."

"And only a wizard could make that happen."

"It's got to be Slado," Rowan said through her teeth, then in sheer frustation thumped the edge of the chart table with the side of one bare foot. "Who else would *hide* like that?"

Zenna leaned back on the pilot's bench and closed her eyes. "We don't know, we don't know, we don't know, we don't know." She opened them. "Shall I say it a few more times? But what I'm convinced of is this: Janus was taken there."

"Then that's where I go."

A thump, as Steffie slid down off the low cabin housing. "Did it."

"Good," Zenna said without looking at him. "Do it again."

He hesitated, opened and closed his mouth, then hoisted himself back onto the cabin, turned to hands and knees, cautiously gained his feet. "Don't lock your knees," Rowan called, just as the boat crossed another set of cross-waves. Rowan noted, pleased, that Steffie managed to fall forward, instead of back off the cabin. "You'll make a sailor of him yet," she said to Zenna.

"My loyal crew. And to think I joined the Steerswomen because I thought I'd never make captain." She looked up. "Ho! Steffie! Clip your line!" He glanced about, found the safety line where it had slid under the edge of the small skiff lashed to the top of the cabin. Steffie retrieved it, dutifully clipped it back onto his harness. Then, with a preliminary deep breath and squaring of shoulders, he set hands and feet into the footholds of the mast and climbed.

"How is his seasickness doing?"

"It comes and goes."

Rowan considered the direction of the wind, and rose. "I believe I'll sit over *there*."

It had taken the travelers six days to pass through waters already familiar to the local fishers. Sails had been sighted regularly at first, then less and less often, eventually dwindling to the occasional small fishing boat, cautiously putting out from one or another tiny settlement along the shore east of Alemeth. Finally, even the most stubborn of these turned about and headed toward shore, its bright green sail a mere chip of color on the west horizon. They never saw it again.

Two days past the last village, Janus's chart indicated that the boat should head to deeper water south. The reason was obvious. The shoreline became more and more fragmented, with crossing wave patterns and foamy whorls betraying the presence of subsurface upthrusts of rock, treacherous to navigation, impossible to predict.

With regret, Rowan watched the shore retreat to a mere shadowy line on the northern horizon. Janus's chart suggested that land was probably continuous from Alemeth all the way to the Dolphin Stair; but no steerswoman had yet been there, and if the area had seen other explorers, their reports had not reached civilized lands. Rowan wondered if the land was inhabited, or if some change in the native life prevented humans from settling there, wondered if Routine Bioform Clearance had ever been used there.

But she was allowed no opportunity to observe. Even before land vanished completely from sight, the winds grew fickle. Many resettings of sails and adjustments of sheets were needed to keep the boat moving at best speed, and all three sailors were kept busy. Rowan had no time for study or speculation.

She tried to allow Steffie and Zenna to handle most of the duties, so that they might learn to work smoothly together. It would not do for them to depend on her assistance. But for speed's sake, she ended up pitching in as often as not. She only hoped that there would be no need for such great hurry, if Zenna and Steffie must return without her.

Soon, rain settled in, and for two days sightings of stars or Guidestars were impossible. When at last the clouds broke, Zenna's reckoning found the ship to be further east than her assumed speed warranted.

"We're in the channel," Zenna said, brooding over the chart belowdecks.

Rowan wished the aft cabin had the headroom to allow her to pace. "And too soon. We've found a current."

Zenna nodded, plied her calipers again. "Hm. Let's check our speed." They donned oilskins and clambered above.

Steffie was delighted to see them appear on deck; the tiller terrified him. He relinquished it to Zenna with gratitude.

Rowan handed him a wood chip. "Take this. Go to the bow. Lean as far forward as you can." Steffie began to look considerably less grateful. "Drop the chip, and when it passes the bow, shout 'Now.' "

"Right."

Rowan stationed herself at the taffrail. Steffie gave his shout; somewhat later, Rowan gave another, as the chip passed the stern. During the four steps that brought her back to the cockpit, Rowan performed a quick calculation; arrived, she found that Zenna's own matched it.

"Definitely a current," Zenna said. "Good. It's helping us."

"Yes, but if we were sailing against it, and the wind were exactly wrong, we'd be having a hard time of it." And this might happen, on the return trip.

"Hm. I wonder if it speeds up further on?"

"It would have to get a great deal faster, if it were the sole deciding factor in ships getting lost in the channel."

"You're right." Zenna tilted her head. "You can come back now, Steffie," she called.

"Oh, good."

"But what this means," Zenna continued to Rowan, "is that we should look for trouble that much sooner."

The sky cleared, and days and nights grew cold. The wind was steady from the southeast, tacks became predictable. Steffie's facility with ropes and sails grew more dependable; and Rowan quite suddenly found herself with nothing whatever to do.

She could not map the land beyond the horizon. There was nothing to amend on the nautical charts. She could not change the winds or make the ship move faster.

She ended up positioned in the forepeak, scanning the eastern horizon for sail.

Somewhere ahead: an unseen wizard's ship—quite possibly on the same course, and certainly with the same ultimate goal.

She doubted that Janus's nameless boat could outpace any wizard's, and the wizard would probably not stop at Janus's anchorage at all but sail onward without pause. Why Janus himself had chosen to travel by foot after the anchorage, neither Rowan nor Zenna had been able to determine. But there must have been good reason, and for caution's sake Rowan would follow the marked path.

All the more reason to speed the voyage. The current and the winds were better than could be hoped for. She ought to be grateful; she was instead, persistently, pointlessly, impatient.

Steffie, however, welcomed the inactivity. He settled down on the deck behind Rowan and exhaled gustily. "Never figured," he said, "that sailing was such a busy thing."

"Have you never been on a sailboat at all?"

"Couple of times. Just to ride." Spotting a coiled mooring line nearby, he pulled it closer with his foot and turned himself around to stretch out in the sun, the coil serving as pillow. "Helped Gwen's dad run his crab traps a few times, but that's rowing."

The steerswoman made a distracted, noncommittal sound. Both were silent for long minutes.

"Funny," Steffie said eventually.

"What's funny?"

"Never thought to wonder before. About sails. With the wind pushing at the sail, how come we can go east? How come we don't just go away from the wind?"

Rowan paused, then revealed to Steffie the surprising fact that the wind was not pushing on the sail, but pulling it forward. Explanations were required, and digressions; then elaborations, and eventually diagrams.

The afternoon passed rather more easily than it might have otherwise.

The weather remained fair, then entered into a pattern of rainy mornings followed by clear afternoons and starry evenings. The ship passed through an area to which Janus had attached the question MERMAIDS? but none appeared, to steerswomen's disappointment and Steffie's relief; mermaids were rumored to bring bad luck.

Zenna drilled Steffie intensively on more and more sophisticated maneuvers. The training paid off. Twice they were caught by storms. The second lasted two days, and at the end of it, Steffie declared that encounters with demons had at least the advantage of being over quickly, and fell asleep in the middle of his dinner.

Rowan took his turn at watch that evening. Just before dawn, she was roused from her stargazing by the distinctive sound of Zenna clambering up the companionway. "You're early," Rowan called to her. Zenna's next watch was not due to begin for another two hours.

"I know." The younger steerswoman had not bothered to bring her crutches above. She reached herself from the cabin housing to the port rail, and made awkward but efficient progress aft by means of long, braced hops. "Go below a moment," she told Rowan, and reached out for an assist to take Rowan's place. "There's a noise. Tell me what you make of it."

Rowan did not hear it when she reached the bottom of the companion-way, nor when she entered the dark aft cabin. After a moment's thought, she lay down in the bunk, its blankets still warm from Zenna's body.

Tick, came through the pillow.

She tossed off the cushion and laid her head directly on the mattress. Tick-tick.

She had felt the sound through her hand on the bunk's wooden edge. She laid her head directly on the wood, and pressed her ear tightly against it.

T-t-tick, tick, and then the sound increased briefly, becoming a con-tinual tapping, quiet and intimate, like the sound of winter sleet against the outside wall of the sleeping room in her childhood home. It faded again.

Beyond the open door, shadows shifted from a moving light. Rowan found Steffie in the passageway, shirtless, sleep touseled, carrying a lantern. "Did you hear that?"

"It sounds like pebbles striking our hull." Both paused to listen.

Nothing.

"Got pretty loud before, up front," Steffie said. They went forward to the sail locker where Steffie had been sleeping. Rowan touched one of the bare ribs curving up the inside of the hull, then the wood between, then moved her hand lower, below the waterline, feeling the rhythm be-neath her fingers become clearer. "Down."

They climbed into the hold, Steffie lifting the lamp as Rowan sidled her way between the crates and barrels. Before she could reach the hull, the sound reappeared, now clearly audible, increasing: a continuous faint clatter, like hail. She stood puzzled, thinking, listening. The sound was louder toward the bow. "We're passing through something . . ." The rough wood planking of the floor communicated it to her bare feet, as well: hun-dreds of tiny collisions.

"Stones, or something like," Steffie commented.

"The sea's too calm to throw up stones from the ocean floor," Rowan said. With her entire body, she could feel the smoothness of the ship's course. "And the seabed's too far down for a current to do this." Then: "Or it was a moment ago." She scrambled back toward Steffie. "Up."

Above, the eastern sky had lightened to dawn pearl. Zenna's eyes were wide. "I'm feeling it through the tiller now."

"Where's the sounding line?" Rowan found it stowed in a compartment beneath the chart table. "We may have entered shallows." She hurried to the foredeck, swung the weight, and let it fly ahead of the ship, let the line run hot through her fingers, ticking off the knots as it sank. Four, eight, twelve fathoms, and then the lead pointed straight down. "Deep water," she called, not waiting for it to strike bottom. She pulled it in again, swung, let fly.

Steffie came up beside her. "Zenna says the ship's getting sluggish."

"I'm not finding shallow water here," Rowan said, and tossed again. She felt the weight speeding downward as the line ran through her fingers—then stopped. The line fluttered loose in the breeze. "I've lost the weight." She pulled in the line. Broken, at less than a fathom. She braced herself for a grounding, but none came.

The east had evolved a lemon haze, and the still-unrisen sun underlit the ragged lines of cloud overhead. The sea swells were deep and even. No shallow water would show a pattern like that.

Rowan returned to Zenna's side. "Sluggish?"

"Just a bit." Zenna was looking past Rowan, abstractedly; all her attention was on her hands. "Almost unnoticable . . . And I still feel those tiny stones." She startled. "More," she said; and an instant later the rattle rose loud enough to hear above deck.

Rowan strode to the starboard rail. "What *is* it?" Steffie was peering down along the hull. He shook his head, seeing nothing.

Rowan thought. "Get the net."

Steffie fetched the hand net, swept it down into the waters and back on deck.

About fifty small brown cones, an inch or so in length, glittered wet in the young sunlight. Rowan bent close, prodded them with one finger.

She recalled Janus's notation on the chart and laughed out loud. "It's little snails!"

Zenna's mouth twisted. "Little snails?"

"We're sailing though a swarm of little snails." There must have been thousands of them, to raise such a racket.

They were not any sort that Rowan had seen before. The shells seemed light, and did not spiral but grew straight out into a dull-pointed cone. Rowan picked one up. The shell had no door, and its inhabitant was cowering just within the entrance. As she watched, it experimentally extruded four veined fins, began waving them in a vain attempt to swim the air.

"Lot of fuss for little snails," Steffie commented.

"How badly is the swarm interfering with our progress?" Rowan called to Zenna, placing the snail on Steffie's upturned left palm. He poked at it curiously.

Zenna tested the tiller slightly, shook her head. "Not much. But I don't like the feel of it. Here, you try it." Rowan stepped over to her.

Steffie yelped.

Rowan turned back. He was shaking his hand. "Bugger *bit* me!"

"Are you all right?"

"Yes. No! *Damn!*" He pounded the heel of his hand on the rail. "Won't let go—" His face was twisted in pain. He tried to pull at it with his right hand, cried out again, stopped, cursing and hissing. "It's digging in—"

Rowan rushed to him. "Hold still, let me see." His hand was slick with blood. The cone seemed rooted to his flesh; she could not get a grip on it. Steffie was making wordless noises behind clenched teeth. Rowan pushed the side of the snail with her thumb; Steffie gasped and stumbled to his knees.

She pulled her sleeve over her hand and grasped, and pulled; Steffie shrieked. She squeezed hard, harder. The shell cracked. A tiny body writhed between her fingers; she crushed it.

Steffie gasped once, then relaxed, dropping to a seat on the deck, breathing through his open mouth, pale, wide-eyed.

Rowan knelt beside him and carefully extracted the creature. Within the wreckage of its body were four sharp spiraled spines, nearly an inch long, and a mouth ringed with tiny black teeth.

She considered it with disgust. "I hardly think," she said, "that 'Little Snails' constitutes an adequate warning."

A sharp whistle from Zenna. Rowan turned.

"I don't like the look of that," the younger steerswoman said, and pointed with her chin.

Rowan looked down. Within the net, all the cones were now upright.

She pushed at one with the toe of her boot. It was solidly attached. She picked up the net; it tore, and the snails remained, rooted to the deck.

She reversed the net and used the wood handle to crush the creatures, pounding and sweeping it along the deck, feeling each shell crack. Finished, she stooped down, finding the spiraled spines each drilled into the deck, some of the small mouths of the dying creatures still feebly grinding at the wood. She rose and exchanged a significant glance with Zenna. "Copper hull," they said, simultaneously.

Neither magic nor mermaids protected these waters. Thousands of little snails, attaching to the hull of an unprotected ship, drilling into the wood, gnawing at it; then leaks, hull breaches, and weakened wood splintering from the pressure of the sea.

No ship entering these waters would survive; no ship would return to give warning to others. Only Janus knew how to protect his ship.

Steffie was still seated on the deck, nursing his hand, viewing the mass of crushed snails with disgust and suspicion. Rowan helped him to his feet. "Let's go below and clean your hand." She led him to the companionway, and followed him down toward the hold and the freshwater barrels.

With one hand still on the top rung, she stopped.

Freshwater. Barrels of it.

Crates of salt fish. Another of dried fruit. Three more barrels, of pickled pork. Bread, sacks of wheat and maize flour. Two sides of smoked beef. And water, especially water.

Weight.

A crew of three, not one; provisions for three, not one. Three times the weight Janus generally carried.

She opened her mouth, closed it. Out loud, she said, "How low are we riding?"

She hurried up again, went to the railing, looked down. "I can't tell."

Zenna was puzzled. "What's wrong?"

The copper sheathing and the first foot of hull above it had both been painted black. Rowan could not tell where the copper ended: above the waterline or below.

A boat hook was stowed nearby. She grabbed it, reached down to drag it alongside the hull, meeting a multitude of small obstacles, the long wooden pole rattling in her hands.

Three long steps took her to Zenna's side. She thrust the boat hook into Zenna's hands, began lashing the tiller in place. "We're riding low," she began; but the other steerswoman needed no further explanation. Zenna lurched to the rail, leaned over, began thrusting and thrashing with the pole.

Rowan found Steffie in the hold by an open water barrel, a clean wet rag in one hand. He startled at Rowan's arrival: she had jumped the last three feet. "Find something to throw overboard."

"What?"

She grasped him by the arm, urgent. "We're riding low. The top of the copper is below the water. The snails are attaching. They'll eat through."

He stood gape mouthed. "Oh, no." He quickly tied the rag around his hand.

Rowan looked around, desperate. "What can we lose?" Not the freshwater. She pointed. "Can you handle those alone?"

The smoked beef. "No."

"Then this." A crate of salt fish. "Go." She took another.

They flung them overboard, making splashes pitifully small. "More."

On the way back down, Rowan paused to enter the aft cabin, emerged with her sword and Zenna's.

She passed the second sword to Steffie. "Use it to cut the beef in half."

"Right."

Rowan was about to follow him down but stopped: the cabin's table, the two chairs.

She hacked and split them with her sword and feet, carried the shattered wood above and sent it over the side. Steffie reappeared, flung half a side of beef overboard.

"Here." Zenna was at the chart table, taking the chart from its clips, stuffing it into her shirt. She banged one table leg with the boat hook, saying, "Get that," and went back to the rail.

The table was bolted to the deck. Rowan retrieved her sword from the cabin, tearing off two locker doors to discard while she was there, returned above, set to hacking at the chart table's legs. An axe would serve better, she thought. There was one aboard somewhere, but she could not stop to find it.

Steffie had sent all the smoked beef overboard and was now struggling with a barrel, which he had somehow got on deck. He winced from pain in his hand, but did not slack his efforts.

Shocked, Rowan spotted him. "What's in that?" she called.

He thumped it with his good hand. "Nothing." It went into the sea. "Used to be pork. Dumped it out on the floor."

"Good thinking. Help me with this." The chart table followed the barrel. "More."

All food that had a container lost its container. Most of the loose plank floorboards of the hold were sent up, and over. Lockers and cabinets lost their doors. Rowan and Steffie wasted precious minutes determining that the brick cookstove in the narrow galley could not be dismantled quickly. They set to work on the cupboards themselves, chopping them away from the walls; Steffie had found the axe.

Above, and overboard; and now Rowan could see two inches of cone-encrusted hull rising above the waterline.

Zenna was at the taffrail. "Drop sails!" she called.

Rowan spun on her. "What? No, we should increase our speed, we need to get out of these waters—"

"We're going nowhere if we lose our rudder." The rudder had been sheathed as well to the same level as the hull, no higher.

Rowan helped Zenna struggle with the lock pins. "Steffie, free the sheets." By the time they wrestled the rudder up, the boom was swinging wide and loose, the mainsail and jib luffing. Steffie found another plank, and started using it to dislodge the visible snails from the hull.

The steerswomen considered the rudder. The snails had attacked it in a five-inch span across its width. "The ship needs to rise more."

They hacked out the lockers in the cabin, and the bunk; and all the while, Rowan's body and sailing instincts were warning her, over and over, that the ship was adrift, and that it mustn't be, that it was dangerous. But there was no help for it, and the steerswoman clenched her teeth on the protest.

From above, a rattle, a thump, and the flooring perceptibly rose beneath her feet. She traded a wild glance with Steffie.

They hauled their wood above. "What was that?"

Zenna had worked her way to the bow. "I got rid of the anchor."

Rowan quelled the shouting in the back of her mind. "Good." She saved one shattered plank from the bunk, and used it to attack the snails on the starboard side.

Some she destroyed were immediately replaced by their fellows. "We still need to be lighter."

"Can we lose that?" Steffie pointed: the skiff.

They would need it when they reached Janus's anchorage, to row to shore. "Can you swim?" The chart did not note snails in those waters.

"Yes."

"Zenna?" She had been able to, before.

"Well enough."

"Then yes."

Rowan and Steffie manhandled it to the starboard rail and sent it into the sea, where it immediately became a hazard; with the ship making no headway, the skiff remained in the water at its side, and the waves attempted to dash it against the weakened hull. Cursing, they hauled it back in with the boat hook, reduced it to kindling, discarded the pieces.

Rowan checked the waterline again. "Just a bit more." She rapidly ran down a mental inventory of the ship's stores and fittings, reached a bleak conclusion. "There's nothing more to lose."

"Yes, there is," Steffie said. He adjusted the bloody rag around his left palm, spat on his right palm, hefted the axe, and swung it into the side of the low cabin housing.

Rowan nodded slowly. "I think that should be just about enough."

29

*A*bove the copper strips, the hull showed snail damage in a band nearly five inches wide toward the stern, over six inches at the bow. There were five places where individual snails had gouged through completely; fortunately, the holes were less than half an inch wide and widely spaced. Other spots had been nearly chewed through, mostly concentrated toward the bow.

The travelers sacrificed a floor plank from the cabin, and Rowan and Steffie whittled twenty-four tapered plugs to be driven into the holes and near holes from the outside by a person hung over the side on a rope harness. After some experimentation, it was evident that Zenna was best at the job, and for most of one day she swung above the water in a harness, nimbly propelling herself along the side with her one foot, Rowan and Steffie tending her safety lines. Periodically she climbed aboard so that the stores in the hull could be shifted to counterbalance the weight of three people all standing on one side of the ship.

Repairs completed, they immediately reset the rudder, secured the sheets, and cautiously left the snail-infested waters behind.

They restored the rest of the ship to as much order as could be managed. The aft cabin was rearranged with pallets on the floor, loose gear secured in bundles with ropes. Among Rowan's traveling equipment was an oiled canvas tarp, which she generally used to contrive tents and rain flys; it was now pressed into service as a cover for the absent cabin housing. In this duty it was less than ideal, as its unsupported middle tended to dip, collecting pooled dew in the morning, and later bucket-worths of rainwater. It was laced across with cords, to prevent it catching and rising in the wind.

The chaos in the hold was a larger problem. The remaining floor planks were reset. The water barrels, the heaviest single objects on the boat, were redistributed for best balance. Smaller crates of stores were lashed to the floor's bare crossbeams.

Most loose stores had ended up in the bilge. One of the two bags of wheat flour had burst, and a bag of maize flour was soaked through. The wheat was unusable; the maize had to be chipped into chunks and crushed to be used. The pickled pork was rescued from the bilge, and the travelers, of necessity, dined on it for days; out of its barrel, it would soon spoil.

The preserved fish had gone overboard, and once repairs and rearrangements were effected, the travelers tried to replenish supplies by fishing.

On days of smooth and steady wind, there was little else to occupy them. They took turns at the tiller. Zenna charted their progress. Both women amended Janus's charts with what new information they could find and updated their own logbooks. They coached Steffie on the finer points of seamanship, in which he took serious interest, remembering everything and applying it with more and more confidence. And they fished.

Rowan found an hour's distraction studying a particularly peculiar little creature that had snagged itself on her hook. It bristled with wild spines, which she carefully did not touch, and was striped like the breasts of some sparrows. She brought up her logbook and pens, and began entering descriptions and sketches.

Outskirts, she found herself musing, Inner Lands. The boundaries of the two categories were becoming more and more clear to her. Although it seemed odd to label a sea creature so, the spiny fish she studied obviously belonged to the "Inner Lands" category. It lacked the "four-ness" one found so consistently in Outskirts life.

Beside her, Steffie had found a bit of charcoal and was idly drawing the fish himself on the wood of the deck. Rowan smiled a bit but did not intrude.

She needed better terms for the categories, she thought, as the fish on her page grew more and more like the one gulping air before her. But she could find no satisfactory words to pin down so vague a concept as "more like us" and "less like us." The fish was in no way like a human, but she sensed very clearly that it was closer to humans than were the four-spined, four-finned little snails; the four-legged moths in Alemeth; or the demons . . .

Beside her, Steffie had grown still. Puzzled, she glanced at him.

He was glowering down at his sketch, which, unfortunately, resembled nothing living. Moreover, the spines were too large, so that only three fit on the hump intended to be its back; the stripes ran in entirely the wrong direction; and the circle positioned as the eye seemed to have a white, like a human's.

Hoping that Steffie would not ask for a comment, Rowan tried to look away before he noticed her attention; but she was too late. He glanced up and met her gaze, then abruptly and roughly wiped his foot across the drawing, leaving it a smear of gray. He scrambled to his feet and strode off to the starboard bow.

Rowan hesitated, then returned to her work.

Some time later, he was still there. She set aside her logbook and went to him.

He was systematically destroying the bit of charcoal in his hands, scraping off shards, letting them flutter off in the wind.

"Don't be discouraged," she told him. "It isn't an easy thing to do. I have had some training."

Steffie flung the charcoal away abruptly. "Never mind. It's too late, isn't it?"

Rowan puzzled. " 'Too late?' "

"You have to start young, don't you?" He glowered down at the black speck as it swept alongside and was left behind. "I'm too old."

"Not at all," she assured him. She felt she was missing something. "If you want to learn to draw well, I'm sure you—" But he had turned away and strode angrily past the helm, to stand brooding over the aft railing. Zenna shot him a puzzled glance, spoke a question that Rowan did not hear.

He replied; Zenna caught Rowan's eye and motioned her over, relinquished the tiller to her. "I was fifteen," Zenna replied to another unheard question. She joined Steffie by the rail but called back to Rowan. "You were, what, eighteen?"

Rowan was lost. "At what point?"

"When you entered the Academy."

The meaning of Steffie's complaint became clear. "Yes," Rowan said, then overcame her astonishment. "But, Steffie, there were others who were older. Age is not considered a factor."

"Helen was twenty-two," Zenna volunteered.

"But I'm that come winter," Steffie said. Rowan had thought him somewhat younger. He turned back to lean glumly against the rail. "And this training, this Academy, where's it? Wulfshaven? Take a while to get there."

"It won't be in Wulfshaven," Zenna said. "It's in a different place each time. I don't know where it will be held next."

"Three years from now," Rowan added.

"There, see? I'll be nearly twenty-five. Most likely, I'll be married, with tykes climbing all up me when I come home from work, the wife complaining at me about something or other . . ."

In the silence that followed, Zenna shrugged. "Then don't marry. Use the time to prepare. I'll be there to help. You can learn to read better, and chart and diagram. I can get you started on higher maths."

"Of course!" Rowan said. "With Zenna's help, you can learn a great many things in three years. And then, when the time comes—"

"But that's not good enough, is it?" He looked from one steerswoman to the other. "There's more to being a steerswoman than just knowing things. Anyone can know things. I could work as hard as you want, and memorize all sorts of things, but . . . but I'd be just collecting them. Like pretty rocks, or butterflies . . . that's it. Pinning them down in your head, and then your head all full of beautiful things, but none of them alive anymore." He held his hands as if there were something between them, something that moved, and then was still.

Rowan recalled that among the steerswomen candidates who had failed training, the commonest reason was the very thing Steffie was trying to express; those women, in attempting to acquire knowledge, had instead merely collected facts. "It does take a special sort of person," she admitted.

"But how can I tell I'm that?" Steffie turned his gaze on Rowan: dark, clear eyes under the wild tangle of brown hair. "How can I know I'm not just wishing for things, fooling myself? With me so old already, I don't want to . . . I don't want to waste my heart on something impossible. Can *you* tell?" His gaze now included them both. "Can you two tell if I'm the right sort for it?"

"No," Zenna said honestly, "I can't tell, one way or the other. I've only known you a few weeks. But nothing I've seen tells me you're definitely wrong for it."

"It's much easier to tell who is wrong for it than who is right," Rowan admitted. "And even people who seem perfect for the work can fail training, for any number of reasons. Forget what we think, Steffie—what do *you* think?"

"Me? How am *I* supposed to tell?"

Zenna made to reply; but Rowan held up a silencing hand, thought a moment, then motioned her to take over the tiller. "Hold on a moment," she said to Steffie, then went below.

She returned, and Zenna caught sight of what Rowan was carrying. "Oh, perfect!"

Rowan handed it to Steffie. "Let's try something. Tell me what that is."

He fingered it suspiciously. "Well, it's a bit of paper . . ." A glance at Rowan's face told him she wanted more. "A strip of paper," he went on. "Got its ends glued, so it's a loop with a twist in." He noticed something that pleased him. "Look, it's like your rings! Bigger, though."

"That's right," Rowan said. "And the twist is not a whole twist, it's a half twist. That's important. Look closer, and think about what you see."

Steffie did so: his puzzlement grew glum, and then he shook his head. "It's a Steerswomen's test, isn't it? And I'm missing it."

"I wouldn't call it a test," Zenna said, "not exactly."

"Not in the usual sense of the term. Just go ahead and tell us everything you can about that loop."

He winced, shrugged, then returned to the question with dogged determination. "Right. Well, it's made out of paper and glue. And it's about an inch wide. And a foot long, I mean the paper it's made from was a foot long, before it was turned into a loop. But now it's a loop, so it doesn't have any 'long' to it anymore, it's just got an 'around.'" He blinked. "Two 'arounds.' Around the inside and around the outside." A pause. "With a twist. I mean a half twist." Another pause. His brows knit. "Where the sides . . . switch . . ."

Rowan was attempting to keep her face impassive; Zenna did not bother, but sat half turned at the tiller, watching with a broad catlike smile.

Steffie seemed to derive equal encouragement from both their expressions. "The sides switch," he said more definitely. "So the outside goes inside, and the inside goes outside. Right there." The twist. "But . . ." More thought. "If that half of a twist was there all along, then the outside that's switching to inside was the inside already."

He had ceased addressing his comments to the steerswomen. "Where d'they switch back?" He was asking only himself. "'Cause, I don't see it happening." He stopped turning it and merely regarded it, rapt. And Rowan found it extremely interesting that he did not do as she had, when first she saw such an object: trace the loop with one finger, moving along it until, impossibly, the finger ended its trip precisely where it had begun with no break, no jump, no switching of sides.

Instead, all such action was taking place in Steffie's mind only; and he reached his conclusion alone. "It's . . . the same side, on the inside and outside. Always. That's only one side the thing has." His voice was quiet with wonder. "This is a thing with just one side." He became more excited. "And look here, see?—the twist, that's what makes it *be*. Because you can't just have a side all by itself, can you, hanging on to nothing? Everything else has got two sides—a this side and a that side, leaning right up against each other, sort of, and making the thing *be*. But this one side, all by itself . . ." He grinned suddenly. "Right! That half a twist flips the side over, and lets it lean right up against itself. So that's how come . . . that's how come it's not just an idea you can think about, it's a real thing that you can hold in your hand." He laughed. "Now, that's about the wierdest thing I've ever seen, barring demons. No, forget that; this is weirder even than demons—" He looked up to find the two women regarding him, and seemed a bit surprised to find them there. He recovered. "So . . . did I get it right? I know I did, I'm sure of it. I passed the test?"

"Solving the loop is not a test," Rowan told him. "It's a demonstration."

"Demonstration of what?"

"Of everything you just did," Zenna said.

"But what's the point?"

"The point," Rowan said, "was to make you do it. Tell me: was it hard or easy?" Steffie became wary, but Rowan assured him: "It doesn't matter whether it was hard or easy. But just tell us: Which was it?"

"Well . . ." The loop, hanging from his hand, fluttered in the breeze; he held it more tightly. "Some of it was hard, and some of it was easy. And doing one hard part made some of the other hard parts easy. I wasn't thinking about it being hard or easy. I guess I was too busy." He regarded it again, shrugged. "Mostly, it was just different. Something different to think about. A different way to think about things. Do you have any more?" he asked suddenly.

"More?"

He held it up. "More things like this that make you think different."

"Why?" Rowan asked.

He was taken aback. "Well, because, if you do, I'd like a crack at them."

"Why?" Zenna repeated.

"Why?" He looked back and forth between the women. "I liked it. I want to do it again."

"And again after that?" Zenna asked.

"Well . . . sure."

"For the rest of your life?" Rowan asked.

"Yes." The answer came immediately, and almost inaudibly, as if the word had spoken itself before Steffie could think to take a breath to speak it. He himself seemed surprised to hear it and, with his gaze turned inward, more amazed still by all that lay behind the word inside him.

Then he did take a breath, a deep one as if to shout, but he spoke in a normal tone of voice. "Yes," he said.

Rowan felt a grin on her face and was surprised by the amount of pride in him she felt. "Now, what did you just learn?"

"That I want to know. I want to find out." No hesitation. No uncertainty.

"Then, join us."

"Well," he began, but took a moment to wipe his eyes with the heels of his hands, "I think I'll do exactly that."

The air threatened rain for days, but never made good on its threat. White haze crept up the sky from the southwest, and sunlight beat down on the ship, damp and hot, like a solid, sweltering blanket. Each morning and evening, Rowan impatiently tapped the blown-glass flute of the barometer, in a vain attempt to encourage the fluid level to change. The level stubbornly continued to indicate low pressure.

The Guidestars remained invisible throughout the nights, and in daytime the sun became more and more blurred behind the mist overhead. The steerswomen could not tell direction other than vague east in the mornings and vague, red west in the evenings. The ship crept across the water, with a sluggish breeze three points aft of starboard.

On the fourth day, the horizons began to close in.

Rowan and Zenna stood in the bow, grimly watching the fog move in. "We can't afford to wait this out."

"No."

The women stood regarding the weather. "There's no way to tell where we are."

Rowan sighed. "Let's take soundings. As long as we have deep water, there's a chance we're moving in generally the correct direction." Janus's charts showed the shallower water closer to the north shore of the channel and even had some indications in place on the southern shore. The center of the channel had been too deep to sound.

They set Steffie in the bow with the sounding line, laboriously tossing out the bolt that had replaced its original weight and reeling it in; but his call was always, "No bottom!"

In the afternoon, the breeze lifted, backed, and they permitted the ship to run before it, now not wishing to move more quickly, for fear of running into shallow water too soon to react. Steffie's voice became a comforting rhythm.

Then the wind stiffened, and the fog began to pocket, opening and closing about them. "At last," Rowan muttered, relieved to see clear water in the passing breaks.

Both women startled at silence, when Steffie did not call on cue. "Steffie?" Zenna shouted.

He cried out, wordlessly.

Rowan ran forward; but he was already scrambling aft. "It ends!"

"What?"

"The water, it ends, I saw it in a break—"

"Land?" Rowan was stunned. They must be far, far off course.

"How far ahead?" Zenna asked.

"No, not land! The water just *ends*, in a straight line, straight ahead!"

"That can't be right," Rowan said, "the sea can't simply end—"

He clutched her shoulders, shouted at her, terrified. "Straight across, nothing past it, *dead ahead!*"

"Jibe!" Zenna yelled. "Get the boom, I'm jibing to port, now."

Rowan ran to the mainsail sheet, pulled the knot loose just as Zenna shoved the tiller hard about. Rowan and Steffie grabbed the boom, forced it into the wind, past it. The boom tore from their hands, swinging wide and fast, as the sail caught. They stumbled, clutched the flailing rope, lashed it. The jibe snapped the line taut, the sail filled with a clap like thunder, and the little ship shook and shuddered from the blow.

Zenna fought to hold the tiller, bracing her foot on the cockpit side, then found her balance and the ship's simultaneously. They were heeled wildly over to starboard; but the clumsy vessel suddenly loved the angle and, almost as if surprised, gave itself to a sweep of glad speed.

Rowan found herself braced with her feet in the ropes tying down the tarp, her back against the port side rail, her right fist clutching the back of Steffie's shirt, fingers slipping in old silk. Steffie was scrabbling with his hands, kicking, trying to avoid tumbling into the tarp-covered hole.

Looking out, but feeling from the angle as if she were looking up, Rowan saw that the fog had lifted off the starboard side.

The sea ended.

Perhaps three miles distant: a geometrically perfect line, a false horizon beyond which the gray sky seemed too close. It's fog, the steerswoman thought, a line of fog; but a line a fog so perfectly straight was no less impossible.

Steffie had quieted beside her, found a grip on the railing above him, and turned himself around. The two stayed so, staring, quiet, trembling.

Eventually Steffie said in a small voice, "Met an old Christer once who said the world was flat."

"The world is not flat," the steerswoman said immediately.

"Right."

Between the ship and the end of the sea, gray shapes humped and sank between the waves: one, three, then half a dozen, a dozen. "Big fish," Steffie noted inanely. One broke the water, arced down again.

"Dolphins," Rowan breathed.

Zenna called out, her voice tight from her straining muscles, but her words cheery. "Well, my loyal crew, I believe we've come a bit further than we suspected." And past the clean straight line of water, the fog receded further, lifting, and revealing more sea beyond—but more distant than it ought to be, and seeming further down, as if they were looking past a ledge down some great height.

"The Dolphin Stair!" Steffie cried out, now glad. "It's *got* to be!"

"That's my guess," Zenna said. "And if we don't want to roll over the top"—and the tiller creaked—"someone better help me with this."

Steffie clambered across the tilted deck to lend his back to Zenna's work. But Rowan remained wedged, staring out across the stretch of water, to the far horizon beyond, thinking: *Can stairs be made of water?*

30

They could.

The travelers stood with their backs against the foot of the great cliffs on the northern shore of the channel. The narrow strip of ground at their feet was covered in small, loose shards, fallen through the years from the rocks above.

The straight edge, the end of the Inland Sea, was a mere two hundred feet away; they dared not try to get closer.

The lip ran south by southwest, stretching off to become invisible in the hazy distance. On the far horizon: a tiny, dim, gray shape—another cliff. The eye could not doubt that the sun-silvered line ended at that place.

Seawater poured over the edge, seeming almost static in its smoothness. But the power of the moving water was revealed by the sound: a continual, rushing roar, so loud it seemed more matter than sound. It was as if the noise itself possessed mass, weighting the three people in place under its pressure.

Past the edge of the lip, and down: another expanse of water, spreading eastward, ending in another lip. Past that lip: another, further down. And again, and more as, in a series of unnatural waterfalls, the Dolphin Stair guided the water of the Inland Sea down to join the distant Ocean.

Zenna's grip on Rowan's arm tightened, and when Rowan turned to look, the other steerswoman indicated with a lift of her chin.

Dolphins had been pacing them offshore, possibly the same group sighted three days before. Now they began a series of leaps and dives, then as a group turned toward the edge and raced at it. First one, and then a crowd of dolphins: leaping just as they reached the water's end, each gray, muscular body arcing up and out into the bright blue air. In mid-flight, each dipped its nose downward, and vanished past the edge.

And that, Rowan saw, was how the dolphins used their stair, leaping over edge after edge, eventually to reach the open ocean.

They had found Janus's anchorage that morning, after three days of sailing north, keeping well back of the top of the stair. The anchorage lay between a barren island and a little rocky cove. Rowan had been prepared to dive overboard to search the cove's floor for a boulder large enough to replace the lost anchor, but this proved unnecessary: Janus had sunk a mooring line. The line was marked by a sphere of murky yellow glass, the float from a fishing net.

Alone, Rowan swam ashore, and discovered Janus's camp.

Above the tide line there was a small but solid hut constructed of Inner Lands wood, nestled against a rock wall. Inside: a pallet made of old blankets, a battered chair, a lath crate beside the bed, and a lamp with a tin of oil—conditions hardly different from Janus's room above the cooper's. The steerswoman immediately checked inside the crate and was disappointed to find that it held no papers or charts, only some pots and a boning knife. A small store of firewood, much of it driftwood, lay stacked at the foot of the bed, safe from the elements.

Outside, water barrels crowded against the hut, some holding rainwater, some upended and empty, some in various stages of being reduced to firewood. These last gave Rowan an eerie feeling; there remained here a feeling of work interrupted. Rowan caught herself looking around warily, half expecting someone to suddenly return.

After a moment spent thinking how she herself would arrange such a camp, she immediately found a storage hole, with sacks of vegetables, a crate of salt fish, and a barrel holding sacks of wheat flour tucked inside.

Returning to the water's edge, Rowan waved to her friends and then used an exaggerated version of the wood gnomes' language of gestures to communicate to Zenna that she had found the camp, that there was no danger, and that there was food here.

They spent their first night ashore in three weeks.

In the dusk, by the snapping fire, Rowan studied her copy of the chart of the land past the Dolphin Stair, laboriously comparing it to the smaller version she had drawn in the first pages of her fresh logbook. Should she lose her copies, she did not want to depend on memory. She found nothing to amend but still repeated the action obsessively, until she was stopped by the distinct feeling that she had done all this before, under other circumstances—

Of course: at the Archives, when she and Bel were preparing to depart for the Outskirts. When she had made all the preparations possible; when, nevertheless, the amount of unknown contingency still remained too large to be comfortable with, and she had continued to feel that, somehow, there must be more she could do.

Her mouth twisted. She ordered the charts, slipped them into their tubular case, packed them away in her backpack.

Across the fire, the other steerswoman was involved in her own pursuit: with paper, pens, and ruler, Zenna was calculating the size and strength of the underwater dams that surely must delineate each edge of each step of the Dolphin Stair. The numbers had become huge; she was working now in compressed notation. She turned a moment, to shout out behind her, "Oh, loyal crew, your captain is definitely not going to spend her time tending this stew!"

Steffie emerged from gloom at the water's edge, looking sheepish. "Sorry." He came to the fire, where a small pot was bubbling. He dutifully stirred the contents with a well-worn and half-burned wooden spoon, but again and again he turned back to glance toward the water. Catching Rowan watching him, he said simply, "It's so beautiful."

Rowan nodded, hugging her knees against the chill. In the dimming light, the top ledge of the stair, thread thin, seemed to hang suspended between two blue worlds: the deep shadowy blue of the dimly moving sea and the flat, featureless gray-tinged blue of the sky.

She felt that another such line existed, invisible, that she would cross in the morning. She had gone into strange lands before in her life, but this time it would be with no companion, no friendly guide, no person who knew more than she. She had only the map, and more often than not, its notations were mere indications; what they referred to remained to be discovered.

Steffie began clearing the area around the fire to a wider expanse, preparatory to spreading the bedrolls. Zenna idly assisted him and was about to toss a handful of pulled dry grass onto the fire. Rowan stirred from reverie, her attention caught by the resinous scent. "Don't do that," she said. "That's blackgrass. Burning it will send out very unpleasant fumes."

Zenna looked more closely at the twisty weeds in her hand. "You didn't mention fumes." Rowan had briefed her on the commoner Outskirts plants and animals, on the assumption that similar conditions might obtain in the area of this anchorage.

"They're only dangerous if you burn great amounts." And slowly poisonous if handled constantly for days on end, she reminded herself; and useful to rid clothes of infestations of fleas . . .

To Rowan's eye, this area was a milder version of the Outskirts, oddly mixed with Inner Lands life. The blackgrass was familiar, crowding around the freshwater stream that descended the hill at the back of the cove. She had found no lichen-towers, not even the small ones usually indistinguishable from stones in streambeds; but they propagated by a spreading underground root system, while blackgrass had airborne seeds.

Contiguity, she thought, and access.

The blackgrass did not approach the sea edge itself; normal Inner Lands sea oats grew in the pocket marsh where the stream's water commingled with the sea waves.

The rocks of the shoreline were encrusted with mussels—Inner Lands. Tanglebrush nestled in the damp crevasses of the rocks above the shore—Outskirts.

In the Outskirts, there was very little coexistence of the different life-forms. Here, the difference must have something to do with the sea, or with the absence of the redgrass veldt.

Something nagged at her mind. She could not pin it down.

Above, the first stars were appearing, and to the east, the Eastern Guidestar. Rowan found herself gazing at it; and although she was not aware of any particular thought about it in her mind, the expression she felt on her face seemed to be one of distrust and suspicion.

Zenna was watching her. "Suppose it sends down that heat again?" Steffie looked at Zenna in surprise, then up at the Guidestar, then at Rowan.

Rowan shook her head. "There's no way to be warned if it does. There's no way to tell by looking at it; it could be doing so at this very moment, directed at some other part of the world."

"Heat means light," Zenna replied.

"Not always, apparently."

"It makes no sense."

Rowan's mouth twitched. "Magic."

Steffie stirred the stew. "Got to be some way to tell."

"No."

Rowan had come to understand that the Guidestars were actually objects, and that they moved as the world turned, at the same pace, and so only seemed to stand still in the sky; in fact, the concepts, when they first occurred to her, excited and pleased her. They made sense. They were new knowledge.

But that the Guidestars could do such evil was, to Rowan, a particular and disturbing betrayal. The more she considered it, the more unstable the world seemed. *Our ancient allies: servants of evil.*

A servant does what its master commands.

The original intent of the heat from the Guidestars was beneficial; but that remained an idea difficult to sustain, slipping away when she did not focus on it. The fact that the Outskirts must shift eastward ahead of the Inner Lands seemed logical; but the fact that it needed the intervention of magic to do so was somehow wrong—although she could not see why.

There was something behind this that she was not seeing.

The group ate their stew in silence; the evening grew toward night. "Let's put the fire out." A precaution only; Rowan doubted that any goblins would haunt so damp an environment.

They planned to sleep in shifts, with Rowan taking first watch, so that she might sleep undisturbed afterward and be fresh for her travel the next day. Steffie and Zenna would have their own duties: They must work to repair the ship and lighten it further, and more intelligently, for the return trip. Rowan had alloted them three weeks in which to accomplish this. It was the shortest amount of time she might be expected to reach and return from site four, assuming no delays at all.

She had also firmly instructed them to sail back to Alemeth without her if she had not returned in six weeks.

Steffie covered the fire with sand, and he and Zenna wrapped themselves in blankets, lying down close by the fading heat of buried coals.

Rowan remained sitting, her cloak about her, the rising stones behind her, and the cove before her, where Janus's nameless ship stood on the water. Beyond, the sea roiled faintly, as if to shapes moving beneath. More stars arrived, seeming to coalesce from the pearl gray of dusk, with the continual roar of the Dolphin Stair coloring the air like the sound of the stars themselves.

And an odd thought came to her, and it expressed itself to her as: *In the absence of humankind.*

Wizardly magic destroyed the dangerous life on the blackgrass prairie. In the wake of that destruction: the Face, and later, the veldt. Then, Outskirter life and ways destroyed the veldt, clearing the way for the greenlife of the Inner Lands to spread.

Human actions, all—even the magic.

What might the world be like, in the absence of humankind?

Perhaps like this, everywhere. Perhaps nothing like this. Perhaps stranger.

She tucked her hands under her arms and sat wrapped in her cloak, with the cooling earth beneath, the cooling air falling from above, and the chill sight and sound of the stars all around her.

31

For two days, Rowan doggedly clambered down the jagged cliffs beside the stair.

She coughed and spat almost continuously, breathing a mist so thick she felt she was inhaling water: the spray of the eternally falling Inland Sea. Its thick salt tang burned her throat and made her tongue raw; she soon tied a large kerchief around her mouth so as not to drown in the open air.

She heard no demons, and would be unable to, if one were near.

But these crags and upthrusts and shattered boulders must surely be as daunting to a demon as to a person; and the immense roaring of the stair must overwhelm their seeing ears as a person would be blinded gazing at the sun. She thought they would not come here. And the mist itself would hide her from any human eyes.

The mist became fog, thickening as she descended. The cliffs were a vague gray mass to which she clung, suspended in whiteness, with all the world reduced to the stone above that her hand had just released, the boulder below that her cautiously searching foot had just located.

Night fell at noon, when the sun passed the upper edge of the Dolphin Stair. The steerswoman ate a cold meal, rested, and later slept tucked into a stony niche, wrapped in layers of cloak, blanket, and oil-skin tarp.

She awoke to pink light, a solid, perfect, endless pink the exact color of wild rose petals. A lovely color; half asleep, she could not resist reaching out into it. It remained insubstantial, the length of her arm fading in fog, her fingers completely invisible.

The pink slowly shifted to gold as she breakfasted, and the gold to white as she repacked her gear. She donned her pack, turned, and descended again, her back to the pure, empty white, her face to the jagged tumbles of gray and black stone.

She found level ground abruptly when, standing on what seemed a secure place, her foot could discover no edge to work around or clamber over. Wiping condensation from her face, Rowan stood and turned into the whiteness. Now her feet searched forward, long testing reaches, and she moved on like a blind woman.

When the sound of the stair began to be behind her, when there were no shadows of boulders about her, when her feet found few stones in their path and her boots sometimes sank in sand, the mist began to clear. It did not part but lessened, lifted, coalesced; and at last the sun appeared, high above and faintly blurred.

Rowan slid out of her pack and sat on it as she rested, sipping from her water sack.

Ahead, the shoreline curved toward the south, defining almost a third of a full circle, ending in a rocky spit. Haze erased far details and paled colors close by: a watercolor landscape of gray-blue sea to Rowan's right, pale blue sky above, faded gold and gray distances. Behind, the last step of the stair cut the sky, a white wall of falling water.

Rowan had the eerie feeling that she was surrounded by a landscape wholly imaginary. To dispel the sensation, she reached down to scoop up a handful of the stony sand.

Red-black pebbles, damp sand grains of both golden brown and black, and as many shells and shell bits. Here, the characteristic violet and white of Inner Lands clams; here, too, the fractured black and blue of mussels; but there—what shell would carry a combination of green and pink in tiny alternating trapezoids? These last became smaller fragments under the slightest pressure of her fingers, and dry dust at the slightest bit more.

She brushed her hands together: green and pink ghosted away like smoke; violet and white tumbled to the ground. The steerswoman closed her eyes and listened.

The endless sound of the stair, now quieter; the slap of small waves against stone; the sudden cry of a gull, sharp, like a little knife of sound.

No sound of demons, no voices or footsteps of humans.

Rowan opened her eyes. She rose, slapped sand from her pack, swung it on, and strode away down the misty, rocky shore.

She was several days travel away from site four, where Slado's presumed residence, with its presumed attendants and servants, was located. Still, Rowan might expect to encounter people, or see signs of them, fairly soon. Who knew how far Slado's people might range? She must be cautious.

But as well as danger, people represented opportunities. She might learn from them more of what to expect when she reached Slado's keep, perhaps enlist an ally. Without more knowledge, she could form no plans.

But she discovered that, unless she consciously made an effort, she stopped anticipating human beings. The land felt empty to her, in the way that the area beyond the Outskirts proper had felt, when she had traveled there.

It must be the presence of Outskirts life-forms that inspired the feeling. But this shore was not Outskirts.

Tanglebrush climbed the lee of the dunes she passed, but Inner Lands cutgrass dwelled on the crests. Common sea oats grew here, too, but they had acquired strange companions: knee-high, fat-leaved black fronds with finger-shaped yellow seed heads crowding greedily around the standing water. Rowan decided that they were a coastal relative of the black-grass that covered the prairie beyond the Outskirts, out on the Face.

Past the spit, a true beach appeared, an expanse of gold and black sand sorted and arranged into dizzying interlocking curves that marked the leading edges of past waves. Rowan took a moment to adjust her eyes to the striped ground, stepped onto it cautiously. Beneath her feet, the sand was merely sand, harder close to the water. She continued on.

She passed an object half buried in the sand: a huge, sinuous animal skeleton, nearly twenty feet long, seeming to consist entirely of ribs and vertebrae. The bones were black, their surfaces slightly wrinkled. Shriveled, as a demon's own cartilaginous bones might become, exposed to months of sea air. Rowan hoped that this great creature had posed no danger to humans while alive.

Further along, she spotted what seemed a human-made object; she snagged it as she passed and examined it as she walked: a coarse, stiff fiber mesh, perhaps part of a sieve . . .

Presently she stopped and studied it more closely.

The tiny strands were hollow. Toward the center of each, dark color showed through the pale substance, like old, dried blood within.

As she walked on, she tried to imagine what sort of sea creature this might have been. She failed.

Less than eight miles from the foot of the Dolphin Stair, Janus's map notated a location, with a small, unlabeled x, one of the series of such that appeared intermittently across the route through the four numbered sites. Analyzing the distances involved, the depicted terrain, and considering Rowan's suspicions about encroaching Outskirts-type life, Rowan and Zenna had decided that the marks indicated staging points, likely including caches of supplies and food. At the first of these, Rowan planned to make camp that evening.

She did find a food cache; she also found a crypt.

She was some time recognizing it: a cairn, larger than that covering the food cache. Rowan at first assumed it to mark a second cache.

She also found an old shallow fire pit and a clear area between it and a tall dune. If Janus had used fire at night, either he had avoided attracting goblins by sheer luck, or the creatures did not inhabit this area.

It was autumn. The night would be chill. By the dictates of their natural life cycles, the goblin jills would now be dead, the mated jacks jealously patrolling their egg caches, unmated jacks wandering solitary.

Rowan did not doubt her ability to dispatch a single goblin jack—and did not doubt that any demon-voice would wake her instantly.

She lit the fire, took her dinner of dried fish and bread beside it as the sun set, then took out her logbook, pen, and ink and made her daily entries. This task she completed very quickly.

Above her camp, the stars above were clear, as sharp and bright as on a winter's night. There, the Eastern Guidestar; there, the Western.

Friends of the traveler, reliably giving direction; friends of the farmer, telling the season by what stars lay behind them in the evenings. Timekeepers, winking out in turn, as each passed into the world's own shadow.

The steerswoman regarded them; and they, she knew, regarded her. The Guidestars watched, heeded commands, undertook actions—behaved, in a way, as if alive.

Her face tilted up, Rowan wondered: How alive? She knew they made records of events. Did they ponder the events they saw, did they speculate? In the times between enacting the commands of their masters, did the Guidestars dream?

The idea disturbed her.

The fire writhed its flames upward; the dunes around her lit intermittently, flashing in her peripheral vision.

She was tired, body and mind. She must rest. She rose and went to bury the fire.

Motion. She turned.

Nothing, and then a flicker: shadows shifting among the stones of the second cairn, responding to the moving flames. In one dark hollow between two stones, something white flicked in and out of visibility, illuminated and darkened.

Rowan stood and scanned the night beyond her small circle of light, found it impenetrable. She listened: insect noises, some of which she recognized from the Inner Lands, some from the Outskirts; the snap of the fire; and the pause and rush of breakers. Nothing else.

She pulled a small branch of burning driftwood from the fire and carried it to the pile of stones. Moving it back and forth, she tried to elicit the flicker of white again.

In a gap between rocks, she saw darkness and, peering closer, whiteness. She pulled out two stones that seemed designed to be pulled.

Inside, a human skull gazed out at her emptily.

Rowan quickly drew back and as quickly recovered and leaned forward again. The superstitions of her childhood had long been supplanted, and she had only a moment's distress.

Rowan considered. Then she opened the crypt further.

There were several individuals interred, all of them bones merely, with no clothing, no remnants of flesh. Perhaps they were very old.

But humans had been here. A good sign.

Closer examination must wait until daylight, Rowan decided. She returned to the fire, doused it with sand, and wrapped herself in her bedroll.

She returned to the crypt as soon as the light permitted. There was dew; and a trace of fog.

She pulled out more stones and found the bones inside neatly stacked, in a rather specific arrangement: long bones outlining a square, smaller bones within, each obviously representing an individual. The skulls were separate, lined up around the walls of the structure, each one facing a small chink in the wall. There were seven persons altogether.

There was an undeniable ritual aspect to the arrangements, but it was no ritual the steerswoman recognized.

The condition of the bones puzzled her. In some individuals, most bones were broken, especially ribs and long bones: thighs, shins, and arms. Two of the skulls had been reconstructed from crushed fragments, now held together with clay.

In others, the bones were clean, unmarked, and their former owners apparently healthy and not elderly. The cause of their deaths was not evident . . .

But the spray from a demon would not melt human bones.

The remains interred nearest the entrance were of a woman apparently near Rowan's own age. She seemed to have warranted special care, her bones arranged in her alloted space with an almost obsessive precision. Only she retained a possession from her former life: on top of the overlapping pattern of ribs lay a rope bracelet of complicated knotting, such as sailors made in their idle hours—

Rowan had a sudden vision: a ship, swept by the currents up to, onto, over the Dolphin Stairs themselves, and falling, shattering in the churning water—

And the people: some drowned, some dead of injury, and some few surviving . . . for a while.

A fragment of information presented itself: Among Janus's own people in the upper Wulf valley, it was believed that the dead remained interested in the living world and wished to observe it from the afterlife.

The steerswoman carefully replaced the skulls she had moved, setting each one face out at its own tiny window, and closed the crypt.

Janus's mapped route lay directly along the beach, and at first Rowan followed it exactly. Presently, she altered her plan, for two reasons: first, the dry sand shifted beneath her feet with each step, making walking more tiring; and second, the beach began to stink.

Every seashore had its odor. Persons who lived by the sea either ignored what others called a stench or, like Rowan, grew to positively enjoy it. The scent had pleasant associations for her, and whenever she approached the sea from a distance, her heart would lighten and she would feel a happy thrill when the first wind-borne hint of it reached her.

This was different.

She noticed it first rising from the occasional bit of unidentifiable sea wrack, borne in by the waves and stranded by the ebbing tide. Soon, there was more.

Foot-wide, jagged black fronds glistening with sour-smelling blue oil; yellow hollow spirals wafting up a strong scent that somehow made her think of new-broken rock; red chitinous pentagons, weirdly regular in shape, ranging from the size of her thumbnail to the size of her hand. These last, when overturned by her toe, revealed broken stubs of jointed legs, an abdomen of overlapping plates.

None of them any animal or plant she knew or knew of.

She left them behind; but there were still more ahead. Other offal joined them: rotting debris once alive, now existing apparently only in order to foul the air.

Wondering if it were normal for this new sea to wash up such great amounts of dead matter, Rowan incautiously kicked aside a helmet-shaped green sphere.

The helmet moved, but the former inhabitant, unfortunately, did not. It lay there, yellow, wet, rotting, and emitting a truly horrific odor that seemed to actively clamber up Rowan's nostrils, find a home somewhere behind her eyes, and there apparently attempt to expand—

She fled the water and took refuge in a stand of stunted sea oats, their sweet green scent almost painful in the wake of the helmet creature's stink. Rowan resisted, then succumbed to a fit of retching.

She walked behind the dunes for the rest of that day and for the next; but the following day with the breeze suddenly fresh, she wandered down to the beach before breakfast and found it pristine, marked only by the swirls of colored sand: gold and black, like the markings on a sleeping tabby cat.

The change was eerie, even more unnatural than the offal. But by noon, when she reached the next cache, some litter had returned, in what struck her as a more normal amount: bits of this strange sea's strange plants; coral-like twigs; the odd pentagonal shell, hollow and scentless.

32

She reached the first numbered site; reached it and passed it before she realized she had done so. She paused at a field of boulders, and in confusion pulled out her map.

The boulders were very clearly marked, definitely just beyond the location of site one. Rowan looked back, scanned the landscape. There was nothing remarkable.

The locations numbered one through three had been crossed out on the chart. Something had interested Janus here initially, if not ultimately.

The steerswoman doubled back, circled and searched, and eventually ended at a field of sandy hummocks. She had noticed them on her first pass and had thought little of them. But when she entered the field and stood in its center, she saw what she had missed before.

It was a village—or had been, once.

Five clear paths joined together where she stood. Between the paths, five clusters of sand piles stood, obviously marking the former locations of structures. Of the structures themselves, nothing remained.

Rowan approached one of the groups, prodded the sand with her foot. No wood, no brick. No pot shards. Not a scrap of cloth, not a nail, no single sliver of glass.

Far too clean. Unnaturally so. Had Rowan arrived here a year later, or even six months, the sand itself would have been dispersed by wind and rain, leaving no hint at all of the former inhabitants.

A departure both impossibly complete and apparently inexplicable.

Standing in the center of the former village, Rowan closed her eyes and listened intently.

No sound of demons. The steerswoman left the silent ruins behind and returned to the shoreline.

Strange; but whatever had caused the villagers to leave, and however brief their dwelling here, they must have been very resourceful indeed. Wresting a living out of so difficult a country—

So *extremely* difficult a country. Rowan stopped short and stood surveying the landscape.

No greenlife was present, none whatsoever. She had not noted its passing; she noted now its utter absence.

Where scrub pine and beach plums should stand, now only tanglebrush and some strange, taller blue-leaved bushes, entirely unknown to her.

No sea oats, but maroon-blossomed spike-grass.

Not cutgrass but the new variety of blackgrass, fat-leaved, unmoving in the light breeze.

No sign of humans; no sign of life that would support humans. There seemed no place for people here.

Rowan made her way slowly to the water's edge, slipped out of her pack, clambered onto a boulder that thrust itself up out of the shallow surf. She looked down.

No seaweed, no crabs or mussels. Instead, a collection of lithe, pale blue rods that writhed blind heads just beneath the surface, in motion completely independent of the waves' action. Their lower bodies descended in the clear water to terminate among angular black crystal encrustations.

Rowan captured a passing stick of tanglebrush driftwood, used it to prod at the crystals; the blue rods startled, then communally twisted and knotted themselves around the stick, which Rowan was forced to abandon to them.

She stood. She gazed out to sea for some minutes.

Even the sea seemed strange to her; as well it might, being an entirely different sea. That wave, for instance, breaking far out against a submerged sandbar; who knew what distance it had traveled? Who knew how far away lay this ocean's other shore?

Who knew, in fact, if it even possessed one?

And in a single, elegant movement of thought, so graceful it astonished Rowan herself, the steerswoman created in her mind both the largest map she had ever conceived and the smallest, simultaneously.

The largest was of the world itself, whose shape and size she knew from the secret and intimate interplay of mathematics, but which she now seemed to see whole, all open sweep beyond all horizons, curving to meet itself at the other side, complete, entire—and huge, so huge.

The smallest map was, to scale, that part of the world known by humankind.

The smallest map was crowded; the greatest, nearly empty.

And there, just outside the smaller map, the steerswoman with casual precision marked her own position, as if with a bright, silver needle; and she saw and felt the greater map rock, turn, orient, descend (or ascend, she could not tell which), approaching, adjusting and finally matching, point for point those distant cliffs, those nearer hills, this shoreline, this rock-strewn beach, the spray-splashed boulder on which Rowan stood, wet to the knees, arms thrown wide, head tilted back, breathing salt-tang air, and laughing for wonder.

Two days later, in the evening, she reached Site Two. She moved with caution; the shoreline had evolved into a marshy estuary, and she had certain experience with such areas in the Outskirts. She did not care to meet a mud-lion.

Janus had indicated the best route across the uncertain terrain, and Rowan was required to swing slightly north and then west. She approached the site from the east, sunset dazzling her eyes, the sky above her a raddled pink expanse of herringbone clouds.

Ahead, silhouettes: rounded shapes taller than she stood, clustered. She sidled through clattering tanglebrush, found a path on dryer ground, and entered the village, walking where many feet had walked before her.

Abandoned—but far more recently than site one. And she could see now why so little had remained there.

These dwellings were mere mud huts, the most primitive she had ever seen. Without maintenance, weather itself would eventually reduce them to hummocks of dirt.

In most, the process had already begun. Of twenty-five huts, only a few possessed intact roofs. Rowan approached one, peered into a door that was a mere open oval in the face of the hut.

Light in the back, a series of canted parallel slits at the level of Rowan's waist, emitting pink-gold lines of sun. Useless as windows. Likely designed purely for ventilation.

Rowan set her pack on the ground outside and entered cautiously, uncertain of the state of the domed roof. She paused, letting her eyes adjust to the gloom.

A second door, leading into an adjacent hut, whose own street exit spilled a hazy oval of pink light on the floor. And across that hut, another internal door, visible as a mere darker shadow on the shadowed wall.

A sociable people, apparently. Rowan decided to like them.

She crossed into the second hut, paused before the access to the third.

Dark, there. Walls and roof had collapsed, reducing the room to a lightless and crumble-walled vestibule. But the previous occupant had been less fastidious than his neighbors. Something on the floor just inside—

She did not need eyes to identify it; touch told her immediately. She pulled it out, sat on the floor in the last spill of pink light.

A talisman.

But not like her own nor like any of the other such objects in Janus's room. A short column, flared at top and bottom. Its colors were blotched dark and light, its surface an etched network of tiny hexagons.

Her own talisman held magic, magic that affected demons—and so must this one. Someone with knowledge of demon magic had been here.

Janus. Or . . . one of Slado's minions?

Or perhaps the wizard himself?

Outside, in the falling night, sounds were suddenly sharper, clearer: the clack-clack of a trawler, a chorus of whistle-spiders, hawkbug chirr, tanglebrush clatter, the wind, the sea.

No demon-voice. No human sounds.

She carried the new object out into the open and stood, gazing about at the shadowy dwellings.

So clean, so utterly empty. It would take time to collect every possession. If it had been demons that drove the people from their homes, surely they would have fled quickly, left something behind.

And where were the fire pits? Where were the chimneys? The grain stores, the pens for animals?

And had the people truly owned so little that each and every item could be carried away during their escape?

Or had they, in fact, any possessions at all?

Rowan took one blind step backward, another.

This was no village.

The steerswoman said, in a voice more breath than words, "I'm in a demon hive."

But no demon-voice here. The whistle-spiders had ceased their farewell to the sun; the hawkbug had settled for the night. The trawler now kept silent vigil on its shoot lines.

Only the wind. Only the sea.

And night falling.

It occurred to Rowan that her own safest and most defensible shelter would be found in one of the abandoned hive chambers. But she could not bring herself to sleep here.

She returned to the shoreline and spent the night blanket wrapped on a patch of dry ground, watching the stars in their arcing course above the great ocean.

At Site Three, she found a corpse.

33

The hawkbugs drew her to it. Rowan saw a dozen of them battling high in the air just past a grassy rise—vying for territory that each considered desirable, abundant with food, and worth the fight.

She found it at the top of the rise: a hive of flesh termites, a long white mound two feet high, five feet in length. In the Outskirts, she had seen many such hives, built on the corpses of goblins. But here it was easy to discern in the crusted white shape the angles of the four knees, the sprawl of four arms.

She listened: no sound of a living demon.

The flying scouts of the hive swarmed the air around the corpse. One lit on Rowan's arm, and she suppressed the impulse to slap at it. She endured its bite, and it flew off at speed, hurrying to tell its hive that she was inedible.

Rowan gazed down into a little vale below, where a glittering stream meandered to the sea. Nearly a dozen white-shrouded forms lay scattered on the hillside. From intimate knowledge of the life cycle of flesh termites, Rowan knew that these demons had died less than six months previously.

At the bottom of the vale: clustered domes. No motion.

The steerswoman considered the view in silence, then set her pack on the ground, found the gloves stowed in the top, and pulled them on. Carrying only her sword in her right hand and Janus's talisman in her left, she stepped sideways down the slope.

This demon colony was less deteriorated than the previous. From halfway down the rise, Rowan could see that the domed roofs remained complete; but there was no motion and no demon-voice, which she ought to have heard even from this distance.

She gave another termite nest wide berth as she passed, but was nipped by two of its scouts regardless. And now the air about her was clouded with insects; the termites had been joined by golden gnats, which Rowan also knew were harmless to humans. But they were interested in the moisture in her eyes; the steerswoman waved her sword hilt continually before her face.

Eight groups of five dens. It seemed an unnaturally large number. From her experience and studies, only small creatures tended to live in such large groups.

She came suddenly across another termite hive hidden in the blackgrass and barely prevented herself from stumbling into it. Five scouts immediately tested her; but the workers, disturbed by her proximity, did not wait for word. They crawled from the many exit holes to promenade for her benefit, little abdomens lifted in threatening display.

Rowan snorted laughter at them, inhaling gnats in the process. She spat, then coughed, then spat again.

More scouts lit on her arms; other hives were near enough to be interested. Rowan endured the bites, walked on, was tested again before she went five feet, increased her pace.

The air above the demon colony was thick with flying insects, filled with buzzing and the clacking and chirring of many insect battles. The steerswoman slowed her approach, less convinced of the simplicity of conducting an investigation.

Something moved between two dens; Rowan froze, then relaxed as a knee-high pincer-beetle wandered out. A hawkbug immediately dropped from the sky upon it. A struggle followed, which the beetle won.

From here she could see further into the colony. There were many white-shrouded demon corpses on the ground within and an astounding amount of activity on, around, and over them.

So many termite hives would attract slugsnakes, and harvesters, and trawlers; slugsnakes brought pincer-beetles, some of which could attain truly disturbing size; harvesters and trawlers brought hawkbugs.

Fool-you bugs would lure and ambush hawkbugs. Snip-lizards would burrow under the fool-yous to attack their undefended bellies. Goblins considered snip-lizards to be very tasty and could hear them underground for a remarkable distance.

And this was naming only the creatures whose sight or voice Rowan recognized. What else might be feasting in the colony? Some coastal equivalent of swarmers, perhaps, or even mud-lions, neither of which she cared to meet.

She found she had stopped, standing knee deep in blackgrass, in a cloud of golden gnats.

Investigation was impossible. She might never know what had killed so many demons.

The steerswoman turned back and left the dead colony behind.

Janus's next food cache had been raided.

Rowan slipped out of her pack and stood surveying the wreckage. Less than a week old.

Only Inner Lands creatures would be interested in food of this kind. Humans, or the animals they brought with them: dogs, cats, possibly escaped pigs.

She picked up an oilcloth wrapper, smelled it: dried meat of some sort, probably venison. The smell was old, but the wrapper might just as easily have been dug from a garbage pit.

She searched. She found the garbage pit, undisturbed. Animals would have gone for the garbage pit, as well.

Rowan loaded her pack with as much unspoiled food as she could find and fit, to make a new cache further on.

It was time to increase her vigilance. She walked more cautiously now, keeping near the dunes, constantly scanning the beach ahead, smelling and tasting the air for a hint of woodsmoke, and listening. For human voices and for demon; she must be alert for both.

At least a demon could not sneak up upon her unawares. As she made her way along the slanted beach, her pack doubly heavy with the extra supplies, it came to her that demons must have no natural predators. Any such predator would find its prey far too easy to locate.

But surely there must be predators, she thought.

And she smiled to herself, stopping short only in her mind. The sea— demons were designed for the sea, but now walked on land. Perhaps they did so in a species-wide escape from some ocean-dwelling predator.

Rowan imagined a fish, hanging in the lightless deeps: huge, silent, intently listening—and hungry. She was surprised at how much pleasure the image gave her.

With supplies already in hand, Rowan put as many miles behind her as possible before stopping for the night.

A west wind rose, sending high clouds scudding. Lower clouds crept up from the south simultaneously, and sunset became a mere matter of increasing darkness.

Rowan moved off the beach and wound her way through the dunes, eventually finding a site on the back of one dune, open to the landscape to the north and east: A wide field of blue-leaf bushes, grown nearly to the size of trees; low hills, windswept bare on top; and at the horizon, the pale blue line of far mountains.

She made her camp simply, merely arranging her bedroll, and dined on cold food. So close to the wizard's keep, she dared not announce her presence by lighting a fire—but her vantage might allow other people to announce theirs. She sat, her back against the slope, munching cheese and bread, doggedly chewing jerked beef, and watching the world darken before her.

Rain would come before dawn, she knew; but she waited for the last glimmer of light before setting up the canvas tarp that served her as rain fly. Then she sat late in its open end, watching for lights in the hills to the north, on the brushy fields, among the valleys.

None came.

She watched long. Still, none came.

Eventually, she resigned herself to sleep.

34

*D*id she trust the talisman?

Rowan lay on the crest of the dune, in the black-grass, peering out between the blades. On the beach below, five demons were crossing the sand, moving toward the water.

Did she trust the talisman?

They did not behave like a group; each seemed to ignore the others. One strode into the sea, dropped to a horizontal position in the waves, then vanished from sight.

Did she trust it?

Another moved off to the left, down the beach. Rowan watched it out of sight. Three demons remained, standing in the sand, arms waving vaguely.

Presently, one retraced its previous route, back inland.

Did she?

One of the remaining pair shuffled its four feet, sending up sheets of sand, then abruptly dropped to a seat, knees high all around.

The last wandered desultorily away to the right, reaching down now and then to pick through bits of sea wrack.

Its route would bring it opposite Rowan's position.

Did she trust the talisman?

She watched it walk: a nightmare creature, headless, faceless, with no recognizable front or back and armed with deadly, burning spray. The memory of its effect was very present in her mind.

Rowan was more than a hundred feet away. She was safe from the spray.

She wished she could place the talisman somewhere in the demon's path and observe the monster's behavior, but could not risk it. There were other demons near, many others, somewhere out of sight. She could hear them.

Site Four had announced itself well before she reached it. Quietly at first, and she had been a long time recognizing the sound. In Alemeth, she had only heard one demon's voice at a time. It had not prepared her for this.

A mass of low notes at first but so blended as to seem one quiet, complex tone, rising and falling on the wind. Closer, the tones grew more steady; closer still, higher notes appeared, seeming to move above the others—an illusion of distance and obstacles, perhaps.

And here, this close, she felt the sound was almost a visible cloud hanging in the air above the still-unseen keep. She felt it ought to have color or pressure, so great, constant, and specific it was.

She did not yet know how many demons Slado kept here. More than had lived at Site Three, she was certain. It would take many more than forty demon-voices to create a sound that could be detected fully four miles away.

Down on the beach, the solitary demon continued its stroll. Slowly, with her sword in her right hand and the talisman in her left, the steerswoman rose to her feet.

She must move closer. She did not wish to. She wished herself far away from the monster—or for it to be dead.

She forced herself to take one step over the crest of the dune—and was committed, the steep slope shifting under her feet. She half stepped, half slid down to the tide line.

The solitary demon had moved farther down the beach, walking slowly along the edge of the waves. Rowan took a parallel route, close to the dunes. Moving slightly faster than the creature, she closed the distance by increments.

When she was sixty feet away, the demon stopped; Rowan did the same, heart pounding, waiting.

The creature lifted its arms slightly. Rowan tightened her grip on her sword.

The arms waved gently, slowly, each in turn around the demon's body.

A wild thought came to Rowan: she must move even closer, to give the demon a better look at the talisman. She could not bring herself to do it.

They stood so, some forty feet apart, for what seemed to Rowan like a very long time. Then the creature moved.

Away from Rowan, along the beach, back in the direction from which it had come.

The talisman worked.

Rowan let out one harsh breath, a breath she had not known she was holding. She breathed twice more quickly, almost long gasps.

Then she fell in behind the monster, following in its broad, flat footprints. Her teeth were clenched, stomach writhing within her like a separate living thing; she followed nevertheless. They walked the length of the beach together, sixty feet apart, then fifty.

The demon that had earlier been sitting on the sand was now gone. When Rowan's demon passed that place, it turned left and climbed the slope of the beach, toward a group of sandy hillocks.

The steerswoman stopped. She remained in place, watching the demon as it entered a gap between two hillocks and vanished from sight.

She was alone on the black-and-gold-striped beach.

She set her sword point down in the sand, wiped her face with her sleeve, forced herself to breathe deeply, slowly, felt her calm return. She looked down at the object in her left hand.

Magic.

No change in the talisman, no visible change, no sense of force or power. Still, she had been protected.

And somewhere beyond the hillocks, still out of sight: the location Janus had marked FOUR.

Rowan shivered; she had left her steerswoman's cloak at her campsite, knowing that it would be too typical and recognizable from a distance. She had assumed that Slado's human servants were allowed some freedom of movement, and had hoped that the casual eye would take her for one of their own, idly wandering the beach.

But the casual eye, Rowan considered, might be rather alarmed at the sight of a stroller carrying a naked blade. She pulled the sword from the sand, sheathed it, and proceeded east on the beach. The talisman she kept in her hand, carrying it as naturally as possible.

She had encountered not a single soul so far. Hardly surprising, since apparently Slado's pets were permitted to ramble about freely. Likely the people generally stayed within the precincts of the keep itself; and that explained the absence of outlying homes.

And the absence of roads. She found only one, leading up from a harbor.

It was the first human-made structure she had seen since the crypt, and a rough one at that: a breakwater, a mere double line of stone built out from the shore, with the space between filled with earth. Just east of this, the action of waves and currents had carved into the seafloor to a depth sufficient for small- and medium-sized sailing vessels. There were neither wharves nor piers, but a smaller ship would be able to draw quite close to the shore here.

No ship was present. Whatever vessel had delivered Janus and his captor had departed.

The road from the harbor was muddy, leading into the tall blue-leaf bushes that stood above the harborside. Rowan waited, leaning back against the first of the breakwater stones, watching the gap in the foliage suspiciously for some time. Just as she had decided that it was deserted, she saw motion and turned, scuttling like a crab to crouch behind a larger boulder.

Another demon. It walked a few paces toward the harbor, then stopped. Rowan could not tell what interested it; she hoped, not herself. Should it come nearer, she would stand, and display the talisman.

It came no nearer. It remained frustratingly motionless for several minutes, then returned up the road, disappearing among the blue leaves.

It was late afternoon; Rowan must attempt at least to locate the keep before nightfall. She wished the geography were different here; she wanted a hill, with brush cover, where she could scan the land from a height, sight the keep from a distance, and observe it before approaching. But the beach gently sloped, and the dunes were not high enough for a useful overview.

She took the road.

It curved in a broad arc, with blue-leaves and tanglebrush close beside. She could not see through the brush, could not see past the curve ahead.

But she could hear; and the demon that had left the harbor was somewhere up ahead. Rowan slowed her pace to keep out of direct sound sight.

But presently she heard that the creature had stopped. To go further, she must pass it; and she knew of no other road, and one could not bushwhack through tanglebrush. Rowan unsheathed her sword, held the talisman before her, took a deep breath, and continued on.

At first she did not see the demon, even though its voice became clear, frighteningly nearby. Then she sighted it: half submerged at the far end of a pool of water just off the side of the road. Its arms were spread, drop elbowed, its fingers just above the surface. Rowan fought the impulse to back away, to escape back down the road. Instead, she paused.

Motionless, the demon was even more bizarre; without action as a cue, it no longer seemed even to be an animal. More like a strange plant, Rowan thought, a freakish four-branched tree sprouting from the water.

The motion, when it came, shocked Rowan's senses: a single arm snapped down and then up, a wet, black, many-legged creature clutched in its fingers.

Whether crustacean or insect, she could not tell. The demon lifted it into the air within reach of the other arms, and long fingers snapped off each leg. The remaining carapace undulated in three segments. The demon pushed the creature down into its maw, the cracking and crackling audible above the humming voice, the fallen, severed legs of its prey stubbornly continuing to twitch on the stones at the water's edge.

The steerswoman felt a twist of nausea. Even though the demon's actions must be as natural as those of a mantis or a spider, they disturbed her. Inner Lands animals, and even insects, showed something in the nature of their motions and the very configuration of their bodies that told her she was kin to them. But this creature remained strange, wrong, different to the core.

The demon returned to stillness and to its hunting pose. To pass it by, the steerswoman must come within thirty feet of it. Much closer than to the demon on the beach.

Did she trust the talisman?

She did, but to what degree?

Make a virtue of necessity. Test how far the talisman would protect her.

She had an escape route; the demon had little room to maneuver. She thought that she could kill the monster, if she needed to; in fact, feeling as she did now, killing it might come as a positive relief.

She approached the pool.

It was rock-ringed, she saw now; no fine workmanship, merely enough stones roughly stacked to hold in the water that fed in from a small fresh rill and exited through a gap on the opposite side. Efficient. And kind of Slado, Rowan thought ironically, to relieve his monsters of the need to forage.

The demon was near the opposite edge of the pool. Rowan stepped up to the near edge, paused, then stepped up again, to stand atop the rough rock wall, her talisman held close in front of her body. She was perhaps twenty feet away, rising well above every other object. It was impossible not to be perceived.

The demon crunched on, indifferent or oblivious. Good.

Rowan stepped to her right, brought herself a quarter turn around the pool. Still no reaction. Another step.

The demon had finished crunching and reassumed the hunting pose, fingers above the water. Rowan waited for the splash and snatch, stepped again just as the demon again raised its prey above its missing head.

She was no further than fifteen feet from it; the demon repeated its previous actions with no variation other than the direction in which the severed legs fell.

A step . . .

The demon paused; Rowan froze.

The demon resumed eating. Rowan took one more step.

With its dinner still writhing half in its mouth, the demon freed its arms to spread them wide but not lifted to spray. The arms weaved, lifting, then falling, each in turn.

Human and monster remained for a long moment, during which time the demon's dinner, its segmented body flexing, escaped from the creature's mouth to fall on the rocks. There, legless, it calmly attempted to escape, inchworm fashion, bending its remaining hinge to drag its half body back toward the water.

The demon snatched it up again, lifted it to its mouth, and resumed dining, somewhat more slowly.

Her gum-soled boots silent on the rocks, Rowan took another step.

The demon rose from the water. Its voice grew louder, its arms weaved. Jaw clenched, Rowan stood her ground, ready, waiting for the lift that would precede a spray attack.

The demon paused, lowered its voice. It took one step away from her, paused again, then exited the pool.

Watching it go, Rowan passed her sleeve over her brow and was surprised when it came back soaked.

The demon continued down the road, moving at an easy pace now. Rowan paused to stretch every limb, breathe deeply—and then followed at a distance.

Another monster was somewhere near, further ahead; Rowan could hardly miss its approach, humming as it came. Then it appeared, its voice blossoming overtones as it rounded the curve ahead.

It was a smaller animal, slightly over half the first demon's size. Its body was smoother, and its color was more uniform: a dull bluish gray, where the first demon's was pale gray and faintly striated with brown. The two creatures approached each other, displaying no more sign of recognition than might two snakes crawling over the same rock.

The smaller creature might be an example of demon offspring. Rowan wondered what to call it: not a cub, a kit, a chick, or a whelp. She settled on "calf."

As they were about to pass each other, the larger demon stopped and abruptly reached for the smaller; from the suddenness of the movement, Rowan assumed that she was witnessing an attack and prepared to back off if they began using their spray.

Then the two engaged in such activity as demonstrated that the smaller demon was not a calf but a male.

The act was perfunctory. Neither creature showed passion, animal heat, nor even any great interest that Rowan could detect. Coupling took place four times, once with each set of organs, after which the female thrust the male away roughly and continued down the path.

The male remained, crouched on the ground with its knees high all around, its arms tucked in a knot above its body, its fourth organ still half extended. To pass it, Rowan would need to leave the path and circle into some brush, which would give her a less convenient escape route. She waited instead.

The male had retracted its organ, and with its arms still tucked in a knot, was now engaged in flexing and bending all its knees in unison, resulting in its entire smooth, columnar body being thrust up and down, over and over, which action Rowan, inexplicably, found unbearably obscene.

She retreated down the path, stepping backward. She passed the curve, and with the male out of sight she paused, scanning and listening for the approach of other demons.

Only the great hum of the mass of demons somewhere out of sight. No single demon was near. Rowan mastered her disgust, walked cautiously past the curve again, carefully displaying the talisman.

The male demon's actions were slowing.

Perhaps it merely suffered from cramped knees. As well it might.

And perhaps males were less sensitive, or more sensitive to Rowan's presence. Perhaps the talisman worked differently on them. The idea ought to be tested.

Rowan moved closer, paused.

The only result was that the male ceased its flexing, which perhaps it had been intending to do of itself. Rowan experimentally took two more steps, then another, which placed her as close to it as her closest approach to the female.

The male raised itself slightly; its arms unknotted, spread, and began to weave; its voice increased in volume.

When the female had done the same before, no attack had followed. Rowan decided that the behavior represented confusion. The male was puzzled, but could not identify any threat.

The arm weaving ceased, but its body began to sway, slightly. It trudged to one side of the path, stopped, trudged to the other side, repeated the actions.

The path behind Rowan led back to the feeding pool; possibly the male was hungry after its desultory sexual exploits and wished to dine. The steerswoman moved to the left side of the path.

The male demon immediately crossed to the right, stepping off the path entirely to avoid Rowan's sphere of protection, exactly as if some physical object that had blocked its way was now shifted. Rowan nodded to herself.

When it was opposite her, it slowed, stopped.

It took one step directly toward her. Appalled, Rowan took a matching step back.

The male took another slow step, and another.

A crowd of tanglebrush stood behind Rowan; she could remove herself no further without rattling their branches. She did not risk the noise and watched as the male took two more hesitant steps toward her. When it was no more than six feet away, it stopped and stood.

She could smell it. She could taste its strange breath on the air. Should it reach out its hand and Rowan reach hers, they would touch fingers. At the thought, every nerve in her body seemed individually to twist, to attempt to draw back from the monster.

A long minute passed, during which neither moved. Then Rowan's sword point rose as she tightened her fingers. She stepped forward.

The male stepped back.

She stepped again; the male retreated again.

It would not attack her; it could not.

She had magic. She was invincible.

Rowan stepped forward twice, raising her sword to strike.

The male took two quick steps back, then a third—then fled, back up the path. With a dark, fierce satisfaction, Rowan watched it go.

She let it live. She could kill it later, at any time, if she cared to.

She had magic.

Ahead, the female demon was still visible through thinning underbrush, plodding along. The male, at a staggering run, caught up to it. With sudden shock, Rowan realized the deep, the very deep stupidity of her actions.

A dog would bark warning to other dogs. A wolf would run to the pack leader. Even a crow would scream danger to others at the sight of a cat.

The male knew that something strange, something frightening, was nearby.

It came to a stop by the female; it reached up, clutching at the female's fingers. The female thrust it away, continued on. The male caught up again, reached again.

Rowan found that she had herself retreated, stepping back down the path, sword point dropped, talisman held directly before her.

The female stopped walking. Rowan prepared to run.

The female demon paused long; then it lowered itself, spreading two knees in mating stance.

The male disengaged its fingers, retreated a few steps.

The female rose, then continued on its way. After a pause, the male followed, more slowly.

Rowan watched them out of sight, their voices fading to blend with the distant demon song.

In the quiet of their absence, she became sharply aware of the sky, the air, herself: muscles tensed, nerves tuned to painful tautness, listening so intently that every leaf and insect noise struck her ears with a tiny shock.

She could kill a demon; she could kill two. But if three, five, nine were all around her, and in a panic?

But the male's warning was not understood. How very lucky for Rowan that these animals were so stupid.

She backed down the path some twenty feet before she remembered that, with the demons gone, there was no need to walk backward. She turned and managed to keep herself from running the rest of the way to her camp.

She had set up among the dunes.

She did not know if demons slept, but she must do so. She had needed a place where she would be protected on three sides, so that she could place the talisman on the open side, where it would deter the approach of any passing demon while she slept. Such a location was difficult to find. She had hoped for a cave with a single opening, but there were no cliffs, no visible outcroppings of rock.

Physically, her camp was comfortable, in a little cul-de-sac among the maze of grassy dunes; now, it felt like a trap.

She sat on her bedroll, wrapped in her cloak, studying with narrowed gaze the talisman flickering in the firelight before her.

Did demons, she wondered, have a sense of smell? Could the male demon track her here? Would others follow, perhaps out of curiosity? Would she find herself mobbed?

Or would the male remain so frightened that its master would notice, suspect, and investigate?

How stupid, how unutterably stupid to have drawn attention to herself, and then let the creature go. She ought to have killed the male demon immediately.

Perhaps the talisman's magic worked in both directions. Perhaps she had been under a spell of some sort herself.

She rejected the idea with an almost physical disgust at the rationalization. It was power, merely power. She had become drunk on power.

Perhaps that had been Janus's own mistake. Perhaps that had been what gave him away to the wizard.

Perhaps she had just done the same, herself.

If only there were two persons traveling, to take turns watching the night. If only Bel were here.

Rowan rose, arranged her pack behind her, to prop her into a sitting position, sat with the talisman at her feet.

Outskirters could sleep deeply, sitting up. She could not.

The night was long.

35

No mob of demons came to her camp. Light grew slowly, mist white, until the first sliver of sunlight caught every speck of dew, strewing the blackgrass, the dark tanglebrush, the brown sand with constellations of pink, then gold.

A sole whistle-spider set up its tune, pausing to wait for replies that never came. A hawkbug had spent the night on Rowan's pack. She chased it off; it crawled away awkwardly, wings still too wet to fly.

The road from the harbor remained Rowan's only clue to Slado's keep. She breakfasted, filled her water sack, slung it over one shoulder and her sword over the other. Then she slipped on her gloves, took up the talisman, and left camp.

The beach was deserted of both people and monsters, as was the road, when she reached it. She passed the rock pool, and was wondering what sort of natural schedule demons kept when not under magical control, when she first heard, then sighted up ahead six demons assembled in the middle of the road.

She waited, sword drawn, talisman carefully displayed. She would not repeat yesterday's mistake.

The demons did nothing whatever; and finally, one by one, they left the road, entering and disappearing down a rough path that led into the undergrowth.

Rowan wondered what mission they were on: their own or the wizard's. Perhaps she ought to follow them.

But this road must lead to the keep. She continued.

The curve of the road remained very smooth, continual, its arc unchanging. If it did not change farther on, Rowan thought, it would eventually complete a circle.

Glimpses through gaps in the blue-leaves on the left told the steerswoman what lay within the circle: the domed roofs of demon dens showed through, intermittently, the brown and black color of native earth. The mass of demon-voices was louder now, closer, an invisible edifice of noise, directly in her left ear. The comparative quiet in her right made her slightly dizzy.

Paths led from the dens to the road, and Rowan had to pause, again and again, to permit demons to cross in front of her and move out into the countryside. Twenty-six of them passed her in this fashion, singly and in small groups.

The massed demon song seemed undiminished by their departure. Rowan adjusted upward her estimation of the demons' numbers.

And still no sign of people.

She went on. She passed another rock pool, and then another. She considered the distances, surmised a pattern, and immediately found it confirmed. The next pool contained two male demons, breakfasting at their leisure. Rowan kept her distance.

But beyond the far edge of the pool, the undergrowth was less dense and shorter, and the steerswoman acquired a very good view of the countryside to the north.

An undulating slope of blackgrass, blue-leaf, and tanglebrush crossed by a brook, threaded by vague paths through the grass. A flat meadow beyond, with the humped shapes of small and larger lichen-towers. A series of low, shrub-covered hills with higher, more distant hills beyond. Above: the white, overcast sky.

No fortress visible, neither near nor far. No structures at all. And no paths well-worn enough to betray an important destination.

But not every wizard possessed a keep. And, now that Rowan thought of it, for what purpose would Slado need so great a thing as a fortress, when the demons—and the hostile countryside itself—secured his isolation?

Very well: her target was smaller than she had thought. A low-built mansion, perhaps, with a small adjacent compound for servant quarters and livestock. Quite possibly, it sat directly among the dens kept by Slado's pets, protected from them by his magic.

Rowan turned back and continued down the road.

But she could not simply wander about aimlessly until she stumbled over Slado's doorstep. She needed clues.

Magic: magic was the supposedly inexplicable. Look for the inexplicable.

She found it, almost immediately.

Talismans. Dozens of them.

She had expected another rock pool here. Instead: a large area, flat and completely free of brush and grass, some fifty feet in diameter—and talismans, strewn and grouped all across it.

Even to the eye alone, the material of these objects was clearly the same as that of her own; but not a single spell resembled hers in shape.

Some were small, low, and individual; others stood in cluttered clusters; still others were large indeed, spun up into bizarre constructions with flutes, filigrees, risers, and ribbons.

The steerswoman stood, stunned, the point of her sword dropped to the ground. A wind rose, ruffled her hair with casual intimacy. Diffuse sunlight cast her vague shadow across, into, and among the objects.

There they merely stood, matter-of-fact, weirdly innocent. Rowan half expected them to make some sound; but the only sound, other than the endless hum of the demons, was a single demon-voice, somewhere nearby.

Then motion, on the far side of the area: a female demon emerged from behind one of the higher constructions. Rowan watched nervously.

It ambled. It merely ambled among the spells, pausing now and again, and then moving on and doing, apparently, nothing.

Rowan skirted the limits of the area, studying the animal's every movement with fierce concentration—and learned nothing. It wandered and paused, wandered and paused. Only that.

Rowan had frankly hoped for something more obviously purposeful; but she could not fault the situation for inexplicability.

A growing voice announced another demon's approach. It soon appeared; a male, this time. It paused on the road, then changed direction and stepped into the spell field.

And proceeded to do exactly as the female did. It ignored the female and Rowan, moved at its own pace, wandering, pausing, moving on.

Rowan cautiously took a sip from her water sack, let it linger in her mouth, continued watching. The female demon continued its amble; the male did the same.

Exactly the same.

Rowan swallowed, moved cautiously along the edge of the area for a better view.

As she watched, the female demon approached and paused before a collection of low, angular spell objects. After a moment, it moved on. Just over a minute later, the male arrived at the same collection and also paused, then continued.

A winding route among the objects, with many small pauses, eventually brought the female to a large, complex construction. The creature stood by it, and for a brief moment its arms weaved in the reaction Rowan had equated with confusion or puzzlement. Then the weaving ceased, and the demon stood quiet for a long moment, and then passed on.

The male demon traced the identical winding route, arrived at the same construction, and showed the identical reaction. Had the male wished to reach the construction earlier, it would only have needed to take four steps west of its previous location. Nevertheless, it walked exactly where the female had walked.

The steerswoman watched, dumbfouded, as step-by-step the two demons marked out the route of an invisible maze.

Eventually, the female's route brought it back to the road, where it stood motionless. Soon, the male reached the same location, paused exactly as pointlessly. Then the female departed.

Follow the inexplicable.

Rowan sidled around the talisman field, trying to keep a comfortable distance between herself and the male when she passed it. But the male moved abruptly; Rowan froze.

The male demon reentered the maze and, moving with an odd quickness, retraced its entire previous route—backward. Rowan watched with utter incomprehension.

It did not pause in each place it had before; but each time that it did pause, however briefly, it reached down, picked up one small spell, and ate it.

When it arrived at the road again, Rowan had already stationed herself at a distance; and when it completed its apparently obligatory pause and moved on, the demon had acquired a silent companion.

It led the steerswoman directly into the demon colony.

36

S he moved like a rat through the streets.

She sidled along the dens, slinked from one structure to the next, shifted abruptly to opposite sides of the den-lined pathways when demons emerged from entrances or intersections, kept her back against or directed at walls, bushes, rocks.

At fifteen feet away, females ignored her; twelve feet for the males. At twelve feet, the females retreated; the males, at six.

She must not disturb these creatures. A crowd, a panic, and one of them could slip behind her, where her own body would hide the talisman.

Where she was unprotected. Where she was blind.

And all the while, entirely, as good as deaf.

Demon-voice was everywhere: tones so deep they trembled in her chest and throat, so high they dizzied her. She felt she could not breathe for the sound; the sound was an ocean; she was at the bottom of it. She had the bizarre impression that if she opened her mouth, the sound itself would wash into her throat, her lungs, and drown her.

And this with the street nearly empty—two females walking far ahead and the male that Rowan followed at a distance of twenty feet. All the other noise—pouring down between the dens, falling, it seemed, from the sky itself—was voiced by demons out of sight.

Rowan's guide had stopped halfway along the path, and now sat on four heels, four knees high all around, on the ground outside one of the dens. The steerswoman moved back, leaned against the den opposite, breathing shallowly, trying to focus her thoughts amid the din, and failing. She tried again, more forcefully, but achieved only a macabre intellectual detachment in which all sensory information seemed distant and irrelevant—a state so dangerous of itself that a sudden thrust of fear brought her back to reality.

Beside her, an opening between two dens. Down it, an open, marshy space clotted with sea blackgrass, empty of demons. Behind the shield of her talisman, Rowan rose, backed down the gap and out into the marsh, half stumbling over clots of blackgrass.

She stopped in the center of the area, trees and demon dens all around, demon-voices still filling the air, and only fractionally quieter.

"I can't do this," she said. She said it out loud, realized the fact, spun around to see if any of the monsters had heard. None were visible.

Something must be done. She stared at the talisman in her hand.

Then, cautiously, glancing all around, she set it on the ground, kneeled in the mud beside it, and removed her right glove. With the flat of her sword propped against one knee, she clumsily used the edge to slice off the last two fingertips of the glove. She put a daub of mud inside each, folded them tightly, and stuffed them in her ears.

Relief.

Not silence but near it. Intimate sounds only: her own breath, her slowing heart, a rough hiss as she ran her hands through her hair.

There was a breeze she had not before noticed, coming from the south; and it was cool, carrying the now-familiar odor of the strange sea-weed and seawrack of the great ocean. She drank it in and felt better, cleaner, saner. Even her vision seemed clearer.

She dipped her kerchief into the dirty marsh water, wiped its coolness down her neck, across her forehead. Then she donned her glove, took up the talisman and her sword.

A shield and a weapon. No traveler or warrior could ask for more.

And her goal was near, so near.

When she emerged from the path, she found her guide still seated by the side of the den, its arms now knotted above its maw. At this proximity, she did hear its voice; but only its lowest tones came through the obstructions in her ears. Exactly enough to be useful. She lowered herself to a seat opposite it, resting her sword across her knees.

But now she was entirely unable to hear quieter sounds: distant human voices, say, or human footsteps. And humans were immune to the talisman.

Any person, either wizard or wizard's servant, would also be carrying a talisman, Rowan assumed. A simple thing for Slado to provide. But she still had yet to see a single human being.

Her route into the colony had taken many turns; each street was crossed by others, at wide intervals. Her guide had turned corner after corner, never hesitating, before coming to rest here.

The steerswoman tried to reconstruct the route in her mind—and was startled to find that she could not. Her mind had been too muddled by noise; she had been too intent on maintaining a safe distance from the demons she had passed. She had no idea at all where she was. The feeling was strange to her, and deeply disturbing.

Meanwhile, her guide still had not moved. Rowan began to wonder if the creature had fallen asleep. If so, it hummed in its dreams.

Rowan pulled more tightly against the den at the approach of two demons, both female. Their only reaction to her presence was to move as far as possible to the other side of the path, jostling the male as they passed. Other than that, they ignored Rowan, the male, and as far as the steerswoman could tell, each other.

Time passed. More demons came and went, behaving exactly as the others had. Rowan became restive.

Her guide stirred; she became intent. Then it defecated, moved three feet to the left away from its own excrement, and returned to motionlessness. Rowan suppressed a hiss of frustration.

Somewhat later, another passing demon paused by the male, picked up the feces, dropped them into its maw, and continued on.

Cleaning the street. Insects, birds, and even some mammals would clean their nests in exactly the same fashion. Nothing inexplicable there. And all the while, her chosen guide inexplicably continued to do nothing whatsoever.

Surely it was asleep. Rowan resisted an impulse to go over and prod it with her foot.

With the street otherwise deserted, the steerswoman had nearly decided to abandon the male and continue alone, when one more demon turned into the street.

A male. Males were marginally less sensitive to the spell. Best to wait.

The demon plodded the length of the street to the next intersection, where it paused, then abruptly executed the eerie, unturning demon reversal of direction. It approached again. Wondering if something had alerted it to her presence, Rowan slowly rose, sword held at the ready.

The demon arrived at Rowan's napping guide; the other demon stirred, unknotted its arms, and rose.

Each demon reached out one arm, touched fingers, then intertwined them. With another arm, Rowan's guide reached up and then down into its own maw, extracted something, and passed it to the reaching fingers of the other demon.

A spell-object. Rowan's astonishment was complete.

The second demon ate it.

The demons repeated the action three times. Then they immediately parted, in opposite directions.

Rowan dithered briefly. Which demon was more inexplicable? Which action more bizarre?

For familiarity's sake, she followed her original guide, hurrying to safe distance, then pacing it, slinking and side-stepping.

Apparently, the demon had not actually digested the spells it had earlier taken, but had been carrying them, conveniently in its maw, as a chipmunk carried nuts stuffed in its cheek pockets.

This creature was merely sharing food. An entirely natural action, and not directed by magic—

The male was not leading her to the wizard.

She stopped, allowed the male to proceed without her. It passed through a trio of approaching females, took the next intersection, and was gone.

Rowan must find Slado's residence herself, and for safety's sake, as soon as possible. She took a sip from her water sack, and narrowed her eyes in thought.

Very well; if Rowan herself were a powerful wizard, with the ability to utterly control the actions of these monsters, where might she choose to live?

If not close to her demon servants, then among them; and if among them, where else but directly in the center?

She grimaced. An unpleasant prospect, to move so deep among these creatures. And how was she even to locate the center, when she did not know where she was?

By the sun's angle she knew the cardinal directions, and she had entered the colony from the north. She decided to try south.

Easily said, less easily accomplished. The streets seemed intentionally designed to prevent any straight-line movement. She took turn after turn, zigzagging, knowing only that she was going in a generally southerly direction.

The steerswoman passed demons; they passed her: singly, in pairs and groups. Rowan found herself falling into a pattern: step to the right as a demon neared; turn to place her back against a den; wait for the demon to leave the street. Repeat and repeat. It became second nature.

Dangerous. She must not become too accustomed to this.

When demons were numerous, she walked sideways, her back against a den, the talisman held centrally. Far more awkward, but it did serve to keep her alert.

Then, at the next intersection: a crowd of demons, seven of them. Rowan paused, wondering how best to pass.

In the middle of the group stood a single spell-object, as tall as Rowan's waist. It was complex in structure, standing on many feet like tree roots, combining and rising to a single striated flute. Rowan noted that the animals had oriented themselves so that no demon blocked another's view.

Each of the demons stood completely motionless. Perhaps the spell had placed them in a trance.

Rowan doubled back to the intersection, took a different turn, then another, continuing to work her way south.

She came upon her erstwhile guide again, recognizing the demon by the stippled pattern on its torso and the fact that it was once again napping in a deserted street. She almost felt glad: a familiar face, so to speak. When she left it behind, another male was entering the street; when she glanced back, she saw it receive a spell object from the cache in the first male's maw.

She went on. Intersections began appearing at closer intervals. A good sign, the steerswoman decided. She envisioned the perimeter road as a huge circle, the demon dens within; she overlaid the streets she could see, surmising repetition of pattern.

Something like a network emerged, wide at the edges, tighter toward the center. But the streets curved; she curved them on her internal map. And alternate streets curved in opposite directions . . .

The pattern blossomed in her mind: lovely, perfect. The crisscrossing streets were each a spiral segment. Each street ended in the center.

All roads led to Slado.

She ceased bothering to take any turns at all; but now she became even more cautious, more tensely alert. Here, among these close-set intersections, so near the residence, here would be the worst place to be surprised by one of Slado's people, with monsters all about and her own presence so unexpected.

But still she saw no one.

But surely Slado had servants. Surely a demon, however precisely controlled, could not cook a meal, do the laundry.

Passage became more difficult. Streets were narrower, intersections ever more close and sharply angled. Out of sheer exhaustion,

Rowan backed up against a den and allowed the traffic to find its own way around her.

A thought passed through her mind as if from afar: What if the count of left-curving streets and right-curving streets were adjacent Fibonacci numbers?

She stopped short.

What if?

Rowan had been introduced to the peculiar sequence of numbers mysteriously named Fibonacci in her second year of training. Each element was the sum of the two previous: 1, 1, 2, 3, 5, 8, 13 . . . extending infinitely.

An intellectual oddity, she had then thought, charming but useless, until the teachers Arian and Edith had independently begun pointing out examples of the numbers in nature.

Petals on a daisy. The spiral growth of snail shells, ram's horns. Leaves on a grass stem, seeds on a pinecone, the double spiral of a sunflower. The sequence seemed to appear everywhere, either as simple integer counts or as ratios.

Even Outskirts life: the number of the outermost twigs on a tangle-brush was always a Fibonacci number, and the count of branchings from the original stem was 1, 2, 3, 5, continuing in an unbroken sequence. Blackgrass leaves were offset from each other by five-eighths of a turn around the stem.

People do not typically build in spirals nor cause spiral streets to be built. Humans liked straight lines, square buildings, and even numbers—and direct routes to important places.

The demons had created these streets themselves, by a natural process. Uncontrolled, undirected.

Apparently, in daily matters, the wizard ruled the monsters with a very light hand—

Assuming he was here at all.

No. These were Slado's creatures. He was here. He must be here.

Janus had been taken from Alemeth; and this was the last mark on his map.

And Janus had possessed a magical spell. Other spells were here. Magic was here; a wizard was here, or must be . . .

The center. The center would tell her.

She reached it sooner than pure mathematics predicted, simply because it was no abstract point. The steerswoman stood at the edge, looking down.

A depression, nearly one hundred feet in diameter, sloping at an angle of about twenty degrees, down to a flat area some thirty feet across. Packed earth, all around.

Along the slope, a few demons, scattered.

Below, a few demons, gathered.

Among them, a number of the spell objects.

Nothing else.

And all around the circular edge of the area: demon dens and street entrances—and nothing else.

Above it all, the wide white sky, a pearl overcast, the sun a haze of brightness in the west.

Nothing else.

Far below, one of the motionless demons stirred, moved, and began climbing the slope in Rowan's direction. With no thought whatsoever in her mind, Rowan watched its slow approach.

It stopped in front of her. Human and demon stood for some time, neither moving.

Eventually, Rowan herself moved. She took six steps to the left.

The demon entered the street whose access she had been blocking, walked its length, turned a corner, and was gone.

Rowan watched it go. She turned back and regarded the great, empty center for some time.

Then, slowly, the steerswoman walked: down, across, then up, to the street that natural geometry told her would exit the colony closest to her camp, and left the center behind.

On the beach she stopped; she stood on the black-and-gold swirl-patterned sand, watching the surging of the strange and possibly endless ocean, gazing at a sky where no birds flew, and feeling that she was dreaming the entire scene—or dreaming herself.

She twisted her mouth in derision, stabbed her sword point down in the sand, pulled the plugs from her ears. Reality flowed in with the sound: rush and crash of waves, whistle and scree of insects, clatter of leaves, and the soft sift of the wandering, wind-borne sand. She snatched up her weapon, strode down the beach.

No sign of humans found during her original approach from the west; no sight of roads, buildings or even woodsmoke in the open countryside, north, east, west.

In all this wilderness, no sign of human habitation at all; and Site Four was merely a remarkably large demon colony.

Slado was not here.

And so, neither was Janus.

Rowan found she had reached the water, and had stopped. She was gazing blindly out to sea. She turned and gazed less blindly at beach and hillocks.

"But he *was* here," she said, her own voice sounding almost plaintive.

And perhaps recently, as the spell objects testified. Magic had been enacted at this place and then abandoned. And it was important, important enough to change Janus utterly; important enough to Slado to cause Janus to be snatched away from Alemeth . . .

But not brought here.

Janus was likely dead. If not dead, as good as dead, because there was no way in the world for Rowan to find him.

She walked up the beach again, more slowly.

He really ought to have spoken. He really ought to have asked for help, long ago. Now he was lost.

Very well, then. If she could not save Janus, could not find Slado, Rowan would, at the very least, recover the information Janus had found here, the precious secret that the wizard so vigorously protected. She could follow her lost comrade's footsteps in this strange and dangerous country, her single advantage a magical protection so complete that she might as well be invisible.

She stopped short, stood with the cooling wind ruffling her hair. Some natural pause in the waves' pattern caused the ocean itself to be, for a moment, breathless.

Invisible. What a very interesting idea.

Was it possible, through magic, to hide an entire fortress? To obliterate all clues, disguise all roads, so confuse the mind that one could stand within sight of something that must surely be the equivalent of a small town and simply not see it?

Her grip on the talisman tightened, her other hand clenched into a fist around her sword hilt, and she said out loud through clenched teeth, "*Parameters.*"

But who could know what the most powerful wizard in the world was capable of?

Janus had found *something*. Perhaps the fortress. Perhaps he had, somehow, circumvented Slado's magic.

By using . . . more magic?

She looked at the talisman in her hand. It was the only magic she had.

She pushed her sword tip in the sand again, leaving her right hand resting on its hilt. She took a deep breath, attempted to clear her mind of all confusion and misconceptions, held the talisman before her, and looked.

Slowly. In a circle. Step-by-step around her upright sword.

The beach to the west. South, the sea. East, the beach again and the breakwater. The dunes. The sandy hillocks, with the demon colony tucked behind and the distant hills rising far beyond. Dunes again, and the cat-striped beach running down to her feet—

She stopped.

A spell.

A *talisman*. Like her own.

Sitting, simply sitting, abandoned on the beach.

She pulled out her sword and walked slowly to it.

It was larger than hers, nearly three times the size, but—and she lay down her weapon, knelt in the sand, reached out to touch it—the same: the truncated pyramid, the swirling striations, and, to the two bare fingertips of her right hand, the exact gum-and-sand texture.

Color was different: still black and gold but in blotches that in no way matched Rowan's talisman.

Of course. Color was irrelevant to demons.

She set down her own talisman, and with one hand on each side of the new object, tried to lift it. She could not. She ran her fingers under the edges; it seemed rooted to the sand. Digging harder, pressing inward, she felt something give way, and her two bare fingertips were suddenly cold, and wet.

The fingers immediately itched, first mildly, then madly. She yanked her hands out, struggled to free her water sack, and drenched fingers and gloves, thrust them into the dry sand, drenched and thrust again. The sensation subsided. Wiping the sand off on her trouser leg, she sat regarding the object.

Then she took up her sword, prodded at one of the slanted faces. The surface dimpled. She pushed harder, punctured it.

Clear fluid spilled out around the blade.

Rowan thrust further in, feeling no resistance. She sliced the object completely across, levered it open.

Within: transparent spheres more than an inch across, perhaps a hundred of them. Large enough and clear enough that she could see plainly inside each one the small, curled form, the gray line of backbone, the pale arms trailing forward, the tiny fins furled back.

Rowan had a sudden urge to snatch up her own talisman, fling it away from her, in a sudden fear that it might split and hatch a horde of little demons onto the sand all around her.

Impossible.

Impossible: it was a *made* thing, it had to be. She could make no sense of this, none at all.

"It does work," she said out loud, slowly. "It does protect me."

How?

Magic. A wizard made it.

Made it of the same material a demon uses to cover its eggs?

Apparently . . . Apparently, and why not? Who knows what properties in this substance a wizard might find useful?

Made it in the same shape?

"But it works!"

How?

"Magic . . ."

And when exactly did you come to believe so easily in magic?

But it had not come easily, not easily at all. It had taken a jewel of impossible origin, a statue that moved without life, blasts of destruction destroying an entire fortress, invisible heat from the sky killing everything in its path . . .

But before that—and had it been so long ago? When, standing on the deck of a ship, she had said to Bel: *The few times I've been faced with something called magical, it seemed simply mysterious . . . as if there were merely something about it that I didn't know.*

What did she know, here and now?

Next to nothing.

Sometimes I feel people call it magic, she had said, *because they want magic.*

What did she want?

"No." She spoke aloud. "What I want is irrelevant. A steerswoman sees what *is*."

Then, look.

A cache of demon eggs in the sand, surrounded by a protective covering. A smaller object, resembling the cache.

"But why would this protect me?"

Why assume your own importance in this? Remove yourself from the equation.

A demon does not approach or harm the so-called talisman. Therefore, a demon does not approach or harm a cache of eggs. Preserving the next generation: the simple logic of survival.

Look at what is.

She did. She looked up. She looked at the landscape all around, but now with her mind so nearly empty that she seemed to herself not to be present at all. Absent; and absent also every wish, every want, every hope. Only her sight remained, uninhabited.

Endless wilderness. No humans. No sign of humans. Nothing that referred to or reflected humankind. No magic.

Rowan remained, still, silent, empty, for many minutes.

A troop of seven female demons emerged from the colony and made their way toward the ocean. Rowan's only reaction was to shift her talisman to the other side of her body, toward the demons. This she did without thought.

The creatures passed, entered the water, vanished.

Finally, the steerswoman rose, picked up her sword and the object which she had carried with her from the Inner Lands, and returned to her camp.

She sat on her bedroll in the sand in the flickering dark, arms around her knees, staring into the fire.

Nothing she was seeking could be found here.

Janus had acquired no magic at all, merely a dried stunted egg case.

Something else about him had attracted Slado's attention.

The steerswoman said out loud, "You *fool.*" No—there was no reason, none at all, to think that it had been Slado who had taken Janus from Alemeth. Rowan had only assumed so because of the apparently magical inaccessibilty of these lands.

But even that had a natural explanation. Little snails.

Her tin stew pot clattered its lid; stew hissed down its side into the fire. She ignored it.

Some other wizard could just as easily have taken Janus—anyone with the power to command animals. Jannik in Donner, for instance; he controlled dragons. Why not demons as well?

Oh, and what a simple thing that would have been, to sail from Alemeth to Donner. She might have accomplished Janus's rescue weeks ago.

The steerswoman ran her fingers roughly through her hair, dropped her hands to her lap, sat gazing at them, watched as they clenched into fists.

She had wanted it to be Slado. She had wanted her search to be over.

"I," she said out loud, "have misled myself at every turn!"

She was indifferent to the noise she made. Should a demon approach, she need merely become silent, show it the egg case. It would go away.

Her stew was burning. She muttered a curse, snagged it out of the fire with a bit of tanglebrush driftwood, set it on the sand to cool.

And now what?

Janus had inspired someone to cause him to be captured. The only unusual thing that he had been doing: wandering in the demon lands.

Wandering and charting, as any good steerswoman would. A difficult and dangerous task—but if he had resigned from the order, why bother?

Why does anyone do anything?

The answer from her early training spoke itself. "To make one's life better; to prevent one's life from becoming worse." Neither alternative seemed to apply.

Leaving her—and she pulled the tin pot closer to her, began to attack her dinner with unnecessary viciousness—leaving her wandering the demon lands herself.

Accomplishing nothing. She ought to leave in the morning. She ought to be hunting Slado, sifting for clues; she could be reunited with Bel, they could be working together again. Instead—

She stopped short, a spoonful of stew suspended halfway to her mouth.

Instead, she was in a new and unknown country, seeing new, strange, and wonderful things.

This was what she wanted, all that time in Alemeth. In the chaos of the Annex, mired in books and mundane town life—this was what she had been yearning for.

She looked about her.

Pack, bedroll, stew in the pot, pens and ink and logbook—her camp, a little miracle of comfort in the wilderness. Firelight catching the glints of yellow in the strange black dunes that rose about her. A clear and open sky above.

Insects speaking in voice and motion: some she knew, others whose names she was free to invent. The gentle grumble and hiss of a new and unexplored ocean. And the very voice of strangeness itself: the unending hum of demons, coming to her across the hills and sand.

Someday, in the Inner Lands, there would be war.

Someday, the Outskirts would no longer support its people; and they would move inward.

Someday Rowan's people and Bel's people must fight: either against each other or by each other's side, against a power whose scope Rowan could not even imagine.

And so much to be done before that time; to prepare or prevent or at the very least learn the nature of the fight.

But here, now, there was only the wide, wild unknown country—and one human being with a heart hungry for wonder.

It came to Rowan that with all struggles and duties that lay before her, this might well be the last time in her life that she could be, merely and purely, a wandering steerswoman.

She would spare one more day.

Quickly she finished her meal, cleaned her utensils, stored them, re-arranged her campsite, repositioned the talisman, crawled into her bedroll with her folded cloak as a pillow.

She slept soundly. She rose early.

37

*R*owan took a new route into the colony: north from her camp, northeast across a huge meadow of sea blackgrass to where she knew that she would find a street leading to the eastern section. She had passed through that area quickly the previous day, while her mind had been clouded by the noise. It was worth closer examination.

In the meadow she gave wide berth to a troop of eight female demons moving off to the northwest, a hunting group, perhaps. They trotted, which action Rowan observed with amusement. The creatures seemed not designed to trot; their columnar bodies rocked wildly backward and forward, their arms whipping about loosely. On rough terrain, they would certainly fall over at this speed. Nevertheless, they trotted.

Rowan paused again at a rock pool and considered its construction in the light of her new understanding. Simple, efficient, but no more surprising now than a beaver's dam. And the breakwater at the so-called harbor—merely another example of a similar process.

She followed the elegant, predictable street from the perimeter inward— and chided herself for continuing to refer to it as a "street." Still, she needed some convenient term and could think of none more apt.

With no fear of being sighted by humans, she was able to concentrate on observation—and on remaining safe among demons. It was its own sort of skill, she decided, requiring great care but manageable—although the earplugs were necessary.

She passed demons cautiously but safely; they passed her, on what errands she did not know. Curious, she selected one female, followed it on its wandering route, and discovered that it was industriously collecting and swallowing feces left by other demons.

Interesting. Division of labor suggested a hive structure, like bees. Still, an unpleasant profession. At an intersection, she let the street cleaner go on without her, and looked about, attempting to acquire an overview.

There seemed to be no difference in the level of activity this morning from that of the previous afternoon. Possibly night and day had no meaning for the animals, other than difference of temperature. She wondered how their instincts reacted to the changes of season and was sorry she did not have the time to discover it. She stepped up to a den to closely examine its structure, and decided that it would stand against snow, at least for one winter.

She moved aside to allow a restless and confused female demon access to the den entrance, feeling almost apologetic.

They were, she decided, amazing animals.

Dangerous, yes, and she must remain cautious. But if she did not come near, the creatures acted exactly as if she were invisible. She wished she could move among other creatures with such freedom. What could one learn of wolves, birds, or even fish, invisibly? What volumes of knowledge would that experience speak to her?

She selected a street, followed it toward the center.

The so-called spell-objects remained a mystery—and she did need some other term for them. "Egg case" would not do; none of the ones within the colony looked like egg cases at all, nor had the same effect on demons.

Further on, she had the opportunity to observe a female demon creating one of the case-objects. The action was simple; the creature merely reached down and extracted it from a lower orifice. Rowan nodded to herself, now recognizing the purpose of the internal protrusions she had discovered during the dissection in Alemeth.

But the purpose of the act itself was not evident. Three other demons nearby grew suddenly still; although Rowan had no reliable clue as to the direction of their attention, she could not help assuming that they had noticed the object. If so, their interest was brief, as all four demons then simply wandered away.

With only a single demon remaining further down the street, Rowan went to the object and stooped down to study it, gaining no new information whatsoever. But as she rose, she noticed that the demon, a male, was pacing the street from side to side.

Odd. It was far out of her talisman's range.

Then she recognized the stippled pattern on its skin; the male from the maze, the food distributor. Interested, she slowly backed away from the object.

When her sphere of protection moved away from the object, the male stopped, lifted its arms suddenly—but not in attack; his arms immediately dropped again. Then the male remained in place, unmoving. Rowan continued to back away.

Abruptly, the demon broke into a run. Startled, Rowan backed against a den, lifted her sword.

Not even pausing, the male snatched up the object, dropped it in its maw, passed her, turned at the next corner with its taloned feet scrabbling the earth, and was gone.

Rowan stood bemused. The case-objects were edible, obviously; perhaps fresh ones were tastier.

Still, the male had displayed rather a lot of urgency—competition within a hive? She could think of no other creatures that did that.

As she continued further into the colony, it occurred to her that it was perhaps less than useful to attempt to find analogies for demon behavior or try to identify parallel behavior in other animals. Demons were not insects, were not birds, were not reptiles or fish, and appeared not to be mammals. Perhaps their organization and behavior were unique to themselves; or perhaps they paralleled the behavior of other, unknown animals dwelling in these Demon Lands. Perhaps one day, when she or another steerswoman finally came to learn about those other animals, that person would say: See how similar to a demon they are?

The idea pleased her.

She finally did find demon calves, two of them. Both seemed to her to be female. Although one was nearly the height of a male, it was less blocky, more lithely muscular, as females were. The second calf was smaller still, but shared the same physique; and its skin was paler, almost translucent. Rowan could see its hearing organs as small, pale bubble shapes under its skin.

Both calves wandered the street, apparently at random. The passing adults seemed not to notice the calves; but there was no way to determine where any demon was directing its attention, if indeed it divided its attention at all within the circular sweep of its seeing ears. But by stance and body language, the adults seemed indifferent to the calves and largely indifferent to each other.

A passing demon immediately disproved Rowan's assumption by pausing to hand to each calf one of a clutch of black chitinous legs that the adult was carrying atop its maw. The legs were of no creature that Rowan recognized.

The calves thrust the legs into their maws, the smaller clumsily, the elder more efficiently. The legs protruded above, waving back and forth to the action of the grinding plates within, like a rigid fifth arm engaged in some urgent, ludicrous semaphore.

The elder calf finished its meal first, paused, then snatched away the bit of leg that still stuck up from the younger's maw. The victim of the theft quickly lifted and dropped its arms—startlement, Rowan decided. It seemed not to connect its loss with the presence of its companion, now munching away again. After chewing on empty air for a while, the younger calf took to wandering about aimlessly and was six feet away from Rowan before she realized that the little creature was absolutely unaffected by the talisman.

She backed away quickly. A mistake; the calf noticed and became interested. It followed. Rowan moved left; the motion startled the calf. It jerked its arms once in surprise, then threw them high in attack stance.

Rowan did not wait to see if its spray was as deadly as the adults': she quickly thrust her sword into the creature, severing its central backbone. Its voice stopped abruptly, and it fell. The steerswoman backed away again.

As soon as her protection moved away from the fallen calf, the elder immediately executed the arm jerk of surprise and stepped up to the still-flopping form. It prodded at it curiously, and then with no further preliminaries picked it up and attempted to push it down into its maw.

The corpse was too large; it remained half outside the elder calf's maw, its limp arms flopped over to one side. The grinding plates working on its lower half caused the corpse to jiggle obscenely.

Sickened, Rowan backed herself against a den, side-stepped away quickly and quietly.

But she had gained some valuable information. The avoidance instinct did not operate universally. She must keep a very sharp eye out for the youngest calves.

Two thirds of the way toward the center of the colony, Rowan noticed an unexpected break in the pattern of roofs. Somewhere ahead, no dens had been built for a considerable space. But far more interesting was the sky above that space.

A swarm of little flying things was arriving, coming from the north and descending beyond the roofs. As Rowan watched, they came in handfuls, in straggling lines, and then abruptly in a single great stream overhead and then curving sharply down.

She wove her way through street after street until she reached the gap and found herself facing the rocky lip of a little ravine. No demons were near; she side-stepped around the edge to the north side to stand just under the swarm and looked up. Insects, apparently; they continued, undisturbed. Reaching up, Rowan snagged one out of the air.

A moth.

The same as those in Alemeth and on Spider Island: four-legged, four-winged, body striped in a pale green that Rowan knew would shine in the dark. As she held the one, the rest streamed above her like bats, descending in front of her. Rowan leaned over the lip of the ravine and looked down. Below, the slanted floor was overgrown with blackgrass and scrub blue-leaves, all laced throughout with branches of something that looked like yellow, spiny coral.

The moths poured down, doubling back to apparently disappear somewhere directly under Rowan's feet. Thousands of them; their refuge must be large.

Here was the cave she had earlier been hoping for, right in the colony proper. No matter; her camp in the dunes had served her well, and she would be leaving in the morning.

She wondered what inspired them to gather. If they were night hunters now returning home, they were rather late about it; it was mid-morning.

She released her captive; it made two small, quick circles, then oriented and headed for the cave. As if at a signal, the entire overhead stream sank to the ground. The steerswoman suddenly found herself in the heart of a living current, the small bodies striking her softly, almost silently. Through the earplugs, she heard them only when they gently thumped her head, rustled her hair. They were unharmed; she was unharmed. She caught herself laughing in delight, stopped the risky noise with the greatest difficulty.

She arrived at the edge of the colony's center and stood gazing across its sweep; then settled down to sit with her back against a den, the talisman standing guard at her feet.

More demons were present than on the previous day. Perhaps thirty were scattered about the slope, with three groups at the bottom clustered around collections of case-objects. Rowan watched for some time, but the only activity immediately identifiable below was intermittent spates of mating.

That might be the purpose of this area, despite the mating she had witnessed at the perimeter. These circumstances seemed much more formal. In fact, the setting even weirdly resembled a rough amphitheater—with the demons on the slopes as spectators? She found herself entering into a series of hilarious speculations, which she forced herself to stop for fear of laughing out loud.

But perhaps she was not far from the truth. In the Inner Lands, many animals enacted complex mating rituals. And often—and she became interested in the idea—these included offerings of gifts.

And case-objects were edible. Of course.

If demon behaviors did parallel that of Inner Lands animals after all, one might, by studying two so different kinds of life, actually distill a set of behaviors universal to all animals. An exciting prospect. The steerswoman leaned a bit forward, hugging her knees, grinning as she watched the scene below.

Some of the case-objects, here and elsewhere, were quite large; obviously, she now realized, made of several smaller ones joined together. Less easy to eat, but as a prelude to mating, quite attention getting. Certain birds in the Inner Lands constructed huge, complex, and purely decorative bowers solely for the purpose of catching a lady's eye.

Apparently demons reversed the Inner Lands protocol; only females could create case-objects.

And the spectators were certainly an interesting innovation. Rowan recalled her evaluation of the inhabitants of site two: a sociable people after all.

Two of the spectators, both female, were seated twenty feet away from Rowan, with half a mud-lion carcass on the ground between them. They alternated tearing off oozing chunks, stuffing them down their maws, in a weird parody of a picnic.

Lunchtime in the demon lands. And what a good idea. Rowan laid her sword across her knees and extracted from a second kerchief tied at her belt a cold baked potato. It was one of several small items she had carefully selected as being very silent food.

From across the way, she could see motion in one of the groups below, as one demon seemed to touch a tall case-object with one hand. Improving on it, likely. While she finished her lunch, the steerswoman studied the arrangement of demons on the slope around her and decided that with enough care, she could manage to get closer.

She could not avoid passing quite near the dining females; when she was twelve feet away, both abandoned their meal to wander away, in no apparent distress and in no great hurry.

When she was past the carcass and some ten feet beyond it, a male seated nearby gave the quick arm lift of surprise, then rose, hurried over to the mud-lion, and rapidly tore off gobbets of meat to push down its throat. Rowan continued; and when she was far enough away, both the females displayed the same sharp arm lift and drop, and jogged back to chase the male away from their meal.

The males were on the low end of some demon pecking order, Rowan decided. Size alone could account for the fact.

But as she neared the bottom of the slope, Rowan grew more and more nervous. At the moment, she could keep herself positioned so that her own body did not block the talisman from any demon's hearing sight, but soon that would be difficult.

And there seemed little to see at the bottom of the amphitheater. The demons merely stood, for the most part, apparently admiring their constructions. Occasionally, some would copulate—and not always in mere pairs, Rowan noted. At long intervals, one or another female demon would produce a case-object and either set it on the ground by itself or attach it to one of the larger constructions. The other demons in the group would grow still, then return to a more natural stance, raising and lowering their arms slightly, gently.

A number of calves were scattered about, either wandering aimlessly or sitting on the ground, four knees high, four arms tucked above their maws. Rowan became distracted by the need to watch their movements closely and stay far from the youngest.

One calf, considerably larger than the others, stayed long at one particular group, seeming to take part in the pause that the others were presently enjoying. Eventually, possibly bored with inaction, it began vigorously scratching itself. The slightest lift in the arms of the adults revealed that the action was not lost on them. The calf was concentrating its activity on its lower orifices; perhaps it would produce its own case-object, or perhaps it was mature enough to be viewed as a new sexual rival by the others. This could be interesting.

An adult standing near the calf reached down one of its own hands, and Rowan discovered that she could clearly tell, from the stance and arm position of the other demons, that they were paying close attention to the act.

The demon, casually and smoothly, reached into its own case orifice and pulled something out: a small column, six inches high, four down-looping branches above, four flat-footed supports below.

Rowan's first stunned thought was that, bizarrely, the creature had given birth—but no, demons were egg-layers. Nevertheless, she saw, with an inexplicable twist in her stomach, that the object resembled a tiny demon.

Rowan could find no explanation for this, none at all. She moved closer, but demons all along the slope were now shifting position, and the steerswoman suddenly found that she must move to protect her undefended back. She sidestepped, then backed off into a clearer area.

More motion in the demon group, from the calf. It must have produced a case-object. Rowan could not see the result, but reaction from the demons was immediate.

They threw up their arms—every demon present.

Rowan scanned wildly, found a clear route, and fled up the slope.

She was out of the amphitheater and halfway up a street before she realized she was not being pursued; nor had she been sprayed.

She stopped and waited, heart pounding; a close call. She had not been the target.

Eventually, with the greatest caution, she returned to the end of the street and looked down.

Below, and all around the center, demon arms were raised up high, waving, writhing, long fingers curling and uncurling. Demon bodies rocked, swayed. The animals were like trees in a sudden wild wind; and only the calf, entirely unharmed, stood quietly, its arms gently lifting and falling, one by one, all around its body.

The steerswoman attempted explanation and failed. She attempted hypothesis and finally wild speculation; nothing satisfied.

But as she turned to leave, she concluded, at the least, that it would be wise to stay very far from the center of a demon colony.

Throughout the morning, the sky had been developing a high, thin haze; now it thickened, lowered. The sun, a pale lemon yellow, acquired faint sun dogs on either side.

Just past noon, but rain would come by evening, Rowan thought. She still had a good part of the day left, but her close call at the center left her jumpy and deeply unsettled.

Up the curve of the street, motion. Rowan backed herself against a den. Two female demons were approaching, dragging something behind, something that struggled.

Rowan thought for one wild moment that it was a human child—then relaxed when she recognized it as a young goblin jack, perhaps a year old.

One of the demons was also carrying above its maw a round object: the goblin's severed head. Goblins were so stupid it took them many hours to realize they were dead.

Rowan stood quietly, permitted the demons to pass her. They dragged the jerking corpse into a nearby den, and a moment later, flung the head into the street.

A calf, one within the safe age range, stood by the next intersection; it jerked its arms in surprise. Then it ambled over to the head, picked it up, and stood turning it over and over in its clever fingers, prying at it with its talons. Goblin heads had no convenient access to their contents, as Rowan well knew. But the calf, doggedly probing and poking, finally managed at last to extract a fingerful of blue-white paste from the place where the neck had connected.

As Rowan sidled past the persistent creature, the thought came to her that perhaps she ought to take the skull herself and make a mandolin from it, as the Outskirters did. The idea amused her.

The instant she had that thought, she felt as if they were near: not only Bel but the entire, marvelous, wandering village that constituted Kammeryn's warrior tribe.

But then she passed the corner, where a cross street brought a breeze that smelled of blackgrass, crushed blue-leaves, the strange, musky taste of the great ocean—and all thoughts of humans vanished. Beyond that intersection and along the street with dens all around, she smelled only the sandy dust and oil of the dens, the salt and musk of innumerable demons.

Rowan's steps slowed, then stopped. She stood, vaguely puzzled. She looked back.

Only the calf, now attempting to crack the skull by stamping on it.

Rowan turned back, walked back past the calf again.

And stopped.

Outskirters; why was she now thinking of Outskirters?

And what was that smell?

She pictured the Outskirts in her mind, the rolling, rattling red and brown—

Ghost-grass. No, not quite; and there was no redgrass here to rot into ghost-grass at the touch of decaying corpses or Inner Lands animal or human excrement. But something associated with ghost-grass . . .

Cessfields. Outskirters were profligate with their wastes, and not only redgrass died from it. Blackgrass, tanglebrush, mudwort, lichen-towers:

any native Outskirts life within the perimeter of a cessfield would die and then smell exactly like this—

But only under that precise circumstance.

There was an alleyway between two dens. With a glance at the calf, Rowan crossed the street and entered. The alley wound around behind the dens. A left-hand jog, and then a right, and she found herself in a little pocket garden.

Blue-leafs, tanglebrush, broad-leaf, blackgrass. But the blue-leafs had turned dusty orange, branches on the ground crumbling amid now-brown leaves; the blackgrass had gone stiff and shriveled; half the tanglebrush had dropped their leaves and stood as mazy skeletons. The scent was strong, the particular smell of plants not of the Inner Lands decaying.

She had found one of the places where the street cleaner demon deposited its loads. Waste lay across the entire floor of the area, in an arrangement so weirdly tidy that it seemed inspired by some obscure mathematical formula.

The demon waste was nearly odorless; this close, the human waste was not. It was not difficult to locate.

It was three days old. And Rowan had herself arrived only yesterday.

The steerswoman rose. Surrounded by the backs of demon dens, in the midst of the dying plants with the darkening sky above her, she felt herself crowded by theories, hypotheses, wild speculations—and hopes.

No. Look at what *is*.

She forced aside all preconceptions; the result left her weirdly blank and pure.

And she turned, in the end, to pure workmanship.

She searched the colony. She was systematic.

In short order: three more cess gardens. And from the evidence at hand, Rowan knew another human was in the colony and that person was alive as of yesterday. And that was all she knew.

How do you find a man?

Animals live by pattern. Human presence would disrupt the patterns. Look for the break, for the unexpected, the unnatural.

She found it. It was a crowd.

Twenty-four female demons and half as many males were gathered together, nearly filling the street from one intersection to the next.

Halfway along the street, case-objects were grouped haphazardly about the entrance of one den. None were large, and some seemed remarkably

ROSEMARY KIRSTEIN

341

similar; the first time Rowan had seen any such close resemblance. As she watched from her safe distance, one demon stirred and removed a new case-object from one of its lower orifices, placing it among the others. The others stilled, then stirred, arms slowly raising and lowering.

She could not pass among so many demons so close to one another. She could not protect her back in the crowd.

The males seemed to be keeping to the fringes; but one male entering the street from the opposite end trod in a straight line directly through the thick of it. Nearby demons shifted, arms jerking, fingers splaying. Agitation? Annoyance? When the male reached the den entrance and the thickest grouping of case-objects it halted. All demons present became quiveringly attentive.

The male stretched out its four arms wide all around, then high, stood in that pose for a long moment; then jerkily reached down into its maw and extracted one, two, three small case-objects. These it placed on the ground, then took two steps away.

The other demons killed it.

The act seemed entirely passionless. The creatures simply closed in on the male and methodically tore its arms and its legs from its body, thrust taloned fingers into its torso and pulled out fistfuls of viscera. Their victim showed no resistance and only flailed once and collapsed when one deep-thrust hand reached and severed some vital core.

The corpse was rendered into convenient pieces and eaten. Those who had participated in the killing jostled for the best segments, but once satisfied generously stepped aside to allow others to dine. One male took three pieces and carried them to the edge of the crowd not far from Rowan, where it handed two to a male and a female. All three sat down in the dirt and shoved the pieces into their maws and remained at their ease, chewing.

The steerswoman stood watching, understanding nothing, knowing only one thing:

She must get into that den.

All dens had ventilation slits. Some dens had pocket gardens behind them.

She began carefully to back off; but the demons became attentive again. Even the happy trio nearby ceased their chewing and rose, arms weaving as they watched.

Something emerged from the den entrance. Rowan stopped, then sidled to her right, seeking a clear view.

Merely a single female demon. Rowan found herself disappointed.

But the demon stood at the entrance for a long moment, motionless, while the others slowly grew equally still, and Rowan suddenly had the freakish impression that this creature was about to take a breath and declaim some great speech, and that the other demons were waiting for it to begin.

Naturally, no such thing occurred. The demon stepped away from the entrance, moved left, picked its way through the crowd, and eventually disappeared around the curve of the street.

There was no cess-garden entrance on the street around the next corner nor around the next or the next—and then Rowan was back at the crowd again on its opposite side.

For the entire block, the dens were completely contiguous. There was no access from the back.

But contiguous dens, Rowan recalled from site two, were interconnected inside. Enter one, and you enter them all.

Rowan backed away from the crowd again and around the corner.

This street was deserted. Rowan crossed and very cautiously pressed the side of her head against one den.

A hum through the bones of her skull; a demon within.

She tried the next and the next.

The fourth: no hum.

Rowan waited while two demons passed, dragging an entire mud-lion that trailed its own viscera from its slashed abdomen; waited longer while the calf that followed them snagged a loop of intestine, resulting in a brief tug-of-war; waited again as the calf, after slicing its prize free, slowly fed the entire length up, and then down into its maw; waited an eternity while the calf indulged in one of the typical, incomprehensible demon pauses; waited while it took its own time wandering down the street; waited until it was gone; waited until she was sure it was gone; and entered the den.

nd waited while her eyes adjusted.

Diffused light spilled through the entrance, casting a hazy oval on the floor; slanted slits showed on the back wall.

There were no interconnecting doors. This den was isolated.

Rowan set her talisman on the ground, slightly back of the center of the chamber. Protection spilled invisibly out the entrance, guarding her back.

The uppermost slit in the wall was just below eye level, but the aperture was too narrow to afford her any good view. Nevertheless, where there was light, there was access to the sky. An open area, perhaps, like a central air shaft or courtyard, with dens all around.

Lower down: more slits, closer together. By stooping and rocking from side to side, the steerswoman acquired an assembled image of the area beyond.

Flat, earth-floored, the backs of other dens beyond, a number of objects that seemed constructed by the same method as the dens but standing perhaps three feet tall and showing no openings.

No demons visible.

Rowan inserted the point of her sword into one of the slits, applied a slow pressure, checked the result.

A small nick. It might take an hour or more to create an opening sufficient for her pass through, even on hands and knees. And the act was surely not silent; she had felt the abrasive rasp as her weapon cut through the sandy material.

The talisman would not protect her through the wall: any demon that entered the central area would hear her sawing sword instantly. There was no chance of being overlooked by an animal with no front or back, and with "eyes" completely around its body.

But none at all on top.

How very interesting.

Picking up the talisman on her way out, she crossed the street and stood regarding the roofline of the row of dens.

Some sort of rope seemed called for. Unfortunately, she had brought none.

Still, the den before her was only seven feet tall at the top of its dome. A handhold or foothold might help.

She used her sword to chip at the face of the den, quickly creating a two-inch-deep gouge at the height of her own head. She backed off and stationed herself at some distance, to observe the reactions of passing demons to this wanton destruction.

Four individual creatures passed down the street, showing no interest. A fifth executed the surprise motion, then crossed to inspect the niche, prying at it with its talons, paused motionless for some moments, then walked away.

The creature was apparently not instinctively directed to immediately repair the damage.

Rowan then waited, with great impatience, while some natural flow of traffic caused no less than twelve demons to pass down the street, in groups and singly. Eventually there was a pause.

She could not waste the moment. She sheathed her sword, backed against the opposite den to acquire the best amount of running room, and ran.

A jump, and up, and her toe caught in the niche, pushed her higher, and she scrambled up the slope. Finding a stable position, she turned around to sit on the curve just shy of the crest of the dome.

She waited to see if any creature had noticed her act. She thought she had been very quiet.

So far above the demon line of sight, it might be possible for her to tuck the talisman into its kerchief, freeing her other hand—and she found a dozen reasons not to take the risk. Like an awkward, three-legged, inverted spider, Rowan cautiously worked her way around the dome toward the courtyard.

She rested, gazing down. No living thing was visible.

Three dead things were, however: an entire adult goblin jack; the skull of a mud-lion; and one limb, either arm or leg, of some unidentifiable other animal. All of them stank.

To jump down would be easy; to escape the same way with less running room, and objects to dodge, more difficult.

There must be access from the courtyard into at least one of the other dens. But she might need to fight her way out; she needed to be sure it was worth it.

Her sense of smell had helped her before. Resisting the impulse to close her eyes, she breathed slowly through her nose, letting her mouth fall open, smelling and tasting the air.

There, under the other odors: Urine. Human. Male.

She jumped—and rolled, drew her sword, and moved back against the wall—

And spun away again, swinging and striking at the creature standing behind her, then retreating to give herself sword-room—

The creature, a goblin, did not advance; nor did it fall. Rowan stood waiting for it to move. It remained in place. She lowered her sword, stepped forward.

The goblin was already dead, had been so for months. It stood upright against the wall, in a pose weirdly natural, held at critical points by thick wads of sand and gum. Rowan eyed it suspiciously, then cautiously crossed the courtyard.

The enclosed area was approximately thirty feet across, with three knee-high constructions spaced across it, each some five feet long, four feet wide. Touch confirmed that they were constructed as dens were, but they seemed solid.

Atop one: the first goblin-corpse, which she had sighted from above. She had assumed it was whole, but now she saw that each joint had been cracked or severed, and the pieces laid down in their proper configuration on the raised surface. She prodded the head with her sword tip; it rolled free, fell to the ground, scattering a group of small case-objects.

The severed arm appeared to belong to some massive relative of a pincer-beetle. A number of case-objects stood beside it. The mud-lion's skull was reduced to mere black bones, its huge jaws lying separate, displaying the fearsome triple rows of needle teeth. A single, simple case-object lay in the cracked hollow where the creature's brain would have been.

All around: the slitted back walls of dens. Only one showed an entrance. Rowan backed away from the center of the courtyard, approached the entrance by sidestepping around the walls, needing at one point to sidle past the upright goblin corpse, its dead arms outspread as if to embrace her.

Above, a cloud obscured the weak sun; the courtyard grew gray.

Good. Her eyes would need less time to adjust.

At the entrance, she paused to listen: no demon-voice. She sent her left hand with her talisman into the opening before her, then cautiously looked inside.

Only a chamber, empty but for five distinct groups of case-objects on the floor. No exit to the street outside, but there were two apertures, to left and right. Rowan entered the chamber, checked the left exit: another chamber, with another door and case-objects but no demons. The right aperture: another chamber with a similar configuration, also abandoned.

Which way?

She followed her nose. It was not difficult. Left.

Three, four, five chambers, connecting only to each other and never the outside. Some had case-objects in neat collections about the walls. Others contained bits of trash: empty pentagonal seashells, little chitinous leg joints, the odd branch of tanglebrush or blue-leaf.

No demons, neither by sound nor sight.

She estimated the size of each room she passed, noted its doors, set it in place in a slowly growing map in her mind. She marked the angles of the turns she took, found she was doubling back into a parallel set of chambers, far darker than the first. Air became stale and still and fouler, and ventilation slits no longer admitted outside light.

Eventually her sense of smell told her that she had come too far. She turned, retraced her steps.

The chamber she stopped in seemed empty. But the odor was strong, rank, and fresh; and if he was not here now, he had been recently, and for a long time.

The odor included that of old blood.

Trash all around, difficult to identify in the dim, twice-filtered light. No sound of a demon.

By the far wall, one pile showed a faint and incongruous splash of pale green. Rowan approached it, reversed her sword hilt, reached with the fingers she could spare from her grip.

The glove on that hand lacked two fingertips; her skin touched old silk.

No motion, and then sudden motion, all violence. She scrambled away, back against the wall beside one of the exits.

He was a vague, dim shape; but her senses were so keenly attuned to demon movement, demon shape that the human form and human stance almost glowed with logic. She half-saw half-reasoned that he was crouched back against the wall, left hand flung out on the wall beside him, right arm forward, fending her off, protecting his face, his head tucked downward.

Demon-voice, but distant; but she must stay silent.

She moved toward him; he shrank back.

Because she had recognized shape and movement in the dimness, she thought he might, also—so she stood erect, arms spread, giving herself the most human silhouette possible.

The warding arm dropped slowly, the head was raised. She could see the moving glint of his eyes, first on her shape, then on her sword, then on her face.

She approached. He permitted it.

Close up, his eyes were wide, wild. The green silk shirt was stained dark in places. Rowan paused to listen to the distant demon-song that still did not approach, and then risked saying, in a voice of only breath, "Janus."

She thought he would faint. Then he did.

She dropped her sword, set the talisman down behind her, searched in panic for his heartbeat, felt it stuttering too rapidly beneath her hand, too close behind the sharp bones of his chest. She felt his face, his head: old, scabbed scratches across forehead and one cheek; hair in mats, some damp, some crusted. His shirt adhered to his body in places. She thought he was holding his right hand in a fist, but touch informed her that under the crusted wrapping of torn silk the fingers of that hand were missing. She drew back her own hand sharply.

He was, at the least, alive. Rowan sat back on her heels in the gloom, calming herself, thinking. Even half starved, Janus was far too heavy for her to carry.

She unknotted the kerchief at her belt, wet it from her water sack, applied it to the hollow of his throat, wet her bare fingers and let water drip onto his lips.

She waited, looking around the littered chamber: two exits, to adjacent chambers. She reviewed the route back to the courtyard.

But even conscious, Janus would not be able to clamber up the walls to escape. They must find some way out to the street.

The only street exit of which Rowan had certain knowledge led directly into a mob of demons.

And there was at least one demon, inside, somewhere. She could hear its voice growing fainter, then closer, then fainter again, as it moved among the other chambers.

But no voice was nearby. And she could deal with the one demon, should it come here.

Movement, from the corner of her eye; Janus was stirring. She turned back to him, wet his lips again, helped him to sit up, then held the water sack while he awkwardly drank.

Movement, again. She turned.

Nothing visible; and the demon-voice was still far.

And again, motion; across the chamber by the other exit. Rowan left the water with Janus, left the talisman to guard him, picked up her weapon, rose.

Across the room, something was slowly unfolding.

A sound, behind her. She spun.

Janus, drawing back from her sword, then half falling forward, clutching at her, and the sound was his voice, he was speaking. No—he would draw the demons, he must be silent. She put her hand on his mouth, but he fell back against the wall, free of her.

And then his voice became a shout, and she could hear him clearly. *"Kill it!"*

She turned back; and somewhere outside, clouds thinned before the sun; the twice-filtered, diffuse light grew, slightly.

The thing in the room with them was a demon.

But silent, it was silent.

Then she saw: marks on its skin but arranged exactly, precisely where, beneath, the fluid-sacs of its seeing ears lay.

Not marks; wounds. This demon had been blinded.

From behind, Janus clawed at her right hand with fingers suddenly strong, wrenched her sword from her grip, thrust himself away from her, toward the creature.

But he staggered, stumbled, fell hard, full length, and she felt the shock of it through her feet. The blind demon startled, threw up its arms. Rowan made a wild guess where the spray would strike, threw herself to the ground.

The demon was damaged; its spray was weak; it could not see. It missed.

Outside the chamber, not far, and growing nearer: the voice of another demon.

The talisman—where was it?

She cast about in the trash on the floor, found it; she scrambled across to Janus, now struggling to his knees, and took her sword from his hand.

The blind demon swayed, knees trembling; then it flailed its arms, groping, slicing the air with its talons. It took a stumbling step toward them.

The second demon entered the chamber.

Janus gained his feet, fell again, back against Rowan; she caught him in her arms, held him half erect against her. He fought her weakly.

One of the blind demon's thrashing arms struck the second creature, which caught the striking hand between two of its own. The blind one startled, then clutched the hands, pulled at them.

Janus struggled for balance; Rowan adjusted her hold around his waist, pulled him back—

And stopped.

The talisman was in her left hand, pressed against Janus's body. Covered. They had been seen.

The second demon raised its voice, louder, its arms rising and falling. Janus shouted without words.

And Rowan in pure, stupid instinct, raised not the talisman but her sword. She thought only, regretfully: Too late.

Rowan and the monster gazed at each other. The pause seemed eternal, during which time nothing at all moved in Rowan's mind.

Then the second demon moved.

In one fast motion it gathered the blind demons arm's down tight against its body, pulled the creature back against itself, held it close, stepped back one step—and stopped.

Another pause. Rowan's charge struggled weakly in her grasp. The second demon's did the same.

A thought slowly rose to Rowan's awareness and stayed there, alone, for a very long time.

The thought was: What am I looking at?

Then Janus subsided, trembling in her arms. And, with the slightest of motions, a mere outward rotation of her wrist, Rowan displayed the talisman.

And the creature stepped away, as it must, pulling the injured one with it, until both stood against the far wall. There, the blind demon ceased to struggle, began to shudder. The shudders diminished to trembling; the trembling stopped. The other demon slowly lowered the limp form.

Rowan used her sword arm to steady Janus, kept the talisman displayed. Together, they left the chamber.

They moved toward greater and greater light, and had passed through five chambers before it occurred to Rowan to wonder why, after showing the talisman, she had not then killed both demons.

Rowan and Janus emerged into gray light, thick, damp air.

Case-objects, dozens, all in a wide sweep on the earth before their feet. Beyond that, twenty-four demons, seated and standing, out to the dens opposite, out to the intersection to the left and to the right.

And a demon-voice in the den behind, now approaching.

She half led, half dragged Janus left; their feet scattered the little objects. She leaned him against the den, held her talisman before them both, pushed him on with her shoulder. They moved slowly, step by shuffling step, along the den, the demons they approached slowly moving back, and back.

They had gone some ten feet more in this fashion when Janus's knees gave. He slid to sit. Rowan stepped in front of him, knelt on the ground, sword held out to her right, talisman centered before her.

Janus was safe behind her. She glanced back to check his state.

What she saw, out in the chill air, was the exact extent of his injuries and his physical condition.

He would not make it back to the camp in the dunes.

She waited. The creatures around them adjusted, slowly, eventually defining by position, as clearly as if on a diagram, the exact extent and limit of the talisman's influence.

From the den entrance, a demon emerged—the same that Rowan had seen inside and the same, she now realized, that she had seen in front of this den earlier. It paused, made some movement—she could not see what through the crowd of monsters about her—then stepped right, wove its way through the gathered demons, and was gone. Rowan returned her attention to the creatures around her.

They were shifting.

Slowly at first, a few at a time; the clear line eroded, grew less clear, seeming to open outward, as more and more demons departed.

And then the street, amazingly, was clear.

A thin drizzle began to fall.

Rowan stepped out and faced Janus, freed enough fingers of her sword hand to half grip his shoulder, shake him slightly. She was appalled at the amount of pain the motion caused him, hoped desperately that he had not cried out; but she got his attention. She could not interpret his expression, but he was, at least, looking at her.

It occurred to Rowan that he might think he was hallucinating her. From his condition, she judged that he had good reason to assume so.

Still no demons about. Rowan turned back, laid her sword across Janus's lap, placed her freed hand on the center of his chest, fingers spread. He jerked back at the touch, but his gaze did not leave her face.

She mouthed, slowly and as clearly as she could: *I'm real. Come with me.*

He glanced left, right, looked up at her; his face twitched and his breath huffed in a helpless half laugh Rowan hoped was silent.

She took his left hand, placed it on her right shoulder, took back her sword, and turned again to face the street.

Eventually, Rowan felt the hand on her shoulder grow heavy, felt the other hand join it, as Janus braced himself and got to his feet. Rowan rose with him. With Janus behind her, Rowan began to sidestep, felt him following.

On the next street, demons, moving in a plodding, flat-footed pace. Rowan, eyes tight in thought, studied their spacing.

Searching. The demons were searching for something walking among them. Only the females.

But even so, none came within the talisman's safe circle, and those that Rowan and Janus came near altered their steps, staying instinctively clear. And yet, they continued to search, exactly as if they had not noticed their own change of course, exactly as if the humans' presence remained unknown to them, as if Rowan and Janus were invisible.

But there were so many. And Janus could not keep this up much longer.

They managed to get past three intersections before he fell. Rowan could do nothing but wait. They stayed in place for half an hour, with the demons too occupied to notice that the den entrance before which Janus lay crumpled was now inaccessible. When she saw him stir, Rowan struggled clumsily out of the loop holding the water sack, used one foot to push it toward his hand; she did not dare put down her weapon. She sat with her back toward him, to maintain the best position for the talisman. But some time later, she felt his hand on her shoulder again.

They rose; they continued. He walked with an arm draped completely over her shoulder, his body close against hers. She felt the water sack between them; he had managed to loop it over himself.

Her camp in the dunes was half a world away.

Perhaps they could take over a den or a cess-garden, find some corner somewhere to hide in while she gave him what food she still had, more water, let him rest. Someplace with a single, defensible opening—

When she abruptly changed direction, he stumbled, all his weight suddenly on her. She waited while he adjusted. They continued.

They paused four times. Each time, Janus seemed stranger, eventually moving as if completely blind and aware only vaguely of her motions.

When they finally reached the little ravine, Rowan wondered how to get Janus down without his falling into it. She could not prevent it, and he fell. She scrambled down after him, kicking up dust, then stood over him, breathing through clenched teeth, talisman held before her, sword high and ready to strike down any creature that came to the rattle his falling had made.

A male appeared at the end of the ravine, paused, departed. Another appeared at the edge above, and another. Rowan raised the talisman; the males left.

A female came to the lip. It stood for a long time, until it was joined by a male that reached up to urgently tug at its fingers. Both departed.

Rowan might have no other opportunity; she must be quick.

With desperate speed, she sheathed her sword, put the talisman down the neck of her shirt, got her arms beneath Janus's shoulders, pulled. He seemed to come awake, seemed not to know who she was, tried to fight her. She got him half up, put a hand over his mouth, shook him. She hoped her hand muffled his cry; but he did see her, recognized her as at least human if not herself, let himself be helped up. They made their way through the brush toward and into the jagged opening of the cave.

Inside, green light blossomed around them as Janus fell to his knees, light that swirled and spun; small, soft bodies struck at them. Rowan felt tiny feet touch her face and arms, spring away again, taking away motes of cool brightness that circled back, then away.

Rowan pulled the talisman out of her shirt and placed it just inside the cave's entrance. She sat on the floor, her hand on Janus's back as he gasped and coughed.

The moths took their light further back; the cave opened wider in that direction into a short passageway, the far end just as defensible as the opening, and more secret. Rowan retrieved the talisman, half dragged Janus toward the back of the passage.

By the time they reached it, the moths had settled, dimmer when still. Rowan reached a hand up to the low ceiling, stirred them to brief brightness again, and examined their refuge.

The steerswoman breathed, "Oh, no."

The chamber was wide, deep, and low, and it slanted downward. Across the entire uneven floor in small groups, large groups, immense agglomerations reaching far into the deep recesses of the cave: case-objects.

Rowan stood, half stooping. If there were a demon in here now, she must kill it. But she could hear nothing, nothing.

But demons would come.

If they could not enter this place, what would they do? Stand forever at the entrance? Gather, waiting? Gather in the dozens, the hundreds?

If she left now, left Janus behind, she could escape. She turned back to him.

He was on knees and one hand, his damaged right hand held before him, regarding it as if it were an object entirely new in his experience. Rowan said, "I hope you're worth it," and was shocked at the sound of her own voice in her head. He looked up at the sound, then around, his gaze utterly uncomprehending. He spoke, but she could not tell from his lips what was said.

Demons would come. She could kill each one as it entered; but she and Janus would starve before the process was complete.

She looked around again, brushed her arm against the ceiling to get more light.

Let them come.

Go to the back. Far back. Against a wall. Use the talisman. Be invisible.

Let the demons freely come, and let them go. Hide. Wait. Let Janus regain some strength. Leave when you can.

She sheathed her sword again, tucked away the talisman, went to Janus, took him by his good hand. "Not yet," she told him. "You can rest in a moment. Just a bit further."

She saw her name on his lips. He followed her.

39

Rowan moved through a nightmare in which she was surrounded by demons, each of them carrying a pole with a banner at the top, each banner a different color. The hands holding the poles were human hands at the end of demon arms; they snapped and swirled the colors high above. The demons' voices filled the air and, it seemed, the inside of her own head; but they were human voices speaking human words, which Rowan, with completely inexplicable terror, found she could not comprehend.

She awoke, and the contrast between the cacophony of her dream and the silence of her waking world shocked and confused her, and she could not place herself. She flung out her arms, striking Janus's still form on one side, cold stone and soft, small objects on her right. Moths startled at her touch; their light and their flight showed her where she was.

Underground. The cave.

Janus had not stirred. She checked, found his heartbeat, but could not hear him breathing.

She removed the plugs from her ears. Janus's slow, harsh breaths; her own easy ones; the stuttering rustle of moth wing; and somewhere back and to her right, the distant tapping of water falling. No demon nearby.

The green, dim light shifted and fluttered; the moths still swirled in a loose, rising column above her head. She looked up. It seemed that some of the moths were rising and not descending again. A high, narrow chimney, she surmised, with perhaps a small outlet above.

She found the water sack, tested its weight with great dissatisfaction, and wet Janus's lips again. He stirred but did not wake.

She sat back on her heels, regarding him. He must wake at some point, eat, drink; he must regain some strength. She could not carry him back to camp.

Her ears felt almost painfully sensitive to sound after the silence of the plugs. Even the sort of false noises one's own ears manufacture in silence seemed absent. She heard every stir of moth wing, the rustle of her own clothing, even a tiny crack and creak that might be the sound of the stones themselves.

And, distantly, outside, the single massed voice of the demon colony.

Rowan chose a far low corner of the cave in which to relieve herself, and with nothing else to do, went back to sleep.

She awoke to the feeling that someone was watching her. It turned out to be true.

Janus was awake, sitting with his body hunched over. Only his head was tilted up, the whites of his eyes pale green in moth light, the rest of his dark face visible only from reflection across the forehead, the cheek-bones. Rowan felt she was looking into a mask.

She rubbed her own eyes as if the action would bring more light, or light of a different color. She found the water sack again, rose to hand it to him.

He drank thirstily, wiped his mouth. "How far are we from the city?" His voice was cracked, hoarse, hardly recognizable as his own.

Rowan retrieved the sack and set it down behind her.

"Rowan?"

She turned back to him.

"I thought I was going mad, when I saw you." He closed his eyes, dropped his head, becoming effectively invisible. "Where is this place?"

She turned away again, looked up into the moth-still dimness. "It must be night. There's an opening somewhere above. I believe that if it were day, we'd see some light."

He did not speak. She turned back to find his regard upon her again, now wider eyed. "I'm dreaming," he whispered.

"If that's true," she said, "you'd do us both a favor to wake up."

He shuddered, huddled forward. He shifted his arms, elbows on knees, trying, she assumed, to find some position that did not cause him pain. He could not. He threw back his head, breathing in slow gasps. "Why are you here?" It should have been a shout; his voice was not up to it. It came out half cry, half hoarse whisper.

The remnants of her lunch were still in the kerchief at her belt. She pulled out a bit of dried meat, brought it over to him. She sat on her heels, holding it out. "Can you manage this? You must eat, if you can." He stared at her as if she were some object, unidentifiable, terrifying.

He did not know what was happening, he could not integrate these events, and she was providing no help.

She sighed. She said, "I can't answer your questions."

His expression slowly became recognizable: disbelief. He made a small sound in the back of his throat and another; perhaps it was laughter. "Do you think I care about your stupid little rules *now*?"

She was a moment mastering the sudden flare of anger, and another finding a reply that did not answer the question. "Janus, it is only by thinking like a steerswoman that I managed to find you at all," she said tightly. "And as we are not out of this yet, I plan to continue functioning as a steerswoman. Now, eat." She took his left hand, placed the dried meat in it, closed the fingers; and noted that her own movements were harsh, abrupt. She forced her temper down. "And rest," she added more gently. "We may need to move soon, and we may need to move quickly. And there's still a long way to go."

He sat looking at his own closed hand. Words came, as if against his will. "How much do you know?"

"How much do *you* know?" A flick of white as he glanced up, then down again. "It doesn't matter," Rowan continued. "I don't need you to answer anything. Whatever you discovered in the demon lands, I assure you, I can discover just as well. Better."

There was a long silence. Then: "But you haven't yet, have you? No." He closed his eyes. Whispering, his voice seemed his own again, remembered, familiar. "Did you ever wish," he said, "did you ever wish that you could see ahead, to future days? Did you ever wish to be magically transported forward in time or placed in a magical sleep to wake twenty, fifty, a hundred years from now, to see how we will be then, what we'll know, what the world will become? I used to." He opened his eyes, staring past her up into the dark. "I don't anymore. Now I wish, oh, I wish"—and his cracked voice became like the grinding of stones—"I wish all time would freeze and hold us still forever; I wish the sun would rise on the same day, over and over, forever; I wish we could repeat and repeat, and the human race remain *stupid*, and never again learn a single new thing; and nothing, *nothing* ever change—" He tossed his head back, threw his arms up, as if to guard his face against some sudden, intolerable brightness; but only the steerswoman was there, watching from her place in the shadows.

Then he twisted away and threw himself down on the ground, his face against his arms.

Presently, Rowan rose and placed the rest of the food by his head. He did not stir; asleep or unconscious, she could not tell which.

"I do know one thing," she said, expecting no reply. "We were *allowed* to escape."

40

*T*hat was why she had not killed the demons in the den.

The second demon had stopped the first. It had prevented the blinded one from harming Rowan and Janus. It had secured their escape.

The animal had acted with intelligent purpose. Someone, somewhere, had directed the demon's actions; and the demon itself was Rowan's only link to that person.

She waited.

Eventually, in the flickering dark: demon-voice.

First one hum, then two more, frighteningly clear to her unmuffled hearing. Rowan listened closely to the sound, how it filled the space, extending, rebounding on itself, until it became itself a shape almost tangible, until she felt she herself could sense the exact size and formation of the cave and all objects in it by sound alone.

Only three. She placed herself between Janus and the voices, sword across her lap, talisman standing on the ground before her.

Rowan ought not kill them if she could avoid it, not here. The animals came to this place regularly, that much was clear; they would certainly be alarmed by corpses.

A long pause at the entrance, as the demons evidently indulged in one of their inexplicable pauses; then the sounds split. Two departed; one moved deeper into the cave.

Taking up sword and talisman, the steerswoman quietly rose. She wished she could stir up the moths, acquire more light; but if the moths took to flight, the disturbance might be noticed. But light did increase, following the location of the approaching voice. Apparently the sound itself disturbed the moths slightly.

And now she could see it, overlit and shadowy. Not the female from the den but a male, moving among the piles of case-objects, carrying something in one hand.

She waited, very still, silent. The demon came nearer. It arrived at a nearby group of case-objects and placed something on the pile. Then it paused.

Rowan shallowed her breathing. Hesitantly, the male took one step in her direction. Rowan felt as if her veins were filled with a sharp and sour fluid, and she recognized the sensation as fear only by an effort of intellect.

The demon took another step.

Was she blocking something that the demon wanted to reach? Was there something it expected to see, that was now behind her, protected, as good as invisible? But there was nothing there other than the up-slanting moth-lined shaft, and Janus.

Another step. The demon's voice blossomed feverish overtones.

She could not move further back; she must not move to the side. She must not expose Janus.

She moved forward, one crouching step.

The male stepped back. It stepped back.

It ran.

She scrambled after it, half stooping under the uneven ceiling. The male, shorter, moved faster and freer, its wild rocking motion making its hands thrash among the sleeping moths; and then the air was filled with spinning motes of green light, and soft bodies battered against Rowan's face. She shut her eyes, pursuing sound only, stumbling and scattering piles of case-objects; then her ears told her that the creature had found the exit and was gone.

The demon knew that something was in this cave; but she had seen a male's primitive warning ignored once before.

No. She could not risk it. She could catch it outside, she was sure of it.

It was half stumbling down the rough slope, rattling the tanglebrush, clutching at blue-leaves as it descended to the floor of the ravine.

Humans were nimbler than demons; a far better body design for a land-dwelling creature, Rowan thought with a fierce glee. She clambered along the wall, outflanked the demon, arrived at the entrance to the ravine, showed the talisman.

The male slowed, stopped. It moved left, right, as if seeking an exit now rendered invisible.

The great hum of the demon colony poured into the ravine like water; but no other single demon seemed near.

She had this creature entirely in her power. She could kill it anytime she chose. She was invincible, invisible.

Invisible?

In the den, the second demon had not restrained the blinded one un-til Rowan's talisman had been covered. Only then, she realized, had it clearly seen her.

Whatever power had been controlling that demon, it had seen her through demon senses only.

Might it also be working through other demons?

If this demon could not see her, it could still hear.

After careful thought, and with no other demons near, she decided to risk it. "I don't know who you are," she said, and she felt foolish for ad-dressing an animal, "but if you can hear what I'm saying," and the form of her statement made her feel as though she was praying; she despised the sensation, "please . . . give me a sign."

At the first sound of her voice, the creature had stopped pacing, but had resumed immediately, even more urgently seeking escape. "Any-thing," Rowan went on, "anything at all. Something this animal wouldn't normally do." But the animal merely ceased trying to find the exit, and moved away from her.

Perhaps the unseen intelligence could not discern her words over the hum of the demon's own voice.

Rowan realized there was one act that would provide the proof she needed immediately. She slowly drew in her left hand, and hid the talis-man against her shirt.

The demon's arms jerked in startlement, jerked again and again. It stopped. Then it stood, knees trembling, its arms slowly rising and falling, one after the other.

It did not spray.

Rowan let out the breath she was holding, slowly. "I believe," she said, barely audible even to herself, "that I can take that as a sign."

It began to rain. The demon seemed indifferent to the fact, as fat drops struck its waving arms, its speckle-skinned body—

Rowan said, amazed, "I *know* you." It was the male she had seen in the maze, collecting case-objects, snatching them up from the streets, dis-tributing them to other males.

Perhaps she had been right from the first; she ought to have been following this creature all along.

Whatever power controlled the demon now knew where the steers-woman was hiding. Someone who helped once might help again.

It began to rain in earnest, and now the demon clearly did not like it; it quickly folded its arms in a peculiar arrangement, hands to its maw, elbows out all around, resulting in a ludicrous skeleton umbrella. Rowan huffed a laugh.

But the rattle of water would cover the approach of other demons, ones possibly less benign. The steerswoman moved aside; the speckled male swayed, hesitated, then jogged to the end of the ravine and left her.

Back in the cave, Rowan removed her shirt, which seemed less wet on the inside, used it to dry her face and hands as best she could, shook it out, and with no better way to dry it, put it back on.

Janus had not moved; Rowan became disturbed at the length of his sleep. With effort, she shook him to groggy half awareness and convinced him more by action than words to drink. Immediately after, he weakly struggled away from her supporting arms and lay curled in upon himself, breathing deeply through teeth clenched even in sleep.

Shivering, the steerswoman sat beside him, rubbing her arms, the moths around her stilling toward darkness. Eventually she raised her head to gaze up the shaft, finally discerning far above a tiny crack of white sky. She watched it fade to gray, then black.

Demon-voice woke her; but by the time she had collected sword and talisman, it was gone. She tried to convince herself to sleep again, but found that restlessness and curiosity would not permit it. She stirred the moths for light, went toward the entrance.

The groups of case-objects she had disturbed before seemed to have been reordered. Ducking low, she entered the vestibule and, holding her talisman before her, peered outside.

Stars above; the outlines of demon dens visible at the edge across from her. She thought she discerned movement toward the entrance to the ravine, but could not be certain.

Possibly the animals' instinctive search for an intruder had ceased; but Rowan could not negotiate the streets in darkness.

As she made her way back inside, her foot struck something that rolled away. Case-object, she thought, and was back in the main cave before recalling that she had not yet seen one round enough to roll.

She returned to it. It was a raw potato.

There were two others, and a small block of mold-encrusted cheese, in a neat pile by the entrance. Rowan carried them to the alcove at the back of the cave, carefully trimmed the mold from the cheese, halved it, placed one of the halves beside Janus's inert form.

She said to him, "By the hospitality of a friend."

He slept on.

She thought she would not have long to wait. She was correct.

Demon-voices outside the cave, many; then one, inside.

Rowan nodded. She drew a breath, rose.

Another voice, inside the cave. Rowan stopped. Another, and more. She grew disturbed.

After counting six, she could no longer separate individual voices.

She had planned to leave her sword and talisman behind; she changed that. Carrying both, and with her ears blocked by the glove-finger plugs, she made her way toward fluttering, shifting green light.

Seven individual demons stood in the clear area by the entrance.

This could not be good. The person controlling the demons would surely not need so many creatures at once. The steerswoman waited; the demons remained, arms waving slightly.

Then the tallest reached down and emitted a case-object. The others, all males, Rowan now realized, froze, then shifted, returned to stillness.

The green light was confusing; but Rowan studied the males and—yes, there: the speckled male she had encountered before. And the female; possibly the one from the den. It had been gray, shaded with tan in daylight; it was green shadowed with green here.

So many, and in such an awkward space: if logic had led Rowan wrong, she and Janus would die, very soon.

The steerswoman slowly moved forward, half-bent until the ceiling rose as she neared the group. At twelve feet away, she did exactly what the tiny, needle-sharp, agonizing voice of instinct told her not to do: She covered the talisman.

Lifts of startlement. One male raised its arms to spray; but another immediately interposed itself between that one and Rowan. The nervous male subsided. The demons stood, arms gently raising, lowering.

Rowan said, "I suppose you can't actually hear me through these creatures. I'm not surprised. I couldn't hear a person through this noise myself." But her own voice, in her blocked ears, was loud, thick, seeming to come from the base of her skull.

Perhaps she should write; but she had nothing to write with or on. And if her mysterious friend saw only through demon senses, writing would be useless. Words on paper did not echo sound.

She ought to gesture—but both her hands were full. And she could not, yet, bring herself to set down either her weapon or her only protection, still clutched tight against her chest.

The female demon stepped forward, away from the males, and Rowan forced herself not to back off and managed by sheer will to allow the point of her sword to drop. Five feet away, the demon stopped.

The last time Rowan had stood so close to a living demon was in Alemeth. Two separate creatures; and both times she had approached so near only to drive her sword into them.

The males had shifted, spreading themselves in a line to left and right. Rowan began to dislike the configuration.

The female reached down; this close, the movement was startling, the structure of the arm so freakishly wrong that Rowan took two steps back, teeth clenched, sword again raised. The demon paused; then continued the motion and withdrew a case-object from one lower orifice. This it placed on the ground. Beyond, the males shifted again, spreading further, and two of them moved a few flat-footed steps closer.

The object was vaguely conical, tilted, covered in small bosses. Rowan regarded it blankly; then she looked up at the female, wishing deeply that she could read the face of the mind behind this creature.

The demon stood, headless, branch-armed, strange-legged; but Rowan had studied demons closely the previous day, enough to learn the patterns of body posture and some hint of emotions behind them.

The demon was waiting.

The demon *itself* was waiting, and watching her.

Not some distant controlling power; not some outside guiding force.

Rowan felt abruptly empty, as if something had left her; a noise, perhaps, a constant internal noise of which she had not been aware. Or perhaps it was her strength; for she felt, at the moment, incapable of any motion whatsoever.

The steerswoman said, weakly, "There's no one here but us." It was no more than a whisper. Even through the bones of her skull, she could not hear her own words.

The only human mind present was Rowan's. She was alone, underground, with seven monsters—who were watching her and waiting.

Eventually, they stopped waiting. The female reached down—and Rowan found she was unable to retreat or even raise her weapon.

The demon picked up the case-object, passed it to the opposite side of its body, and held it out. One male took it, stood turning it over in its twiggy fingers, then carried the object away, into the recesses of the cave.

From the corner of her eye, Rowan saw moth light following the male's movements.

When it returned, the female emitted a second object, set it down.

Smaller, simpler in form. Rowan glanced at it, looked back up at the female demon, wishing for, wanting desperately a face to speak to. "I don't understand," she said, louder. The smallest male startled at her voice, stood jittering, arms twitching. The speckled male reached and caught one of its narrow-fingered hands in two of its own. The act calmed the smaller one. The two remained, behind the female, holding hands.

Waiting.

And for no reason she could explain, the speckled male's action calmed Rowan as well. She looked down at the case-object again, then slipped her talisman into its kerchief at her belt, and stooped to one knee to see better.

It was a half-dome, with four blunt-pointed extrusions on top, one much longer than the others. Rowan picked it up, turned it over awkwardly, one handed; the other hand still held her weapon.

She learned nothing. She looked up. The demons still waited. With nothing else to do, Rowan set the object down again.

The males froze briefly; and she had seen that response before. But the female did not. It retrieved the case-object, which was again passed to a male, carried off into the cave.

Shuffling its feet, the female rotated its body a quarter turn and emitted a third object. The males jerked their arms in surprise.

Four inches tall, stooped and folded, one small knee up, the other on the ground; one tiny hand dangling from an arm whose elbow rested on a knee, the other hand clutching a small, straight stick—

Rowan felt the shock like a blow, found herself breathing shallowly through clenched teeth.

It was herself. Tiny, perfect, eerie; a little manikin, with the folds in the clothing, the characteristic cant of the head, all in miniature, all green in the green, shuddering light.

The hair on the left side of its head was disheveled. Dazed, Rowan reached up and smoothed her own hair. Its eyes were shadowed. Rowan did not pick it up, nor lean closer; she did not want to see, as she knew she would, her own features on its thumbnail face.

The demons waited.

"I don't understand!" Rowan spoke helplessly, uselessly. "What does this *mean?*"

Meaning. It must mean something.

Herself. This is you.

"I can't do as you do, I can't make something. I have nothing to give you." She looked at herself, at her two hands.

An object with meaning. "Here." Quickly she pulled off her left glove, dropped it, pulled off her silver steerswoman's ring, set it on the ground. "There. *That* means me!"

As one, the demons threw up their arms, high.

The spray-vents were exposed. Rowan found she had risen to her feet, was standing with arms flung out to each side, and she thought: Now I will die.

No spray came.

The arms writhed, waved, thrust upward, fingers curling and uncurling, as demon bodies swayed, hands straining toward the ceiling, or perhaps the sky beyond the ceiling: all the creatures, together, caught in the throes of some overpowering demon emotion.

Rowan had seen this before in the amphitheater. It continued, long.

Then slowly, the demons subsided to stillness, but for the smallest male, still trembling in the aftermath.

Then, using a hand on the side of its body away from Rowan, the female reached down—and, Rowan assumed, produced another object. The males came closer to it.

The steerswoman could not see it from where she stood, and so, quite simply, she stepped up to and around the female. One of the males shuffled aside to make way for her.

It resembled nothing that she recognized.

She stood beside the female. The air was faintly cool around the creature and smelled, in the dank earth scent of the cave, like the great ocean. Rowan felt no fear, only utter, helpless incomprehension.

The female produced another case-object, touched it to the first; it adhered instantly. Another and another; the structure became more complex. The males reacted with lifts of surprise, gentle waves of interest; the speckled male positively jittered excitement.

The female stopped. Human and monsters stood, the one in silence, the others in what passed in them for silence, regarding the object.

Then, all at once, the males scattered like a flight of bats, off into the angles and crannies of the cave.

Rowan was alone with the female. She turned to it, feeling she ought to say something, make some sort of comment; but it would be useless. She went to retrieve her ring, but it, and the eerie manikin, were both gone.

The males were not absent long. At a dead run, one returned and placed a case-object beside the last one the female had produced. A small object, simple in form. Then another male returned, and another, each with an object of its own. The speckled male returned with apparently none, then pulled six out of its maw, squatting on the ground and using all four hands to arrange them in a neat semicircle. The other males crowded around, jockeying for a clear view, and swayed as they studied the collection, clearly impressed.

The female produced one more, also small but with a complex surface. Then it rotated itself a quarter turn, and reached down as if to emit another.

No result.

Naturally, Rowan thought; made of egg-case covering. The female demon would certainly not have an unlimited supply of the material. It must run out at some point.

And the males—they had no supply whatsoever.

Something shifted inside the steerswoman; she felt an internal drop, a moment's vertigo, as if she were on a ship that had unexpectedly crested some great wave.

She felt she ought to be surprised; she was not. She said only, "Oh, of course." And then, like a slowly growing light, a slowly growing joy. "Oh, of *course*!"

The female shifted its previous case-object on the ground, reached out with two other arms, and selected from among those arranged by the males. It placed the three in an arc. The demons stood, considering the arrangement.

And—Rowan turned to look—out in the low cave's dim shifting light: hundreds, thousands of case-objects. Piles of them. Collected, sorted, according to what system or logic she did not know—

Words. Language. The demons were speaking.

Or the female was; the males could not produce the egg-case material. They could not speak, not as females did. They must use words already uttered by others—like saving a note written by a friend on the chance that someday one might wish to say the same thing oneself . . .

But why store them here? Why not in a den, or a series of dens, convenient?

Secrecy. Rowan had seen a male killed for speaking in public. Rowan was in a secret place.

But this female was privy to the secret, seemed to encourage the males; certainly she aided them, handing them the words that she spoke, for the males to add to their secret hoard.

Sharing. Sharing knowledge.

The steerswoman gave a weak laugh. "I think that you and I are very much alike." She turned back.

Then she said, "Or perhaps not."

The female, unfortunately, was engaged in mating, employing two males simultaneously on opposite sides of her body.

Rowan stood watching the unerotic coupling, winced in embarrassment. "Well," she admitted, "customs do differ."

41

"What is this place?"

She turned; he stood, head ducked under the low ceiling, his left hand steadying himself against the stone above. Moths fluttered about the hand, a dizzying little pocket of light. He flinched when they flew close to his eyes.

Rowan held up the object she was examining. "Does this look like a tanglebrush to you? It rather does to me, from a certain angle."

He gazed about, toward the dimmest recesses where no moths stirred. "We're underground." Light moved too quickly across his face for her to discern his expression.

"Yes." She returned the object to its grouping, rose, brushed the ceiling to improve the light. "But we're not home free yet."

"I've never seen this." Janus looked blankly at the collections of case-objects—of utterances—that lay all across the cave floor. "This is one of their places."

"Yes." She studied him in the brighter light. He seemed a bit dazed, a bit unsteady on his feet; still, quite an improvement. She took his arm, led him back toward the alcove. "Did you find the food I left by you?"

"No . . ."

"You should eat. And drink more." She sat him down, handed him the cheese. He reached for it with his right hand, stopped, took it with his left.

She felt his forehead: slightly warm but dry. She knelt beside him, gently felt his right arm again, down to the wrist. "I don't understand why this hand isn't horribly infected." She had not dared to unwrap it; she was certain to cause pain, and there was not water enough to clean it properly.

"I put it in the bug pond."

" 'Bug pond?' A pool of water, surrounded by rocks?"

"They brought me there every day. They couldn't bring me water, so they brought me to the water."

"Well, you seem to have done some good by it." She released the arm, shifted to sit facing him. "Do you want to explain to me what you said earlier?"

"How far are we from the city?"

Only people built cities. "I see that you've figured out that these demons are not animals."

He looked at her blankly, but he said, "Unfortunately."

Her gaze narrowed. "Why unfortunately?"

"If this is one of their places, they'll come here soon. We can't stay long."

"We won't be staying long. What do you mean by 'unfortunately'?"

"I can walk now, if we go slowly. You still have the talisman. Let's go now."

She sighed, but it was through her teeth. "Janus, one of us must answer the other's questions—really, one of us must. And since it can't be me, it must be you."

"I can't bother with your rules."

"They're not rules, they're principles. You know that." She forced her anger down. "I want to understand you, I truly do, but you're not giving me any help." He did not reply. She rubbed her forehead, pushed back her hair, reminded herself that he had undergone a horrific experience, the like of which she could scarcely imagine, and she could not expect him to behave in an entirely rational fashion.

Then she realized, suddenly and apallingly, that she could imagine it, easily: if, months ago, she had acquired a live demon to study, it might well have received similar treatment at her hands.

She said, "They thought you were an animal." He did not reply. That was why the female demon had let them go, Rowan understood; Rowan herself must have done something that demonstrated clearly that she was no animal.

Janus was watching her closely. She could not help asking, "Why you? They could have captured any number of humans to study. Why come all the way to Alemeth—" She suddenly saw that they must have used a blinded demon to capture Janus. "The talisman—" And a blinded demon had guarded him in the den; another, or the same one. "But why—" They must have feared that his immunity would somehow return; they did not know that it could not; they did not know at all of what Janus's original protection had consisted.

"What *is* this?" She picked it up from the stony floor, held it up between them in the dim, shifting light. "Other than a word, or a sentence? How can they obey it unless they perceive it? How can they perceive it and not know what it is?"

He did not look at it but sat merely regarding her, expressionless. "They're not like us," he said.

She flung out one arm. "I do believe I've noticed that already! But what is it, what does it *say?*"

Then he did look at it, brows knit slightly. And then, head tilted a bit, he gave the question such calm, unhurried, careful, thoughtful, and complete consideration that Rowan understood that his mind was far less stable than she had assumed. She must deal with him cautiously.

Eventually, he arrived at his conclusion; the discovery seemed to please him. He smiled at her. "I believe," he said, "that it means . . . 'Holy, holy.' "

Silence. Then, "I see." She carefully set the talisman down again. "And . . . have you managed to decipher any other statements?"

He looked at her as if she were simple. "I don't want to *talk* to them," he told her.

"I see . . ." she said again. She decided not to argue the point. "Now, Janus, listen carefully. I am going to get you home. There's a ship waiting for us at the Dolphin Stair. All we need to do is cross the Demon Lands . . . and you know that will take some time. You have to cooperate with me, you have to do what I say, and everything will be all right."

"It's impossible to cross the Demon Lands."

"No it isn't," she pointed out, carefully patient. "You've done it, several times. And I've done it."

"No, you haven't. You only think you have."

She was a moment finding a reply. "Well . . . you're free to correct any misconceptions I might have. In fact, I'd welcome it. But I do know how to get us back to Alemeth."

"Good. Let's go now." He started to rise.

"No." She placed a hand on his shoulder. "Not yet. This cave is located inside the city. They're patrolling the streets outside; I've checked recently. There are a lot of them, and they're being very systematic. I don't want to get into a situation where we might become surrounded. We'll wait until they relax their guard. Then we'll leave."

He studied her face. He took a breath as if to speak, released it word-lessly. He nodded.

"Good."

He discovered the food in his hand, began eating, with rather less ur-gency than Rowan expected from one as obviously starved as he was. She did not consider this an encouraging sign. She wondered how much to tell him in his present uncertain condition; but she must say something, and soon. "Janus, shortly demons will be coming here. You mustn't be afraid."

He continued eating. "We have the talisman."

"That's right. And if you like, you can stay behind it while they're here."

She watched as the implication of her statement dawned on him. Eventually he said uncertainly, "And you must, too . . ."

She took a breath. "That depends on which demons they are. A de-mon helped us escape from that den you were held in; and she and her mates are still helping us. They've brought us food, twice now—from my camp or your nearest cache, I suspect." He looked aghast at the cheese in his hand. "I believe we can trust them," Rowan said.

"Trust?" He dropped the food, clutched her shoulder. "Rowan, if they're feeding us—"

"Please, calm down—"

"—then this is just another prison!"

"A prison we can walk out of, any time we like? We still have the talisman—"

"All they need to do is block off the entrance—"

She placed her hands on his shoulders, held his gaze, spoke distinctly, stressing each word, "But they haven't done so." He subsided, but his eyes remained wide. "We've been here two days," Rowan went on, "and the other demons are still searching the city for us. Tan and the males are keeping our presence secret." She saw astonishment on his face, spoke before he could ask. "I call her 'Tan' for her color. I must call her some-thing, if only in my own mind."

He dropped his hand, sat stiff under her grip. "Skies, Rowan, you've *named* the thing!" he spat, with sudden fury.

"Yes! Yes, I have. In fact, I believe she's named me, as well. We had a very interesting conversation while you slept—I'm sorry you missed it. Apparently, I was both brilliant and eloquent." She released him. "Unfor-tunately, I have no idea what I said."

He was so long silent that she grew disturbed. Eventually he said only, quietly, "You fool."

"Why? Why am I a fool, Janus?" No reply. "Very well, then. But this fool, as you call her, is going to get you out of this alive."

Demon-voice.

She expected him to startle or show fear, but his expression did not alter. He held her gaze.

She glanced toward the entrance, shifted to sit beside him, placing the talisman in front of them both. "They're probably dropping off more food. Here—" She had cut two more finger-ends from her right glove; she found them, passed them to him. "Put these in your ears; it will help with the noise." He did so, awkwardly, one-handed. They waited, she watching the light grow and fade as the moths reacted to the demons' movements; and he, when she glanced back, watching her, his face unreadable.

The voices went on: three of them. They continued too long to be a simple food drop. Rowan began to wonder if these demons were strangers to her, and she grew concerned. She found her sword, gestured to Janus that he was to remain where he was, and took the talisman. Stooping, she slowly walked forward, carefully keeping Janus protected directly behind her.

The light and voices had moved deeper into the cave, among the case-objects. Rowan approached near enough to recognize three of Tan's males.

She returned to Janus, placed the talisman before him, and indicated that he was not to move. He made no response, neither by gesture nor nod. She left him.

Three bizarre creatures—the strangeness struck her even more forcefully now that she knew that they were intelligent. She had, while Janus slept, spent a long time considering the idea, examining it, with a deep and very steerswomanly delight . . .

But seeing the demons again, she realized that in her own mind she had subtly altered their shapes, adjusting them toward the human form, even to the addition of a shadowy suggestion of a head above the arms. How could you guess what a person was thinking without eyes to watch, a face to read?

No heads, no faces. Columnar bodies. Arms sprouting from the top. Quadrilateral symmetry. It was very hard to see people in those strange shapes.

But these particular people were doing something, and having a lot of difficulty at it.

She approached slowly, not wishing to startle them; the smallest male did seem startled nevertheless, arms jerking upward and dropping several times during her approach.

She decided it was a habit of his. Some people, she told herself, are just nervous. But she stopped ten feet away.

The second demon, the largest and darkest colored of the three, was dragging something along the ground. It was nearly as large as he was.

The third demon was the speckled male; he stood to one side, either watching the dark male, watching Rowan, or regarding something else entirely—or doing all three. Rowan studied the gentle rise and fall of his arms, wondering what emotion or state of mind the movement might indicate. When, by pure guess, she decided that the males were accustomed to her presence, she came a bit closer; and even the jumpy male did not seem bothered by her.

The dark male was attempting to add the object he was dragging to one of the groupings of utterances. Unfortunately, it was so large that it immediately displaced all the other objects. All three males set to rearranging the collection around it.

Rowan sat on her heels, observing the process.

She had already determined that the utterances were not grouped by size or shape. Some other method of organization must operate, if the males were to have any chance at all of knowing where to find the ones they sought. The only other method the steerswoman could think of was a conceptual organization, with similar or related ideas grouped together. The males had obviously decided that this new object belonged among these others. Eventually, they completed their adjustments, and they stood around the group together in a moment of motionless demon regard.

Rowan's mouth twitched. "I suppose I ought to be able to learn something from this," she said, unable to resist speaking aloud, "but somehow, it seems unkind to leave it there. I don't think it's going to be very useful to you."

It would, however, be extremely useful to her. It was her pack.

She could wait until they were gone; she decided not to.

She moved closer again, by inches, and thought that the stirring of arms must indicate that she had their attention. "Here." She reached out one hand cautiously toward the pack; the dark male and the speckled one moved further apart to allow her access. The nervous male, on the far side of the grouping, startled three times in succession, then backed away rapidly.

Rowan found herself addressing the speckled male wryly. "Please tell Twitchy over there that I'm not going to eat him." Twitchy himself startled once more at her voice, but immediately grew calmer, and even dared to draw a bit nearer again. She found herself admiring him for overcoming what was obviously an urgent, and perhaps instinctive, need to flee or spray.

Twitchy. And that made two demons she had named.

And why not? They could certainly hear, better than she could. They might come to learn to recognize human words. She pointed. "Twitchy." And to her left, the dark male, "Bry," after a big black dog she once knew. And on her right—

The speckled male had moved slightly closer, and stood with his nearest two arms gently arched, fingers delicately dangling, just high enough to not obstruct the hearing eyes beneath his skin. Rowan studied him a moment, considered his actions in the case-object maze and on the streets of the city. She smiled. "The Thief of Words."

Unfortunately, she soon found that it was impossible to determine whether the act of pointing had any significance to demons. Only when she pointed to the ceiling did they show any reaction, and that a decidedly negative one. Possibly they feared she might try to spray them.

"Well." She pulled the pack from the grouping, careful not to disturb the other objects, and knelt down beside it. "Look." She untied the closure, flipped open the flap. "This is not a word. Nor a sentence—" She was startled when a demon hand reached into the pack, and she moved back quickly; she was even more surprised to discover that the hand was Twitchy's. He boldly thrust it deep in the pack, pulled out Rowan's spare blouse by one sleeve, and immediately fed the length of it into his maw.

Rowan mastered her surprise and watched, bemused. "I'm sure that's not good for you." Her little tin cook pot followed the blouse. "And you're definitely going to have trouble with that." The Thief and Bry were standing well aside, arms rising and falling slightly, in what Rowan decided was a watching-something-interesting stance.

Presently Twitchy thought better of his actions, and extracted the pot and the blouse. He dropped both to the ground, the blouse a sodden, tattered mass. The three demons shifted positions—to gain a better view, Rowan realized. All three stood motionless; then all three walked away.

Well. At the least, Rowan had identified two different demon body postures: watching-something-interesting and the Thief's clearly directional closely-observing-one-specific-thing. Progress of a sort.

As she tied the pack closed, it suddenly occurred to her that Twitchy had assumed that the pack, not being an utterance, must be an animal carcass, and had attempted to dine on its entrails.

Still, she had her pack. Her logbook, pens, and ink would keep her occupied until it was safe to leave. No blanket, nor cloak—she had not completely dismantled her camp, planning to stay one more night—but a woolen vest would help Janus stay warm. There was a packet of dried meat and at the bottom, a precious canteen of water—

The demons returned. Bry arrived first and, choosing a clear space between two groupings, set down three utterances. Then he stepped back from them and stood, shuffling his feet slightly, resulting in a slow rotation of his entire body, for what purpose Rowan could not even begin to guess.

Rowan rose, went somewhat closer, considered the objects. She made a noise, whose purpose even she could not identify: frustration? Longing? One would think that a language of physical objects would at the least contain components that resembled the things to which they referred, as the wood-gnome's gesture language sometimes did.

Wood-gnome. She could not emit shaped objects, but she could shape her hands. And demons had hands.

Twitchy arrived, an utterance in each hand. He stood for a moment, perhaps considering Bry's statement, then placed his own beside it. Bry became motionless, then returned to circular shuffling.

The Thief returned, and as Rowan expected, had carried his own statement in his maw. But he first paused, and having seen it three times now, Rowan identified the specific looking-at-a-new-statement pose. Then he extracted his own statements, arranged them; and all three first looked and then, perhaps, contemplated, arms slowly rising and falling.

Rowan waved her hands as wood gnomes did to get one's attention; an alteration in the demons' arm movements suggested that it had worked. Then Rowan gestured: You, me, speak.

But *you* and *me* consisted merely of pointing. *Speak* was gestured at the mouth, and would have some significance only if these demons knew she communicated with her mouth—or for that matter, even knew that it was her mouth. Or knew that her mouth was located on her head. Or knew what her head was.

And in two days of observations in the city, she had never seen any demon gesture in any fashion. How was she even to assign signals to objects if she could not point at them?

She slapped the pack beside her, signaled *pack*. She went to Twitchy's discarded meal, rapped the pot with her knuckles. The sound was not loud enough to pass through her earplugs, but, predictably, it caused Twitchy to startle again. *Cup*, Rowan gestured, having forgotten the wood gnome gesture for pot. Cup would do.

She was completely unable to determine what impression, if any, the demons gained from her antics. She thought they were watching her; they might as easily have been regarding each other, the statements they had made, or the furthest walls of the cave.

Abruptly, the Thief froze in the look-at-a-statement pose. The others noticed, did the same, then shifted to "watching." With obvious hesitancy and caution, the Thief approached Rowan.

The steerswoman forced herself not to retreat, with difficulty. Three feet away, with the pot and blouse between them, the Thief stopped.

She was sitting on her heels; the demon loomed above her. She found herself looking up at him, to where his face ought to be. Nothing there; but below that, between the shoulders, two puckered spray-vents, pulsing slightly, weirdly.

The Thief tucked his feet close, lowered himself, and sat, four knees high all around, in a demon version of Rowan's own posture. Delicately, he reached out his nearest hand, folded the fingers, then rapped once on the pot.

"Yes!" *Cup, cup*, Rowan gestured rapidly; but the Thief, ignoring her, picked up the pot, passed it to his opposite hand, and walked back to the other demons.

Arrived, he placed the pot beside the utterances. All three entered into "look," and then "contemplate."

Rowan thumped one knee with her fist. "No, it's not a *word*." She crossed over to them; Bry and the Thief politely shifted, to allow her to join the contemplative circle. "No, it's—" she knelt on the stony floor "—it's a thing, an object, a tool—" She had seen no tools in the city, no implements of any sort: even the hunting party had carried no spears. Other than utterances, the only made objects she had seen were dens, the tables in the courtyard, the rings around the rock pools, the rough stone breakwater.

"It doesn't mean anything," she said helplessly. "You use it . . ." She picked it up; the demons increased their attention. "It's a container . . ." She turned it over, used it to cover one of the case-objects—

Startlement, from all three, so sudden, so extreme that Rowan instinctively ducked, wrapped her face in her arms, remained in a trembling ball, waiting for spray or attack.

None came. She unfolded herself.

Twitchy was gone; moth light deep in the cave showed where he had run to seek his words. Bry stood, arms rising and falling one at a time in sequence all around his body: a curious weaving motion that Rowan had seen before.

The Thief had the pot. He was lifting it, lowering it, lifting and lowering, covering a different case-object each time, and displaying with each uncovering the identical degree of extreme startlement.

Rowan sat back, wrapped her arms around her knees, watched. "Apparently," she said presently, "this is an entirely new concept in your experience, am I right?"

Twitchy arrived, precariously carrying eight utterances, which he immediately spilled to the ground and set to arranging. The Thief demonstrated the pot trick, which caused Twitchy to weave his arms as Bry did. Bry discovered an urgent need to comment, and hurried off to find the means of doing so, leaving a trail of moth light on the ceiling behind him like a comet's tail.

What an incredibly inefficient means of speaking, Rowan thought. Less so for the females, of course, but even so: how carefully one must choose one's statements, how slowly information must spread! On the other hand, once something was said, how easy to transport the utterance itself, like writing and speaking simultaneously . . .

The females' utterances were far more complex, more sophisticated. Possibly a great deal of information could be carried by one discrete object. The males must be speaking a simplified version, perhaps as clumsy as baby talk; and what a shame that their quick minds had no easier expression.

"Clay," she said to the demons. "What you boys need is clay. Why have you not discovered clay?" The next steerswoman who came here would certainly introduce its use; although that might inspire antagonism from the females . . .

Bry approached, a case-object in each hand. At the least, Rowan decided, she would have some idea of what he was talking about . . .

Bry stopped. He dropped his words. The Thief and Twitchy paused.

All three demons walked away.

Rowan puzzled. "Now what?" Light rose behind her; she turned.

She had only an impression of movement, the flash of steel; words scattered. Then he was past her, clumsy, stooped.

"No!" She scrambled to her feet, threw herself at him. He had nearly caught up with Bry. She clutched his shirt, swung him around. The talisman fell from his right hand, where it had been awkwardly balanced on the bandages. "Are you insane?" It struck the ground, landing at an angle that displayed only its underside.

The demons saw him, threw up their arms.

"No!" She swung Janus behind her, wrenched the sword from his grip, shoved him to the ground, turned back, interposed herself, held up one hand to the demons in a useless, meaningless gesture, spoke out loud, helplessly, "No, he doesn't know what he's doing!"

The demons hesitated, during which moment Rowan seemed to have a great deal of time to contemplate exactly how foolish it was to place herself in such a situation. She thought she ought to go for the talisman; she also thought—and this very clearly—that she ought not move at all, not the slightest bit.

Twitchy had already made his escape. The Thief stood near the door, arms raised. Bry, the largest and strongest of the males, had his two near arms raised high, his far-side arms spread low and wide, taloned fingers forward, guarding the retreat of his companions.

The Thief relaxed, slowly; Bry did not. The Thief shuffled a few cautious steps forward, reached out one hand, wrapped the fingers around one of Bry's. He tugged gently.

Bry allowed himself to be led away, keeping his near-side arms high enough to spray, high enough to keep a very clear view of exactly what he was leaving behind.

Rowan turned back to Janus; he lay half sprawled among scattered case-objects, watching her with a wild gaze. "You idiot," she said. "They're *helping* us." His mouth moved; she could not hear him. She pulled out her earplugs. "What?"

"You should have killed them."

She composed herself with difficulty. "Janus . . ." She went to him, reluctantly offered a hand to help him up. "I know that demons hurt you, but you've got to understand—it wasn't *these* demons." He stared at her hand, seeming not to recognize it. Then he took it; she pulled him up. "Demons aren't animals, Janus. They're intelligent, just as humans are. They're people. You can't just go about randomly slaughtering *people*—"

And realization struck her so hard she felt blinded.

A village, inhabitants vanished, structures reduced to dust by wind and rain.

Another, emptied of life.

A third, with its dead lying in the streets, on the hillsides.

And an innocent line on a traveler's map. Janus's route, with its simple notations, each crossed out: ONE. TWO. THREE.

Janus, sailing away from Alemeth in his copper-bottomed boat. Janus, with his perfect protection from demon attack, walking the demon streets like a ghost, impervious, invisible.

His face was inches away; his hand was still in hers. She flung it away, stepped back, and back. She gasped once, said, "No."

He watched her; he said nothing.

"No! No, tell me you didn't!"

No answer; his face was blank.

"But, but"—and she pleaded—"you didn't know, did you? You didn't know they were *people*—"

Silence. Silence, and his empty eyes.

He had known.

"Are you *insane*?"

No words.

She threw her sword down; it clanged on stone, loud. "Why?" He said something; she did not catch it. "What?"

"Payment."

She flung out her arms. "For what?" A crypt in the wilderness. "Your shipmates? The ones who survived the wreck? Demons killed them?" Revenge, yes, that she could understand. "Oh, but, Janus, surely," and she said, "surely *one town* was revenge enough—"

No visible remorse, no visible shame, not even any anger; and on his face, in his eyes, not one single visible thought.

"Oh, no wonder, no wonder they came for you, hunted you." She clutched her own arms, tight, shaking. "All those poor people . . . You're, you're some kind of creature, a monster from the Inner Lands! Murderer—" Her voice cracked in her throat, painful. "I should leave you here to *die*—"

"Why don't you?"

She could not answer; she could not even find the answer that she was not permitted to speak. She made some sort of sound; she heard it. But even she did not know what it meant. She shut her eyes.

Three dead towns. Insects and animals, feasting on corpses. "Janus . . . why . . . ?" She opened her eyes.

He stood, green light shuddering about his head, shadows beyond and around, demon thoughts lying scattered about his feet. And at that moment, what seemed to Rowan impossible, incomprehensible, and terrifying was merely: his human shape, the thinking tilt of his head, the slight knit of his brows as, with every appearance of calm rationality, he carefully considered her question.

Then he said, in a perfectly reasonable tone of voice, "Sometimes, Rowan, one pays in advance."

42

*H*e would say no more than that; eventually, she ceased to ask. She waited. She could do nothing else.

Tan did not return. Of the males, only the Thief visited in the night, bringing food and leaving immediately after. He did not attempt to converse.

Rowan waited.

She tried to fill her time. She wrote in her logbook, made sketches of the four demons she had named and of selected groups of case-objects. She drew the formal demon body stances she had identified: *surprise, confusion, regard an utterance, contemplate.*

She searched the cave for her ring and her name. She did not find them.

She gave Janus food, when the Thief brought it, and her woollen vest, when it grew cold. And she waited.

She slept close to the entrance, so that demon-voice would wake her before Janus. She kept the talisman, kept her sword close by. A night passed, and a day, and another night.

The next morning, Rowan woke to find herself blanketed in delicate moth wings which crumbled under her touch. The entire cave floor, and all the beautiful, organized words, were covered in drifts, as if from a pale green snowfall. On the ceiling, the wingless moths were clambering, seeking each other, mating.

Rowan also drew all this. It was easy to do. The moths' light was now bright and steady.

When demon-voice came, she checked the location of the talisman without thinking, merely reassuring herself of its presence. It was in its kerchief; she stood ready to reveal it if the demon was a stranger.

It was the Thief. He saw her, paused by the entrance, then made his way toward the groups of utterances. Rowan followed.

He did not go far; and at a nearby group of very small case-objects, he stopped, selected one, set it on the ground before her.

A canted cone, striated, with tiny projections on the point.

She spread her hands uselessly. "I don't understand."

The Thief replaced the object, walked toward her, and then past her. She turned to follow him. "No, let's try again . . ."

He stopped. She waited; and then he moved away from her so suddenly and smoothly that she checked the talisman, checked her sword, looked behind her.

The talisman was still hung at her belt, covered. Her sword was sheathed at her back. Janus was nowhere in sight.

At the entrance, the Thief paused again, then exited.

And immediately returned, approached her, paused, backed away again.

No, not backed—demons had no front or back. He was merely walking.

Rowan followed a few steps, paused. The Thief paused as well. Then, in a lovely motion as graceful as a spider's, he swept three arms back to the far side of his body, and slowly stretched out the remaining arm toward her, fingers extended.

Rowan hesitated, then reached out her own hand. Cold, hard fingers found hers, intertwined with them, talons gently brushing her palm.

The Thief tightened his grip. He tugged.

Rowan glanced about the cave once, turned back to him. She allowed him to lead her outside.

When she returned she went directly to the back alcove, where Janus was idly sifting drifts of moth wing. "Do you want to live?"

He looked up. He was rather long replying. "Yes."

"Then come with me. Ask no questions. Do exactly as I say."

A pause. "All right."

Rowan did not display the talisman when they left the cave; no other demons were present in the ravine. Nor did she when they reached the street; there were no demons in the street, nor in any street visible around the edge of the ravine.

They followed the Thief of Words. Each street he led them to was deserted.

At one intersection, he turned right; Rowan knew that the quickest exit from the city would be accomplished by turning left. She paused at the intersection, looked left, saw no one.

The Thief noticed they were not following, stopped, returned, led right again, and paused, waiting. Rowan thought.

She had her sword in her right hand, the talisman in her left, pressed against her blouse, shielded, to prevent the Thief from being driven away. She gestured to Janus with her sword hand. Wait here. She went left.

The Thief startled, then jogged after her, kicking up small clouds of dust, brushing past Janus, who shied back against a den wall, eyes wild.

Rowan displayed the talisman; the Thief fell back. She maneuvered her body to block it from him, and continued on. When she looked back, the Thief of Words had fallen in behind her, clearly nervous, from the twitching of his fingers.

Just past the curve of the street, at the next intersection: four female demons moving in a slow, searching formation. Rowan backed off until the curve hid the searchers from view, then tucked the talisman against her blouse again, and jogged back to Janus.

The Thief caught up with them, paused, and with an almost emphatic deliberation, led right again. Rowan waved Janus forward, and they followed.

They took many turns; every intersection they passed, every street they entered, was empty. At one point, the Thief stopped in the middle of a street, for no reason that Rowan could discern, and waited, long; but when they crossed yet another deserted intersection it came to Rowan that the demon, with his exquisite sense of hearing, could certainly tell when nearby streets were occupied; could likely tell in what direction those demons were moving; and quite possibly, Rowan realized with wonder, could recognize specific individuals many streets away, purely by the sound of each voice.

The search had been relaxed but not discontinued entirely, as Rowan had seen. There might be places where many searchers were concentrated; but the Thief of Words knew how to lead them out.

They passed down street after street. The emptiness grew eerie. The great city began to feel to her like the pitiful, empty dens at Site Two.

And if Janus had not been stopped, he would have rendered it exactly the same.

She glanced back at him; his eyes were wide and wary, his clothes tattered and filthy, his hair and beard wild. He seemed half a wild animal, the only touch of civilization Rowan's own neat and sturdy steerswoman's pack. She needed her own hands free; but she had lightened the pack as much as possible by tossing out half the clothing and by carrying the water sack herself, refilled from the discarded canteen. She had made sure Janus had no weapons.

The Thief had paused again, and now abruptly doubled back to the last intersection and chose a different street. Rowan surmised a search party nearby.

They moved, for a while outward; then, suddenly nervous, the Thief doubled them back, crisscrossed eastward, and moved more calmly and easily.

Rowan could not share his confidence; by her reckoning, the new route would bring them quite close to the center of the city.

But the streets remained empty, even when by their length and curvature Rowan knew they had come closer to the center. The Thief moved more quickly but without fear; and Rowan began to notice something. It took her some time to identify.

Her earplugs had muffled the single combined voice of the city; now she heard it again. And it seemed to be no longer everywhere but focused, directional.

When by her calculations she and her companions were merely three streets away from the center, it became clear: many, many demons, perhaps most of the city's population, were gathered together in the amphitheater.

The Thief crossed an intersection, waited for Rowan and Janus in the middle of the next street. Rowan glanced at him, caught Janus's eye, and with a lift of her chin directed him to go ahead. Janus's gaze narrowed, but he complied.

Only three streets away . . .

Rowan held out the talisman, turned to face the sound, and walked forward.

She did not need to go far. Past one intersection, then up ahead between the buildings, a narrow view of the center.

Demons all down the near slope and up the opposite slope and, Rowan surmised by sound, all around, nearly elbow to elbow, like a huge grove of strange trees, branches moving gently.

Down at the bottom, on the flattened area, on the stage: Tan. She was building something.

The structure spread around and to one side, and it was nearly as tall as Tan herself. As the steerswoman watched, the demon reached down to her speaking orifice and drew forth a case-object.

A word, Rowan thought, or a sentence, a statement? How much can a demon say in one utterance?

Tan held the utterance before her briefly, and the shifting of arms told of the watchers' attention. Then she placed it atop one section of the structure; it adhered instantly. Tan took a half-rotating step to one side, clearing the view for the audience.

Rowan watched as more than two hundred demons simultaneously entered the identical stance: the specific demon pose of Regarding-an-utterance. And then, like a smooth wave, the stance of Contemplation.

And then, waiting; waiting, Rowan saw, with interest, eagerness. Individual demons shifted for a better view.

Tan continued her work.

Tan was making, Rowan realized, not many statements, but one great statement, one single thing that grew before the eyes of the crowd, each watcher waiting for the next idea to be added to the rest, linked to the rest, made part of the whole.

Imagine it, Rowan thought: to say something and have it stand before the eyes of all, to be judged by all, as one unified expression.

So many demons—people, but no kin to her—held by words.

Is it beautiful to them? Rowan wondered. It must be, to hold them like this. Is it a song? She thought of Bel standing by a campfire in the Outskirts, tilting her face to the stars as she sang, the truth of her words riding on the beauty of her voice, riding up and out to the sky.

It must be beautiful. And it must be the truth.

And in that moment, the steerswoman felt she could not breathe for the weight of the yearning that lodged in the hollow of her throat. She wanted to stay. Even utterly uncomprehending, she wanted to remain until Tan had finished, to see completed the single great statement.

She could not stay.

She and Janus had needed a diversion to make their escape from the city. Tan was providing it.

She must leave; and suddenly she found that she could.

Only because she knew that humans would return. If not herself then some other steerswoman, someday.

Invisible, she nodded to them, to all the people, silent yet endlessly singing, and she said to them, with her lips if not her voice: We'll be back. We'll learn. We'll speak to you, and we will come to know each other.

She began, carefully, to back away. She glanced over her shoulder—Janus, directly behind her.

Not looking at the demons, looking at her; at her face; at whatever, at that moment, her expression revealed to him.

She saw him jerk, saw him gasp, draw a breath, heard him shout, "NO!" He snatched out; she moved the sword out of his reach.

But it was the talisman he went for; snatched it from her hand; flung it over the den roofs. Then he stood, shuddering, half bent, fists clenched, eyes closed, making wordless sounds—

And the demons came.

Rowan shouted, turned, struck out, contacted nothing, and fell, wondering why she fell.

Then she had no room left in her mind to wonder; all she knew was pain.

43

*R*owan fought.

She twisted, flailed, struck out at the bodies around her, clutched and tore at the fingers gripping her. Her feet scrabbled on the ground, but whenever she put weight on her left leg, something sharp and bright flared in her brain, blinding every sense, and she ceased, briefly, to think at all.

She fought nonetheless. She heard a sound, loud: it was her own voice. She was shouting, cursing. The curses became more vicious, her voice wilder, and her words evolved until she said, in more a scream than a shout, "*I am not a wild animal!*"

Then stop acting like one.

She relaxed so abruptly that the demon who held her staggered and nearly fell. Narrow, taloned hands reached out from all around, caught, and steadied them both. The steerswoman shut her eyes, blindly searched for her balance, could find it only with one leg. She stood canted, half propped against the chill, smooth demon body behind her.

She opened her eyes to a forest of arms. The sun was too bright; the dusty air felt like lemons on her skin. She was dizzy and nauseated. She was shuddering with cold, despite the fact that she seemed, somehow, to be standing in fire.

She said, in a voice thick in the confines of her own skull, "Very well. You have me. Exactly what are you intending to do with me?"

But the demons' attention was elsewhere.

Down below, at the focus of the amphitheater, Tan was demolishing her construction.

Tan's fingers pried and tore. She hurled the fragments out into the crowd. Where the pieces fell, demons stepped quickly back. Along the slopes, the movements of arms told of shock, distress.

Tan cleared the stage completely of the remnants of her great statement. Then she spoke again: one small case-object.

That said, she stepped aside, sat, arms knotted above her maw.

As one, the audience entered into Regard and then Contemplate. At the edge of the amphitheater, Rowan stood among demons, held by demons, and tried, with strange difficulty, to focus.

Burned; she had been burned. She looked down, and discovered the damage. She must do something.

Her arms were held close to her body, but her hands were free. She clutched the water sack, tore the mouthpiece from it completely, pulled the opening wider, aimed as best she could manage, and emptied it.

There was darkness.

There was light. She was standing. The steerswoman lifted her head.

A demon stood before her. Rowan recognized Tan, and said weakly, "Oh . . ."

She looked down: on the dirt, a case-object. She looked up again. "I—I don't understand." She tried to study Tan's pose, the movement of her arms, for clues as to thought, emotion.

Waiting. Tan was waiting.

Rowan shifted, found that some demon was holding her, from behind. It was the only reason she was able to stand.

Two female demons stood near Tan, also waiting.

Past Tan: more demons. Left, and right: demons.

Rowan was at the bottom of the amphitheater.

"I can't answer," Rowan said to Tan, helplessly. "I can't speak as you do . . . I'd have to speak like a man."

One of the two other females made a statement. All present Regarded, then Contemplated. Rowan gazed about, blinking in the glaring, painful sunlight.

The demon holding her, a female, had three companions, also female. All four stood tense and alert, their attention apparently only on Rowan. Close by: another group, in a similar configuration, with Janus at its center. He had lost the pack but seemed unhurt, but Rowan could not be certain—she could not see well, it was too bright, there was no air . . .

Rowan turned away, suddenly dizzy and unable, for a moment, to understand why she hurt so much. She closed her eyes, forced her breathing steady.

When she next looked, Tan had spoken to her again. The case-object resembled nothing Rowan could identify. The three demons with Tan still waited.

Rowan said, through clenched teeth, "This won't work!"

Prove you are a person. But Rowan could not.

The ring; the steerswoman's ring had impressed Tan, whatever she had thought its meaning. Tan's men had taken it. Tan must get the ring or send one of her men—

To the secret place? Now, with the whole city watching?

No. That should not be done.

"Then say the word, the word that protects, the talisman. We'll take it, we'll leave you . . ."

But demons did not understand about the word, did not know what drove them from it.

But where had it come from? How had it ever been spoken?

The two females with Tan ceased to wait and now displayed anger. Tan tried once again, and this time, Rowan recognized the word.

A small word: a tiny human shape. Rowan herself.

What else did people do? Rowan scanned the crowd wildly. Other than speech, what showed these people as thinking beings?

Rowan's guard still held her; but Rowan now found that when she moved, the guard permitted it. Awkward on one leg, leaning back against the demon, weak with pain and shock, the steerswoman raised her arms. As best as a human being could, she entered into the demon stance of Regard and then, Contemplate.

Startlement, like a wave moving up the slopes of the amphitheater. Then, arm-weaving, the sequential lift and fall, all around each demon's body.

Wonder, Rowan suddenly understood, that's *Wonder*.

Her guard released her, stepped back. Rowan fell; and for an unknown space of time, could not think.

When next she could see again, there were many more words on the ground than before; more people had spoken. But Tan—Tan strode among the statements, tossing them away with her hands, kicking them with her broad, taloned feet.

The two females nearby were watching, one quivering with rage; she entered attack stance.

A guard moved forward and quickly, smoothly, efficiently, killed her.

All present paused to eat. Those nearby politely passed portions to those further away. Tan dropped a choice segment down her maw, and stood chewing slowly and, it seemed to Rowan, thoughtfully.

When she was finished, Tan began to speak again. Rowan pushed herself up on her hands to watch.

One case-object; another, attaching to the first; a third, joining them at the top ... Tan proceeded to construct a new statement. The crowd displayed Watching-with-interest.

But the slain female's companion did not wait for Tan to finish. She uttered a small statement of her own, and stepped away from it, sat, her arms tucked above her maw.

Regard, from the audience. Contemplate. Tan paused.

Tan spoke again: a single, self-contained utterance.

Regard. Contemplate.

And, at the top of the slope, at the edge of the crowd: movement, a small pocket of agitation.

The dissenting female unknotted her arms, rose, approached Tan's new statement. She uttered a case-object, attached it directly to Tan's. Both stood considering the result.

The motion moved down the slope, though the crowd, toward the stage. Annoyance from those its passing disturbed.

Tan's opponent took advantage of the pause in the proceedings. She stepped to the edge of the crowd, selected a male, and engaged in intercourse.

Tan continued to consider the combined statement. Then her arms lifted slightly as she, and simultaneously Rowan, recognized the demon pushing through the crowd toward the stage. The Thief of Words.

It came to Rowan that she must stand; if the Thief were bringing her ring, then whatever mysterious and important statement it would convey to the demons, Rowan must at the least be standing when they saw it.

She was half sprawled on the ground. She looked about: her guard was still beside her. As if it were the most natural act in the world, the steerswoman reached up, grasped one of the demon's arms, and tried to pull herself to her feet.

She nearly fell again; the alteration in the pain in her leg made it seem new, and it nearly overpowered her.

But she found herself standing, the guard demon supporting her with all four hands. Rowan stopped the strange sound that was coming from the back of her own throat, gasped, breathed deeply, and said, "Thank you." Painfully, and needing great concentration to do so, she managed to turn around to face the audience.

The Thief of Words arrived at the stage. None of the demons watching approved of this, and Tan's opponent was herself so amazed that she ceased mating, and her arms quivered anger.

The Thief's hands were empty. Rowan was suddenly shaking and found herself pleading, so breathlessly even she could not hear, "No, no, don't take it from your mouth . . ."

In the sight of fully half the city, the Thief reached up and down into his maw; not with one hand but four.

Four words. He reached again.

He did not complete the motion.

From the edge of the stage moving inward, from behind Rowan moving forward, from all about, demons converged on the Thief. They did not spray: they slashed with talons, tore with thin, strong fingers. He fell, and Rowan could see him no longer.

Then one was thrown back, violently, and another, and another. The rest, startled and panicking, retreated—

And it was Tan, alone beside the fallen Thief, holding the killers back with an attack stance so wide and high that it seemed to be directed at the entire city.

Startlement, all around, in a visual stutter, as the crowd showed surprise—showed it over and over, as if there were no way to move past an astonishment so great.

But Tan was too late; the Thief of Words lay, legs tangled, arms sprawled, a spread of bloody viscera fanning out beside him on the dirt. The words he had not spoken lay spilled between his arms, mute and meaningless.

Keeping three arms raised, Tan reached down with the fourth, twined her fingers among Thief's limp ones, gently lifted the slack hand. She stood a moment so, with all the people watching in stuttering startlement, and slowly, eventually, in stillness.

Then she dropped the hand and stepped over the corpse. Using all four of her hands, Tan laid out the words the Thief had brought.

One long arc of nine discrete utterances. Within the curve: a second, small arc of three simple words. Tan took two steps to one side, stood quietly, passively; and even her body no longer spoke to Rowan.

But the steerswoman understood. With a sudden, glowing clarity, she knew—not the meaning of the words but the meaning of the act.

She knew exactly what to do.

Her breath was shuddering; she had not noticed. It was from pain; but pain was irrelevant. When she took a step forward, the pain flared through her, inhabited her completely, drove out thought. But that did not matter; she did not need to think to do this.

Standing free of her guard, in the center of the stage, the steerswoman threw up her arms.

She waved them, she twisted them, writhed them. She curled and un-curled her fingers, straining toward the glaring blue sky above. She swayed.

And it seemed to her that it now took no effort to do this; she could not stop if she wished. She shut her eyes; she gave herself to it. It was right, it was pure and true, and it was the one way to express this emotion.

She knew what it meant. She had seen it done twice:

For the child she had seen in the amphitheater; for Rowan herself, in the cave. She knew what it meant:

First words.

One who was silent has spoken.

One we had thought without thought, now shows us, now shares with us, the thought that is within him.

He is like us. He is one of us.

Rowan said, gasping, "Welcome," through the pain and through the joy, "oh, welcome . . ."

When she opened her eyes and saw the demons again, it was through tears. When she shook the tears away, she saw, across the amphitheater, isolated spots of wild motion, waving, twisting. And when she looked again, more: every male present, and females—a few, and then more, and then more . . .

One who was silent has spoken. Welcome.

But on the stage, in the midst of the great and joyful motion all around, Tan herself did not join in. She merely stood beside the words quietly, and it seemed to Rowan, with immense dignity: accepting, in her husband's place, the welcome of his people.

But not all of his people.

Demon words come too slow for a shout of warning; Rowan's shout meant nothing to Tan; but Rowan shouted, "No!" She stepped forward; her left leg gave way; she sprawled to the ground.

Demon legs all around, flat feet shuffling, all pale in the whitened light of shock. Rowan pulled herself half up, agonizingly. She clutched at demon knees to raise herself. No one killed her for it. She was vaguely amazed.

But by the time she stood, it was over.

Before her: a guard member, dead, two other females nearby, dead—the three who had attacked Tan. Some people were already dining on them.

A cluster of demons around Tan: not striking her but supporting her, hands gripping her arms, others under her shoulders. Rowan pushed some aside; they permitted it. She reached out; she became one more among the many who held Tan, who tried to lift her up, who did not want to let her fall.

Rowan's gloved hand was on Tan's torso, sliding in yellowish demon blood. Rowan tried to slip a supporting arm about her; her human arms were stronger than the demons' thin ones.

But her leg was not, and she staggered, crying out. She gripped another demon for support. Thin fingers encircled her arm, held tight.

But when she had touched Tan, she felt at once, even through the glove, that Tan's endless voice of sight had ceased. And the demon's wound was wide and deep.

Tan's knees slowly folded, and she collapsed to sit in the dirt. Her arms dropped, moving vaguely, fingers trembling.

Rowan turned to the demon beside her, expecting, somehow, to find a face to speak to. But she only looked down, into the creature's maw.

Far down. This demon was short. A male. Rowan could not tell which one.

"She can't die," Rowan said to him. "I've just *met* her."

He released her arm, stepped away. Rowan fell.

Tan lay sprawled in the dirt. Rowan half crawled, half dragged herself to Tan's side, and the people stepped back.

Tan still lived; her feet shifted, searching for the ground. Her arms tried to lift and fell.

"I'm here," Rowan said; but voiceless, Tan could not see her. Rowan found one thin hand, held it. The fingers gripped hers; and the people moved back.

And back.

Rowan looked down.

On the ground, beside one angled, trembling knee: a truncated pyramid, swirling grooves on each side . . .

A talisman.

Rowan said helplessly, "Now? Why *now?*" Tan's fingers released Rowan's; and the people continued to move away.

Tan's wound was a wide, gaping slice. With brutal casualness, a part of Rowan named the internal organs visible, learned so well from her dissection of the first demon in Alemeth.

Rowan wondered at that demon, that person, wondered what strange dangers she had faced to track a monster all the way to its distant home.

The people moved back.

She wondered at those who had followed after the one who did not return. So many miles of land and sea, and hunger . . .

To capture the beast—not merely kill it, but bring it back, so that the people could learn its exact nature, its mysterious power—

Never realizing that the power was their own word.

And Rowan remembered: in the dark den, how, when the blinded demon collapsed, Tan had held that one, had lowered her so gently.

A friend. That had been Tan's own friend.

Sitting alone in the dusty air, in the bright sunlight, Rowan knew why Tan had recognized her as a person. Rowan had held Janus exactly as Tan held her own wounded friend; and Tan knew of the miles and dangers that Rowan herself had crossed, to help a friend.

And knowing both types of beings now as people—then, surely, whatever evil had been done, had been done in error. And if not all the people could understand and believe, then at the least, Tan must help the strangers escape, so that no more need die.

Rowan looked up.

Corpses strewn about the stage, some half eaten; the quiet, singing people, forced back helplessly, standing in a wide circle all around.

And nearby, alone, blinking at the sunlight, seeming stunned, blind, uncomprehending, stupid: the creature, the monster from the Inner Lands.

The amount of hatred the steerswoman felt was beyond her ability to measure. She wished him dead.

She did not have her sword. Unfortunately.

Also, she wanted to live. She needed him.

She got herself to him, dragged herself erect against him. He looked down into her face, seeming not to recognize her at all.

With Tan's last word in one hand, Rowan put an arm around Janus's waist, twisted her fingers into the cloth of his shirt, held tight, took three hissing breaths through teeth clenched against pain and hatred, and said, "Let's go."

The people parted before them. None followed.

44

She fell twice before reaching the edge of the city. Janus gave her no help, standing each time passive, blank as she pulled herself back to her feet against him, using him like an object. She was almost glad; she was free to feel no gratitude.

At a rock pool, she staggered forward, allowed herself to fall in, managed to pull herself to sit leaning back against the stones. She did not think she screamed when the water first touched the burn. But she could not be certain.

She sat, half submerged, as waves of dark and light passed behind her eyes. She did not know whether, during one of the dark waves, she had fainted; but in one wave of brightness Janus was standing, and in the next he was seated on the stones.

Tan's word lay on the stones beside him. Janus could have taken it, left her; he had not. He merely sat, his gaze empty. Perhaps he had lost whatever sanity had remained to him. Rowan found that she did not care.

She dragged herself from the water, recovered the talisman, shoved Janus to his feet; and together they went on.

It took a very long time. They saw no demons.

At the beach, Rowan spoke three times. She said, "Go right here"; and later, "Right again"; and then, "Through there." But by the time they reached the camp, pain so inhabited her mind that she no longer knew what she did.

She later understood that she must have done something; because, by stages, she became aware of darkness and a fire, which seemed somehow very small and far away. She was lying on her bedroll with her cloak over her.

A tiny Janus sat on the other side of the tiny fire, his face tilted up to the sharp, bright stars.

* * *

Light woke her. She found herself facing a weird, insect gaze: a hawkbug had spent the night on her chest. Her face was cold, her body hot. Her leg hurt more than she knew how to express.

She pushed off cloak and hawkbug, wondered why the whistle-spiders were silent.

She warmed her cold face against her hot hands. She gathered her thoughts. They were few and came with difficulty.

She had rinsed the burn twice; good. She must bandage it.

She did not have her pack. What did she have?

Blanket, cloak; empty water sack, still strung about her, its spout missing. Kerchief tied to her belt. Her field knife.

Her field knife. She had had it all along. She could have used it to kill Janus in the amphitheater.

He was nowhere in sight. Tan's word—

It was on the ground, beside her, protecting her. Good. Let demons kill Janus.

He appeared; she had not heard him coming. He sat down by the embers of the fire, regarding her.

She discovered that she was carefully, rationally, weighing the satisfaction of killing him now against the impossibility of traveling back to the Dolphin Stair alone. A small, quiet, internal analysis; an interesting process, whose progress she observed with a detached and rather pleasant curiosity.

Janus was still gazing at her. Something very subtle altered in his expression; she could not identify the change. But it suddenly came to her that, right now, her mind was functioning in exactly the same fashion that his did—and he knew it.

The shock of the fact brought her back to her senses. She pushed herself up, sat hugging her right knee, studying the damage to her left leg. "You might lend a hand here," she said, and her own voice was oddly loud, thick, the only sound in existence.

She pulled out her earplugs, flung them on the ground. Whistle-spiders were racketing. A tanglebrush clattered. The hum of the demon city was steady in the windless air. Waves, past the dunes, were distant but deep throated.

Janus did not answer her. "Very well," Rowan said. With shaking hands she pulled off her gloves and took her field knife.

The burn was an inch-wide line, seven inches long, a curving diagonal starting at the outside of her upper thigh, ending lower at the front.

Redness all around, blisters across the length, and in two small areas, appalling glimpses of her own muscle tissue. She shut her eyes and lay back again.

A burn; unfortunate that it was a burn; burns were very different from incised wounds. She had been trained for such situations; the training came to her, but distantly, dwarfed against the overpowering presence of the pain.

But still, the information was there and more: it moved. Smoothly, like a tiny run of clear water. She followed it.

Bread-mold would help reduce the infection; there was no bread at this cache. She must drink a great deal of water, with salt; her salt was in her pack, gone.

Her trouser leg was already partly severed; she could use her knife to complete the process. It was the largest piece of cloth that she could spare, but it was not clean. Janus in his present state was probably unable to undertake a task as complicated as boiling water without a cook pot. And Rowan was not up to the task herself.

She had no salve, and no way to make any. Once in place, the bandage would adhere. It would be impossible to change it. Whatever she did right now must last until she reached the ship.

Presently, shuddering, clenching her teeth so hard she thought they might crack, she forced herself to sit up, wrestled the water sack up and off, and flung it at Janus. It struck him in the chest, hard, fell to his lap. He looked mildly startled. "Get water," she told him. After a moment, he rose and left.

Rowan rested her head against her knee. She felt as if her entire body were trying to twist to the left, to draw itself toward and completely into the pain in her leg. She thought that if she did not force herself still, it would do so, and she would vanish, utterly.

When Janus returned Rowan drank half the water, was immediately gripped by agonizing stomach cramps, and, reasoning that she could not possibly hurt any worse, poured the rest of the water on the burn.

When she regained consciousness, the sun was in her eyes, directly overhead. She was nauseated and thirsty. She tried to remember what food she had left at the campsite, tried to match it against the food that the Thief of Words had brought, tried to guess how much was left, and found the analysis completely beyond her.

But the thought of the Thief, and of Tan, tore the curtain of Rowan's physical shock; and for a space of time she lay with her eyes closed, seeing only the slow-speaking, singing people, hearing their distant song, and feeling only sorrow and anger.

Anger. She must live. She must live to tell the steerswomen.

She must act.

She sat up again. Her knife, cloth, and water sack were exactly where she had dropped them. Her cloak was not; it was at some distance, and Janus was on it, asleep. In the warm sunshine he lay curled tightly, as if against cold.

In small stages, with many pauses between, Rowan completed her arrangements as best she could. She sacrificed the sleeves of her blouse to lay against the wound, covered that with the trouser cloth, tied all in place with strips cut from her other trouser leg. It would have been best to allow the burn to heal in open air, but she would be traveling across sand, and she expected to fall down many times.

Janus still had not moved. Rowan flung the water sack at him again, finding immense satisfaction in the fierceness of the motion and disappointment that he did not startle or cry out. Perhaps he had already been awake. He seemed to know what was expected of him, and left again.

Rowan began to feel more herself; but she knew well that this would not last. She must take advantage of what strength she now had, as soon as possible.

She managed, on hands and one foot, to get to where her tarp lay folded square and weighted down with stones. She opened it, refolded it long, tied the ends together to form a loop.

When Janus returned, she drank; and seeing his blank regard, she told him to do the same, which he did, after a pause that contained no visible thought.

She gave him the tarp, told him to loop it around himself; he did not seem to understand, so she pulled herself erect against him and pulled it over him herself. Her bedroll, with a slit made in the center, went over his head as a makeshift cloak, which he seemed to understand better. She tied off the mouth of the water sack with a loop of its strap, and slung it about herself, not trusting him to tend it. Then, balanced on one foot, she swung her cloak about her, which oddly, she managed to do smoothly and easily; it was that familiar a motion to her body.

She tied the talisman in the kerchief at her belt, put Janus's left arm across her shoulder, which he allowed; it lay loosely across her.

He stank. He had been unwashed for weeks. She put her arm about his waist and held tightly.

"Let's go," she said. More because she took one shuffling step herself, and they both would have fallen if he did not move, he walked.

And when he did, Rowan realized that even injured, she was, at the present, much stronger than he was. But that would change.

She did fall; and she soon lost count of how many times it happened. It began to be routine.

She found herself making various small noises, intermittently, which first vaguely annoyed her, then began to seem merely a part of the environment.

Presently she noticed that it was sometimes better to let herself fall rather than to force herself forward when her energy was spent. It allowed her to recover a bit quicker, or so it seemed. Possibly the phenomenon was entirely illusory.

Eventually, she stayed down for a long time, during which Janus first merely stood by and then finally sat in the sand.

She realized that the growing darkness was outside herself, not inside. On hands and one foot, she got herself up to the dunes and wrapped herself in her cloak. The instant she decided to sleep, she did so; it was like a door closing.

When she woke, it was night. Starlight lit the foam edges of small breakers; they seemed to move according to some formula with which she was familiar, but could not be bothered to solve at the moment. The entire sky lay before her, each star voicelessly speaking its own name; the ocean past the breakers seemed another sky, starless. She was very cold.

When she woke again, she was not cold, and there was shuddering yellow light: a fire nearby, and Janus beside it. She was sorry for the fire; it made the stars less bright.

A number of little creatures were moving at the edge of the waves. She could not see them, but she heard clicking and chitinous creaks.

She thought there was a small, hot animal under her cloak with her; and only by an act of concentration so intense it seemed physical did she recognize it as the pain in her left leg. It seemed to have acquired a spherical boundary and its own identity, separate from her own. She could not recall whether this was good or bad. For no reason she could think of, the left side of her nose hurt, and there was a line of pins and needles along the left side of her jaw.

And Janus was looking at her. It startled her. She did not know why, until she saw that his face showed some dim expression, where before there had been none. She began to wonder if she were in danger.

The expression was one of mild and distant speculation. Then, equally faintly, he seemed to reach some conclusion, and turned away to regard the sea.

She realized that she could still hear the demon city. They had traveled less than four miles; perhaps as little as one.

She suddenly felt very hot, but knew it would be foolish to toss off her cloak. She found the water sack, and drank, and slept.

When she woke, she was drenched in sweat and hot, except for her fingers. The bandage on her left leg showed a wide dark line where the burn lay underneath, damp in the center, stiff at the edges. When she attempted to shift her leg, the cloth lifted free, and she made an unpleasant noise that she did not like to hear and wished would stop.

When it did, her mind was unnaturally clear.

She realized that she had not relieved herself for a long time and did not need to. At the least, that was convenient.

When she attempted to stand, she found she was too weak; and then, she was standing. She discovered, startled, that Janus had helped her up.

They regarded each other, he with the same mildly speculative expression; she did not know what her own face showed. Then he looked west down the beach, looked back at her, and moved to her right side.

After a moment, and because there was simply nothing else to do, she put her arm about his waist; he put his arm about her shoulder, and they made their clumsy way down the beach, her dragging one leg, half stumbling against him with each step.

She fell even more often, but not always to the ground; sometimes he held her as she regained her balance.

She thought they were walking in the dark; she wondered if this were true. She became interested in the sound of their steps. It was a remarkably curious pattern: crunches, hisses, and a long hiss separate from the others.

She could not hear the demon city. She said, "I can't hear the demon city."

She stopped walking. It was hard to do.

She wondered why she had stopped.

She opened her eyes. Light hurt. The view was flat, without depth. The only colors were yellow, white, blue, black.

Something in her mind shifted, matched, shouted.

Pattern. The landscape.

"I think I left some food around here," she said and fainted.

It was still daylight, but she lay in shade. Long shadows pointed east. A whistle-spider attempted a tune, found itself alone, and went silent. High above, a hawkbug climbed the wind like a kite, pink wings glittering.

Every part of her was cold; every part of her was damp with sweat.

She turned her head; she could not integrate what she saw. The world was sideways. She closed her eyes, felt them flick back and forth behind her lids. When she moved her head back, the sensation subsided. She lay watching the hawkbug.

She attempted to speak, but made no sound. She tried harder and said, quite clearly but distantly, "I know I left some food near here."

His voice came: "Probably."

"You should look for it."

"I don't think so."

With very great effort, she turned her head again.

He had built another fire, and was feeding it with sections of tangle-brush. He had, she noted, the sense to strip the leaves off first.

"I don't," she said, then forgot what she intended to say. "I think," she began again; then felt a rush of heat through her body, and could do nothing but lie still under it.

Janus said, "Take your time."

She did. "I think"—but she could not finish the statement.

"Yes," he said, "your leg is infected. Inevitable, really."

"Why are you speaking?"

He took his time replying. He continued to feed the fire slowly, using sections unnecessarily small. His image wavered in her sight; but she saw him shrug. "No reason not to anymore."

Was there before? she asked, then realized she had not asked it but only thought it. She decided to speak again, gave the matter careful attention, prepared exactly what she was going to say, drew several breaths. "You really should look for that food, Janus, I don't feel particularly hungry, but I know I need to eat, and you do, too, I marked the cache with some stones— it's just past the dune line and a little west." Many more words came out than she had planned. But when she breathed again, more came. "You're not in your right mind. I know you can't see it, but you're not, and you really do need to do what I say—" She was abruptly exhausted and nauseous, and she lay with her eyes closed until it passed. "You should look for that food," she said.

"There's no point."

"I have no intention of dying!"

His voice was quiet, mild. "I really don't see how you can avoid it."

Somewhat later, he said, "There's water, if you want it."

She had to think long to find the word. "Yes."

He held her head while she drank, lowered it gently when she was done. She looked up at him; he was studying her with, it seemed, kindly interest.

She said, "Why?"

"You'll have to be more specific."

Why everything? "Why water but not food?"

"Because you don't feel hungry, but you feel thirsty. No reason to suffer more than necessary." He rose, stood above her, gazing out at some distance invisible to her. "I think that when you're gone," he said, "I'll just walk into the sea. Yes." He nodded to himself. "Perhaps something will eat me, eventually."

"If it does, it will die."

"All the better."

Then it was dark, and it occurred to her that she ought to simply go and get the food herself; so she rose and walked, and found it exactly where she had left it. She brought it back to camp, having no difficulty at all walking in the night; and this was because there was a strange, cool, beautiful light in the sky high above her.

When she arrived at the camp, she discovered that she had dreamed the entire event.

But she was sitting up, her left leg stretched before her, visibly swollen beneath the bandages, and her right knee drawn up.

Janus was by the fire. He seemed always to be beside the fire. He watched the flames.

She said, "Murderer."

He looked up. "I used to think that. Now I think I'm a soldier."

"There is no war."

He turned back to the fire. "Yet."

"Soldiers only fight in war."

"Well, then, I am a murderer after all." He seemed indifferent to the matter. "Although," he went on, "if you kill the child that will later become the enemy soldier, what is that?"

"Arrogance."

He made a noise, a small laugh; and he spoke again, but she was suddenly weary and let her head drop.

Somewhat later, by the change in stars, he was either speaking again or still speaking. "Shut up," she said.

She thought he turned to her, but could only see a dark shape where he sat. The fire was too bright, leaving blue spots and streaks on her vision. He said something, something about the future.

"What?"

"It's not a good thing to know the future."

"Change," she said; the future can be changed.

He seemed to understand her. "You can't change the whole world, Rowan."

"All the time." The world was changing all the time, was *supposed* to change all the time. That was important; why was that so important?

"Look around you."

"It's dark."

"Then remember," he said, but she was suddenly thirsty, not for water but for air; and she leaned her head back and drank the cold night into her lungs.

"They can't go further south," he said.

"Who?"

"The people in Southport. I never got there. It was supposed to be my route. I read everything about it."

Tanglebrush, she remembered reading at the Annex: tanglebrush in Southport. Outskirts life. Demon Lands life.

It would stop them. No redgrass. No goats.

The world is supposed to change, all the time.

The stars were going out; no—clouds. "Rain."

He glanced up. "Not for a while, yet."

"Put up," she said, "the tarp."

He turned to study her. "Let's wait," he said. "By the time the rain comes . . . I think you won't need shelter any longer."

After a long silence, she said something. She could not hear what it was. She wondered, and so she said it again. "No trees." What an odd thing to say . . . and then she remembered.

Wulfshaven, market day, a tinker's fortune-telling booth. She and a friend, Artos, laughing, having their fortunes told. "You will die far from your home," the tinker had told her, "and someone will plant a tree on your grave." And Artos, first amused, then intrigued. But Rowan was from the north; she had the manners and accent of the north; and in the north, one did that. One planted trees on graves. The tinker knew this; he was playing them. No mystical ability.

North. The cold, hard desert.

She was not aware she had spoken; but Janus replied, "Yes, and west."

Mountains. Impassable.

East: the Outskirts. Beyond: blackgrass prairie and no life that would support humans.

North, where the only life that grew was life brought by humans; where the funeral groves were planted as far out as possible, and the farms, carefully fertilized, cultivated, slowly grew out to embrace and overtake them. And beyond the desert?

"The same," she said.

"What?"

She found she was looking at stars again; the ground was hard against her back. "South," she said. The same.

He was beside her. "Beyond," she asked him, "beyond the mountains?"

He smiled down at her with, it seemed, pride. "There, you see? Now you understand. We're surrounded." He looked out at the dark land. "They fit, here. We don't. And all the way around the Inner Lands—oh, if not demons, something else or someone else. Life that fits.

"But we grow, we're made to grow. And some day we'll come up against them. And we'll fight. And they'll win. Because they fit, and we don't. It's their world, Rowan. It's a Demon World."

She said, "Routine Bioform Clearance."

"What?"

She could see the Eastern Guidestar through the clouds past his shoulder. It was different from the other stars; she could not remember why. It seemed to her like a person, a strange person who could kill or help, and was supposed to help. A person who did not feel or think as she did.

Everything should be bright, she thought, because it was so very hot. Heat should glow, and this heat, this heat should blaze.

"Heat," she said. "Heat. From the sky."

A sound from him; if it was a word, she did not understand it. Perhaps it was no word.

He moved but not far, shifted, she could not see how; but her hand was cool now, and she thought it was because he was holding it, and she hated his touch, she wanted to pull away, but she did not, because his hand was so very cool. She held on to it as a cold person holds on to a warm stone. "That's what it's for," she said.

"What?"

"Heat. From the sky. From the Eastern Guidestar." But she could not see the Guidestar anymore. Then, suddenly, she saw everything, briefly but with perfect clarity, and she thought that the cold light from her dream had arrived; but seconds later, there was a distant rumble. "It kills everything. Everything that's there. Then we go there."

His beautiful cold hand was on her forehead. She closed her eyes. "What are you talking about?" he said.

"Routine Bioform Clearance. Every twenty years. Kills everything. Clears the way. Then we go. But it stopped."

"Heat . . . from a Guidestar?"

"Yes." Something was wrong, something was very wrong. What? She could not identify it.

"Why have I never heard of this?"

"Outskirts. Over and over." What happened over and over? She could not remember. But she said it again. "Over and over . . ."

"How can heat come from a Guidestar?"

"Magic . . ."

"Magic," he said quietly. Then, more quietly, and after a very long time: "The wizards . . ."

Magic to save us, Rowan thought; magic to kill us.

Magic to kill demons.

Something struck her face: small, and it burned, not with heat but with cold. She made a small sound of gratitude. Another came and another; she loved them. She counted them, because it seemed the correct thing to do.

His hand moved away from her face; she opened her eyes.

He rose and stood gazing up at the sky. "I think," he said, "that I will put that tarp up after all."

45

She thought she was back in the Outskirts. She heard rattling, like redgrass, endless in the wind.

She thought she was under the tarp, and there was a sick person there with her—that would be Averryl; she and Bel were caring for him; he had been injured by a goblin; she remembered now. He had a fever, that was why it was so very warm here. But it should not be this warm. That was wrong. She tried to tell Bel, call Bel's name. She managed to do so, but the name stood all alone in the air, and the rattling continued.

She thought she was running. Then she was not; someone was stopping her, pressing her to the earth. But she had to run, run from the killing heat from the sky. She fought.

Then she did not, but her body moved nevertheless, and the motions made no sense and she could not stop.

"Be still," a voice said.

There was brightness, and she was thirsty and very cold. She drank but not water—something warm and salty and musty and somehow brown-smelling.

After that, she drank water.

After that, she slept.

She lay watching him for a long time before he noticed. He faced away from her, sitting by the fire, working with something she could not see. He glanced back, as if he had been doing so regularly, and noticed her regard. "I see you're awake. Good." He put aside his work, picked up something, brought it to her. "Can you manage more of this?"

It was a cup of sorts: a little framework of twigs, holding a scrap of cloth in a pocket. There was liquid inside.

She did not reply, but he helped her to sit, held the cup to her lips: broth, with tiny shreds of what had once been dried beef. When he let her down again, she saw that the cloth that had bound his ruined right hand was gone. He noted her glance, inspected the hand himself. "Not very pretty. I'll have to cover it later, but for the moment, I think the air will do it good." He studied her. "Rowan, you're coherent at the moment, or I think you are, but you know that won't last. And there's not enough food here to allow us to wait to see if you're going to live or die. So we're going to have to move soon."

She heard a high hum, realized she had been hearing it for some time. She groped at her belt, at the ground around her. "What do you want?" Janus asked her. She found it behind her head, wrapped in a kerchief: Tan's last word. Rowan managed to take it out, set it down beside her, and lay back.

Janus puzzled, looked about, looked at her again, huffed a small laugh. "Your ears are ringing. From the fever. There are no demons here."

He returned to the fire, brought something back. "Here." A square scrap of cloth—cut from the tarp, she saw—and on it, a baked potato, smashed into pulp. "Try this, if you can." She did not respond; but when he took a bit onto his fingers to bring to her lips, she managed to turn on one side and pull the makeshift plate closer herself. When she finished, he took the cloth scrap, cleaned it with sand, set it and the cup into the center of the tarp. A small packet joined it: the rest of the food she had cached. After a pause, he took the kerchief and talisman and tied them to his waistband. Then he rolled the tarp, tied the ends, slung it across his body. He came to her, handed her something. "Here." A length of tangle-brush taproot, trimmed to a thick stick. He held out his hand to her.

She stared at the hand for a long time; then she gripped it, rose, and fell immediately. He caught her, nearly fell himself. She cried out at the sudden increase of pain. "Careful," he said. Her leg had been splinted with strips of tanglebrush root and straps of cloth. "Take this." He picked up the stick, put it in her hand as a cane. He stepped away from her experimentally; she did not fall but stood weaving dangerously. He took the moment to quickly pull on the bedroll and put her own cloak about her. The weight of it nearly felled her again.

Then he held out his left arm.

She did not respond.

He came to her side, took her slack right hand, put it around his waist, put his left arm over her shoulder, and waited. She gazed at the face so close to her own; and there seemed to her at that moment to be no thought at all in her mind.

Eventually, her fingers wound tight into the cloth of his shirt, and they went.

She could not count how many times they fell, both; he was only marginally stronger than she. Sometimes they rested long on the sand before rising again.

When the fever came back, he dragged her up past the tide line; it took a very long time. She did not remember the rest of that day, or the night, except that at some point, under stars, with the sea sounding in her ears, she ate, and drank, and drank again.

In the morning, she needed his assistance to relieve herself, which fact she found hateful beyond all description.

In the afternoon, they went on. The day was no different from the previous or the next.

She began, in slow stages between pain and dreams of fire, to notice a change. They fell less often; and this only because when she stumbled, he did not, but held her against him until she either regained her balance or collapsed completely.

And then it seemed that for a very long time, she did not move, other than in dreams. But when she woke, she found she was moving after all, and through no effort of her own. She did not know how long this continued. It might have been minutes; it might have been days.

Then they walked again, for a while; nearly half the afternoon. The sun blazed in her eyes as it descended toward a dark line at the horizon.

Janus was talking. Perhaps he had been talking for a long time. But she heard it now, and the sound made her stomach twist in hatred.

Somehow, he noticed. They paused. Then he pulled away a bit, turned to study her face. "Ah. I see you're back. How do you feel?" She did not answer. He looked mildly disappointed. "Really, Rowan, you ought to answer my questions now—you've no reason not to." Still no answer. "Well, never mind," he said kindly. "I suppose I can understand. It's all that you have left, really, poor thing."

She struck him.

The blow had no force, but his face went suddenly, utterly blank, and she thought: There he is, that's the Janus I know, better than the other one.

He stood back. He released her. She dropped to the sand.

His shadow fell on her. "Rowan," he said in a toneless voice, "at the moment I have no reason to leave you here." He stooped close. "Don't give me one."

She wept; the fact of it shocked her even more than the sound. She wept from pain, hatred, frustration, weakness.

He remained where he was, until she finished.

Then they went on.

She only spoke to him once.

They were in a windless place: a house, she thought, or a room—

It was a demon den.

Site Two.

The walls were lit by the flickers of a small fire. Just past that, at the entrance, standing guard against what voices might come in the night: Tan's last word.

"What is it?" Rowan asked.

Janus seemed not surprised to hear her. But he shifted a bit, shifting them both. He was seated with his back against the wall, she was leaning back against him, his arms holding her in place: an embrace, but as sexless as that between a mother and child. The bedroll was a cushion beneath them, the cloak a blanket across them both.

His voice came from behind her invisibly. "A word. A cry. A warning. A curse." He breathed once, a sound not quite a sigh. "The voice of instinct, perhaps . . .

"They're not like us, Rowan. They don't always think. Or instinct and thought work together in them. I don't know how.

"But I know they can go mad. Hunger will make them mad, make them become all instinct." He was silent a moment. "As it does with us all, I suppose . . .

"One of them must have been very, very hungry. The other—the other was sitting in the sand, and I didn't know then why it wouldn't fight or run.

"And the first came at it, tearing at it, to kill it and eat it." He shifted again. "And the second fought, but it would not get up. Then it died. As it died, it said . . . that." His voice became a whisper. "And the mad demon walked away."

Outside, animal clicks and clatters; a rustling that paused and continued, paused and continued. She could not hear the sea.

"I know now, but I didn't then: even a mad demon cannot disturb a cache of eggs—if it sees it. But the mother was still laying them and hadn't made the covering, and the mad one could not see. So the mother told it. She said it completely. She said it so perfectly that a demon starving and mad with hunger could not even stay to eat her . . .

"What must it be like, to say something that completely? To say something in a way that cannot ever be denied? I wonder . . .

"I didn't know it was a word, not then. I just saw what it did. I had been hiding. I was so very still—I'd learned that you have to stay still. I learned it, watching the others die. One by one. Burned . . .

He shifted again; they shifted together, locked. "I was starving, myself. Starving and trapped. I know I wasn't in my right mind. I don't think I would have done it otherwise: just walk right up to the thing and pick it up. And carry it over to the mad one . . . and see the demon walk away.

"I followed it, and it always walked away. Then I killed it." She felt his heart beat, against her back. She felt his breath, beside her face. "I used stones. It was all I had. Then I found a stick. And I went to where the others lived. And I killed them all.

"They ran, at the end. When they saw each others' corpses, first they ate them, then they fought each other, and then they ran, toward the sea. I caught up with them. I killed them in the sand . . .

"And when I was all done, and all the little animals came out to eat them, I thought, That's good. That's enough. I can die now. So I sat in the sand by the sea, and I waited to die.

"That's when I saw the ships."

He fell silent. Only two things moved: the fire and Rowan. She felt herself trembling, slightly but continuously.

"Twenty ships." Silence again. Then: "Not like ours. No sails. More like huge rafts, and demons pulling and pushing them. But so many . . .

"Demons from across the sea. Demons on all the shores of the world's great ocean. Demons enough to kill all of us, burn us to muscle and bone.

"It would happen. I could see it all, happening. And nothing I could do would stop it.

"But it came to me, their great ships passing by, their dead ones around me, and me half dead myself . . . I could hurt them. It was the only power I had. They would suffer, for what they were going to do. And keep suffering, as long as I had the power . . .

"So I couldn't die, as I wanted to. I had to survive. But there was no food."

She could not stop trembling. It felt like a force outside herself, entering her, more intimate than Janus's embrace.

"I went back to where Riva was. It wasn't demons that killed her—she'd been running, something broke under her, sent up spines."

Rowan was not cold, was not warm, but when she breathed a long breath out, she felt the breath stand hot before her face like a burning ghost.

"So I knew that there was no demon poison on her."

Rowan made a small movement, subsided.

"Instinct, I suppose," Janus said. "There's always something, Rowan . . . there will always be something that can drive us down to instinct. You should remember that."

The trembling had become shudders: hard, continuous.

He leaned forward, looked at her face. "I don't think we'll be traveling tomorrow. It looks like you're taking a turn for the worse."

She knew nothing but heat, and cold, and motion, and sometimes, food.

It was all there was; it was all there had ever been.

Then, at last, there was light and stillness.

She looked about, seeing sand, stones in a ring around charred wood—

A campsite. She knew about campsites. This was one.

That was good. A steerswoman, alone, outdoors, at a campsite. That was proper. All was well. She closed her eyes.

But she was supposed to be doing something. She could not recall what. But it was urgent, necessary, and wrong that she was not doing it.

Going. Moving. Yes. Steerswomen went. That was it.

She ought to be going somewhere. She did not know, at the moment, where. Still, one went. After resting, always, one went on.

She pushed off something that was on top of her, in her way, stopping her from going. She rose; but then found she had not risen. She tried again, and again. Finally she turned on her hands and clambered to her feet, and fell.

She needed something. Something like a stick. She found one, by her. It was the right size.

Where was her pack? She could not see it.

She was forgetting something—what was it?

Move. That's what it was. Move.

She did; then she got up and did it again.

She passed something; it took a long time. It's a house, she thought, just a house. But she did not like the people who lived there, did not like the way they peered out at her through their little windows.

No, no stopping there.

She got up again. She moved.

And it seemed the whole world opened up in front of her, the wide horizon that she loved. And all she had to do was go, walk out endlessly, and there was nothing more to the world, nothing else that mattered.

She got up again. She moved.

"We'll walk for the rest of our lives," Janus said.

Of course we will, she replied, how else can we see new things?

She did not hear her own voice; but Janus did, apparently. How clever of him. "Well, that's the whole point, isn't it? But how many new things can a person see before even new things are familiar?"

That was a young thing to say; how very young he was. He was just a boy, with his new cloak and his soft boots and his map case jutting out of his pack. She was so much older than he; how did she get this old?

"Get up," Bel said.

Yes, Rowan said, and did so.

She was explaining something to Bel; she often explained things to Bel. Rowan wondered what she was saying, since her own voice made no sound at all. But Bel listened, tilt headed, nodding, striding along beside Rowan, as ever; and all was right, all was well.

"Get up," Bel said. Rowan got up.

And then there was music, but she could not tell if it was Janus's flute, or Bel singing, and that was strange, because she ought to know the difference. Perhaps it was birds; Rowan loved birds—where were they?

"Get up," someone said in a voice that scratched and cracked and hurt Rowan's throat. "Get up get up get up."

Yes.

There was light, far ahead, white light all around the horizon; air flickered and shuddered above it. Something moved inside it: a person in the distance, very far ahead, but she could not see him clearly, and he would not stand still.

No matter. She was going the same way. She would get there, in the end. And she would see what he saw, know what he knew.

And then, she would go on.

Bel said, "Get up," and Rowan said, Yes, and got up.

There were people with her.

They walked beside her, behind her, all moving together. A quiet people. So many; she could not count them.

They had no faces. That was all right; not everyone had a face.

Get up, Bel said again, and Rowan did not answer, but she knew what to do. She did it.

Then Bel said, Get up, and Bel said, "Be still." She said them both at once.

Make up your mind, Rowan said.

You have to move, Janus said; and Rowan said, Yes. One of the quiet people handed her, Get up; and Rowan handed back, Yes; and Bel said, Get up; but Bel said, "Stay put."

And then Bel rose, and her shadow blocked the sun, and she waved her arms wide. There was a sound, not far off; Rowan did not know what it was. Bel bent down again. "Stay put, you fool, you can't walk like that."

Clattering, hisses, thumps. "What's she doing way out here?" Steffie asked.

"I don't know. She's out of her mind. Lend me a hand."

Rowan felt herself lifted half up, found water in her mouth. She swallowed, coughed. "You're real." They were alone, the three of them, under a sky of bright and painful blue.

"Of course we're real," Bel said, "and we had the devil's own time finding you. You were going in the wrong direction."

"She should have stayed where Janus left her," Steffie said. "How'd she expect us to find her, wandering off like that?" He looked down at her, his face twisted in distress. "Fool woman, why didn't you stay put?"

Rowan looked from face to face, leaned back in Bel's arms, breathed in, breathed out.

"Instinct," she said.

umming.
     Demons.
     No—music. A rich, dark voice.

Rowan opened her eyes.

Bel was seated on the floor, leaning back against the wall; she noticed Rowan's gaze, stopped humming. She picked something up off the floor, slid herself closer. "Here you go," she said cheerfully. "Let's try some more." She levered Rowan up, held a mug to her lips.

Fish stew. "Actually," Rowan said in a rather small voice, "I'm not very hungry at the moment."

Bel regarded her with something like astonishment. "All right," she said, and set it aside, eased Rowan back down. She studied Rowan's face carefully. "How do you feel?"

Rowan searched for adequate words. "My leg hurts," was what she finally settled on. She had no idea where she was.

Bel made a noise. "That's no surprise. Zenna had to do some nasty work on it. You were a mess."

Rowan looked down at herself. Her hands lay atop a thick wool blanket. She was lying on a mattress that lay directly on the floor—no, the deck, the deck of the aft cabin, where the bunk housing had been torn out. Packets of gear hung in rope-tied bundles from the ceiling. They shifted, swinging slightly, and Rowan recognized the sweet motion that had comforted her in sleep.

And beside her, Bel. The Outskirter's face was evolving a grin. Rowan observed the process with interest. "How long have I been sleeping?" she asked.

"This time? A few hours."

" 'This time?' " Rowan tried to sit up, and managed only the slightest shift in position. The action caused her left leg to feel as if some extremely large and cruel person were sitting on it.

Rowan blinked, breathed, waited for the sensation to pass. "How long have I been here?"

"On the ship? A week or so. Almost two since we hauled you up the cliffs."

Rowan attempted to piece together events, found it impossible. She seemed to have no memories that she could trust. "How did you ever manage to find me?" From the deck above, thumps, voices.

"Well, it wasn't easy, with you crawling around the landscape. But Janus had told Zenna and Steffie exactly where he left you, so we started there and worked outward."

Rowan attempted to translate the peculiar images in her mind. "The first cache?" she ventured. "The camp by the crypt?"

Bel nodded, her short dark hair sifting forward and back. "I like that crypt; it's very poetic."

Things began to make more sense. "But, Bel," Rowan said, "how did *you* get here?"

Laughter. "Mostly, at sword point," the Outskirter said. "None of the sailors in Alemeth were willing to take me, so I slipped aboard one ship at night and made them do it. Just as far as a fishing village. Then I went ashore and kidnapped some fishers and got farther. Then I did the whole thing again. We always stayed close to the shore. I was only a day or so behind you at first—I saw your sails once or twice. But when the fishers got more afraid of the sea than of me, I had to let them go. I walked the rest of the way."

And there she was, an Outskirter, cross-legged on the plank floor, barefoot, wearing a huge gray silk shirt Rowan recognized as Steffie's. Her thatch of brown hair, her dark eyes, the neat muscularity of her form, even while sitting, all stunningly familiar, missed, welcome.

"Have I mentioned," Rowan said, grinning, "how very glad I am to see you?"

Bel nodded broadly. "Every time you woke up. At first it was flattering, but then it got to be embarrassing."

Rowan laughed: a thin sound but laughter nonetheless. "Well, I don't remember it." But then, suddenly, she could: a collection of discrete images and sounds and sensations, strewn about randomly in her mind. As if on command, they ordered and connected themselves into nearly contiguous, and extremely unpleasant, memory.

The memories included rather a lot of irrational behavior on her part. Rowan watched herself, in retrospect. "Oh, dear." Bel made an amused noise.

Still, if anyone could survive the trek through the wild lands, it was certainly Bel. "How did you know where to go?"

"I took those maps you left behind."

Something about this statement disturbed Rowan; she was a moment identifying it. "Bel," she said eventually, "those maps were originals."

"Yes, and you needn't lecture me. Zenna already did. But her heart wasn't really in it. The maps got me to the anchorage, and as far as I'm concerned, that's the best use anyone could put them to. But by the time I arrived, Steffie had already gone down the cliffs after you."

"Alone?"

"Yes."

"He wasn't supposed to do that." The idea of Steffie wandering the demon lands alone was appalling; he was Rowan's responsibility; she ought not have led him into danger. She ought—somehow—to be able to protect him, and Zenna as well. "He was supposed to stay with Zenna." Rowan thought she was speaking sternly, but discovered, by the sound, that she had achieved only a sort of plaintive petulance that embarrassed even herself.

"Wonderful. And how were you supposed to get back to the Inner Lands? Janus couldn't get you any farther. And you couldn't walk. And you were trying to go in the wrong direction. Not to mention conversing with rocks and bushes, as near as I could tell." Bel leaned over her. "You know, Rowan," she said, "you can't expect to do everything by yourself. Sometimes you just have to shut up and let your friends help you."

Rowan looked up at her. "I suppose you're right," she said. "I'm hardly in a position to argue. Oh, my . . ." This when she attempted to sit up again, to no visible effect whatsoever. The effort left her suddenly, completely, drained.

"What do you need?" Bel asked immediately.

"Um . . ." Rowan was a moment recovering words. "Water?"

Bel rose, thumped on the ceiling three times, sat again. Above, the murmur of conversation ceased. Footsteps crossed the deck toward the companionway. "Hey, ho," Steffie called as he descended. Rowan heard him in the pantry; then he entered the cabin with a cup in his hand. "Here you go, then," he said to Bel, and passed it to her.

"Have a seat. She's talking sense."

A glance in Rowan's direction. "See how long that lasts."

"As long as I can manage to stay awake, I should think. And don't worry: I don't intend to greet you like a long-lost brother, as I seem to recall having done so a number of times already." It took a great deal of effort and concentration to make so long a statement, but Rowan was rather pleased with the effect.

Steffie sat right down where he had stood, opened his mouth, closed it again. "That's the most she's ever said in one go."

"And she's been at it for a while now."

"It *is* possible to address me directly," Rowan said. Bel held the cup and steadied Rowan's head as she drank. The water was cool and delicious, and Rowan felt herself somewhat stronger.

"Well," Steffie said when she was done, "sorry. Zenna was saying that things'd settle down for you pretty soon. Guess she was right. She could be a healer, if she wasn't a sailor, except she's a steerswoman."

Rowan lay back again, nodded. "Can you send her down here?"

"Why?" Bel sounded suspicious.

"I'd like to find out where we are . . ."

"We're on the water, and we're on our way home. That's all you need to worry about right now."

"I was thinking more of our actual position . . ."

"Um . . ." Steffie said; and then he announced the ship's position, down to minutes of longitude and latitude. "Except not any more, because that's from dawn. Couldn't see the Guidestars after that."

Rowan regarded him with pride. "That's a very good job of remembering numbers," she said.

"I'm not likely to forget those, 'cause Zenna made me watch while she figured them out three times through, and then made me do exactly what she did. Five times through. And I got it right the last time. Well, the last-and-a-half time."

"I see she's been keeping you busy."

"You don't know the half of it. And here I'd thought we'd be taking things easy, myself. With so many people around, I don't have to haul a sheet every time Zenna wants to tack. Guess she showed me."

"I suggest you get used to it." Rowan discovered that she had closed her eyes again. It seemed like a good idea. "I suppose Janus has recovered enough to pull his own weight?" she said.

Silence. Then, someone took a breath to speak; but Rowan spoke first. "He's not here, is he?"

"How did you know?"

Rowan found herself unable to organize her explanation, and lay regarding the back of her eyelids. After a pause, Bel amplified. "He jumped ship, two days ago. We had gone close to shore to bring in some fresh water, and that night Steffie heard him go."

"We were still near shore," Steffie said. "Close enough for him to swim for it, but none of us fast enough swimmers to catch him."

"Zenna's upset."

"Can't think why he did it. Rotten thing to do to Zenna," Steffie went on; but he spoke to Bel, and quietly, as if having decided that Rowan was asleep. "Her coming all this way, just to help him out of trouble, and all. Couldn't see Gwen doing that for me."

"Hm." Bel shifted, stretching her legs, by the sound of it, and moving the cup to do so. "Would you do it for Gwen?"

"Well, sure." Steffie sounded surprised. "You don't leave people in trouble, if you can help it. Even if you don't like them much. Well, don't like them any more. I mean . . . well, I'll always have a soft spot for Gwen, and all—"

"What did he tell you?" Rowan asked.

A pause. "Janus?" Bel asked.

"Yes. About the demon lands," Rowan said.

They did not immediately reply; then Steffie said, "Well . . . everything."

"No," Rowan said, "what *specifically* did he tell you?"

"Are you sure you want this now?" Bel asked.

"Yes." Rowan drew and released a deep breath, forced her eyes open, turned to regard them. "Right now, please."

Something in her expression gave them pause. They traded a glance, then told her.

The story was long. They took turns relating it. Rowan needed at first to concentrate very hard to follow the tale; shortly, her anger made it easy to do so. She listened, staring blindly at the splintered bunk above her.

When the tale was done, Rowan hardly knew where to begin. Bel and Steffie watched her uncomfortably. "That's not even slightly true," Rowan said at last.

"What, none of it?"

"No." She was immediately, immensely, weary.

"You didn't rescue him from the fortress?"

"There was no fortress."

"No wizard either?"

"No."

"But you did get burned by a demon."

"Yes. But not while I was rescuing Janus. While someone else was rescuing us both."

"What, one of those people from the fortress?"

"She said there was no fortress."

"Oh . . . right . . . But, why make up some story? Makes no sense, does it?"

To gain their confidence. To travel with them for as long as possible.

To hide his crimes. "He's a murderer." This brought no response. When Rowan looked, she found that Steffie and Bel had acquired expressions of disappointment, resignation, and extreme patience. "I know I've said that before," Rowan said, and it was suddenly difficult to speak so long a sentence, "but it actually is true."

"But, Rowan, you've got to see that makes no sense—"

Bel said, "Yes it does." Steffie looked at her in astonishment. "He jumped ship," Bel went on. "He knew Rowan would get her wits back at some point and give us the truth."

"So . . . what she said before, about corpses in the streets, and blood in the sand, and bugs and things eating the people? That's the real story?"

"I'm starting to think that steerswomen tell the truth even when they're delirious."

"Interesting idea," Rowan said. The words were not at all clear. And her mind was wandering; she forced it back. There was something still to be said; she searched, found it. "Wizards," she said, with great concentration. "He's going to the wizards. Did I say that before?"

"Um, no . . ."

"Why?" Bel asked quickly.

"Because . . . he can't kill enough people by himself . . . He needs magic . . ."

"Routine Bioform Clearance?" Bel was suddenly very near; her hand gripped Rowan's shoulder. Steffie made a wordless noise of protest. "The heat?" Bel demanded.

"Yes . . ."

"Who? Who does he want the wizards to kill?"

Bel's face was close; Rowan looked up into the dark eyes, understood. "Not your people," Rowan said. Bel relaxed somewhat. "And not mine."

Bel released her, leaned back, her gaze speculative. "Who else is there?"

"Everyone else . . . the rest of the world . . ." Rowan could fight it no longer. Her eyes closed.

"Rowan—"

"Let her sleep," Steffie said.

"But—"

"We'll get the story later. Not like we can do a thing about it in the middle of the ocean, is there? Let her sleep."

Perhaps Rowan did sleep, but she seemed to herself not to. If she dreamed, she dreamed herself where she was: amid the smell of ocean and the wool blanket, the sound of ocean and ship's creaking, and the particular flutter of wave-reflected light against her eyelids.

True dreams crowded about her; but one stepped forward, spoke to her urgently and silently.

She found herself trying to rise. "Where . . ." She cast about weakly.

Bel was still beside her. "What do you need?"

"Did he take it? I had it with me. In a kerchief . . ."

"Take what?"

"Here," Steffie's voice came, and the sound of objects being shifted. He drew near, stooped down. "See? Right here, safe and sound."

"The magic spell?" Bel said.

"No . . . not magic . . ."

Steffie knit his brows. "No?" He regarded it, lying in his hand, on folds of crumpled Alemeth silk. "Then what is it?"

Rowan sighed. "A cry," she said. "A prayer. A warning." She closed her eyes again. "A demon's dying word."

ABOUT THE AUTHOR

Like so many people in the twenty-first century, ROSEMARY KIRSTEIN makes her living in information technology, having served variously in programming, user training, tech support, and technical writing. And like so many other authors, she has also acquired a satisfyingly random array of peculiar past jobs: field laborer among migrant workers in the tobacco fields; airport security guard; wielder of the "green" brush in a hand-painted watercolor factory; truck loader for UPS; dishwasher in a nursing home; and, inevitably, waitress.

More importantly and continuously, she remains a singer-guitarist, playing hot acoustic fingerstyle guitar and very occasionally turning out an original song. Early in her career, she was involved in the folk-music resurgence centering around the Musician's Cooperative in New York's Greenwich Village and was contributor to and sometime associate editor of the *Fast Folk Musical Magazine*, a monthly combination magazine/vinyl LP. Back issues of FFMM are planned to be reissued in CD format and will include some of Ms. Kirstein's music.

She is a member of The Fabulous Genrettes, which, despite its name, is not a girl band, but a writer's group based in the Boston area. She reads science books for fun.

She lives with two cats and mostly writes at night, when the telemarketers stop calling.